THE BLACK LUNG CAPTAIN

THE BLACK LUNG CAPTAIN

A Tale of the *Ketty Jay*

Chris Wooding

GOLLANCZ

LONDON

Copyright © Chris Wooding 2010
All rights reserved

The right of Chris Wooding to be identified as the author
of this work has been asserted by him in accordance with the
Copyright, Designs and Patents Act 1988.

First published in Great Britain in 2010
by Gollancz
An imprint of the Orion Publishing Group
Orion House, 5 Upper St Martin's Lane,
London WC2H 9EA
An Hachette UK Company

A CIP catalogue record for this book
is available from the British Library

ISBN 978 0 575 08517 6 (Cased)
ISBN 978 0 575 08518 3 (Trade Paperback)

1 3 5 7 9 10 8 6 4 2

Typeset at The Spartan Press Ltd,
Lymington, Hants

Printed and bound in the UK by CPI Mackays,
Chatham ME5 8TD

The Orion Publishing Group's policy is to use papers that
are natural, renewable and recyclable products and made
from wood grown in sustainable forests. The logging and
manufacturing processes are expected to conform to
the environmental regulations of the country of origin.

www.chriswooding.com
www.orionbooks.co.uk

One

An Escape – 'Orphans Don't Fight Back' –
Pinn Flounders – Destination: Up

Darian Frey was a man who understood the value of a tactical retreat. It was a gambler's instinct, a keen appreciation of the odds that told him when to take a risk and when to bail out. There was no shame in running as if your heels were on fire when the situation called for it. In Frey's opinion, the only difference between a hero and a coward was the ability to do basic maths.

Malvery was to his left, huffing and puffing through the undergrowth. Alcoholic, overweight and out of shape. Pinn, who was no fitter but a good deal dimmer, ran alongside. Behind them was an outraged horde armed with rifles, pistols and clubs, baying for their blood.

The maths on this one were easy.

A volley of gunfire cut through the forest. Bullets clipped leaves, chipped trees and whined away into the night. Frey swore and ducked his head. He hunched his shoulders, trying to make himself small. More bullets followed, smacking into earth and stone and wood all around them.

Pinn whooped. 'Stupid yokels! Can't shoot worth a damn!' His stumpy legs pumped beneath him like those of an enthusiastic terrier.

Frey didn't share Pinn's excitement. He was sick with a grey fear, waiting for the moment when one of those bullets found flesh, the hard punch of lead in his back. If he was especially unlucky, he might get blinded by a tree branch or break his leg first. Running through a forest in the dark was no one's idea of fun.

He clutched his prize to his chest: a small wooden lockbox, jingling with ducats. Not enough to be worth dying for. Not even worth a medium-sized flesh wound. But he wasn't giving it up now. It was a matter of principle.

'Told you robbing an orphanage was a bad idea,' said Malvery.

'No, it was *Crake* who said that,' Frey said through gritted teeth. 'That's why he wouldn't come. *You* thought it was a *good* idea. In fact, your exact words were: "Orphans don't fight back." '

'Well, they don't,' said the doctor defensively. 'It's the rest of the village you've got to watch out for.'

Frey's reply was cut off as the ground disappeared from under his feet. Suddenly they were tumbling and sliding in a tangle, slithering through cold mud. Frey flailed for purchase as the forest rolled and spun before his eyes. The three of them crashed through a fringe of bracken and bushes, and ended up in a heap on the other side.

Frey extricated himself gingerly from his companions, wincing as a multitude of bumps and scratches announced themselves. The lock-box had bruised his ribs in the fall, but he'd kept hold of it somehow. He looked back at the moonlit slope. It was smaller and shallower than it had seemed while they were falling down it.

Malvery got up and made a half-hearted attempt at wiping the mud off his pullover. He adjusted his round, green-lensed glasses, which had miraculously stayed on his nose.

'Anyway, I've reconsidered my position,' he said, continuing his train of thought as if there had been no interruption. 'I've come to believe that stealing from a bunch of defenceless orphans could be seen as a bit of a low point in our careers.'

Frey tugged at Pinn, who lay groaning on the ground. He'd been on the bottom of the heap, and his chubby face was plastered in muck. '*I'm* an orphan!' Frey protested as he struggled with Pinn's weight. 'Who were they collecting for, if not me?'

Malvery smoothed his bushy white moustache and followed Frey's gaze up the slope. The forest was brightening with torchlight as the infuriated mob approached. 'You should tell them that,' he said. 'Might sweeten their disposition a little.'

'Pinn, will you *get up*?' Frey cried, dragging the pilot to his feet.

Even with the moon overhead, it was hard to see obstacles while they were running. They fended off branches that poked and lashed at their faces. They slipped and cursed and cracked their elbows against tree trunks. It had rained recently, and the ground alternately sucked at their boots or slid treacherously beneath them.

The villagers reached the top of the slope and sent a hopeful barrage of gunfire into the trees. Frey felt something slap against his long coat, near his legs. He gathered up the flapping tail, and saw a bullet hole there.

Too close.

'Give up the money and we'll let you go!' one of the villagers shouted.

Frey didn't waste his breath on a reply. He wasn't coming out of this without something to show for it. He needed that money. Probably a lot more than any bloody orphans did. He had a crew to look after. Seven mouths to feed, if you counted the cat. And that wasn't even including Bess, who didn't have a mouth. Still, she probably needed oiling or something, and oil didn't come for free.

Anyway, *he* was an orphan. So that made it okay.

'Everything looks different in the dark,' Malvery said. 'You sure this is the way we came?'

Frey skidded to a halt at the edge of a cliff, holding his arms out to warn the others. A river glittered ten metres below, sparkling in the moonlight.

'Er . . . We might have taken a wrong turn or two,' he ventured.

The precipice ran for some distance to his left and right. Before them was a steely landscape of treetops, rucked with hills and valleys, stretching to the horizon: the vast expanse of the Vardenwood. In the distance stood the Splinters, one of Vardia's two great mountain ranges, which marched all the way north to the Yortland coast thousands of kloms away.

Frey suddenly realised that he had no idea where, in all that woodland, he'd hidden his aircraft and the rest of his crew.

Malvery looked down at the river. 'I don't remember this being here,' he said.

'I'm pretty sure the *Ketty Jay* is over the other side,' said Frey doubtfully.

'Are you really, Cap'n? Or is that a guess?'

'I've just got a feeling about it.'

Behind them, the cries of the mob were getting louder. They could see the bobbing lights of torches approaching through the forest.

'Any ideas?' Malvery prompted.

'Jump?' suggested Frey. 'There's no way they'd be stupid enough to follow us.'

'Yeah, we'd certainly out-stupid them with that plan.' Malvery rolled up his sleeves. 'Fine. Let's do it.'

Pinn was leaning on his knees, breathing hard. 'Oh, no. Not me. Can't swim.'

'You'd rather stay here?'

'I can't *swim*!' Pinn insisted.

Frey didn't have time to argue. His eyes met the doctor's. 'Do the honours, please.'

Malvery put his boot to the seat of Pinn's trousers and shoved. Pinn stumbled forward to the edge of the cliff. He teetered on his toes, wheeled his arms in a futile attempt to keep his balance, and then disappeared with a howl.

'Now you'd better go rescue him,' Frey said.

Malvery grinned. 'Bombs away, eh?' He put his glasses in his coat pocket, ran past Frey and jumped off the cliff. Frey followed him, feet first, clutching the box of coins. He was halfway down before he thought to wonder if the river was deep enough, or if there were rocks under the surface.

Hitting the water was a freezing black shock, knocking the wind out of him. Icy spring melt from the Splinters. The sounds of the forest disappeared in a bubbling rush that filled his nose and ears. His plunge took him to the river bed, but the water cushioned him enough to give him a gentle landing. He launched himself back upward, shifting the lockbox to one arm and swimming with the other. Only seconds had passed but his chest was already beginning to hurt. He panicked and struggled for breath, clawing at the twinkles of moonlight above him. Finally, just when it seemed there was no air left inside him, he broke the surface.

Sound returned, unmuffled now, the hissing and splashing of the river. He sucked in air and cast about for signs of his companions. With the water lapping round his face he couldn't find them, so he struck out for the bank. The river wasn't fast, but he could still feel the current pulling him. He vaguely hoped Pinn was alright. He'd hate to lose a good pilot.

He hauled himself out, dragging the lockbox with him, which had inconveniently filled with water and was now twice as heavy as before. Jumping in the river had seemed a good idea at the time, but now he was sodden and cold as well as being dog-tired. He was beginning to think that getting lynched would be preferable to all this exertion.

Once he got to his feet, he spotted his companions. Malvery was swimming towards the bank with one hand, in great bear-like strokes. He was towing Pinn, fingers cupped around his chin. Pinn had gone limp, giving himself over to Malvery's strength.

Frey squelched along the bank to where the current had carried them, and helped them both out. Pinn fell to his hands and knees, retching up river water.

'You rot-damned pair of bastards!' he snarled, between heaves.

'Oh, come on, Pinn,' Frey said. 'I've seen you take down four aircraft without breaking a sweat. You're scared of a little water?'

'I can't *shoot* water!' Pinn protested. He burped noisily and another flood spilled over his lips.

'There they are!' someone yelled from the cliff-top. Bullets pocked the bank and threw up little fins of spray from the river.

'Move it!' Frey scrambled away towards the trees. 'It'll take them ages to find a way round.'

He'd barely finished his sentence before the villagers began to fling themselves off the cliff. 'We just want our money back!' an unseen voice called. 'It's for the orphaaaaans!' The final word lengthened and trailed off as the speaker pitched over the edge and plummeted into the water.

'I'm an orphan!' Frey screamed, infuriated by their persistence. He'd done enough to deserve his escape. Why couldn't they just let him go?

His words fell on deaf ears. Angry faces broke the surface of the river and came swimming towards them.

'Don't those fellers give up?' Malvery complained, and they ran.

It was more luck than design that brought them to a familiar trail, which led them back to the *Ketty Jay*. The villagers had stopped shooting – their guns were soaked – but they showed no signs of abandoning the pursuit. In fact, they were gaining. A lifetime of unhealthy habits and too little exercise hadn't equipped any of Frey's team for a lengthy foot chase. Their waterlogged clothes weighed them down and chafed with every step. By the time they made it to the clearing where their companions waited, Malvery looked like he was about to burst a lung.

The *Ketty Jay* loomed before them, dwarfing the two single-seater fighter craft parked nearby. Frey had long ceased to see her with a judgemental eye. He'd never have called her beautiful, but she wasn't ugly to him either. After fifteen years she was so familiar that he no longer noticed her squat, hunched body, her stub tail or her ungainly bulk. He knew her too well for appearances to matter. That wasn't something Frey could often say about a female.

Harkins, Jez and Crake stood before her, shotguns and pistols in their hands.

'Get to stations!' Frey panted as he entered into the clearing. 'Harkins! Pinn! Up in the sky, right now.'

Harkins jumped as if stung and fled towards one of the fighter craft, a Firecrow with wide, backswept wings and a bubble of windglass on its snout. Pinn lurched off towards the other: a Skylance, a sleek racing machine, built for speed.

'We heard gunfire,' said Jez, as Malvery and Frey approached, soaking and bedraggled. She eyed the doctor, who was unsuccessfully trying to catch his breath. 'Has he been shot or something?'

Malvery's retort was little more than an irate wheeze. He staggered off towards the cargo ramp on the *Ketty Jay*'s far side.

'Robbing the children didn't go to plan, then?' Crake asked the captain, one eyebrow raised.

Frey shoved the lockbox full of coins into Crake's hands. 'It went well enough. Where's Silo and Bess?'

Crake regarded the leaking lockbox disapprovingly. 'Silo's in the engine room, trying to fix the problems we had on the way over here. Bess is asleep in the hold. Should I wake her?'

'No. Get on board. We're going. Last one in, shut the cargo ramp.'

He spared a moment to check on his outflyers before boarding the *Ketty Jay*. The Firecrow and the Skylance were rising vertically from the clearing as their aerium tanks flooded with ultralight gas. Satisfied they were on their way, he ran up the ramp.

Malvery was beached and gasping just inside the hold, surrounded by a large puddle. Frey paid him no attention. Nor did he spare a glance for the hulking metal form of Bess, standing dormant and dark by the stairs. She'd long ceased making him uneasy.

He sprinted up the steps to the main passageway. It was cramped and dimly lit, the cockpit at one end and the engine room at the other, with doors to the crew's quarters and Malvery's tiny infirmary between them. Hydraulics whirred as the cargo ramp closed, sealing the aircraft.

He pushed into the engine room, a small space cluttered by black iron gantries, allowing access to all parts of the complex assembly overhead. It was warm and smelled of machinery. Frey cast around for signs of his engineer, but the only crew member in sight was Slag the cat, a scraggy clump of black fur, watching him from an air vent.

'Silo! Where are you?'

'Up here, Cap'n,' came the reply, although Frey still couldn't see him. He guessed his engineer was working around the other side of the assembly. The *Ketty Jay*, like most aircraft, had two separate sets of engines: aerium for lift and prothane for thrust. Both were tangled together in this room in a confusing jumble of pipes, tanks and malevolent-looking gauges.

'Are we ready to go?' Frey asked, addressing the room in general.

'Wouldn't advise it, Cap'n.'

'Can she *fly*?' he persisted. 'It's a bit urgent, Silo.'

A short pause. 'Yuh,' he said at last. 'Gonna fly like a slug though.'

'That'll do,' said Frey, and pelted out of the engine room, his feet squishing in his boots.

Jez was already at the navigator's station when Frey bundled into the cockpit and threw himself into his seat.

'Destination?' she asked.

'Up,' he replied, and boosted the aerium engines to maximum. The *Ketty Jay* groaned and shrieked as her tanks filled. Frey leaned forward and peered through the windglass of the cockpit. The first of the villagers had reached the clearing now, but they were too late. The *Ketty Jay* was dragging herself off the ground and into the air.

Some of them aimed rifles and tried to fire, but their weapons were still too wet to work. One of them made a suicidal dive for the *Ketty Jay*'s landing struts as they retracted. Luckily for him, he fell short. The villagers raged and yelled and threw what stones they could find, but the *Ketty Jay* kept rising.

Frey felt secure enough to make an obscene gesture at his pursuers. 'Thought you had me, didn't you? Well, let's see you yokels fly!' He slumped back in his seat as they cleared the treetops. Deep relief sank into his bones.

Jez got up from the navigator's station and stood next to him, staring into the night sky with sudden and worrying intensity. Frey followed her gaze.

There were several small, dark shapes in the distance, coming closer.

'Tell me those aren't what I think they are,' he said.

'Yeah,' said Jez. 'It's the villagers. They've got planes.'

TWO

A Ramshackle Squadron – Technical Difficulties –
A Moment Of Clarity – The Fruits Of Persistence

Frey stared out of the cockpit at the dim shadows of the approaching planes. He was getting toward the end of his tether. The paltry amount of money he'd stolen from the orphanage could *not* be worth this level of aggravation.

'Planes,' he said, in the dull tone of one perilously close to going berserk. 'Jez, explain to me how come a bunch of backward country folk have their own air defence force.'

Jez narrowed her eyes. 'Cropdusters modified for fighting forest fires. Mail planes for local deliveries. Personal flyers. There's a small cargo craft in there. Some of them are prop-driven.' She counted. 'There's eight of them in all.'

'Propellers?' Frey scoffed. 'Any of them have guns?'

'Not that I can see. Some of them are open-cockpit two-seaters, though. The passengers have rifles.'

Frey could barely make out the shape of the aircraft at this distance and in this light. But it was no surprise to him that Jez could see every detail. Her eyesight was, literally, inhuman.

He glanced at his navigator. She looked like a normal young woman. *Very* normal, he thought uncharitably, since his habit was to only pay attention to the pretty ones. She wore practical, shapeless overalls and kept her brown hair in an unflattering ponytail. But she was more than she appeared to be. Frey had made it his business not to think about what she actually *was*, but the fact that she had no heartbeat was a pretty hefty clue that something wasn't quite right.

Still, all of them had their secrets, and on the *Ketty Jay* you didn't ask. She was an outstanding navigator and as loyal as you could want. She was the only other person aboard who was allowed – or indeed able – to fly his beloved aircraft in his absence. That decision had taken a lot of trust on Frey's part. Trust didn't come easily to Frey. But she'd been on the *Ketty Jay* for over a year now and she'd never let him down.

In the end, it didn't matter *what* she was. She was crew.

Frey fired up the prothane engines and swivelled the craft, presenting her stern to the approaching planes. 'They really think they're going to catch us in those junkers?' he said. 'Let's show 'em what a *real* aircraft can do.' Jez braced herself against the back of his seat as he lit up the thrusters.

The expected acceleration didn't come. The boom of ignition was far feebler than Frey was used to hearing. At first the *Ketty Jay* didn't move at all, struggling to shift her own weight. When she began to push forward, it was like moving through treacle. The clearing full of angry villagers slid away beneath them, but not half as fast as Frey would have liked.

'Silo wasn't joking about the engines,' he murmured.

'You ever heard him joke about anything?'

'Suppose not.' He leaned back in his seat and bellowed out the cockpit door. *'Malvery! Get up here!'*

The *Ketty Jay* was picking up speed, but far too slowly. There was a silver earcuff lying in an ashtray set into the brass and chrome dash, between the dials and meters. He snatched it up and clipped it to the back of his ear.

'Harkins. Pinn. Can you hear me?'

'Yes, Cap'n, I'm, er, you startled me a bit, I mean, loud and, erm, I can hear you, yes,' came Harkin's babbled reply.

It sounded as if he was standing right next to Frey, instead of sitting in his cockpit fifty metres away. He was wearing an earcuff of his own, as was Pinn. When one of them spoke, the others could hear what they said. It was one of Crake's little tricks. Sometimes having a daemonist on board came in handy.

'What's up with the *Ketty Jay*?' asked Pinn. 'Her thrusters are barely lit. Might as well strap a gas stove to her arse for all the acceleration you're getting.'

'Technical difficulties,' Frey replied. 'We've got incoming craft. They've a couple of rifles, that's all. No real danger, but the *Ketty Jay* isn't going to outpace them till she builds up speed. Keep them off me as best you can.'

'I'll keep them off you, alright,' Pinn said eagerly. 'I'll—'

'And *don't* shoot them down. I don't want them madder than they already are.'

'We can't shoot them down?' Pinn cried. 'What are we supposed to do? Hypnotise them with fancy flying?'

'It's a bunch of cropdusters and mail planes, Pinn,' Frey told him. 'They're not much of a threat, and I could do without the Navy coming after us. We've managed to stay beneath their notice since the whole Retribution Falls thing. I'd like to keep it that way. Let's keep the needless slaughter to a minimum, eh?'

'You, Cap'n, are a pussy,' said Pinn.

'And you're scared of water.'

'He's scared of *water*?' Harkins crowed eagerly.

'Don't you start, you jittery old git!' Pinn snapped. 'You're scared of *everything*.'

'Not water, though,' Harkins replied, with an unmistakable note of triumph in his voice.

'Everyone shut up and fly!' said Frey, before they could get into an argument. Pinn subsided, grumbling.

The *Ketty Jay* had picked up a respectable amount of speed now. Malvery appeared at the door of the cockpit, still red-faced from his run earlier.

'You bellowed, Cap'n?'

'I need you up in the bubble. There's planes on our tail. Don't shoot at them unless I give the word.'

'Right-o,' said Malvery. He returned to the passageway and climbed the ladder that led to the autocannon cupola on the *Ketty Jay*'s hump. From there, he could act as Frey's eyes astern. Frey wished there was a better way to see what was going on behind his craft while he was airborne, but if there was, he hadn't found it yet.

'They're catching us up, Cap'n,' Malvery reported. 'You might want to go a bit faster.'

Frey swallowed his reply and concentrated on flying. The Vardenwood lay for hundreds of kloms in all directions. In the far distance he could see the grand city of Vaspine, a crown of lights on the highest hilltops. Below them was the forest, cut through with steep, sharp valleys that joined and divided haphazardly.

'What's the plan, Cap'n?' Jez asked.

Frey hated being asked that, usually because he didn't have an answer. 'Well, they can't really do much. They don't have guns that can penetrate the *Ketty Jay*'s hull. Pinn and Harkins can stay out of their range. We just need a bit of time to pick up speed, then we'll leave them behind.'

Jez returned to the navigator's station and began looking at her charts. Frey watched Harkins and Pinn drop back, behind the *Ketty Jay*, out of his line of vision.

'Er, one of them's coming up on us awfully fast, Cap'n,' said Malvery. 'Cropduster, by the looks.'

'Put a few warning shots across his bow,' Frey called. '*Warning* shots, Malvery.'

'Got it, Cap'n.' The autocannon thumped out a short burst.

'Hey, how come Malvery gets to shoot?' Pinn complained in Frey's ear. Frey ignored him.

'Doesn't seem to have done much good, Cap'n,' said Malvery from the cupola.

Frey pulled the flight stick sharply left. The *Ketty Jay* responded with an unsettling laziness.

'That didn't do much, either,' Malvery said. 'He's gonna pass over us.'

'You see any guns?'

'No.'

Frey frowned. He wasn't quite sure what the pilot of that plane thought he was going to do to a craft the size of the *Ketty Jay*. He was still wondering when an avalanche of dust hit the windglass of the cockpit, and he found himself flying blind.

'Cap'n!' Malvery yelled. 'I can't see for buggery up here!'

'What in damnation just happened?' Frey panicked, wrestling with his flight stick. The thrusters were labouring. The *Ketty Jay*'s Blackmore P-12s could usually chew through anything, but in their present state, they were having trouble unclogging themselves.

'He dumped his tanks on you!' Pinn told Frey. 'All his fire-fighting dusty stuff. Can't hardly see you in the cloud! Ah, there's more of them coming in now!'

Frey banked again. He heard Malvery open up with the autocannon above him. 'Malvery! I said no!'

'Oh, *now* you've found your morals?'

'You've seen how they are! If we kill one of 'em, they'll never leave us alone.'

'Cap'n, we should—'

His reply was cut short by a heavy thump from above, that shook the whole aircraft. Frey felt the *Ketty Jay* plunge a few metres.

'You've got to be joking,' he muttered to himself.

'Cap'n!' Malvery, slightly hysterical this time. 'He's trying to land on us!'

The *Ketty Jay* rocked again. Frey swore under his breath. The pilot wasn't trying to land on them. He was trying to force them down, bumping them from above with his undercarriage wheels. What kind of crazed idiot did anything *half* that dangerous?

'Can we *please* just shoot them?' Pinn cried.

'I've just robbed a bunch of orphans!' Frey snapped. 'I don't want anything else on my conscience today!'

'I thought you said *you* were an orphan?' Pinn said. 'Doesn't that make it alright?'

Frey bit his lip and sent the *Ketty Jay* into a dive, venting aerium gas from the tanks to add speed to his descent. The dust had sloughed off the windglass, smearing as it went. It was enough to see through, barely.

'Lose 'em in the valleys?' Jez suggested.

'Lose 'em in the valleys,' Frey agreed.

Frey was getting angry, and when he got angry he got reckless. He dearly wanted to machine-gun the villagers out of the sky, but he was too afraid of the consequences. His specialties were minor smuggling, petty theft, a gentle bit of piracy where nobody got shot and not too much was taken. They were soft crimes which the Navy were far too busy to concern themselves with. Once in a while somebody died, but usually it was a guard too stupid to drop his weapon or a criminal who probably deserved it anyway. People who accepted the risks and were paid to take them.

Frey didn't count himself in that category, of course. In some vague, ill-defined way, he thought himself more noble than that.

Innocent folk, however, were another matter. These villagers only wanted their money back. Their dogged persistence made him feel guilty, and he was mad at them for that. Theft was only fun if you didn't have to think about the consequences. He didn't actually want the orphanage to close or those children to starve. He'd sort of assumed that the villagers would stump up to cover the shortfall. But since they were so desperate to get it back, he began to wonder whether they could actually afford it.

Bloody yokels. They were ruining his first successful escapade in months.

The valleys in this part of the Vardenwood were deep and narrow. A complex river system snaked through trenches between the hills, banked by sheer, rocky slopes. Down on the valley floor the walls pressed in tight. The waters thundered through, swollen by the spring floods, glittering silver-grey in the moonlight.

Frey knew the *Ketty Jay* was operating well below par, but he could still fly better than any amateur could. It took nerve to race through enclosed spaces in an aircraft at night. Nerve that he was betting his pursuers didn't have.

'They're taking potshots at us, Cap'n,' Pinn said in his ear.

'Follow me down into the valleys. Buzz them when you can. Just keep them occupied.'

Pinn muttered something Frey didn't quite catch and then shut up again.

Frey rubbed at his earcuff absently. The early versions of the daemon-powered communicators had leached energy from their users, tiring them out the more they talked to each other. Crake had refined them since, giving them better range and minimising the draining effect. Now they could gabble on to their heart's content, but that only meant they argued and bitched more. Frey wondered if he hadn't preferred the way it was before.

'How's that cropduster, Malvery?' he called.

'Falling behind,' the doctor replied from the cupola.

Frey smiled. The *Ketty Jay* had finally built up some speed. Not enough to outstrip the villagers' craft, but enough to make them work to keep up. Still, it was going to be difficult flying through the valleys in her condition. Since the *Ketty Jay* took so long to accelerate, he couldn't use his air brakes. He'd be forced to take every turn at speed.

Just be extra careful, he told himself, knowing that he wouldn't be.

The *Ketty Jay* swooped into a valley. Slopes of grass and rock blurred by on either side, punctuated by scrawny trees hanging on at unlikely angles. Frey boosted the aerium engines – at least *they* worked fine – and pulled back on the flight stick to level out a few dozen metres above the river. The valley floor was wide here, and there were small, isolated farming communities on the banks, their windows dark. The *Ketty Jay* roared past them, kicking up spray and panicking their sleepy herds. Frey took a small, malicious pleasure in that.

'Malvery? The cropduster?'

'He's gone. Pulled off. Can't see him now. Others are coming in though.'

Well, at least we've scared one of them off. Let's see how long the rest of them last in the valleys.

Frey looked up and saw several of the villagers' rustbucket aircraft angling down towards him. Harkins and Pinn were doing their best to harass them, but the villagers' resolve was unshakable.

Jez was rustling charts at her station. 'Valley branches right up ahead, Cap'n. That one's narrower.'

'We'll take it,' said Frey.

The villagers intercepted them before they got to the fork, descending from above to surround the *Ketty Jay*. Suddenly Frey found himself in the midst of a swarm of small aircraft that buzzed around him like clumsy bees. He wiped at the inside of the cockpit windglass in a futile attempt to clear the dust that stubbornly clung to the other side. He didn't dare take evasive action. The villagers were flying too close.

He heard the sharp tap of a bullet hitting the *Ketty Jay*. 'They're shooting at us,' Malvery called, sounding unconcerned.

'Let 'em, if it makes 'em happy,' said Frey. The *Ketty Jay*'s armour plating could take a good deal more than that.

'Turn coming up,' Jez warned him.

Frey flexed his hand on the flight stick. 'Pinn! Harkins! Keep going straight on. Take as many with you as you can. I'm going right.'

'Got it, Cap'n!' said Harkins. Then he screamed.

'What? What?' Frey demanded.

'Something hit me!'

Frey searched for Harkins among the planes that surrounded them, and located the Firecrow. It appeared to be undamaged. Then his eye fell on a nearby villager, who was riding shotgun in an ancient open-top biplane, above and to the left of Harkins. As Frey watched, the man lobbed a small object out of the cockpit. It dropped through the air and bounced off the Firecrow's wing. Harkins screamed again and banked in panic. He almost collided with a one-man flyer that was hard on his tail.

'It happened again!'

'They're throwing stuff at you,' Frey informed him. 'With pretty extraordinary accuracy. I think the last one was a wrench.'

'A *wrench*?!' Harkins shrieked. 'What . . . how . . . I mean, what kind of madmen *are* these? I don't have to take this! Cap'n, I've got a bad feeling . . . I mean to say . . . It's just . . . Allsoul's balls, I'd rather fight the Navy than these lot!'

'Turning coming up *now*!' Jez said.

Frey saw it. The branching valley was a *lot* narrower.

'Everyone, get out of the way!' Frey yelled at the craft around him. 'I'm coming through, like it or not!' With that, he wrenched the flight stick to the right. Planes scattered as the *Ketty Jay* slewed away. Frey and Jez were pressed into their seats. There was a raucous series of crashes as every unsecured object on the *Ketty Jay* tipped over. The artificial horizon on Frey's dash tipped sideways.

We're going too fast!

The rock and scree slope raced to meet them as the *Ketty Jay* curved gracelessly into the tributary valley. Frey hauled on the stick as hard as he could, but the turn was just a fraction too tight, and he knew they weren't going to make it. He hit the airbrakes and boosted the aerium tanks at the same time, lightening and slowing the craft.

Too little, too late. There was no way he was going to miss that wall. With that realisation came a flash, a moment of stunning clarity in his mind.

What will I leave behind?

Then the *Ketty Jay* screamed into the tributary, her belly almost scraping the valley wall. Frey blinked. Not dead after all.

There was no time for shock. He levelled the craft, hit the thrusters and tried to make up the speed he'd lost. He could tell Jez was staring at him in disbelief, but he didn't want to meet her eyes right now.

'Malvery! Are they still on us?'

'Two of 'em! We've lost the rest!' Malvery was still in good humour, apparently unaware of their near-death experience. 'One coming up on us fast!'

Jez shook herself and went back to her maps. 'Another tributary coming up. Hard left. The angle's steep, but the tributary's wider.'

Frey's eyes flickered over the valley. Rock and grass and water. The world beyond the smudged windglass seemed startlingly sharp, yet he was flying in a daze.

'Cap'n?' Jez prompted.

'Hard left. Got it.' He tapped his earcuff. 'Hey, Harkins, Pinn? Still there?'

'We're still here.'

'You've done enough. Get going. We'll meet you at the rendez-vous.'

'At bloody last,' Pinn said. 'Bye, bye, country boys!'

Frey heard him whoop as he pushed the Skylance to maximum, then he faded out of range. Harkins would be gone too. The villagers' planes couldn't come close to the speed of the fighters.

He spotted the turn ahead of them. Plenty of space, especially as they'd shed some velocity. He was lining up for it when one of the villagers pulled in front of him. It was another two-seater, powered by thrusters and aerium like all modern craft. In the back seat was a man with a rifle, levelling up for another shot at the *Ketty Jay*. Frey gave him a glance and ignored him, concentrating instead on the up-coming manoeuvre. Let him waste a bullet. Since the pilot was ahead of him, he wouldn't be able to match Frey's sudden turn.

Ready . . .

Ready . . .

Now!

Frey banked hard, and at the same moment the windglass of his cockpit cracked noisily, making him jump. Between the dust, the dark, and the crazed shatter-pattern on the windglass, he could hardly see a thing. Yelling in fear, clinging to his flight stick, he pulled the *Ketty Jay* through the turn more by feel and luck than anything else.

'He shot my damn windglass!' Frey cried. He jerked his head about, searching frantically for an unshattered section to see through, and found one just in time to spot the cropduster come flying directly towards him along the valley. He yelled again, threw his whole weight on the stick, and the *Ketty Jay* dived, hard enough to send the cropduster shooting over their heads.

'What the bloody shit was that? It almost killed me!' Malvery shouted from the cupola.

Frey levelled the *Ketty Jay* with trembling hands. 'He tried to ram us,' Frey said in disbelief. 'He tried to *ram* us!' Then his face and voice hardened. 'Alright. That's *it*!' He turned in his seat. 'Jez. Take the *Ketty Jay*. Turn on the belly lamps and put her down on the valley floor.'

Jez didn't question the order. She got up and switched with him in the pilot's seat. Frey heard her decelerating as he stormed out of the cockpit and into the passageway. He went past the ladder that led to the cupola, where Malvery's feet could be seen dangling.

'Cap'n?' Malvery said, but Frey swept by him, heading for the cargo hold.

His jaw was set tightly as he stamped down steps and passed along gantries. The hold was all but empty, full of echoes. The whine as the *Ketty Jay* extended her landing struts was loud in here.

Crake was at the bottom of the steps, still holding the lockbox full of coins Frey had given him. He was clinging on to a handrail. There was a bruise on the side of his head.

'What's going on out there, Frey?' he asked. 'I'd have come up, but I didn't dare take the stairs, the way you were flying.'

'Don't worry about it. Give me the box.'

Crake did so. Frey felt the *Ketty Jay* sink and slow, then there was a jolt as she settled on to her struts. He grabbed an emergency flare from a half-empty rack and pulled the lever to lower the cargo ramp at the *Ketty Jay*'s rear. Hard white brightness flooded in from the landing lamps on her underside. Beyond was the deep green grass of a wild meadow.

He went out into the meadow and stood in the full glare of the lights. Three planes were coming down the valley towards him. He thrust the box in the air with one hand.

'Here's your money, since you want it so much!' He threw it sulkily on the ground, lit the flare, and tossed it to the earth next to the box. 'Now leave me alone!'

He went inside, closed the ramp, and headed back to the cockpit. Jez slipped out of his seat and he took the *Ketty Jay* up again.

'Doc!' he called. 'What are they doing behind us?'

'Most of 'em are breaking off,' Malvery said. 'One's landing where you left the flare.'

'Does it look like they're coming after us?'

'Doesn't look that way, Cap'n.'

'Good. Make sure they're not following, then you can come down.'

'Right-o.'

Frey pulled the *Ketty Jay* out of the valleys and into the sky. A profound depression had settled on him. After a long while, Malvery clambered down from the cupola and headed wordlessly off to his infirmary. Jez got up and stood by Frey's shoulder, peering through the ruined windglass at the moon beyond.

'You know what's worse than robbing a bunch of defenceless orphans?' Frey said. '*Failing* to rob a bunch of defenceless orphans.'

She patted him on the shoulder. 'Brave try, Cap'n.'

'Oh, shut up.'

Three

Thornlodge Hollow nestled among the hills and trees of the Vardenwood, minding its own business. It was a town of moderate wealth and prosperity, situated far from the main trade routes. The houses on the riverside were tall and narrow, with tall, narrow windows to match. Cobbled lanes meandered past serene shopfronts. Winding paths led away through the forest to farms and smallholdings and miniature satellite villages. Pretty bridges spanned picturesque streams. The folds of the hills concealed glades and meadows.

It was a pleasant and perfectly normal place. Most people didn't know where it was, pirates and smugglers included. A good spot for the crew of the *Ketty Jay* to hole up and lick their wounds for a while.

The landing pad was some way out of town, on a hilltop, hemmed in by tall trees. Its perimeter was illuminated by gaslit lamp-posts, which cast a yellow light on the underside of the leaves. It wasn't large, but there wasn't much traffic in a place like Thornlodge Hollow. Twenty craft of various sizes rested there, from small one-man flyers to a pair of cargo barques that occupied a quarter of the pad by themselves. A portable oil-powered generator grumbled away next to the dock master's hut, where there was a spotlight to guide down aircraft. Night breezes pushed through the evergreens, carrying the smell of new growth.

Jez and Silo walked a slow circuit around the *Ketty Jay*, studying her as they went. She was a shabby thing to look at, patched up in a dozen places, a bastard combination of a heavy combat craft and a cargo hauler. Yet there was a defiance about her, a certain blunt strength that Jez was fond of. She was built tough, a survivor. Like the cat that patrolled her air ducts, she was scarred, ugly, and invincible.

Over the previous few days, the windglass of the cockpit had been replaced and the *Ketty Jay* had been cleaned. Silo and Jez had carried out numerous minor repairs on the craft's systems: soldering loose plates, oiling rusty mechanisms, running tests. Jez wasn't half the engineer that Silo was, but she was the daughter of a craftbuilder and she knew enough to lend a hand. Silo, for his part, had been mostly occupied with fixing the engine trouble that had made their last escape such a fiasco.

Silo stopped when they came to the *Ketty Jay*'s starboard side. He scrutinised the hefty thruster above and astern of her wing. The tall Murthian was hard to read, as ever. That umber-skinned, hawk-nosed face was like a mask. Immobile and impenetrable. It was a surprise when his expression changed, like seeing a statue suddenly move.

'Need parts,' he said in his rumbling bass voice. After working on the engine for days, this was Jez's first hint of a diagnosis.

'Expensive parts?' she asked.

'Yuh.' He took out papers and a pinch of herbs, and began putting a roll-up together.

Jez watched his long, clever fingers at work. 'What's wrong with it?'

'Timing on the fuel injectors. All wrong. I keep fixin' it, but it gonna get worse.' His accent was slow and hard, consonants like jagged rocks in the lazy tide of his vowels.

'Ah,' said Jez. She understood. Timing was everything in a prothane engine. If the mechanism was faulty, then it would need replacing. But the *Ketty Jay*'s engine was from a workshop that had long since closed down, and the parts could be tricky to find. She doubted Frey had the money to buy them anyway.

'Will it hold up?' she asked.

'She hold up for now,' said Silo. 'But she could go any moment.'

Jez sighed. That pretty much summed up their whole operation. Held together with elastic and luck, straining at the edges, always ready to snap. Yet somehow it never happened.

Silo offered her a roll-up, out of politeness. She held up a hand and gave him a smile of thanks. Even if she smoked, she wouldn't smoke that. Silo's roll-ups were a blend from Murthia, strong enough to induce hacking coughs and limb spasms in even the stoutest of men. They were all he had left to remind him of the land of his birth, thousands of kloms to the south. Silo was an exile, unwanted every-where, who'd found his home on the *Ketty Jay*.

As have we all, Jez thought.

She gave him a comradely slap on the back and left him staring up at the thrusters while she headed astern. The cargo ramp was down, leading into the hold.

A ball came bouncing out of the shadowy gloom and rolled past her feet. She stared after it, puzzled.

It was only the heavy thump of boots that warned her. She threw herself aside as an eight-foot-high armoured monster thundered down the ramp in pursuit of the ball. Half a ton of dull metal and ragged chain mail plunged past her, missing her by inches.

Bess.

The golem pounced on the ball with a triumphant crash, skidding along the landing pad and fetching up just short of the landing struts of a nearby aircraft. She scrambled to her feet, her short, thick legs supporting a humpbacked, outsized torso. The ball was cupped in her huge hands, held in front of the circular grille that passed for her face. Twin glimmers of light shone in the darkness behind the grille, glittering eagerly as she stared at her prize. Then she raced back up the ramp and into the *Ketty Jay*, ignoring Jez completely.

'*Crake!*' Jez yelled irritably, as she picked herself up off the floor.

The daemonist appeared at the top of the ramp. He was blond-haired, with a close-cut beard, wearing an expensive coat that had frayed and faded with time. His forehead was creased with worry.

Jez regretted her tone immediately. Crake wasn't looking good these days. His face was as worn as his coat. There were lines there, too deep for a man of thirty. Dark bags under his eyes.

'Are you alright?' he asked, wringing his hands. 'I'm so sorry. The game just got away from us.'

Jez softened. 'No harm done.'

'She didn't hurt you, did she?'

Jez waved it away. 'You know me. I'm like a cockroach.'

'Honestly, Jez, that's a little harsh. You just need a dab of make-up.' Crake cracked a smile, and that made her glad. She hadn't seen too many from him lately.

She went up into the hold. Bess was sitting on the floor, her legs sticking out in front of her, patting the ball this way and that. An eerie cooing noise was coming from within her. They watched her together for a moment.

'She seems happy,' Jez offered. Crake didn't reply. She looked at him. 'How are you holding up?'

Crake frowned at her. As if he couldn't understand what might prompt her to ask such a question. As if he couldn't imagine what she might mean.

'Fine,' he said, coldly. 'Just fine.'

Jez nodded and headed up the stairs from the hold to the walkway above. There she paused and looked over the railing. Crake was standing next to Bess, one arm laid over her arm, his forehead leaning against her face-grille. His mouth was moving. Though he was far out of human earshot, Jez could hear him anyway.

'Good girl,' he whispered, sadly. 'Good girl.'

Jez felt a tightening in her throat, and hurried away.

She'd almost reached the main passageway when a blood-chilling scream made her jump. She ran the last few steps and burst into the room to find Harkins lying on the floor outside the quarters he shared with Pinn, gasping, coughing and clawing at the air.

'What? Harkins, what?' she cried in alarm.

'The ca . . . it wa . . .' he panted, unable to draw breath. A moment later Slag padded out of his quarters. Harkins shrieked and backed up against the wall of the corridor. Slag stared at him with an expression of loathing, then caught sight of Jez and bolted towards the engine room.

'Oh,' said Jez, understanding now. 'Cat slept on your face again?'

'That bloody rotting moggy!' Harkins exploded, scratching at his unshaven cheeks to scrape off the moulted fur. His leather pilot's cap was askew, revealing a head of mousy hair that had thinned almost to transparency. 'It just . . . it's . . . even if I shut the door, Pinn comes in when I'm asleep and leaves it open! And even if he doesn't, the cat gets in through the vent! I have nightmares! Suffocation! You know what that's like? Do you?'

'No,' said Jez honestly, since she didn't need to breathe any more. 'Harkins, it's just a cat.'

Harkins' eyes bulged from his hangdog face. 'It's *evil*!' he said. 'It's . . . it's . . . it *waits*, can't you see it? It waits till I'm asleep. It hates me! It hates me!'

23

'You and me both,' said Jez, with a rueful smile. 'I don't get on with animals.'

'It's *scared* of you. That's not the same. It's not even close to the same! It's about as far from the same as . . .' He trailed off, unable to think of a suitable comparison.

'Maybe you just need to stand up to him,' Jez suggested. 'You are about twenty times his size, after all.'

The gangly pilot picked himself up with a resentful glare. He looked twitchily around the corridor and then jammed his cap back down on his head. 'I'll never sleep now. Not for hours,' he huffed. Then he hurried off towards the hold and outside, where he'd be safe from the cat. Slag hadn't left the *Ketty Jay* since he was first brought aboard as a kitten, over fourteen years ago. The only thing that scared him, apart from Jez, was the sky.

She went to her quarters with a smile on her face, shaking her head. *My home. My family. What a curious lot we are.*

As dusk fell, Frey, Pinn and Malvery headed into town, as they'd done every night since they landed here. Sometime Crake went with them, but not tonight. Jez wasn't one for drinking, Harkins was frightened of strangers, and Silo stayed with the craft for everyone's sake. The Second Aerium War was still a raw wound almost eight years after it had finished. Silo's people had fought for the enemy, however unwillingly they'd done so. Murthians were not popular folk in Vardia.

Frey led the way as they followed the well-used path down the hill, through the darkening trees. The light drained from the sky, turning to violet and gold, and the last of the day's birdsong died away as the insects took over. This far south, spring was starting early: it wasn't even the end of Middenmoil yet.

When they got to the tavern, they were greeted by the usual fixed grimace on the owner's face. Frey could see how a little piece of his soul died every time these rowdy strangers pushed through the door, calling for drinks. This was a nice town, a quiet town. The kind of town where people got uncomfortable when grown men began to drunkenly sing shanties at the tops of their voices.

But it was the only tavern in town, so they kept coming back. Besides, Frey liked it. He liked the big windows that looked out over a cobbled road to the black woods. He liked to be able to see his reflection in the glass, thrown back by the soft light of the hooded gas lamps. They always sat at a table near a window, though he never said why.

It was about the point in the evening when Pinn started turning the conversation towards his sweetheart, and everyone else tried to turn it away. But Pinn was not to be deterred tonight, inspired by the sight of several young and moderately attractive females at the bar. Word of the strangers had spread. Since it was Kingsday tomorrow, a day of rest, some of the town's more youthful population had come to see what the fuss was about. The tavern was busier than they'd ever seen it.

'She's worth ten of any of them girls!' he slurred, waving a flagon about. 'That's fact. My Lisinda, she's . . . well, I'm a lucky man. A lucky, lucky man. Some people go their whole lives without . . . without finding true love.' He shook his head blearily. 'But not me. Not me, oh no. I found mine. And I love her. I do!' He thumped his fist on the table, frowning, as if someone had been arguing the point. Then his face softened into a happy leer. 'I miss her lips. Lisinda's lips. Soft as . . . soft as pillows.'

He lurched to his feet suddenly, and stood there swaying, his eyes trying to focus. 'Going for a piss,' he said, then stumbled off through the crowd.

Malvery let his head drop to the table with a thump. 'I may be forced to brain him if he doesn't shut up about that damn girl,' he said, despairingly.

'Please do,' said Frey, without much enthusiasm. He didn't seem to have any enthusiasm for anything tonight. Not even for the pretty redhead who kept glancing over at him from her spot among a group of friends. He knew that look. He counted himself something of an expert in the field of casual seduction. But somehow he just couldn't muster the effort to care at the moment. Drink had made him maudlin.

'Do you think she's even real?' Malvery continued. He took a pull from his flagon and wiped beer foam from his white moustache. 'I mean, how long's it been? Years! Years of him talking about his bloody sweetheart, and all I've ever seen of her is that ferrotype he carries around.' He adjusted his glasses and snorted. 'I say she ain't even real.'

Frey stared into the middle distance as he finished his mug of grog. It was a theory he'd heard many, many times before from Malvery.

'What's up, Cap'n?' Malvery inquired. 'You've had a face like a bowel tumour all night.'

'I'm just not in the mood, Doc,' Frey said. ''Scuse me.'

He got up from the table and walked away. Through a doorway and along a corridor was a quieter room, out of sight of the main tavern area. This was where most of the older patrons had retreated, to avoid the raucous singing that would come later. A guitarist was playing in the corner, and the lamps were turned down low.

The townsfolk stared disapprovingly at Frey as he entered. He ignored them and found himself a stool at the bar. The scrawny young barman eyed him dubiously.

'Grog,' said Frey, putting a few shillies on the bar with a click.

There was a mirror behind the bar, tarnished with cigar smoke. Frey watched himself in it as he waited for his drink.

He was just as handsome as he'd ever been, in a roguishly unkempt kind of way. He had dark eyes, promising wickedness. Women went for those eyes. His hair was black, and always seemed to do exactly what he wanted it to. His cheeks and chin were peppered with just the right amount of grizzle. He'd been born lucky in looks, which was good, because in every other department things had been pretty shit. Abandoned as a baby on the steps of an orphanage, brought up with a bare minimum of education in a dead-end town in the backwaters of Lapin. It wasn't the best start in life.

He showed some talent with words, so they'd taught him to write. But reading didn't interest him. Stories seemed pointless; they weren't real. Instead, he turned his talent to charm and lies. He learned early on how the right words could turn an adult's wrath to indulgent chuckling. He learned, later, how they could induce a woman to take him to bed.

There had been many women since, but only one that meant anything.

The barman put a mug down in front of him. He picked it up and drank from it. His eyes flicked back to the mirror. He couldn't help it.

He needed to check he was still there.

What's wrong with me?

It had started soon after they landed at Thornlodge Hollow. At first he'd thought he was just rattled. He'd nearly flown the *Ketty Jay* into the side of a valley, and that was bound to shake anyone up. But days passed and he still felt the same. He'd scraped past death before and it hadn't bothered him particularly. What was different this time?

It was the thought that sprang into his head, in that moment when he really believed he was going to die.

What will I leave behind?

He couldn't think of a single thing. No property, no family. If he was erased right now, what evidence would there be that he'd lived? What was he worth, except a few drunken toasts from a loyal crew? There were six people in his life he could count as friends, and they were a rag-tag bunch at best.

Suddenly, it didn't seem enough.

What about Retribution Falls, eh? he asked himself. *You pretty much saved the Coalition back then!*

He felt a small surge of pride as he remembered the events of the previous winter, when he'd been framed for the murder of the Archduke's son. In the process of wriggling out of that particular predicament, he ended up averting a coup against the Archduke by leading the Navy to a hidden pirate army at Retribution Falls.

But even that didn't feel like much, if he was honest. He didn't give a toss about the Coalition. One Archduke was much the same as the other to him. He hadn't been acting out of noble intentions; he'd been trying to save his own hide. And besides, the only people who knew about his involvement were some Navy personnel and a few Century Knights. Better that way. If the pirate community ever found out about his rather spectacular betrayal, he wouldn't last long.

It didn't *mean* anything. Nothing *meant* anything.

He swigged his grog. The year since Retribution Falls had been squandered, like all the years before it. The money they made had been spent. And now here they were again, living day-to-day, scrabbling for enough ducats to keep the *Ketty Jay* in the sky. Silo would need parts for the engine, of that he was sure. Frey wouldn't have enough to buy them. It was a miserable state of affairs.

He wondered what would have happened if they'd got away from Retribution Falls with *all* the treasure, instead of the measly portion he ended up with. Would he have used it to buy a tavern, perhaps? Would he have settled down with a sweetheart and raised children? Or would he have wasted it on games of Rake with ever-higher stakes?

It wasn't even a question, really.

His whole life he'd been obsessed with defending his freedom. Freedom from commitments and responsibility. He'd dreamed of a buccaneer's life, of riches and adventure. But somehow the riches always eluded him, and what adventures he had were less than romantic in reality.

Living without anchors had its consequences. It was dangerously easy to drift.

His thoughts were interrupted by the smell of perfume. He looked to his left. There, on a stool, was the pretty redhead who'd been watching him in the other room. She brushed her hair behind one ear and gave him a shy smile.

'Hello,' she said.

Later, when they were together beneath the covers, he tried to make himself care about her. He thought about the hopes and dreams she'd bored him with on the way to her bedroom, and attempted to feel something. That was what a decent man would do, surely?

But whenever he closed his eyes, he saw a corn-haired young woman, as he'd known her before her life turned to death and tragedy. A woman he'd almost married, but ruined instead.

The redhead's slender body moved beneath him, but it was Trinica Dracken he felt there.

Four

A Rude Awakening – Grist's Proposition –
An Explorer's Tale – Risky Business – A Hard Bargain

Someone was calling Frey's name. He snorted and snuffled and did his best not to wake up. He could smell cigar smoke, but he wasn't curious enough to find out why.

'Cap'n!' Jez's voice. Damn that woman! Whenever she woke him up it meant trouble. The cloying muzziness of sleep and the weight of a mild hangover helped him resist the call to action.

'Cap'n, I know you're awake, and if you don't get up now I'll shoot you.'

Frey sighed and opened his eyes. He was in an unfamiliar room, in an unfamiliar bed. Standing at the end of it were Jez and three strangers. One he recognised as the redhead he'd slept with last night. That explained the room and the bed. He struggled to remember her name and failed.

The other two he'd never seen before. One was a big, burly man with a thick black beard and a fat cigar chomped between yellowed teeth. He had a broken, lumpy nose, smudged black with frostbite at the tip, and a cauliflower ear. A heavy cutlass and a brace of pistols hung from his belt, deliberately visible underneath his dirty greatcoat.

His companion was slightly built and better dressed, with an aristocratic look about him. He wore a finely tailored shirt and trousers, loose and casual, and he had a long face and strong nose. He'd gone prematurely bald on top of his head, which made him look older than his face and eyes suggested.

Frey took stock of the situation. The redhead looked rather alarmed and was chewing her lip. She hadn't dared refuse these strangers entry when they came knocking, but now she wondered what she'd done. The last thing she wanted was someone murdered in her bed. Apart from anything else, the cleaning bill would be horrendous.

Jez was standing behind and to the left of the big man. She had her hand on her pistol butt, to let Frey know she had him covered. She shot her captain a look, but it was too early in the morning to decipher what she meant. *Relax? Danger?* He couldn't tell.

'Darian Frey,' said the big man with the cigar. He sounded like he was gargling with gravel. 'You're a hard man to find.'

'That's why I'm still alive,' he said, rubbing a hand through his hair. 'Mind telling me how you did it?'

'Heard about the orphanage. Sounded like your handiwork. After that it was just a matter of askin' around.'

Frey gave Jez a baleful glare. 'And how did *you* find me?'

'Women's intuition, Cap'n,' said Jez, holding up a small compass, out of sight of the others. Frey flopped back against the pillow and groaned. Another of Crake's little devices. The compass was linked to a thin silver ring worn on Frey's little finger. Both were thralled with weak daemons that oscillated at the same frequency. So Crake had told him, anyway. The upshot was that the needle of the compass always pointed towards the ring. Crake had thought it would be a good idea to be able to find their captain in times of emergency, especially as he had a habit of disappearing on three-day drunken Rake sessions without telling anyone where he was. Frey complained that they were treating him like a wayward adolescent, but in the end he agreed because he thought the ring looked good on him.

'Could this not have waited till I got back to the *Ketty Jay?*' Frey asked.

Jez shrugged. 'They said it was urgent. Wasn't any telling when you'd be back. Might not have been till next week.'

'And we ain't got that kind of time,' said the big man. He looked at the redhead and sucked on his cigar. 'Forgive the intrusion, ma'am. We'll be out o' your hair shortly.'

'You're not going to hurt him, are you?' the redhead asked anxiously. Damn, what was her *name*?

The big man chuckled, smoke leaking out between his teeth, rising around his head in a cloud. 'Hurt him? No, ma'am. I'm going to offer him a job.'

★

Thirty minutes later, Frey found himself back in Thornlodge Hollow's only tavern, enjoying a breakfast of chicken, potatoes and a morning beer to shake off the effects of last night's grog.

There were four of them at the table: Frey, Jez and the two strangers. The cigar-smoking man was Harvin Grist, captain of the *Storm Dog*. His aristocratic companion had introduced himself as an explorer, by the name of Rodley Hodd.

Frey was enjoying every bite of his breakfast. Food tasted better when it was bought by someone else. 'Seriously,' he said around a mouthful of chicken. 'Why me?'

'You are *the* Darian Frey, aren't you?' said Hodd. 'The Darian Frey who robbed the *Delirium Trigger* while she was berthed in a hangar in Rabban? Who stole Trinica Dracken's treasure from right under her nose?'

That story had grown in the telling, it seemed. It had been charts, not treasure, he'd stolen. Charts that showed the location of the hidden pirate town of Retribution Falls. But he was happy to claim the glory either way.

'What if I am?'

'Then you travel with a daemonist, don't you?' said Grist. 'A man who controls a great metal golem.'

Frey was immediately on his guard. Crake had been on the run from somebody or something ever since he'd come on board the *Ketty Jay*, but Frey had never asked what. There were plenty, like the Awakeners and their followers, who thought daemonists should be hanged for dabbling with strange and terrible entities.

'What if I do?'

'Then I got a proposition for you,' said Grist. 'A dangerous expedition, it's true, but there's vast wealth at the end of it.'

Frey's suspicions abruptly faded into insignificance. 'Vast wealth, you say?'

Grist chewed his cigar and grinned. 'Vast.'

Frey sat back in his chair and took a swig of beer. Well. For once, it was looking like being a day worth getting up for. 'Speak your piece,' he said.

Grist leaned forward, splaying thick, calloused fingers across the table. The smell of sweat and dirt clung to him, old smoke and new. 'I got certain *interests*,' he said. 'I'm a smuggler, to be plain. Mostly I run Shine and rumble-dust, but now and then I deal in more unusual bits 'n' bobs. Exotic artefacts and the like. Samarlan antiques, Thacian spices. Been known to steal rare aircraft for collectors, when the mood takes me.'

'Can't blame a man for making a living,' Frey said. His ears had pricked up at the mention of Shine. He was partial to a drop or two himself.

'My point is, I get around, and I hear a lot,' said Grist. 'One day I heard there was some explorer shooting his mouth off about something he'd seen.' He thumbed at Hodd. 'So I found him, and I asked what it was all about. Says he found a downed aircraft in a rainforest. A craft full o' treasures, just lying there, abandoned. Waitin' for someone to come take 'em.'

'A rainforest?' Frey asked. He raised his flagon and looked over at Hodd. 'Where were you? Samarla?'

'Kurg.'

Frey choked into his beer, spraying a cloud of froth out of the flagon and all over his face. He wiped it away with his sleeve and stared at Grist.

'You want to go to *Kurg*?'

'Aye,' said Grist. 'And I want you and your crew to come with me.'

Frey blew out air between his lips. Kurg. The vast island off Vardia's north-eastern coast. Impenetrable. Hostile. Populated by beasts so horrible that the mere mention of them made the local wildlife scatter.

You must be joking, he thought. But Grist most certainly wasn't.

'I assume you've got some proof of your story?' Jez asked Hodd.

'Oh yes!' Hodd said eagerly, as if he'd been waiting the whole conversation for this moment. He drew an object from his pack, all bundled up in cloth. He laid it on the table and unwrapped it with a flourish.

It was a piece of black metal, of bizarre and foreign design, the length of an arm. Circles, semicircles and curves, stacked on top of each other or interlinked. There was the suggestion of pattern and symmetry, but Frey couldn't quite force it to make sense. Jez craned in to look closer.

'Ever seen anything like *that*?' Hodd challenged.

'No,' said Frey. 'But there's plenty I haven't seen. Could be from somewhere far off. Peleshar? Nobody knows *what* that lot are up to.'

'I'll tell you who made it,' said Hodd, his voice dropping to a whisper. 'The Azryx!'

Staring at the object was giving Frey a headache, so he stopped. 'The who?'

'Azryx,' Jez murmured, still gazing at the strange design. Her eyes had become unfocused in that strange way they sometimes did. 'A lost civilisation with highly advanced technology. They're supposed to have died out and disappeared beneath the northern ice. At least that's if you believe the rumours. There's never been any real evidence they ever existed.'

'Until now!' said Hodd, stabbing the table with his index finger.

'You appear to know your stuff, ma'am,' said Grist. 'Care to say how?'

Jez blinked as she surfaced from her daze. 'I used to be the expedition navigator for a man called Professor Malstrom. He was an authority on the Azryx. We spent months hauling all over Yortland looking for clues. Never found any.'

'Ah, the Professor! I know him well!' Hodd cried. 'How is the old bugger?'

'You can't know him *that* well. He's been dead more than four years,' said Jez.

Hodd looked awkward for a moment, then made an airy gesture with his hand. 'It's so easy to drift out of touch. Especially when you're off in the far corners of the world.'

Lost civilisations? It was all sounding a little bit ridiculous now, and Frey had already pegged Hodd as a braying halfwit. If not for the presence of Grist, Frey wouldn't be entertaining this fool at all. But Grist seemed like a man who knew his business, so he supposed there must be something to the story.

Frey patted the object on the table. 'Why don't you tell us where you got this, and let *us* decide if it comes from some made-up civilisation or not? It'll give me a chance to finish my breakfast, if nothing else.'

His patronising tone was lost on his target. 'Of course, of course. Allow me to convince you.'

Frey waved a fork at him, his mouth already full. 'Please try.'

'I'm an explorer of some renown, even if I do say so myself,' Hodd began. 'I take on the missions that others won't touch. Men more short-sighted than I will map New Vardia and Jagos while I search for the truth yet unknown, for mysteries beyond imagining!'

Frey glanced at Grist, and was pleased to see the other captain roll his eyes. At least *one* of them wasn't an idiot.

Hodd didn't notice. 'I was alone in the rainforests of Kurg when I saw it. It was—'

'Hold on,' said Frey. 'What were you doing there in the first place?'

'I was engaged in the search for a hidden tribe of savages, mentioned in ancient texts from the days of the Angroms, the first dynasty, founded by Wilven the Successor when he united all of North Pandraca. These texts have lasted almost three and a half millennia, preserved by a curing process unknown to us today. They speak of a people on Kurg who could see the future, by means of an elixir. If such knowledge existed, I had to find it.'

'An elixir that lets you see into the future?' Frey asked, raising a sceptical eyebrow.

'Think of it!' Hodd enthused.

Frey returned to his food. 'Oh, I am.' He wondered if there was a similar elixir that would allow him to reclaim the lost minutes of his life he'd wasted listening to this drivel. 'And you went there alone? To Kurg?'

'Oh, no, not alone. I have some connections, you see, and wealthy investors willing to finance my expeditions. With their help I assembled a team of—'

'And this team, where were they when you found the object?'

Hodd's eyes shifted nervously. 'They . . . um . . .'

'They got eaten,' said Grist. 'The ones that didn't get poisoned by the bad food, or died of the rot in their wounds, or sickened with the chills 'cause they went in winter without the right gear.'

'The chills? In a rainforest?' Frey asked.

'Kurg's cold,' said Jez. 'The northern parts are above the Arctic Circle. It's a bit warmer on the south coast, but it's still no fun in winter, especially at night.'

'Oh,' said Frey. This was news to him. His knowledge of geography outside of Vardia was shocking.

'You're a smart man, Cap'n, and I see what you're drivin' at,' said

Grist. 'Bumble-butt rich folk, more money than sense. This man Hodd couldn't plan an expedition if you nailed a shopping list to his arse.'

'Hey!' said Hodd, looking hurt.

'The issue ain't what he does or how he does it, nor what he thinks about this or that. It's what he *found*.'

They looked expectantly at Hodd. The explorer was sulking and didn't seem in the mood to talk to anyone.

'Ah, come on, Hodd,' said Grist, giving him a hearty slap on the shoulder. 'Don't take offence. It's just how we captains talk. Always makin' fun. No harm meant, eh, Frey?'

Frey put up his hands with an innocent face. 'Like he says. It's just how we talk.'

'I suppose so,' said Hodd, reluctantly.

'But just to be clear,' said Grist, leaning over to Frey, '*I'm* in charge of this one.'

'Right,' said Frey, considerably relieved. He turned his attention back to Hodd, who was rearranging his ruffled feathers. 'So you were making your way out of Kurg, presumably a little the worse for wear, and you found an aircraft crashed in the rainforest. What kind of aircraft?'

'Like nothing I'd ever seen before,' said Hodd. 'Like nothing anyone has ever seen.'

'Can you describe it?'

'Er . . .' said Hodd. 'It was big. Hard to get a good look at, really, all broken and tangled in the forest as it was.'

'Tangled?' said Jez. 'The forest had grown up around it?'

'Oh yes,' said Hodd. 'It's been there a long time. Thousands of years, no doubt.'

'Listen to the next part,' Grist advised Frey.

'As you can imagine, I was thrilled at my discovery,' said Hodd. 'I immediately set about exploring it. The craft was quite deserted, but I was in no doubt that it was of a design unfamiliar to Vardia or any of its neighbours. There was writing, in letters I have never seen. And such strange artefacts! Those alone would have convinced me. I have an extensive knowledge of antiques, you know. My father was quite the collector. There has been nothing like this in our histories or anyone else's.'

'Tell them about the *door*,' Grist said impatiently.

'The door. Yes. Well, despite the vessel's broken hull, I could only access certain parts of the craft. You can imagine my excitement when I found a mysterious door.'

'A mysterious door,' Frey repeated, deadpan.

'Quite so! But when I touched it, the most abominable sensation came over me. My stomach turned, my head swam, and I was flung back, as if by invisible hands.'

'Hmm,' said Frey.

'I tried again, with the same result. I believe it was some form of Azryx technology, meant to guard their treasures. A barrier of some kind, composed of forces beyond my understanding. Despite my best efforts, I couldn't get in. Then I heard some creatures approaching – what kind of horrors, I couldn't say – so I grabbed the artefact you see before you and I fled. Not long after that, I found my way to the landing-site where our aircraft were, and I escaped.'

'Now I know this sounds far-fetched,' said Grist, as Frey opened his mouth to say so. 'Sounds that way to me, too. But before you speak, remember that Hodd here is willing to lead us back to that place. He's gonna *show* us every word is true. And I made it awful clear that if all ain't as he says, then he's gonna be wearing his guts round his neck.'

'Please,' said Hodd distastefully. 'There's no need for that. I'm an honourable man, and no liar.'

Frey gazed coolly across the table at Grist. Grist smiled back. The end of his cigar glowed red.

'So that's why you need my daemonist,' Frey said.

'Whatever trickery they put on that door, the one person who might be able to fix it is a daemonist,' said Grist. 'Am I right?'

Frey shrugged. 'I suppose so. I'd have to ask him.'

'Well, daemonists are a secretive lot, and yours is the only one I know how to find. Word spread of the golem you lot used in Rabban when you took on the *Delirium Trigger*.' He took the cigar from his mouth and exhaled slowly. 'Also, I'm short on time. Hodd here told everyone and their wives about this craft before I found him.'

'I was trying to raise the money to go back!' Hodd cried. 'Nobody believed that what I'd found was a genuine—'

Grist talked over him. 'Regardless, I've wasted weeks trackin' you

36

down, Frey. If anyone's of a mind to take his story seriously, they'll be lookin' for that aircraft too. But what they don't have is Hodd here to guide them.'

'*Can* you find it again?' Jez asked Hodd.

'Most certainly! I'd bet my life on it.'

'You *are* betting your life on it,' Grist reminded him. He tapped ash from his grubby cigar on to the table and scratched behind his cauliflower ear. 'I'll be straight with you, Frey. I don't need you or your crew. I just need your daemonist.'

'We're a package,' said Frey.

'I reckoned as much. So I'll cut you in. Mark me, there's treasure on that craft. Your crew and mine, we'll find it. I can get it to people who'll know it's worth, and that worth is gonna be huge. Whatever I make, we split. Eighty-twenty.'

'That's very generous,' said Frey. 'And what will you do with your twenty per cent?'

Grist's eyes hardened, just a little. 'Seventy-thirty.'

'Fifty-fifty,' Frey countered.

'Sixty-five, forty-five,' Grist snarled.

'That adds up to a hundred and ten,' Jez pointed out.

'Fifty-fifty,' Frey said again, 'or we say goodbye right here. Your "plan" stinks like rancid dogshit and the only evidence of this *vast wealth* you're talking about is a lump of twisted metal and the promises of some half-baked inbreed. Frankly, I'm inclined to forget the whole thing and count myself one breakfast richer.'

'*Half-baked inbreed?*' Hodd squeaked.

'It's just how we talk,' Frey said, dismissing his protest.

Grist rolled his cigar around his mouth. 'Sixty-forty,' he said. 'And it's final. I got to pay Hodd's five per cent out of my cut, and I'm damned if I'm making *less* than you on my own expedition.'

'Five per cent? That's all you're giving him?'

'I had some trouble raising the finance, and I was getting rather desperate,' said Hodd, looking defeated. 'Captain Grist drives a hard bargain.' He brightened. 'But fame is my reward! I'll be the expedition leader on paper. That was the deal. At the least I'll get a lifetime membership to the Explorer's Guild. Probably.'

Frey finished his breakfast and pushed his plate away. This whole idea seemed shaky, and the idea of going to Kurg was deeply unappealing, but Frey wasn't in a position to be picky right now. Something had to be done to lift the crew of the *Ketty Jay* out of their rut. These past few months they'd been purposeless, moving from job to job, hauling cargo here, running escort there. The pay was pitiful, the work generally dull. For a brief time, after the destruction of Retribution Falls, they'd felt like buccaneers, lords of the sky. But then real life had seeped back in. Adventure had been in short supply ever since.

A man didn't get too many chances to make a fortune, and he had to grab them when he could.

This time he'd do it right. *This* time he'd make them all rich. He'd buy himself a place, somewhere. Something solid, firm, real. Somewhere he could come back to between adventures. A home. He'd never had a home of his own. Maybe that'd help. Maybe that'd fix things.

But he'd been burned before. The last time he went for the big money, he'd landed himself and his crew in the worst trouble of their lives.

But we got through it, he thought. *And it made us into a crew.*

He looked over at Jez, hoping to read her. Her opinion would help him decide. But she refused to show him anything. *You're the Cap'n, Cap'n.*

'Kurg,' he said to Grist. 'Monsters and beast-men. It's quite a risky business you're proposing.'

Grist puffed on his cigar. Pungent clouds surrounded his dirty, bearded face. He leaned forward, looming through the smoke with a yellow grin.

'Some things are worth riskin' *everythin'* for,' he said. He held out a rough-skinned, grubby hand across the table.

Frey stared at it for a long moment. Why not? It was better than being bored and poor the rest of his life. He held out his own hand. 'Fifty-five, forty-five.'

'*Done,* you thievin' son of a bitch!' Grist beamed, and clasped his hand in a crushing grip. 'Damn, but your men better pull their weight for that kind o' cut.' He glanced at Jez. 'And your women too, beggin' your pardon.' Then he slapped Hodd on the back and pointed at Frey. 'Now *that's* how you drive a hard bargain.'

Five

Crake's Daemons – Harkins Decides –
Pulp Fiction – Jez And The Manes

The crew took the news well, with the exception of Harkins, who had to breathe into a paper bag for a while until his hysteria subsided. They had a few hours to make what preparations they could while they waited for Grist and his crew to sort themselves out. It was a day's flight to the coast and another half-day across the East Divide to Kurg. They'd be taking off as soon as everyone was ready. Grist was certainly in a hurry.

Frey went to see Crake in his quarters after he addressed the crew. The daemonist had been silent throughout, and Frey wanted to pick his brains in private about the strange barrier on the door that Hodd had encountered.

Crake's quarters, like the others on the *Ketty Jay*, were cramped and spartan, with bare metal walls and a sliding door to maximise space. They'd previously been the passenger's quarters, but they didn't take passengers these days, so Crake had the luxury of two bunk beds to himself. He used the upper bunk to store luggage and books.

'So what do you think?' Frey asked. 'You think you could break that barrier?'

Crake was sitting on the lower bunk while Frey leaned against the wall. 'Can't say without being there,' he said. 'I need to take readings. We'll have to haul my equipment through the rainforest.' His tone was lazy, disinterested. Barely bothering to pronounce his words properly.

'Can Bess do it?'

Crake made a face. 'Bess shouldn't come. She's too big and too heavy for tramping around in that kind of terrain. She'd sink to her knees in the mud the first time it rained. Not to mention she'd knock over every tree on the way.'

Frey hadn't thought of that. He cursed under his breath. Having Bess along would have been their most effective defence against the monsters that were rumoured to dwell in Kurg. 'Just give me a best guess, then. Does it sound like something you could crack? The barrier, I mean.'

'It *sounds* like something a daemonist would put up to keep people out,' said Crake. His words had degenerated into slurring. 'Pretty basic, actually. Repulsion and nausea. But I won't know till we get there. If it's some sort of unknown technology . . .' He shrugged. He made to get to his feet, but his hand slipped on the edge of the bunk and he flopped back down.

'Are you drunk?' Frey asked, surprised. It wasn't even midday.

Crake gave a guilty smile. 'Little bit,' he said. He reached under his bunk and pulled out a bottle. 'Want some? Trade you for some Shine.'

'Shine?' Frey said stupidly.

'Shine. We all know you use it, Cap'n,' Crake said, with an insinuating wink.

'Once in a while, sure, but—'

'Can I have some?'

'Crake, what is *wrong* with you? Used to be you felt like one of us, but you've been acting stranger and stranger for months. Now this? Drunk by midday? You?'

Crake just stared at him with an expression that said: *are you finished?* It made Frey angry all of a sudden. This wasn't the Crake he knew. Not at all.

'You're part of a crew now,' he said sternly. 'You stopped being a passenger long ago. I need my crewmen capable, got it? You're no use to me drunk.'

Crake gave him a surly salute. 'So can I have some Shine now, Cap'n?'

'No!' He grabbed the bottle out of Crake's hands. 'Sleep it off. Get your head straight, you bloody idiot. I want us all coming out of that rainforest alive. *All* of us. So you'd better sharpen up.'

He slid the door shut behind him with as much of a slam as he could manage, and stalked off up the corridor. The whole incident had enraged him unreasonably. It wasn't as if Malvery and Pinn didn't drink themselves silly at inconvenient times.

But it wasn't that. It was the sullen defiance, the mocking wink. That leering man begging for drugs had been a stranger. Damn, he knew Crake had been getting withdrawn recently, but he'd rather hoped it would sort itself out. Every man had their private daemons. Crake's were getting a hold on him, though.

Malvery stepped into the corridor ahead of Frey and eyed the bottle in his hand.

'Starting early, aren't we, Cap'n?'

'We're all coming out of that rainforest alive!' Frey snapped at him. Then he stamped off towards his quarters, leaving the bewildered doctor in his wake.

Harkins sat in the cockpit of the Firecrow, watching the coast slide away beneath him. He had a fine view through the windglass bubble on the Firecrow's nose as the dry, barren duchy of Anduss was overtaken by the sparkling blue water of the East Divide. The sun glittered fiercely on the waves, making him squint. He scratched his head under his pilot's cap and shifted in his seat.

Vardia was behind them. Kurg lay ahead. Harkins didn't feel good about any of it.

The *Ketty Jay* flew below him and to his left. Pinn's Skylance hung close by, its sleek body and wide, smoothly curved wings cutting steadily through the air. On his right was the *Storm Dog*. He wrinkled his nose and stared at it mistrustfully.

It was a Ludstrome Cloudhammer: a heavy frigate, manufactured in Yortland. Long, vaguely rectangular, with tiny wings for steerage set far back on its hull. Ten times the size of the *Ketty Jay*, it was built above all for toughness. A Cloudhammer could run any storm, suffer any weather. Slow and cumbersome it might have been, but it bristled with cannons, and its armour was thick enough to take the best that most aircraft could dish out.

Harkins didn't like it. He didn't like the ugly craft or its ugly crew. But more, he didn't like what they were doing. They were threatening to make everyone rich. And Harkins didn't like that idea at all.

There was only one thing in Harkins' life that he really enjoyed, and that was flying. The only time he felt anywhere close to normal was inside the cockpit of a Firecrow. If he couldn't fly, he didn't have much of anything.

Outside the Firecrow, the world was a frightening and hostile place. Harkins didn't deal well with people. Even before the Aerium Wars shot his nerves to pieces, he'd been a jumpy sort. People sensed his weakness and mocked or ignored him. But he'd always let his flying do the talking, at least until his aircraft was taken away.

It was Frey who rescued him from the misery of a land-bound life after he'd been discharged from the Coalition Navy. Frey who'd given him a Firecrow and, with it, another chance. The crew of the *Ketty Jay* were the closest thing to friends he'd ever managed. And now along came Captain Grist, promising them all riches and fame. Promising change.

What happened if they all *did* get rich? Did anyone think of that? Did anyone think what would happen to their little band then? Would things really carry on as they were?

No. Of course they wouldn't. Things would change. Everyone would leave. Pinn might even go back to his sweetheart. And Harkins would be left out in the cold. Because it didn't matter how much money he had. It wouldn't stop him being scared. He couldn't change the way he was.

What would he do, if he didn't have the *Ketty Jay*? He'd have to try and make new friends. The agony of strangers. Just the thought of it made him feel a little sick.

But there was another reason, too. Jez. Kindly Jez, who never said a cruel word to him. Lately, he'd begun to feel funny whenever he thought about her. An odd, warm sensation, like a smile inside. A stirring in his—

'Harkins!' said Jez in his ear. He jumped violently enough to crash his head against the windglass of the cockpit.

'Yes! Jez! Yes sir, ma'am, sir!' he burbled, blushing scarlet.

'Course correction. Three degrees south, okay?'

He looked around guiltily, as if someone might be there, observing him. 'Three degrees south. Yes! Got it! Erm . . . yes!'

He adjusted the cap on his head and waited for her to speak again, but there was nothing more. After a short while, he relaxed and made the course correction as instructed. He didn't trust those daemonic little earcuffs. He had a creeping suspicion that they let people read his thoughts.

Would that be such a bad thing, though? On reflection, maybe a little mind-reading would help him out. It would all be easier then. He might be able to talk to her, if it wasn't for the words in the way. He could tell her how humiliating it was to be him. How frustrating and infuriating it was, to be dominated by everything and everyone.

He wanted to be brave, but his bravery had been torn away in strips throughout his life. Too many near misses, too many crashes he'd walked away from, too many comrades lost. He wasn't much of a man, he knew that. But then she was a little strange herself, what with all those weird things she could do. Like how she healed bullet wounds in hours and how she was strong enough to lift crates that even Malvery couldn't.

None of that mattered to Harkins, though. He wasn't fussy. All that mattered was that she was kind to him. No doubt it was pity that motivated her, and nothing more, but a man like Harkins would take what he could get. Pity was a start. Perhaps, if he was just a *little* braver . . .

No. It was no good. What woman could respect a man who was bullied by a cat?

Maybe you just need to stand up to him. You are about twenty times his size, after all.

He burned with shame as he remembered the incident in the corridor. That cat. That damned cat.

If he wanted to be brave for Jez, he'd have to see about that cat.

Pinn, for his part, shared none of the concerns of his fellow outflyer. The idea of worrying about something that far in the future was alien to him. He only ever thought one step ahead, if that. He didn't really do consequences.

He didn't have any real idea what to expect of Kurg, but that didn't matter. Despite his near total lack of knowledge, he was confident he could handle it. The prospect of adventure, fame and riches appealed to him greatly. Artis Pinn, adventurer! Perhaps they'd make some pulp novels of his exploits, the way they did about the Century Knights. Pinn had never read any of them – he never read anything – but their covers looked exciting.

He let his mind drift as he sat in the cockpit of the Skylance, the sea below him, empty sky ahead. The roar of the thrusters, steady and unwavering, lulled him into a daze.

He pictured himself as the subject of a novel, his likeness on the cover. He was standing atop the corpse of some monster, pistol in hand, native wench hanging off his arm. He had no indication of what the native wenches might actually look like, and his imagination was too stunted to guess, so he settled on a Vardic woman wearing very few clothes, and mentally darkened her skin to match Silo's umber tones. Yes, that would do nicely.

He'd heard many stories about the strange and savage land of Kurg, and he believed them all. Tales of tribes of elegant seductresses, and of warrior women who sought strong men to mate with. What kind of exotic ladies might he find there? Surely they'd be fascinated by his foreign ways and amazing aircraft? They'd be fighting to get into bed with him.

Not that he'd sleep with any of them, of course. He'd resist their charms, and it would make them want him all the more. They'd be impressed by his utter devotion to his sweetheart Lisinda, who waited for him back home.

Of course, his devotion only ever lasted so long. In the end he'd give in. His body's needs were scarcely his fault. Any man worth calling a man had masculine urges too strong to control. The important thing was that his love was for Lisinda alone. It wasn't cheating if the women didn't mean anything.

He looked at the small, framed ferrotype of Lisinda, hanging from his dash. What was she doing now, he wondered? Was she thinking of him, even now, as he was of her? He traced her face with a fond finger.

Five years since he'd seen her. Five years since the eighteen-year-old Pinn left her to make his fortune. Five years she'd been waiting for him. At least, he assumed that was what she was doing. After all, she'd told him she loved him and, her being a woman, that meant for ever. Women didn't say that shit lightly.

Five years. That was devotion for you. What a lucky man he was.

It wouldn't be some down-and-out pilot she ended up marrying. It would be a hero. The kind they put on the cover of adventure novels.

Artis Pinn. Hero. He liked the sound of that.

'It won't be long, my love,' he said to the ferrotype. 'Soon I'll be rich, and everyone will know my name. Then I'll come back, just like I promised. You only deserve the best.'

'You only deserve the best,' mimicked Harkins in a soppy voice. Frey howled with laughter.

Pinn went pale. Nobody had spoken for so long, he'd forgotten half the crew could hear him through Crake's daemonic communicators. He ripped his earcuff off and threw it angrily in the footwell, cutting off Frey's gales of mirth, now laughing so hard he'd begun to choke.

'Bastards!' he snarled. Then he shook his head and started to chuckle himself.

Jez sat in her seat at the navigator's station, listening to the sounds of the *Ketty Jay*. The ticks and groans and creaks were familiar to her now. Silo's repairs on the engines were holding up, but she was bothered by the tone of the thrusters, which was slightly lower than usual. Frey had noticed it too, and it niggled at him.

Flying in a straight line through calm skies, there was little for a navigator or a pilot to do. Frey yawned. Jez felt like yawning too, but she couldn't. She hadn't been able to since the day she died.

She'd been thinking about that day ever since their meeting with Grist. Perhaps it was the talk of the Azryx and Professor Malstrom that brought it all back. If not for the Professor and his quest to unearth their lost civilisation, she'd never have gone to that blizzard-lashed settlement in the frozen north. How different things might have been then.

They came in their black dreadnoughts and their ragged clothes. The Manes. Feral ghouls from beyond the Wrack, the great cloud-cap that shrouded Atalon's northern pole. They captured those they wanted, turning them into Manes, and killed those they didn't. Jez was one of the captured, but the process of transformation was interrupted. Jez escaped, only to freeze to death in the night.

But by then, the damage had been done. She wasn't fully a Mane, but she was Mane enough. Though her heart had stopped beating, she lived. Or perhaps *existed* was a better word. She'd wandered for years, moving from place to place, until she found somewhere that would accept her. On the *Ketty Jay*, they didn't ask questions. They didn't know what had happened to her, they didn't want to, and she'd never told them.

Probably best that way. Manes struck fear into even the most reckless of men. The crew could deal with the fact that she was different, but she wondered how well they'd take the news that they had someone who was part Mane on board.

'How we doing, Jez?' asked Frey from the pilot seat.

Jez checked her charts. 'Coming up on Kurg now, Cap'n. Be at the landing site in six hours at this speed.'

Frey groaned and shifted his butt around to get comfortable. 'Six hours. Right.'

Jez smiled to herself. The truth was it was more like four, but it would give her captain a pleasant surprise when they got in early. Frey wouldn't mind the deception. He knew she could be pinpoint accurate if she wanted, which was more than he could say for any of her predecessors.

'Land, ho,' Frey said, without much interest.

Jez got up and went to stand by the pilot's seat to watch the coast approaching. A wall of black rock rose up out of the sea, as far as the eye could see. Waves smashed at its base. Thick forest crawled away from the clifftops towards barren mountain peaks. Smoke billowed from the mouth of a volcano in the distance, joining the misty clouds that hung over the vast island.

Even from high above, Jez thought there was something forbidding and dreadful about it. What would they find in there? What was waiting for them?

A prickling sensation swept over her skin. *Here we go*, she thought, and then the world flexed and everything became different.

A twilight had fallen, yet to her eyes everything seemed sharper than before. An unearthly clarity had come upon the world. She could see the hairs on the back of Frey's hand and sense their movement as they trembled. She could hear the *Ketty Jay*'s engines, and pick out the sound of each individual part. Rats scurried in the hold. Crake snored drunkenly in his quarters. Slag dozed in an air vent, his heart thumping slowly.

Beyond the windglass of the cockpit, she could read the wind. The stirrings of the cloud and the ripples in the treetops told a tale that Jez, in her altered state, could decipher. Pressure changes, crosswinds and updrafts laid themselves out in her mind like a chart. She sensed the life beneath the canopy, millions of creatures, great and small, the growling heart of the island.

And in the distance, a terrible sound. The howling of the Manes. Calling for her. Calling her to be with them. To join them, beyond the Wrack.

Don't listen to them, she told herself. *You're not one of them. You're human.*

But the dread of their voices was too much. She had to retreat. In moments, the trance had passed.

She slipped in and out of that strange state easily and frequently now. She'd learned to cope with the flood of sensation, to enjoy the thrill of it. But the Manes were always there, waiting for her, beckoning. She was afraid of their summons. She didn't know if she could resist it forever.

She'd experienced what it was to be a Mane, for the briefest of instants, during her aborted transformation. She'd felt their connectedness, the joy of their companionship. The link they shared, the *togetherness* they felt. After that, it was hard not to feel lonely. They wanted her, not to harm her but to embrace her.

That was why she was afraid. To embrace the Manes would be to give up her humanity for ever. To become one of them would be to surrender herself. And she wouldn't do that.

Frey stirred in his seat, glanced up at Jez, and then back at the island before them. 'There she is,' he said.

'There she is,' Jez agreed.

'You ever wonder if half the stuff they say about this place is true?'

'It's probably not,' she said. 'But still, the Coalition would rather colonise New Vardia – on the other side of the world and the other side of the Storm Belt – than colonise a land mass that lies a pleasant half-day's flight off their coast.'

'Hmm,' said Frey. 'That's not a good sign, is it?'

'Not really.'

'If I get eaten, you can have the *Ketty Jay*, okay?'

'That's very sweet of you. What if you get stamped on, poisoned, or die horribly from some unknown plague?'

Frey gave her a look. 'Just get back to your charts, why don't you?'

She grinned and saluted. 'Right you are, Cap'n!'

Six

C rake pulled the collar of his coat up and hunched his shoulders against the cold. It always seemed to be cold nowadays. On the *Ketty Jay* or off it, there was a chill in his core that never quite went away.

The clouds were iron-grey overhead, and an arctic breeze came from the north, pushing through the rainforest. The *Ketty Jay* sat in a bald, rocky clearing, with tree-covered mountains on either side. Crake stood under her tail, the cargo ramp lying open behind him. In the distance, a waterfall plunged hundreds of feet from a ridge of cliffs. When the wind was right, Crake could hear its dull, sullen roar.

Nearby, the *Storm Dog* was easing itself down. The air was sharp with the smell of aerium gas as it vented its tanks.

The *Storm Dog* was craggy and rectangular, like a beam of black, petrified timber. Its prow was blunt and its hull pocked and uneven, stained with cloud-rime and iceburn. It sank on to its landing struts with an artless crunch and settled in the clearing. The air shimmered and rippled as it wheezed out the last of its aerium in an invisible cloud, then its engines shut off.

For a moment, there was quiet. An awesome, massive silence. Only the stir of the wind sounded over the endless industry of the waterfall. Crake tipped back his head, closed his eyes, and basked in the nothingness.

'Hey, Crake!' Pinn yelled from the cargo hold. 'Give us a hand here! Half of this is *your* stuff!'

Crake's eyes fluttered open. The birds and insects of the rainforest, which had been silenced by the disturbance, began to pick up their songs again. Hydraulics whirred as the *Storm Dog* opened its cargo ramp. The moment had passed.

Too brief. All too brief.

The others were coming down the *Ketty Jay*'s ramp, carrying packs and equipment. Tents, weapons, food, and Crake's daemonist equipment, which they'd need when they reached their destination. Bess came clumping down with an armful of gear and laid it down among the other packs with a child's exaggerated care. Then she scampered over to Crake – as much as a half-ton armoured suit *could* scamper – and settled on her haunches in front of him.

'Well done,' he said, patting her flank. 'What a helpful girl you are.'

Bess leaned in, pushing her face-grille closer. Points of light twinkled in the darkness behind. Eyes like stars. She gave a quizzical coo: an ethereal, other-worldly sound.

'I'm alright, Bess. Don't you worry,' said Crake, forcing a smile.

Bess wasn't fooled. She reached out one gloved hand and stroked Crake's arm clumsily. Metal, chain mail and leather dragged down his coat, almost tearing his sleeve off. Crake felt sudden tears threatening, and swallowed. He gave the golem an awkward hug. She was too big to get his arms around.

'Don't you worry,' he said again.

'Will you stop flirting with your girlfriend and *carry something*?' Pinn yelled from the cargo ramp, as he went back in for another pack.

They assembled in a spot between the aircraft: six from the *Ketty Jay*, six from the *Storm Dog*, including Hodd. Frey wanted Silo to come, and Harkins had volunteered with great enthusiasm to stay with Bess on the *Ketty Jay*. Bess was the *Ketty Jay*'s watchdog, ensuring that nobody but the crew came aboard with all their limbs still attached. But the Cap'n needed somebody human to keep an eye on things while they were away, and he was happy to leave Harkins behind. The pilot was a liability in a firefight and he had a jumpy trigger finger at the best of times. In the rainforest, he'd be a disaster. More likely to shoot himself in the foot than kill one of the enemy.

Along with Hodd and Captain Grist came the *Storm Dog*'s emaciated, bug-eyed bosun, Edwidge Crattle, and three crewmen called Gimble, Tarworth and Ucke. They were a seedy-looking trio, but then Crake had hardly expected anything else.

Gimble was a thin, scowling fellow who said little. Tarworth was short, baby-faced and eager. Ucke had a more eccentric appearance.

He was bulky, with hair sticking out everywhere, and he had offensively bad teeth in all shapes, sizes and angles. When Pinn rudely commented on them, Ucke informed the group that they were actually a false set. Dentures. He'd made them himself from teeth he'd collected from a multitude of bar brawls.

Once the introductions were done, they shouldered their packs, checked their guns and made ready to set off.

'Now I don't want none of you believin' all that talk you might have heard about Kurg,' Grist told them. 'There'll be beasts, for sure, but probably not half as horrible as the tales tell.' He slapped Hodd on the shoulder. 'This man's been in there and come out without a scratch. If he can do it, then us rum sons of bitches ought to be able to. What's in there should be afraid of *us*, not the other way about!'

Yes, he *came out without a scratch,* thought Crake. *It was the rest of his expedition that died.*

Crake loathed Hodd on sight. Frey had told him about his first meeting with the explorer, which was enough to convince Crake that they were dealing with a shiftless rich boy who'd spent his life living on Daddy's money, utterly detached from the realities of the world. Crake had grown up amongst the aristocracy, and he was never afraid to apply stereotypes. In his experience, they turned out to be true more often than not.

Besides, Hodd reminded Crake of himself, and Crake hated that.

Crake had been that way, once. A life of privilege, sheltered from trouble by his father's money. Mixing only with his own kind. He treated lowlier folk with politeness because that was what people with good breeding did, but they weren't the same as him. He couldn't have said why, and he'd never have admitted it aloud, but they just *weren't.*

It had been the discovery of daemonism at university which had prompted his awakening. Before long, he'd grown bored with the vacant twitterings of the social classes. While they were talking about mergers and marriages, inheritances and infidelities, he'd been communicating with entities from another dimension. In the face of that, their preoccupations seemed rather juvenile.

But he'd still possessed the arrogance of the aristocracy. The knowledge that no matter what he did, he'd never *not* be rich. Whatever trouble he got into, someone would look after him.

Maybe that was why he did what he did. He'd not known what sorrow or torment or hardship meant until then. But he learned those lessons well in the time that followed.

'Right,' said Hodd, clapping his hands. 'Are we all ready?'

Belts were tightened, coats buttoned, bootlaces tied and retied. Pinn took a few test steps to check the weight of his pack.

'Off we go, then!' Hodd cried.

'Where are we headed?' Jez asked.

That stumped Hodd for a moment. 'Er . . . to the crashed Azryx aircra—'

'No, I mean . . . Don't you have a map? Directions?' Jez asked. 'You said it would be over a day's walk. I just wondered how you were intending to find it again.' She looked around the group and shrugged. 'Sorry. Navigator. I just want to know.'

Hodd smiled broadly and tapped his head. 'It's all in here, Miss.'

'You remember the way,' Jez said, doubtfully. She eyed the forested flanks of the mountains that surrounded them. 'Are you sure? Once we're in there, we'll get pretty badly lost if you're wrong.'

'Be assured, I never forget a route,' he said. 'I've possessed a rather remarkable talent for pathfinding ever since I was a child. It was what inspired me to be an explorer, actually.'

'And what did Daddy think about that?' Crake asked, and immediately regretted it. He didn't want to have a conversation with this buffoon, but he'd been unable to resist a bitter jibe. It had just come out.

Hodd missed Crake's tone and the implied insult entirely. 'He was rather disappointed, actually,' he said, looking downcast. 'My father sits in the House of Chancellors for the Duchy of Rabban, and my six brothers all work in the field of law. But I had a different calling.'

'An explorer,' said Crake. 'So I see. Ever found anything?' Frey gave him a look, but he ignored it.

'Well, not anything that you'd see on the front page of the broadsheets, but I have led many expeditions to far-flung places, and contributed valuable knowledge in the fields of—'

'And how many people have you lost on your expeditions? Aside from your *entire team* the last time you were here?'

Hodd looked wounded, unable to understand the source of this sudden hostility. 'Sir, I don't know what I might have done to offend you, but—'

'Do you even *know*?' Crake asked. The fury exploded from nowhere. Suddenly he was red-faced and shouting. 'Do you even know how many porters and pilots and natives died while you were playing explorer with your daddy's money? How many *people*?'

The group stared at Crake, shocked. Hodd had gone pale. He looked to Grist, as if the burly captain might defend him.

'Crake,' murmured Jez. 'Leave it alone.'

'People like him!' Crake snorted. 'Other people die for their dreams of glory. It won't be *him* that gets killed in there.'

'Now, now,' said Grist, raising his hands. 'Let's all play nice, hmm? We all trust Mr Hodd when he says he's goin' to lead us to great treasure.' He put his arm round Hodd and gave him a menacing squeeze. ''Cause he knows what'll happen if he don't.'

The explorer grinned nervously. 'It's that way,' he said, pointing. With a few odd looks at Crake, they began to shuffle off towards the forest. Jez gave him a sympathetic glance and then turned away. Crake shouldered his pack and followed her.

I wonder if I'll make it back alive, Crake thought.

He honestly couldn't bring himself to care.

The rain began in the afternoon. It came with considerable force.

Frey had been rained on before, but this was up there with the best of them. Leaves and branches bowed and rocked under the onslaught. A wet mist gathered in the air until it was hard to see anything more than a half-dozen metres away. The forest filled with the hiss of falling water and the hoots and screeches of excited animals in the treetops.

What little good cheer had attended their departure rapidly disappeared. They trudged along in single file, wishing they were anywhere but here. Pinn, walking ahead of Frey, kept up a constant stream of grumbling. The ground had turned to a quagmire, and was attempting to suck their boots off their feet with every step. Their coats had soaked through. Previously warm underlayers were now damp and freezing. Frey could only hope that Crake's equipment was wrapped up better than they were.

The only person who seemed to be having a good time was Hodd.

'Spit and blood, I've missed this place!' he cried, then laughed and shook his fist towards the leafy heavens. 'Cruel nature, do your worst!'

Frey saw Pinn's hand twitch towards his pistol, and grabbed his wrist before he could do anything rash.

'Can't I kill him just a little bit?' Pinn whined.

'He's the only one who knows the way back, Pinn. We need him to get us out of here when we're done.'

Pinn thought about that for a moment. 'Alright, Cap'n.' He poked one stubby finger at Frey. 'But I'm doing this for *you*, okay?'

'Appreciate it,' said Frey. Up ahead, Hodd began to sing a marching tune, loud and off-key. Pinn gritted his teeth.

'I can't take much more, Cap'n,' he said.

Frey sighed, then pushed his way up the line to Hodd.

Hodd was punching the air lustily. '*Oh, brave and strident sol-diers, whose cou-rage none can*— Oh! Hello, Captain Frey.'

Frey nodded in greeting, and leaned close as they walked. 'You've heard of the monsters that are rumoured to infest this island, Hodd?'

'Oh, yes!' said Hodd. 'I've seen several, in fact. One of them damn near had me for breakfast.'

'You've seen several,' Frey repeated. 'That's good. Did you see if they had ears?'

Hodd looked bewildered. 'Ears?'

'The singing, Hodd. Will you bloody can it? They can hear you five kloms away.'

'Ah!' said Hodd. 'Yes, I see. Quite right, Captain. Just trying to keep up morale.'

'And you're doing a fine job,' said Frey. 'Just do it quietly, eh?'

Hodd put a theatrical finger to his lips. Frey turned away, eyes rolling skyward, and moved back down the line. Grist gave him a smoky grin around the butt of his cigar and Frey fell into step next to him.

'Bit of a character, ain't he?' Grist said.

'You know, the animals will smell that cigar all over the mountain, too.'

'Risk I'm willing to take, Frey. A life without cigars ain't one much worth livin', if you ask me.' He started to laugh but ended up in a coughing fit that had him bent double. When he was done, he stood up and wiped spittle from his beard. He regarded his cigar with a teary eye. 'Tobacco. She's a harsh mistress.'

'We've all got our vices,' said Frey.

'Aye? What's yours?'

'I've plenty. But I reckon Rake tops the list.'

'A card player, eh? My men are partial to a game, but me? I'm no gambler. Don't have the luck.'

'It's not luck.'

'Well, whatever it is, I ain't got it.'

'Some days I don't, either,' Frey admitted.

'But you keep goin' back, don't you?' Grist laughed. 'The things a man does to make himself feel alive.'

Frey looked at the man next to him. He liked Grist. There was something solid and impressive about him, a grizzled heartiness in his manner. He had a way of including people that made them feel almost grateful for it. He reminded Frey of Malvery, except he apparently didn't spend his whole life arseholed on grog.

'I've been thinking about that lately,' he said. 'Don't you sometimes wish you didn't *need* to? Like, you felt alright *without* all the smoke and the booze and the cards and everything else? Seems like some people manage okay.'

Grist's brow furrowed. 'Men like you an' me, Frey, it don't do us no good to be thinkin' that way,' he said. 'We live for today. The past don't mean nothin', and the future ain't worth a damn. We could all be dead by sunrise.' His dark eyes found Frey's. 'Ain't that how it is?'

Frey stared at the ground. 'Yeah. That's how it is.'

'Anyway, what's wrong with a little fun? You want to live for ever or somethin'?'

'Actually,' said Frey, 'I kinda do.'

Grist bellowed with laughter, which set off another coughing fit. 'Me, too!' he wheezed, slapping his leg, coughing and laughing fit to burst. 'Me, too!'

The rain lessened slightly as night fell, but the clouds stayed in the sky, and there was no light from the moon. Under Hodd's direction, they pitched camp on a patch of high ground, and stretched a tarpaulin between several trees to act as a roof. Hodd arranged stones to make a raised platform and somehow managed to get a fire going on it.

Jez had to admit, the man knew his survival skills. And he still appeared confident of the route. His manner and his history inspired mistrust, perhaps, but a man didn't spend a lifetime as an explorer without picking up a few things.

The rainforest came alive at night. The treetops were busy with shrieks and wails. Insects clattered and hummed all around them. Bats flitted through the air. Repulsive things slunk and crept.

Jez was among the volunteers for first watch, but she intended to take second and third as well. Her eyesight was better than anyone else's in the dark, and she had no need of rest. Usually she took pains to disguise her condition from strangers. She went through the motions of eating and sleeping so as not to arouse suspicion. But, just this once, she'd plead insomnia. The afternoon and evening had passed without incident, but she didn't trust their luck to hold. She didn't want anything sneaking up on them tonight.

She stood with her back to the camp, her head bare to the elements, black hair plastered to her forehead. The hood of her coat was down, so as not to block her peripheral vision. Behind her, the men were cooking up the last of the soup. Some were huddled close to the fire. Others had already crawled into their sleeping bags, exhausted.

Standing there in the rain, she tried to bring on the trance. When she slipped into that strange state of hyper-awareness, she'd *feel* the forest instead of merely seeing it. She'd be able to sense the animals and identify any threats. In the past, she'd even shared their thoughts. Once, during a gunfight, she'd read a man's mind, just before she shot him.

In the chaos of sounds from the forest, she fancied she could hear the cries of the Manes. But no trance came. She couldn't make it happen. They took her without rhyme or reason, and she didn't have the trick of controlling them. Perhaps she never would.

She heard someone approaching from the direction of the fire. Looking over her shoulder, she saw Silo. Only his beak-like nose showed from the shadow of his hood. Without a word, he sat down on a rock next to Jez. He drew a shotgun from under his coat and stared out into the forest.

They watched the forest together in comfortable silence for a time.

Some of the crew found Silo awkward to be around, but Jez rather enjoyed his company. Everyone else talked a lot, usually about nothing important. Silo talked hardly at all, but she had the impression that he made up the difference by thinking.

'There's rage in my family,' he said, out of nowhere. Jez didn't know what to say to that, so she didn't say anything.

'My papa had it,' he went on. 'And his brother. And their papa, and *my* brother. All them dead now, but they had rage. It'd just come explodin' out o' them, and you better not be in their way when it did.'

Jez was mildly surprised that he'd volunteered the information. She didn't even know he had a brother. She'd been aboard the *Ketty Jay* more than a year, but she still knew hardly anything about him. Neither did anyone else, as far as she was aware.

Silo propped his shotgun against a tree and began making a roll-up, hunching forward to shield it from the rain. Jez wondered if that was the end of the conversation, but then he spoke again.

'My brother, one time, he got the rage when we was all chained up in the pens. Broke his ankle against the manacles, tryin' to get at some feller. Weren't fit for work for a long while after, but he was a strong 'un, so they wanted to see if it'd heal.' He licked the paper and sealed the roll-up. 'Didn't. Bones knitted bad, gave him a limp, so they killed him.'

There was a hiss of phosphorus as he struck a match, then the smell of acrid smoke.

'Papa died the same. Picked a fight with some feller, Murthian like him, while they was haulin' rubble in a quarry. Smashed his head in with a rock. Sammies took him away and he didn't never come back.'

Jez hadn't heard Silo talk at such length before. She was reluctant to speak in case she interrupted his flow, but she felt the moment demanded something.

'Sorry about that,' she said.

'Nothin' to be sorry about. There's what is, and what ain't.'

Jez wished she'd kept her mouth shut. For a while, there was only the sounds of the forest and the rain. Then:

'I got the rage, too.'

Really? she thought. *You? I've never seen you anything but calm.* But she didn't say a word.

'Used to be proud of it,' he said. 'They was afraid of me when I was young. I'd take on kids twice my age and give 'em worse than I got. Every day, I was angry. Angry that they kept us in chains 'n' pens 'n' camps. Murthians ain't like the Daks. Five hundred years and they still ain't tamed us.' He took a drag and blew it out. 'Lately, I got to thinkin' maybe that's the problem. We're so damn proud of defyin' the Sammies, they'll never let us out from them chains. Bit more smarts and a bit less angry, and they'd think we was tame. We'd be like the Daks, in their homes, runnin' their businesses, lookin' after their children.' A pause. 'That's when we'd kill 'em.'

Jez kept her eyes on the forest. She'd always felt a faint bond with the Murthian. Both of them, in their own way, were exiles from their own race. She'd always suspected he felt the same. He spoke to her most out of all the crew, though usually about matters of engineering. Machinery was their common ground.

Now it occurred to her that Silo was reaching out to her. Offering something. Making a connection.

'There was a woman, once,' he said. 'We was both young, but old enough. I hadn't seen anythin' like her. Thought there weren't no finer thing in the world. And she thought likewise about me. That's what she said.' He shook his head, blew out a jet of smoke. 'Hard-headed woman. Loved her fierce but she drove me crazy. We'd fight and make up, over and over. Harsh 'n' sweet, harsh 'n' sweet. She had a temper, too.'

Jez had a horrible feeling she knew where this was going.

'One time we both went too far. The rage got me. Only for a second, but that was plenty. Won't never forget the look on her face, her holdin' her cheek like that. Saw it in her eyes. I'd lost her, right then. Didn't matter how I begged nor pleaded, she wouldn't look at me again. Never.'

Why are you telling me this?

'Damn, I was sick with the rage after that. Like an animal. They had to chain me down for a week. But the madness passed, and when I was well again, things was different. Every time I saw her after that, with some other man in the camp, I'd think: *That's what rage did for you.* And I swore I wouldn't never let it out again.'

'And did you?' Jez had to ask.

'Only one time,' he said. 'Years later. Day I escaped the factory where they had us makin' aircraft. He had a gun, I just had fists an' teeth. Don't remember much of what happened after, but I'm here and he ain't.' He flicked away his roll-up, and it was extinguished by the rain. 'Sane man wouldn't have charged him like that. But I weren't sane, not then.'

He got to his feet. Standing, he towered over her.

'Point I'm makin' is, you ignore your bad side, it eat you up. Like my papa and my brother. You got to face it. You got to make it a part of you, *control* it. Maybe one day it save your life, yuh?'

Jez looked at him, startled. How did he know? How did he have any idea of the struggle within her, the push and pull between human and Mane?

He answered her question before she could ask it. 'Think I don't see you walkin' off on your own, worryin', workin' things out? I see you. You the same as everyone else, Crake 'n' me 'n' all of us. Think you better off keepin' it all to yourself.' He turned to her, eyes dark in the shadow of his hood. 'You ain't.'

Jez met his gaze. Of all the people to tackle her about this, Silo was the most unlikely. Of course, the others knew she was different, but they avoided the issue on purpose out of respect for her secrets. She'd been grateful for their consideration, but it also left her entirely alone. It occurred to her that she was doing exactly the same thing to Crake. Of all the crew she was the only one who knew the grief he carried, yet they'd only ever spoken of it once.

Perhaps she *didn't* have to deal with this all alone. Perhaps Crake didn't, either.

'Thanks, Silo,' she said.

He pulled back his hood and turned his face up to the rain. Water trickled over his shaven scalp. 'In Samarla I was a slave,' he said. 'In Vardia I'm the enemy. This might be the first damn place I ever been where I'm just a man.'

He smiled. An actual smile. Jez almost fell over with the shock.

'Freedom makes a feller talkative, I reckon,' he said.

That was when the screams began.

Seven

A Commotion In The Camp – Crake Is Missing –
Frey Takes To The Trees – A Worrying Discovery

Frey dreamed of a meadow on a hill. He dreamed of a young woman with long blond hair and a smile of such innocent beauty that it melted him to see it.

Trinica was her name. They were mad with the joy of first love, swept up in each other. He chased her through the tall grass, but she was always one step ahead of him, laughing. Finally he caught her, and she turned in his arms, her nose an inch from his as she leaned forward to kiss him . . .

Then she was screaming. Her mouth stretched open, grotesquely wide, exposing rotted teeth. Her breath stank of decay. Her green eyes darkened to black. Hair came away from her head in clumps, the dying locks slithering to the ground. He struggled frantically to let go of her, but his upper arms were gripped by some invisible force. She shrieked in his face, features distorted with horror, her skin white, corpse-like. Frey shrieked with her.

He thrashed awake to the sound of screams, shouting, rain. His arms were trapped inside his sleeping bag. Trinica's howling still echoed in his mind.

Rain hammered against the tarpaulin overhead. A fire flickered nearby, smoking up the air beneath their little shelter. Dark figures moved beyond it, barely visible in the downpour. Frey looked about, trying to reassemble his memories, and found himself in a lumpy, tangled landscape of empty sleeping bags. He'd gone to sleep as soon as he'd had his dinner, exhausted by the afternoon's trek.

What in damnation is going on?

'Over there!' someone cried. One of Grist's men.

'Over where?'

'That way!'

'I can't bloody see where you're pointing!'

'*That* way!'

'Which way is *that* way, shit-wit?'

Frey scrambled out of his sleeping bag, pulled on his boots and snatched up his revolver. Then he pulled his cutlass from where he'd lain next to it in the night, and thrust it into his belt. It wasn't the smartest thing to sleep with a naked blade – he didn't want any accidents where bits of his insides ended up on the outside – but he was paranoid about someone stealing it. That cutlass was his most precious possession after the *Ketty Jay*: a daemon-thralled weapon given to him by Crake as price for his passage. It made even an amateur swordsman into a champion. Which was good, since Frey was very, very amateur.

He emerged from the shelter into the open and was soaked to the skin in seconds. Wiping hair back from his forehead, revolver at the ready, he cast around for signs of his crew. It was dark beyond the firelight, and the rain made it seem as if everything was constantly in motion. A pistol shot rang out, making him jump. He turned towards the sound, but the trees and shadows foiled his sight.

'Sound your names, damn you all!' Grist cried from somewhere.

'Crattle!'

'Ucke!'

'Tarworth, sir! I'm shot!' The young crewman's voice wavered fearfully.

'Hodd! Where are you?' Grist demanded.

'Here!' the explorer replied.

'Gimble?'

Frey heard a rustle to his left and Pinn emerged from the under-growth, eyes bright, chubby face flushed with excitement.

'I saw it, Cap'n! It's *huge*!'

'*What* is?' he asked, but then Grist yelled again.

'Gimble? Are you there?'

'Malvery!' This time it was Jez's voice. 'Someone get the doc over here!'

Malvery appeared out of the rain, hurrying past Pinn and Frey, a lever-action shotgun in one meaty hand, his doctor's bag in the other. 'Malvery!' Frey said. 'What in bastardy is happening?'

'Can't stop. Duty calls,' Malvery replied, heading off in the direction of Jez's voice.

'We're coming with you,' Frey decided. 'Come on, Pinn. Everyone, stay together.' They followed Malvery into the trees, slipping through the mud, pushing wet branches aside. 'Jez! Keep shouting!'

'This way!'

Frey's heart was pounding against his ribs as they forged through the forest. The sense of threat was overwhelming. The further they went from the fire, the worse it got. He could barely see far enough to avoid the trees in front of him. Everything was slick with rain. In seconds, the camp was nothing more than a faint smear of light in the distance.

They followed Jez's voice, and found her with Silo. The two of them were smeared in mud and kneeling over a fallen figure. Frey felt a surge of relief at seeing they were unhurt, but it faded as he remembered that Crake was still unaccounted for. That figure on the ground . . .

Don't be Crake. Don't be Crake.

It was Gimble, the scrawny, bad-humoured crewman from the *Storm Dog*. He was trembling, eyes glassy. One arm had been torn off at the socket. A knob of bone glistened there, washed clean by the rain. Three ragged, parallel claw-strokes were carved into his belly. Vile blue loops of intestine poked through the rips. Blood washed into the mud, coming from everywhere. He hadn't even had time to pull his revolvers from his belt.

Malvery knelt down next to him, wiped his round glasses, looked him over.

'He's done,' Malvery announced. 'Soon as the shock wears off.'

'Can't you do anything?' Jez pleaded.

Malvery grimaced regretfully and patted his shotgun. 'Best I could do is make it quick.'

'Anyone seen Crake?' Frey asked, panicked. Something was out there, in the forest, and his crewman – his *friend* – was missing. He didn't give a toss about Grist's folk, but Crake was a different matter. He called into the night. There was no reply.

Crattle appeared, having followed Jez's calls. He stared down at Gimble, then at Frey.

'We need your doctor,' he said. 'Tarworth's shot.'

Malvery got to his feet. 'Lead on.'

'We need to stay together!' Frey insisted.

'They've got wounded,' Malvery said. 'I can't help this feller, but I might be able to help the other. You lot find Crake.'

'I'll make sure he gets back to you safe,' Crattle told Frey.

'What about *your* crewman? You're just gonna leave him here in the mud?' Frey demanded of Crattle, slightly appalled.

Crattle gave Frey a hard look. 'Don't matter what anyone does for Gimble now. My concern's with the living.'

Jez looked up from where she knelt by Gimble. His ragged breathing had stopped while they argued. 'He's dead anyway,' she said, her voice flat. She got up. 'Let's find Crake.'

'Good luck, eh?'Malvery said. He went off with Crattle and was swallowed up by the rain.

Frey rubbed water out of his eyes. The forest looked the same in every direction, but he could still vaguely see the firelight from the camp. 'Alright,' he said. 'He can't have gone far. We circle the camp. Keep that light on your left. And *stay together*. I'm not losing anyone to this forest, you all hear me?'

'Yes, Cap'n,' mumbled Pinn, who'd been rather sobered by the sight of Gimble's guts.

Frey led them away from the dead man. His mouth was dry and his temples throbbed. He couldn't remember the last time he'd felt this exposed. The rain, the dark and the cacophony of animals and insects conspired to foil his senses. If something was out there, they'd never see it coming.

When he was a child, he'd go sneaking through the corridors of the orphanage at night. Usually it was for a dare; sometimes it was because he needed the toilet and he hadn't gone before bedtime. Either way, the punishment for being caught out of bed was severe. But it was never the staff that he feared, or the prospect of a thrashing. It was the monsters that came out when the orphanage was dark and quiet. The whispering things that scraped and creaked and stalked him, waiting behind every door, hiding in the corners.

That kind of fear, that unreasonable, primal, overwhelming fear, he thought he'd left behind with his childhood. But here it was again. And this time, there was no doubt the monsters were real.

Damn it, Crake, where are you? he thought.

Why wasn't he answering? Crake was a smart fellow, the smartest among them. He'd have a good reason for keeping his mouth shut. Was he being stalked, even now, and he didn't dare call out? Was he lying unconscious somewhere, having slipped on a rock or fallen down a hole?

Or was he like Gimble, lying in a muddy tangle of himself, rain falling on his blind, open eyes?

Frey's mind flinched away from the image. He didn't want to think about that. It was he who brought them to this place, and they were his responsibility. Time was, his crew would have told him to stuff it if they didn't feel like risking their hides on a treasure hunt. But that time was past now. They trusted him to lead them, and he felt the weight of that trust. Coming to Kurg had been his choice. If Crake died, it was on his shoulders.

He called out Crake's name, but he got only silence.

Answer me, you bastard.

'Er, Cap'n, should you really be yelling like that when there's a gigantic horror out there wanting to tear out your kidneys?' Jez asked.

Frey reluctantly conceded the logic of that. 'Can you see anything?' he asked. 'You've got better eyes than the rest of us.'

'Not much,' Jez replied. 'Rain and trees.'

'We should—' he began, but then something lunged across their path in a flurry of leaves. Pinn, who was standing behind Frey, fired reflexively. They caught a glimpse of something furry and fat, the size of a large dog, burrowing into the undergrowth.

Frey looked down at himself. There were two holes in the armpit of his coat, where the bullet had gone in and out. He looked back at Pinn, who grinned sheepishly.

'I'm pretty sure that wasn't the thing that did for Gimble,' Frey said. 'Now that we've established there are other creatures *and people* in this forest, let's all think about aiming before we fire, shall we?'

'Sorry, Cap'n,' Pinn said.

'Well, I reckon we solved the mystery of how Tarworth got shot,' Jez said.

'That wasn't me!' said Pinn. Then he thought for a moment and a guilty expression crossed his face. 'Or maybe it was,' he added.

'Let's keep that between us, eh?' Frey said. 'And you'd better hope that poor bloke isn't dead.'

'No, I reckon I only shot him in the leg,' said Pinn cheerily.

Frey was about to reply when Jez seized his arm. 'Cap'n!' she whispered.

The urgency in her voice made him freeze. She was looking off to their left. Slowly she raised her hand and pointed. 'Over there.'

Silo moved around the side of them, crouching, shotgun held in both hands. He was staring at the same point as Jez. Frey peered into the forest, following Silo's line of sight.

The leaves swayed under the pounding of the rain, but nothing moved except the shadows. At first, he couldn't see anything. But then he saw what was *not* moving.

Eyes. Eyes, set half a metre apart. The eyes of something huge.

It burst out of the foliage with a roar. Massive and shaggy, a monstrous approximation of a bear, but much larger than any Frey had ever heard of. Short tusks thrust forward on either side of a mouth that was all fangs and no lips. There was no snout to be seen, just that pair of eyes. Shark's eyes, round and dead and soulless.

Its sheer, unstoppable size panicked them. Frey heard Silo's shotgun, but they were already scattering out of the way of its charge. Frey flailed through branches, slipped and went face-down in the mud, landing chest-first on a tree root. Gasping at the pain, he rolled on to his back.

The creature had reared on its hind legs, pawing the air, twice Frey's height or more. To his right, he could see Pinn behind a tree, taking aim with his pistol. The creature screeched as the bullet found its mark. It thumped down on to its forepaws, shook itself, then lifted its head and fixed Frey with a glare of terrible intent.

'It wasn't bloody *me*!' Frey protested. Then he got to his feet and ran.

He could hear the creature pounding after him, and he sprinted with all the strength in his body. 'Cap'n!' someone shouted, but it sounded like it came from kloms away. Rain-lashed boughs flashed past. His boots skidded on ground that was alternately slick and sucking. The creature came crashing in his wake with a rattling growl. It had its sights on prey now, and it wasn't going to give him up.

Pinn, you bastard, I'm gonna get you for this!

He stuck his revolver out behind him, glanced over his shoulder, and took a potshot at the monstrous shadow surging through the sodden dark. If it hit, it had little effect. He turned back just in time to catch a branch across his forehead. Stars exploded before his eyes. He staggered back from the surprise impact, dazed and blinking.

The creature smashed through the foliage behind him. He spun to face it. It came to a halt with a roar. Close enough to smell its bad-meat breath and the musky, wet stench of its fur. He flung himself through a screen of leaves as a massive paw swiped at him. He scrambled to his feet on the other side, his revolver lost somewhere in the mud. He didn't stop to collect it.

'Cap'n! Cap'n!' Jez, Pinn and the others. Too distant to be any help. He was on his own now. Just him and the creature.

His pursuer was slow to pick up the chase again, giving him a precious few seconds' lead. His lungs burned and his skin felt red-hot. He looked around desperately for some route of escape. A ravine too narrow for the creature, a stream that might carry him away, anything like that. But the trees blocked his view on all sides, reducing his world to a flurry of rain and bark and leaves.

Damn trees, he thought. Then, a moment later, realisation struck. Trees were high. He could climb one. He felt a bit stupid for not having thought of it before, actually.

Spotting a likely candidate, he leaped up and grabbed a sturdy branch. Fear lent him assistance. He clambered on to the branch and reached up for the next. Cold hands gripped wet bark. Leaves cascaded rainwater down on to his face as he disturbed them. He pulled himself up, and blundered through a spiderweb so thick it felt like it was made of rope. Something heavy and leggy dropped on to his shoulder; he let out an involuntary squeal. The unseen thing scrabbled for purchase and then slipped off his back. He got his legs up on to the branch, felt for another, and climbed higher.

By the time the creature arrived at the foot of the tree, he felt relatively safe. It snarled up at him through the branches, and reared up on its hind legs. But he was out of reach.

'Let's see you get me up here!' Frey taunted, drunk with the thrill of his escape.

The beast tottered back on its hind legs, balanced itself, and shoulder-charged the tree. Frey frantically grabbed on as his perch trembled violently. Some unidentified small animal plunged past him with a squeak and bounced off a lower branch.

'Er . . .' said Frey. 'Don't do that.'

The creature smashed into the tree again, with more force this time. Now there was an ominous splintering noise, and an unpleasant sensation of tipping.

'Shit,' Frey murmured.

The next few seconds were a mayhem of whipping and hissing branches, and the sickening anticipation of impact. Something smacked the back of his head. He felt himself jolted, thrown, rolling. Suddenly the leaves weren't there any more. He ended up on the ground, in the open, gazing at the nodding canopy overhead. His whole body felt like one big bruise.

He lay there for a moment, relieved to be alive, before he remembered the creature.

He staggered to his feet, drew his cutlass and looked around wildly. The fallen tree was nearby, but he saw no sign of his enemy. His head was still spinning from the tumble. He shook it, but that only made things worse. His eyes kept trying to double everything.

A thrashing of leaves behind him. He turned and saw the creature rearing, one huge paw drawn back for a swipe that would take his head off.

Then his cutlass moved, pulling his hand with it. The blade flashed in the rain and there was a shiver of impact. The paw splashed into the mud, detached from its owner.

The creature shrieked and flailed backwards in clumsy retreat, the remains of its forelimb tucked against its shaggy chest. Blood spewed from the severed stump as it turned and fled.

And then Frey was alone in the forest. Soaked, covered in mud and blood. He stood there, breathing in and out, just because he could.

'Not bad,' he said to himself. 'Not bad.'

Distantly, he heard his crew calling his name. 'I'm here!' he called. 'I'm okay!' Then his eyes fell on the monstrous paw lying next to him, and he grinned. 'Better than that,' he said to himself. 'I'm a bloody hero!'

Frey dumped the paw in front of his amazed audience and then sat down by the fire, feigning nonchalance. They gathered beneath the tarpaulin, out of the rain. Grist was working on a fresh cigar. Hodd was wide-eyed with awe.

'That,' said Grist, 'is a big paw.'

'You . . .' Hodd gaped. 'You . . . That's tremendous!'

'I wouldn't go *that* far,' said Malvery, eyeing the paw. 'It would have been tremendous if he killed the *rest* of it.'

'Ah, clam it, Malvery,' said Jez, beaming. 'The Cap'n just slayed his first monster!'

'It's probably not even dead!' Malvery protested, but nobody listened.

'How's your man?' Frey asked Grist.

'He'll live. Flesh wound. Bled a lot, but no real harm.'

'That's good news, at least,' he said. He got to his feet. 'Speaking of crew, I'd better go see to mine.'

'He's over here,' said Jez. She led him to the far side of the shelter; Malvery and Silo came trailing after. Hidden among the packs, trussed up in a sleeping bag, was Crake. Snoring. No one had seen him in the confusion.

Frey leaned close. The stink of rum was on his breath. He pulled open the neck of the bag and saw that Crake was clutching an empty bottle.

'He slept through the whole thing,' said Jez.

Frey harumphed and scratched the back of his neck. It should have been a relief to see him unhurt, but somehow it wasn't. Not like this.

'Can you talk to him, Jez?' he said.

'I'll talk to him,' she promised.

'Me, too,' said Malvery. He thumbed at Jez. 'After all, what does *she* know about being an alcoholic?'

'Alright,' said Frey. 'I'll leave it to you two. Fix him, or something.' He waved a hand vaguely. 'You're all better at this stuff than I am.'

'Will do, Cap'n,' said Jez. Frey saw her exchange a glance with Silo. The Murthian nodded gravely at her.

Something meaningful there? He didn't know. He didn't know what half his crew were thinking. Talking about feelings – *real* feelings – had never been something he was comfortable with.

His hand fell to the hilt of his cutlass. Even blind drunk, the daemonist had saved his life. He desperately wanted the old Crake back. He just didn't know what to do about it. But maybe Jez and Malvery did.

They're looking out for each other, Frey thought to himself. *By damn, my crew are actually looking out for each other. Could you have ever imagined it, a year ago? I must be doing something right.*

Well, perhaps and perhaps not. He was just glad that no one had died. But there was still a good distance to go before they could count themselves safe again.

Some things are worth riskin' everythin' for, Grist had said to him. After the close shave they'd just had, Frey was beginning to wonder if this expedition was really one of them.

Eight

Harkins On The Hunt – A Funeral –
The Expedition Finds A Village – Jez's Correction

'Here, kitty. Nice kitty.'

The *Ketty Jay*'s cargo hold was always gloomy. The electric lighting was pitiful and at least fifty per cent of the bulbs had burned out and never been replaced. Harkins wasn't a fan of dark places at the best of times, but tonight he was particularly on edge. Tonight, he was hunting.

In one hand was a small wooden packing crate, open at one end. In the other was a thick blanket. He stalked through the maze of boxes and junk machinery that had occupied the back of the hold for as long as anyone could remember.

This was the last time he'd be terrorised by a cat. By tomorrow morning, he'd be a man.

'Come on, Slag,' he murmured. 'Nice Slag. Harkins just wants to be friends.'

Bess was watching him curiously from the gloom. She moved back and forth to keep him in view, fascinated by his strange behaviour. Harkins did his best to ignore her, and concentrated on calming his hammering heart.

Slag was in here somewhere. He knew it. He'd spent the night lying in wait, down here in the hold, hoping for his chance. This was Slag's territory. He was bound to emerge sooner or later. To speed things along, he'd left a bowl of food out.

Finally the cat had appeared, slipping out of an air vent, and eaten the food. Harkins had meant to spring on him then, but he found that he couldn't. In the end, it took him half an hour to pluck up his courage, by which point the cat had long since slunk off into the labyrinth of junk.

It was the thought of Jez that made him move in the end. Sweet,

sweet Jez. He imagined her whispering encouragement in his ear, and it made him brave enough to act.

'It's . . . well, it's *nice* outside,' he said soothingly. 'You don't want to spend the rest of your miserable life on an aircraft, do you? No. I mean, I'm going to set you free! All those tasty birds and mice! That'll be nice, hmm?' He lowered his voice to a mutter. 'And maybe something horrible will eat you, you vicious little slab of mange.'

He took off his cap and rubbed sweat from his scalp. There were too many dark corners here. Forgotten things loomed over him. Frey had been promising to clear them out for years but, like so many things aboard the *Ketty Jay*, it somehow never happened.

He swallowed his fear and moved steadily forward. A rustling, thumping, clanking noise attended his footsteps. He looked over his shoulder. Bess froze, caught in the act of creeping along behind him.

'You're not helping, Bess,' he whispered.

Bess sing-songed happily. She showed no sign of leaving, so Harkins decided she could come. He'd sacrifice stealth for some reassuring company.

He moved further into the aisles of junk. Bess tiptoed as best she could. His eyes moved restlessly among the shadows. Could the cat be among the pipes overhead? Was he watching them from some secret corner, ready to pounce? Harkins was seized with terror. He wanted to turn and run. Jez didn't ever need to know. He could come back and try again later.

You can do this, he told himself. *You've lived through two wars. You can handle a small domestic animal.*

Then he heard a rapid scratching, coming from a small gap between some crates and the bulkhead. He stopped still, and put his finger to his lips. Bess imitated him, clinking her finger against her face-grille. The scratching came again.

Slowly, Harkins lowered the box to the floor and took the blanket in both hands. It was Pinn's winter blanket, made of hide, thick enough to resist Slag's claws. With it, he'd smother that damned moggy, and stuff him in the box.

He took a deep breath. Scratch scratch scratch.

A huge black rat darted out of the gap. Harkins yelped in fright. It stared at him and scurried away.

Harkins let his breath out. He was trembling. False alarm. He turned to Bess and managed a nervous smile.

'That was close, eh?'

The cat dropped from the pipes above, landing on his head in a frantic scurry of claws. Harkins shrieked in panic, wheeling away down the aisle, beating at his head as if his cap were on fire. He spun past Bess, still trying to get a grip on his yowling adversary, then tripped over his feet and smashed his head against the corner of a crate.

The next few moments were a blur. He was lying on his back, unable to move, too stunned to work out what had happened. The cat padded over and leaned into his field of vision, peering into his eyes. Satisfied its foe was vanquished, it wandered away.

Jez . . . he thought. *Jez, I failed you* . . .

The last thing he remembered was Bess squatting next to him and poking him, evidently wondering why he wasn't getting up. After that, everything went dark. It was better that way.

It was on a damp, cold morning that they buried Gimble.

The rain had stopped at dawn but the cloud cover was still unbroken, a low grey roof over the land. They put the dead man into the earth in the spot where they'd made last night's camp. An anonymous place among the trees and creepers, where the air was chill and fresh, rich with the scent of soil and leaf.

Grist said a few words in Gimble's memory while the others stood around sniffling and coughing. Most of them had caught colds in the night, and several were sipping a hot remedy that Malvery had whipped up. When Grist was done, they laid on Gimble's chest the severed claw of the creature that had killed him. It seemed fitting, somehow, to show that his death had been avenged.

Not that the poor sod'll know anything about it, Frey thought, as Gimble's crewmates began to fill in the grave.

Last night's other casualty, the eager young Tarworth, was in better shape. He was limping along, using a rifle as a makeshift crutch, but his spirits seemed high. Frey saw him joking with Ucke as they set out. Ucke grinned, showing his uneven mouthful of scavenged teeth.

Pinn looked shifty all morning, but nobody said a word about his little mishap with a pistol. Frey's own pistol had been lost during his flight from the beast, so he'd taken Gimble's twin revolvers. Nobody seemed to mind, and Gimble wouldn't need them.

Their pace was slow, for Tarworth's sake. Hodd assured them they'd be at the crash site by mid-afternoon, but even that seemed too long. Last night's attack had made them wary, and they jumped at every rustle of leaves. Yet despite the sound of animals all around them, they caught barely a glimpse of the local wildlife. The animals heard or smelled them long before they arrived, and made themselves scarce.

'See, boys?' said Grist. 'They're more afraid of us than we are of them!'

Speak for yourself, thought Frey. *You didn't see what attacked the camp.*

At midday, they found the village.

It was dug into a hillside, half-buried by the slope of the land. The trees had thinned out and there was little undergrowth. Sunken trenches with walls of stone blocks formed enclosures and yards. Oversized doorways led into passages, tunnelling into the hill. Scattered about were crude huts of rock and packed mud, their roofs fallen in. It was an abandoned place, empty of life.

'Your lost tribe?' Grist asked Hodd.

'Sadly not,' said the explorer. He blew his nose on a handkerchief. 'This is a beast-man village. Home to the savages that inhabit this island. I passed it last time I was here.' He swept the buildings with a disinterested gaze. 'They have been well documented by explorers before me. Come on. The craft isn't much further.'

They ignored him. Several of them wandered off to investigate the huts. Frey stayed back. Dead as it was, the village was uncomfortably roomy, built for people much bigger than the average Vard. He didn't like the size of some of those doorways. 'So there *are* beast-men?' he asked Hodd. 'That much is true?'

'Oh, indeed,' said Hodd. 'I have seen some from afar. They walk like men, but they are more like animals.'

'What are their women like? Are *they* like animals too?' Pinn asked, nudging Malvery in the ribs.

Hodd merely looked puzzled. 'Their . . . women?'

'What happened to the beast-men who lived here?' Frey asked, changing the subject before Pinn could get really lewd.

Hodd sniffed. 'Perhaps driven away by a rival tribe. They are a violent sort.'

'Cap'n!' Jez called. She was waving from the doorway of a hut.

Hodd rolled his eyes. 'Must we waste all this time? I told you, there's nothing you'll find that the Explorer's Guild doesn't already know. Beast-men have been thoroughly, *thoroughly* researched. There's simply nothing more to say! An exploratory dead-end!'

'Ah, let 'em have their fun,' said Grist. He spat out the butt of a cigar and put a fresh one in his mouth.

'Ooh, look at this! Look at that!' Hodd mocked sourly, in cruel imitation. 'There's nothing worse than watching amateur explorers at work.'

Frey walked over to Jez and joined her inside the hut. It was little more than a circular wall with a floor of mud and rotted rushes, but unlike the others, its roof was still mostly intact. Whatever had been inside had long disappeared.

Jez was crouching by a wall, holding a broken necklace of coloured stone. Frey took it from her.

'Genuine beast-man necklace,' he said. 'Nice work, Jez. Might be worth something.'

'Have it if you want, Cap'n, but that wasn't what I called you over for. Look.'

He crouched down next to her. There was a small circle of stones on one side of the hut, and a shallow fire-pit with the remains of a fire inside. She held her hand over it. 'Still warm.'

Frey tried it too. Faint heat came from the embers. He sat back on his haunches. 'Huh,' he said, neutrally. 'Place isn't as deserted as we thought, maybe?'

'I think they were passing through. Took shelter here last night.'

Frey thought about that for a moment, then got to his feet. 'You want this necklace or not?'

Jez waved him away. 'It's yours.'

Frey walked back to Grist, running the necklace through his hands. Grist was smoking, as ever. Hodd tapped his feet impatiently and looked skyward.

'Oh! A necklace!' Hodd crowed. 'Just like the other *thousand* in the Explorer's Guild archives.'

Frey ignored his tone. 'How much do you think it's worth?'

'That? Next to nothing. If it doesn't come with an Explorer's Guild Seal of Certification, there's no way to convince anyone it's not some fake.'

'Seal of Certification?'

'And they'll only give you that if they've first given your expedition a Seal of Recognition.'

'Seal of Recognition?'

'And they only give *that* to people who can afford their extortionate membership fees and who are willing to pay them a tithe on all expedition profits.'

'And I'm guessing you haven't been paying?'

Hodd sniffed. 'I'm a little behind.'

Frey rolled his eyes and tossed the necklace over his shoulder.

'Might I have a word, Frey?' Grist said. He and Frey walked away a short distance.

'What's on your mind?' Frey asked.

Grist pointed with the two fingers that held his cigar. A short way off, Crake was leaning against a tree, throwing up.

'Your daemonist. He is gonna be able to do what he says, ain't he?'

'Don't worry about that,' said Frey. 'Not a lock in the world that Crake can't get through, given time and tools.'

'Aye,' said Grist, doubtfully. 'Well, I hope so.'

'Did you know there are still beast-men around here?' Frey asked.

'Fascinatin',' said Grist, not fascinated at all. 'If they show their faces, we'll kill 'em. Now round up your crew, eh? We'd best get going.'

Hodd hadn't been exaggerating his skill at pathfinding. He strode confidently ahead of the group, leading them through passes, across streams, up slopes. 'Ah, yes,' he'd say to himself. 'Quite, quite.' After several hours of that, he stopped on a low ridge and put his hands on his hips. 'Here we are.'

Frey was next to join him on the ridge. He swung off his pack, dumped it on the ground and stretched. 'So we are,' he said. 'Good job, Hodd.'

The ridge was six or seven metres above the forest floor. Before them was a narrow, tree-choked defile hemmed in by steep mountain walls on three sides. Clearly visible in the undergrowth was the vast black flank of an aircraft.

It was the size of a Navy frigate at least, and possibly bigger. Most of it was obscured by the trees that had grown up around it, but Frey could clearly see a great split in its hull, bent girders rusting beneath. There was the edge of the foredeck, rimmed with spikes, some of which had broken off. Huge rivets studded the bow. A chain snaked out of the trees, the links thicker than a man's arm. It lay there like some fallen edifice of dirty iron, the sad remains of a time long past.

There were gasps as the others made their way up to the ridge.

'Behold!' Hodd cried. 'A vessel of the mighty Azryx!'

Frey had to admit, he'd never seen anything like it, and he'd seen just about every aircraft there was. But the more he looked, the more he thought that it *wasn't* that old. How long had it been lying here? Thousands of years? Not at the rate the rust was eating it. Frey didn't know much about trees, but he reckoned it wouldn't take more than thirty or forty years for them to regrow after the devastation caused by the crash.

He surveyed the damage to the craft. It had almost torn in half, but that suggested to Frey that it had gently, inexorably, sunk to the ground rather than ploughing bow-first into the defile. It had broken under its own weight on the uneven ground. A crash at speed would have ripped the craft into twisted chunks, and caused much greater destruction.

Jez walked up next to Frey. He turned to her to ask her opinion, but he stopped when he saw the look in her eyes, the horror on her face.

Jez, pale at the best of times, had gone white.

'What's wrong?' he asked.

'That's no Azryx craft,' she said, quietly. But Hodd heard her anyway.

'Of course it's an Azryx craft!' he protested. 'What else could it—'

'I've seen one of those before.'

'Preposterous!' Hodd trilled, indignant.

Grist held up a hand to silence him. He was staring intently at Jez, brow furrowed. 'You've seen one? Where? When?'

'Years ago,' she said. 'In the north.' She looked away, and suddenly she seemed very small. 'That's a dreadnought. It's a Mane craft.'

Nine

The Dreadnought – Curious Cargo –
Frey Gets A Shock – Jez Sneaks Off – Flashbacks

Manes, thought Frey. *What in all damnation have I got us into?*
The narrow passageways of the dreadnought swallowed
the light of their oil lanterns. Rusty iron and tarnished steel
pressed in on them. Grim metal walls. Pipes streaked with mould.
They'd only gone a few dozen metres from the rip in the hull where
they'd entered the craft, but already it was like they were entombed.
Lightless, hopeless. There was a scent in the air, beneath the tang of
burning oil from the lanterns and the smell of Grist's cigar. Decay,
and something else. A dry, musky, unfamiliar odour that set his
senses on edge.

Hodd led the way, followed by Grist and his bosun Crattle. Frey,
Silo, Crake and Jez brought up the rear. The rest stayed outside on
lookout duty.

Nobody spoke. The only sound was the shuffling of feet and the
sniffle and snort of runny noses. Anxious eyes strained in the lantern
light. Pistols twitched this way and that. The forest had been hard on
their nerves, but this was worse.

Frey was scared. There were things that man wasn't meant to mess
with. Like daemons, for example. Seemed dangerous to play with
forces like that. He'd never had a big problem with Crake doing it, but
that was mostly because he made sure not to think about what the
daemonist was up to. Thus far, Crake's tricks had been useful and
generally harmless. Like the ring Frey wore on his little finger, or
Crake's golden tooth that could bewitch the weak-minded, or his
skeleton key that opened any lock.

But Manes? There wasn't a freebooter alive who didn't give a
secret shiver at the tales of the Manes. Stray too far north and you
might get caught in the fogs. And with the fogs came the Manes,

inhuman ghouls from the Pole. Shrieking and howling, riding their terrible dreadnoughts. They'd kill you on sight, or worse, *turn* you. You'd be one of them to the end of your days. And that might be a very long time indeed. They all knew the story of the boy who lost his father to the Manes, only to meet him and kill him thirty years later when the Manes returned to his hometown. Changed though his father was, he hadn't aged at all.

Manes. Their nature was mysterious, their purpose unknowable. That frightened people. More than the Sammies who might be building a great air fleet to the south, more than the strange and hostile people of Peleshar with their bizarre sciences, more than the rumours that came out of New Vardia, of disappearing colonies and sinister portents. Nobody knew for sure what the Manes were, or what they wanted.

He checked his crew. Silo was typically inscrutable. Crake looked ill. But it was Jez who worried him most. She had a stricken expression on her face. Maybe he should have left her outside with Malvery and Pinn, Ucke and Tarworth. But no: he wanted clear-headed and reliable people in here with him, and these three were the best he had.

'You alright?' he asked her quietly.

She gave him a distracted nod and a false smile. 'Fine, Cap'n. Place just makes me jumpy.'

'Keep it together, all of you,' he said. 'There's nothing here but bad memories.'

He wished he could be half as sure as he sounded.

The bow end of the craft had listed away from the stern half, making the floor slope awkwardly. Frey had to concentrate to stop his feet from sliding. He glanced down black passageways, imagining Manes at the end of them, with crooked teeth and hateful eyes.

It was cold here, among the metal and the pipes. Empty. No animals had crept in, even after decades rusting in the rainforest. No insects. Something about this place made them stay away. Frey thought he sensed it too. There was an unease about the dreadnought that troubled his instincts. A feeling of wrongness in the stale air.

It seemed they were on some sort of maintenance deck, though it was hard to tell. There were no signs or similar indicators. The dreadnought's interior was relentlessly bare. Their lanterns pressed light through shadowy doorways, illuminating the flanks of unfamiliar machines beyond.

'Through here,' Hodd announced, and Frey saw that they'd reached the end of a passageway. A heavy iron door was half-open there, wide enough for a slim man to slip through. Hodd struggled to open it further. 'Let me just . . . see if I can . . .'

'I'll do it,' said Grist. He took hold of the door and shoved it open with a squeal of hinges.

'Watch your step,' Hodd advised, as he led the way. 'It's quite a fall.'

Frey understood what he meant when he entered the room beyond. They were on a walkway overlooking a cavernous cargo hold. Due to the slant of the craft, the floor of the walkway tilted them towards that gaping abyss. Only a railing stood between them and the dark. Ahead of them, Hodd was shuffling along carefully, one hand fixed to the railing.

Frey peered over the edge, but whatever was down there was beyond the range of the lanternlight. 'I'd like to take a look at what they're carrying,' he mused aloud. His voice echoed back to him faintly.

'In time, in time, Cap'n Frey,' said Grist. 'First port o' call is this door that Mr Hodd spoke of. The one with the invisible barrier. Somethin' worth guardin' is somethin' worth stealin', I reckon.'

'Fair enough,' said Frey. He turned to Jez, who was close at his shoulder, and whispered to her, 'What can you see down there?'

'Building materials,' she replied quietly. 'Girders, slate, joists, stuff like that. Metals like I haven't seen before.'

'Building materials?' Frey was disappointed. He'd been hoping for piles of gems.

'Manes have a thing about disassembly. They can strip whole factories in a couple of days and carry them off. I mean brick by brick. They used to do that all the time in the North.

'They steal factories?'

'Hangars, refineries . . . anything, really,' she said. 'They'd come in fleets, pull everything apart, load it up and take it away. At least, they used to. Not so much nowadays. Now it's mostly people they come for.'

Frey nudged her to get her attention. Grist was watching her with interest, evidently wondering why she was gazing into the impenetrable blackness. Her uncanny vision was something Frey wasn't keen on explaining. 'Don't be too obvious, eh?' he muttered.

'Sorry, Cap'n,' she said, looking away.

'So what's in the hold is the remains of something the Manes disassembled?'

'I don't think so. Everything's all too neat and new-looking. Looks more like they're going to build something. They've got carts, pumps, piping . . . You want my guess? Down there, you've got everything you'd need to set up a small colony.'

Frey didn't like the sound of that at all. 'A colony? You've got to be kidding.'

'In case you haven't noticed, Cap'n, this isn't exactly the place for jokes.'

It really wasn't funny. The only good thing about the Manes was that they generally stayed behind the permanent wall of cloud that hid the North Pole. If they ever moved out of their frozen hideaway, things were going to get pretty grave.

They came off the walkway and joined another passage. A short distance further on there was a room off to one side. Hodd led them into it. It was a small antechamber, empty of decoration or seating. In one wall was a riveted metal door, much like the others they'd seen.

'That's it,' said Hodd.

Grist's brow furrowed as he stared at it. 'That?'

'The impassable door.'

It looked rather innocuous. Crake shrugged. 'Well, let's get to it then,' he said. He motioned to Silo and Crattle, who were the only ones still wearing backpacks. The rest of them had left their burdens outside. 'Put down the equipment – *carefully* – and I'll get started.'

'Shouldn't we try the door first?' Frey suggested. 'I mean, to see if it's actually the right one, before we waste all this time?'

Crake was busy unpacking a box of wood and metal covered with gauges and dials. 'Be my guest,' he said.

'Any volunteers?' Frey asked.

The faces he saw in the lanternlight were not volunteer's faces.

'I'll do it, then,' he said impatiently. He strode up to the door, reaching for the handle. It was just a door, after all. What could possibly—

The next thing he knew, he was upside-down, in a contorted heap on the other side of the antechamber. His head was whirling and he wanted to be sick. His buttocks slid down the wall and he twisted to fall on to his side. Silo helped him upright. He swallowed as his gorge rose, and managed to keep his lunch down with a heroic effort.

'That's the door, alright,' he wheezed. 'Have at it, Crake.'

He sat down again and concentrated on making the room stay still. Nothing else they'd come across had so much as a lock on it, but *this* door had been barricaded with some unearthly force.

What are they guarding?

There was little to be done while Crake set up his instruments. Jez found the lack of distraction unbearable.

This place was both horrifying and fascinating. She felt drawn and repelled at the same time. The evidence of the Manes was in every-thing, all around her. There was something *familiar* here, a faint, lulling scent. It soothed her, the same way the smell of an aircraft sometimes evoked fond, warm childhood memories of her father in his hangar. She was appalled that she could draw a comparison between that time and this, but she couldn't deny it. The feeling was the same. Safety. The unquestioning faith and trust of a little girl in her father.

A trick. This was *not* the same. It couldn't be.

Ever since she'd laid eyes on the dreadnought, she'd felt like she was about to tip into one of her trances. But the moment hadn't come. Instead she hovered agonisingly on the edge. Wanting to fight it off but not knowing how. She didn't dare slip, not here. The Manes were all around her. If she let them get a hold of her, who knew what might happen? Maybe she'd lose herself for good. Maybe she'd become one of them.

Maybe she'd turn on her friends.

She wished she could explain to the Cap'n what she was, what a danger she might be to them, especially here. She wished she could tell him how she was trying so hard to stay human, how she was afraid it was a battle she'd one day lose. But she couldn't say a word. She was too afraid he'd send her away. The *Ketty Jay* was the only home she'd found in her years of wandering since the change. She couldn't lose that.

She was standing at the back of the antechamber. Everyone was watching Crake as he assembled various rods and connected them to a complex brass device. Unnoticed, she sneaked away from the group.

She carried her lantern with her, for appearances' sake, even though she had little need of the light. Manes didn't need it, after all. There were no electric lamps in the walls or ceiling. Even in the midst of a battle, this place would be dark as a mausoleum.

This craft was empty, but it still resounded with the *feel* of them. She was searching for something, but she didn't know what.

I'm part of them. They're part of me. But I don't understand them at all. I don't know what they are.

She found a set of stairs and climbed them. Light grew as she neared the top, and she stepped into a long room. Six huge auto-cannons lay dormant before her, ranged along the port side of the hull. Grey daylight crept in through the open gunnery hatches in the dreadnought's flanks.

She approached the nearest autocannon. There was a seat for the operator mounted on the side, and a rusted control panel. She ran her hand over the seat, her fingertips scoring trails in the dust.

How do they live, these creatures? Do they argue, hope, love? What do they think? Do they think at all?

She pulled her hand away. Risky to even consider questions like that. The temptation was too great. She remembered the feeling of connection, of kinship, that she'd experienced when she was on the verge of turning. In that moment, she'd known how lonely and isolated she really was. How lonely *all* humans were. The Manes were linked, each one to every other. To be included in that was intoxicating.

It had been only the briefest of instants, but she'd never forgotten it. A moment of sight for a blind woman, before being thrown back into the dark. How could she not want more? And yet, what would be the price to get it? If she became a Mane, she wouldn't be human. If she was one of a collective, she wouldn't be an individual. She refused to be assimilated by anyone.

I am human, she thought, addressing the empty craft. *Damn you for trying to make me otherwise.*

She moved on, through the cannon bay. Beyond, she found a

ladder leading to an upper deck, and climbed it. At the top was another slanted passageway, as chill and black as the others. Several doorways led off from it.

Protruding from one of them was an arm.

Jez stared at it. A forearm, visible up to the elbow, lay on the floor of the corridor. A torn, ragged sleeve. Yellowish, waxy skin. Long, cracked nails.

She went closer. The arm was attached to a body. The body lay in a room. And in that room . . .

There were dozens of them in there.

The room beyond the doorway had a large brass globe in the centre, showing the land masses of Atalon in obsidian relief. Beyond it was a porthole, overgrown with vines, but not enough to completely choke the daylight. There were charts on one wall, a desk, a bookcase. The books had been thrown from the shelves in the crash. Now they were scattered on top of the pile of Mane corpses that were heaped against one wall.

It was the captain's quarters. And there, among the pile, in a tatty greatcoat and boots, was the captain. Dead like the rest of them.

How can the dead die twice?

They'd lain here for decades. She knew that by the rainforest that grew around them. Yet they were perfectly preserved, as if they might get up and walk at any moment. The rot that infested the dreadnought hadn't touched them.

She stepped over the corpse in the doorway. It was similar to the one that had tried to turn her: human in appearance, but twisted. Yellow-red eyes stared, unfocused, from a wizened face. Sharp teeth were exposed in a snarl.

Some of the others were more hideous, others less so. Some had the look of monsters; some could have been human. One, even, was handsome, with a cold, eerie serenity to his face. Some wore rags; some were clad in motley armour. Some wouldn't have looked out of place on a street in Lapin; others wore fashions from times long past. There was not a mark of violence on them, except for the way they were heaped up on top of each other. As if they'd been thrown against a wall, limp and inanimate as the books that followed them.

The smell, that awful, comforting odour, was strong here. Dry and animal-like. The smell of the Manes.

She looked away from them. They were painful to see. Something about them inspired a sad ache in her chest.

They didn't even seem dead, not really. They'd just . . . *stopped.*

Her eyes fell on the books, scattered about the room, lying open, their pages bent. Some of them were in Vardic. Classics, many of which she'd read. Several were in Samarlan and Thacian, languages she recognised but couldn't speak. But most were in a script she'd never seen before.

She picked up the nearest and studied it. The text was elegant and complex, all in curves. Circles and semicircles, speared through by arcs. Not a straight line to be seen.

Where did this come from? she thought. It was printed, professionally done. She frowned at it, trying to puzzle out where it might have originated. Peleshar? Well, maybe. It was possible.

But maybe the Manes had printing presses. Maybe they made books.

Maybe they had their own literature.

The thought dizzied her. Jez had seen them come from the sky to murder or kidnap the entire population of a small Yortish town. Feral creatures, springing from the rooftops, flickering and flitting like stuttering flames, sometimes moving too fast for the eye to follow. They'd mobbed men like animals, torn them apart with inhuman brutality.

But these same creatures built and flew aircraft. They stole buildings, and presumably rebuilt them. And now, it seemed, they wrote stories.

She let the book drop from her fingers. Nothing made sense. She'd been inducted into a club without knowing anything about its members or what it stood for. The idea of the Manes as a civilisation didn't match with their thoroughly deserved reputation as vicious, merciless raiders. No one, to her knowledge, had ever heard them speak. So what were they? Animals? Humans? Or something else?

For that matter, what was *she*?

She squatted down next to the pile of corpses. The captain was bearded, his face half-covered by a hat, eyes fierce and red, teeth sharp. Driven by some compulsion she didn't understand, she reached out toward his hand.

Just to prove I'm not afraid. Just to prove they'll never have me. Just to know if I can.

Her hand closed around the captain's, and the images burst into her mind as if through a dam, a deluge of screams and pleading, sweeping her away.

—a captain, a rebel, a man made Mane who didn't want to be—

—no more raids, no more murder, no more taking of people. No more Invitations. No more—

—they are turning away from their brethren, severing connections, a crew setting out for a new world, a new life, isolation, peace—

—but then came the loss, the lack! Once part of many, now they are few, too few—

—Once they were beloved, but they turned away. The horror of their mistake overwhelms them but it cannot be undone and still they go on—

—into the loneliness, the endless, all-swallowing loneliness—

—too much to bear—

—too much—

She washed up on the shores of reality to find herself back in the captain's quarters, freezing cold. She scrambled away from the corpses, tears gathering. The captain's dead eyes stared past her. She knew now what was behind that gaze. She'd been brushed by the tragedy, the inexpressible sorrow of this crew. They'd been Manes, and chose not to be. They cut themselves free. The loss of it killed them.

They lay down and died here, together, she thought. *They died of loneliness.*

She heard a footstep in the doorway, and looked up. Silo was there, lantern in hand. A flicker of concern passed across his face as he saw her.

'Cap'n sent me lookin',' he said.

She flung herself at him suddenly, hugged herself tight to his chest. All that she felt, all the fear and horror and sadness . . . she couldn't keep it in any more.

Silo didn't say a word. He just held her, while she cried like a child.

Ten

C rake could smell himself. Stale alcohol leaked from his pores as he worked. His stomach was sore, and felt swollen. He couldn't tell if he was hungry or not. Even the small exertion of setting up his equipment was making his heart pound. His knees hurt from kneeling on the floor of the antechamber.

Damn it, he needed a drink.

Working by lanternlight, he leaned over and shifted one of the tuning poles a fraction to the left. It was important to get them right. If they weren't all equidistant from the door, the readings would be skewed. There were five poles, thin slivers of metal standing on round bases, in a semicircle around the door. They were linked by cables to an oscilloscope, a small wooden box with a half-dozen gauges on its face.

Next to the oscilloscope was his portable resonator. It was another box of roughly the same size, wired to a damping rod: a smooth globe of metal, standing on a short, thick pole, which was set in a heavy square base. Like the oscilloscope, it was covered with a bewildering array of brass dials, gauges and switches.

He was conscious of the others watching him as he made his final adjustments. He ignored them as best he could. They'd all come to this horrible place because of him. Grist only sought out Frey so he could get his hands on a daemonist. If he failed here, he'd let them all down. Maybe the whole expedition would be ruined then, and that fellow Gimble would have died for nothing.

Keep your head down. Keep working. Prove you can do this. Prove you're good for something.

They watched him work, and none of them had any idea how loathsome he really was.

85

Jez had disappeared and Silo had gone after her. That was good, at least. He could do without the Murthian's silent scrutiny. Silo had a way of making it seem like he knew something about you that he wasn't telling. And he could certainly do without Jez. He wished he'd never told her about that day, when he did the most terrible thing. She'd never said a word since, but it didn't matter. He couldn't stand her looking at him. Was it disgust in her eyes? Pity? He didn't know which was worse.

He rubbed his forehead with the back of his hand. He wanted to be sick. Maybe he'd feel better if he was sick.

Grayther Crake. Look what you've become. Look where your fascination with daemonism has got you. How your dear brother would laugh.

But his brother wouldn't have laughed. His brother had hired the Shacklemores, the best bounty hunters in the land, to hunt him down. They'd almost caught him in the Feldspar Islands a year ago, at Gallian Thade's Winter Ball. He'd stayed ahead of them ever since, but he couldn't ever let down his guard. They always got their man in the end, the Shacklemores. They were well known for it.

Never able to relax, never able to forget.

He couldn't close his eyes without seeing her.

'Crake?' said Frey. 'You alright?'

He realised that he'd stopped working, wrapped up in his private misery. He gritted his teeth and forced himself to concentrate. 'I asked you to be quiet,' he said, irritated more at himself than Frey.

There's a job at hand. Get it done. Don't think about anything else.

He connected the oscilloscope and the resonator to a chemical battery. Sparks crackled as he attached the clips.

'I need absolute silence from now on. Any noise is going to upset the readings.'

Grist chose that moment to have a minor coughing fit. He tried to suppress it, but that only made it worse. Eventually he had to leave the room, eyes watering. They heard him barking his lungs up outside. Crake sighed and waited till he was done. He came back with his cigar clamped between his lips, took a soothing drag, and exhaled with a brown grin.

'Apologies, Mr Crake,' he said. 'I'll be good now, for a while at least.'

Crake pushed a lank strip of hair out of his eyes and got to work.

First, the oscilloscope. He took hold of a dial, lowered his head, and listened. Millimetre by millimetre, he turned the dial. When the needles on the gauges began to tremble, he shifted to another dial and began turning that, picking out the harmonics that the door was emitting. Once he had the bottom and top end of the harmonics, he began closing in on individual frequencies. At that point, his devices gave way to old-fashioned intuition.

He turned the dials a fraction at a time, attending to his instincts. Each time he nailed a frequency, the sense of strangeness grew. The fine hairs on the back of his hand stood up. He got the feeling he was being watched, which deepened into outright paranoia as he progressed. A faint whine, like the buzzing of a mosquito, started up in his ears.

The human body reacted to the presence of the unnatural. A daemonist learned to listen to that. Behind him, the others shuffled nervously. They were discomfited, even scared, but unsure why.

He lost himself in concentration. It had been a while since he'd had a puzzle like this to work on. It was good to bury himself in the Art. With no possibility of a proper sanctum aboard the *Ketty Jay*, he'd been using crude, portable equipment this past year, working in a corner of the cargo hold. It limited him to small, simple effects, like the earcuff communicators, which were comfortably within the range of his skill. But thralling a daemon was one thing; subduing someone else's was a different matter.

Finally he was satisfied that he'd accounted for all the elements of the complex, dissonant chord emanating from the door. The chord was like a cage, binding the daemon there. It was a weak entity, this one. Barely more than a spark of other-worldly life, set to a single task.

He scanned the settings on the oscilloscope, then sat back on his heels. 'Well, if it isn't daemonism, I don't know what it is,' he said. Now he had the readings, silence was no longer necessary.

'What do you mean?' asked Hodd.

'I mean, it's no kind of special technology or anything else. It's straightforward, thralling-a-daemon-to-a-door daemonism.'

'You mean the Manes have daemonists?'

'Just telling you what's here.'

'Can you break it?' Grist asked, eagerly.

'I should think so,' said Crake.

He set to work again, this time on the resonator. He turned the first dial, tuning in to the frequency he wanted. The damping rod hummed as it sent out frequencies of its own, interfering with those that bound the daemon. Crake saw one of the gauges on the oscilloscope drop to zero. One frequency neutralised. He sought out the next. He had the readings from the oscilloscope, so homing in on them was easy. With each frequency he matched, the damping rod hummed louder. He could feel the vibration in his back teeth, his stomach, his bowels. The brainless daemon thralled to the door was fighting to escape back to the aether. It made him want to be sick again.

The last gauge on the oscilloscope dropped. The chord that chained the daemon was countered. Crake felt his skin prickle, then there was a sensation of lifting in his body, as if there had been a pressure on him these past few minutes which had suddenly been released. The paranoia dissipated. All was normal.

The daemon was gone.

He made a cursory scan for frequencies with his oscilloscope, then reached over and unclipped his equipment from the battery.

'It's done,' he said.

'You're a damned marvel, Mr Crake,' said Grist, stepping past eagerly. He reached for the handle of the door, hesitated, then grabbed it. When nothing happened, he chuckled. 'A damned marvel.' He pushed the door open.

'Hey, we should see what's happened to Silo and Jez,' Frey said, but Grist ignored him and went on through, with Crattle and Hodd close on his heels. Frey shrugged and followed them. 'Suppose they can take care of themselves.'

Crake trailed along behind, with one last look at his equipment. He didn't like leaving it lying around like that, but he didn't want to be left here on his own.

Beyond the door was a short corridor ending in a small room. Grist was already at the other end, his lantern illuminating the way. Crake followed his captain in.

It was not what he'd expected. The room was entirely unimpressive. Simple, square, and featureless. In the centre was a thin pedestal, a metre high, and on top of that was a metal sphere about the size of a grapefruit. There were no other exits.

Frey looked around disdainfully. 'I'm not seeing any of this vast wealth you spoke of, Captain Grist.'

Grist was studying the sphere. 'Mr Crake, do you know what this is?'

Crake looked closer. It was made of black metal and appeared smooth. Silver lines ran across its surface in curves and circles. The pattern had no symmetry, and there was never a straight line. It gave him a headache just to look at it.

But there was something more. At this distance, it was impossible not to notice. His finely honed daemonist's senses were quivering with the presence of unseen energies.

'I have no idea what it is,' he said. 'But that little ball is putting out a lot of power. Makes the barrier I just broke through look like a card trick.'

Grist's eyes glittered hungrily. His cigar moved from left to right in his mouth. 'Curious,' he said. 'Real curious.' He reached out to pick it up. 'Perhaps we should—'

He was arrested by the tip of a cutlass, which flicked through the air to press against his throat.

'Perhaps we should pause a moment, Captain Grist,' said Frey, 'so you can tell us exactly why we're here, and what we really came for.'

Grist's gaze slid down the length of the blade to Frey. Frey met him with a defiant stare.

'Now what you're doin' might be thought by some to be an unfriendly action,' Grist said, his voice a gravelly snarl. 'One deservin' of recriminations, if you take my meaning. You'd best not be plannin' to rip me off, Frey.'

'Odd,' said Frey. 'That's just what I thought you intended to do.'

'Gentlemen!' Hodd said. 'Can't we be reasonable?'

'Me and my crew were brought here under false pretences,' said Frey, never taking his eyes off the other captain. 'This man owes me some answers.'

The suspicions had been there from the start, of course. They always were. Frey never trusted anyone outside his own crew, least of all strangers who came bearing promises of great wealth. He'd been burned that way before. Ever since he'd met Grist, things had been adding up and adding up until there was no doubt left in Frey's mind.

He knew the ways of liars and cheats. He'd done enough of both in his time. He didn't always figure them out straightaway but, given time, he'd spot them. And as much as he liked Grist, he knew when he was being taken for a ride.

It was that look in Grist's eyes that did it. That unguarded moment, when he reached for the sphere. Greed. Naked lust. It was like the poor saps he'd seen entranced by Crake's gold tooth. Spellbound.

Grist knew what that sphere was. Frey would have bet his life on it. In fact, he thought, that was probably what he was doing right now.

'What makes you think I ain't honest, Frey?' Grist said. A barely suppressed rage had darkened his face. Frey was used to seeing him full of bullish bonhomie, but now he caught a glimpse of the other side. Grist was capable of terrible, towering anger. Frey would have to be very careful from now on.

'I'll tell you,' said Frey. 'But first, tell your bosun that if his hand gets any closer to that pistol, you'll be smoking your next cigar through a hole in your throat.'

From the corner of his eye, Frey saw Crattle's hand drift away from his revolver.

'Now,' said Frey. 'Let's begin at the beginning. Fifty-five, forty-five. You remember that?'

'Course I do,' Grist said. 'That's the split we agreed.'

'Right. You agreed to cut me in on forty-five per cent of a fortune. Almost half your money. It was your operation; you were just bringing me in. Nobody offers terms like that. I'd have been happy with seventy-thirty.'

'So you've a blade to my throat 'cause I was *generous*?'

'I'm not done. You could have come here with your own crew and kept it all. The only reason you needed me was because of Crake. A daemonist. Because you thought a daemonist might be able to get through this mysterious door Hodd found. In fact, you offered me forty-five per cent of the profits on the off-chance that my daemonist could help you out. People only offer that kind of money if they aren't intending to pay it. Easy to make promises you don't have to keep.'

'If you say so, Cap'n.'

'You made out you had no idea of the nature of that barrier, or even if there was something worth finding behind it,' said Frey. He leaned closer to Grist, smelling the sweat and smoke of him. 'But you took a pretty big risk and went to a lot of trouble to get my daemonist here. And it just happened to be right up his alley, isn't that right, Crake?'

Crake nodded uncomfortably. 'Straight daemonism. Nothing to it.'

'You said yourself, you're not a gambling man,' Frey said to Grist. 'So I reckon you knew. You knew what this craft was, and you knew what that barrier was. In fact, you knew a lot more than you were saying.'

'I knew,' said Grist. 'Now take that damned sword out of my face. No one's gonna hurt no one, are they, Crattle?'

'No, Cap'n,' said the bosun. He relaxed a little, but his bulbous eyes were still wary in the lanternlight.

Frey let the point of his sword drop away from Grist's neck, but he kept it hovering nearby. Just in case.

Grist sucked resentfully on his cigar and glared at Frey. 'I knew she were a Mane craft. Knew it from Hodd's description, first time I met him. I come from the North; we all know about the Manes, more than you southern boys. They're just a spooky story to you. Us, we got to live with the threat of 'em. I even seen a dreadnought once, though it were gone in the fogs before I could decide to chase it or run.'

'You knew that door was protected by daemonism. That's why you needed Crake.'

'Aye,' said Grist. He was calming a little now. His tone had lost some of its darkness. 'Ain't the first time a Mane craft got downed. Back in the early days, when the Navy used to give a shit, they'd run patrols all over the North. They shot one down, got a good look at it. Then its mates all turned up. The Navy got out of there sharpish, but they took some gear with 'em, and they tested what they found.' Smoke seeped out between his teeth. 'Daemonism. Everyone thought the Manes might be daemons, but the Navy pretty much proved it decades ago. Never got round to telling nobody, though. Reckon they didn't want the panic.'

'You know a lot about it, though,' Crake put in. 'Navy reports on a crashed dreadnought? How does a man like you get access to information like that?'

'A man like me?' Grist said, with a dangerous stare. 'You don't know nothin' about me. I got my ways.'

'So you knew it was a Mane craft and you knew you needed a

daemonist,' said Frey. 'I suppose you also knew your promise of treasure was worth dogshit, then.'

'Not true,' said Grist. 'Ship like this, it'll be full of stuff. Genuine Mane artefacts? They'll fetch ducats like you won't believe.'

'Not without the seal of the Explorer's Guild,' Frey replied. He looked at Hodd, who cowered a little. 'That's what you said, isn't it, Hodd? Back at the village? You didn't go through channels, did you? You haven't been paying your Guild membership. Nobody actually knows what Mane artefacts look like, so no one's going to believe we didn't just make the stuff ourselves if it doesn't come Guild-approved. We won't get a tenth of the value, selling it through fences.'

'You'll still make your money, and get your split,' said Grist. 'Fifty-five, forty-five. I been dealing with you fair.'

'It's hardly *vast bloody wealth*, Grist!' Frey cried. He was getting angrier as Grist's fury diminished. He was annoyed that he'd allowed himself to be played for a fool. He turned his wrath on Hodd, who was an easier target than the burly captain. 'What were you *thinking*?'

Hodd quailed. 'Erm . . . well, I was rather hoping . . . I mean, once we came back with all those artefacts, they'd have to listen to reason. They'd have to let me back in!'

Frey, who knew next to nothing about the Explorer's Guild, looked at Crake for confirmation. Crake shook his head. 'They wouldn't,' he said. 'Probably wouldn't even let him in the building. If you're not a paid-up explorer, you're not allowed to make discoveries. Best you can hope for is that someone else who *is* Guild registered recreates your expedition and steals the credit.'

'Aye,' Grist agreed. 'What a system. Makes me glad to be a smuggler. At least it's honest work.'

'But surely . . . I mean . . . it's a crashed Mane dreadnought!' Hodd blustered. 'It's only been a few years I haven't been paying the fees! They'd make an exception!'

Silence. Sceptical stares. A raised eyebrow from Crake, as if to say: *Really? Would they?*

Hodd turned on Grist, flailing his arms about in a huff. 'Well if you thought that, why did you come at all?'

'That was my next question,' said Frey.

Grist indicated the metal sphere with the nub of his cigar. 'That thing,' he said. 'You could've taken whatever you wanted. But that would've been part of my share. I came here for that.'

'I figured that much out,' said Frey. 'So what is it?'

'It's a power source,' Grist said. 'Like nothin' you've ever seen before.' His eyes drifted to the sphere, and they took on that hungry look again. 'When them Navy boys looked over that dreadnought they shot down, they couldn't find nothin' that looked like a prothane engine, nor any sign of aerium neither. The science fellers reckoned it had to be powered by somethin' else.' He scratched at his bearded cheek. 'Somethin' like this.'

'This is what you came looking for?' Crake asked, peering closer at the sphere.

'Ain't it enough?' Grist asked. 'A power source that don't need aerium or prothane? If you could figure it out, you could power a fleet with these things. You'd never need to refuel. Allsoul's balls, it'd be a revolution! The Fourth Age of Aviation!' He nodded his head towards the sphere. 'You know what this is worth to the right people? There ain't enough numbers in the world.'

'I've got some. Fifty-five, forty-five,' said Frey. 'Like we agreed.'

'Aye,' said Grist, reluctantly. 'Fair's fair. I reckon even fifty-five per cent'll be more money than I can spend in a lifetime.'

'Don't forget my five per cent!' Hodd chimed in hopefully.

'Aye, yes, five per cent for you,' said Grist, waving him away.

Frey lowered his cutlass. 'The deal stands, then.'

'The deal stands,' Grist agreed.

Frey slid the blade back into his belt. The tension in the room eased down a notch.

'Better let me run some tests on that sphere before anyone touches it,' Crake suggested. 'Don't want anyone dead. I'll go get my equipment.'

'I'll come with you,' said Frey.

Frey was at the doorway when Grist spoke. 'One more thing, Cap'n Frey,' he said quietly. 'Draw a blade on me again and it'll be the last thing you do.'

'If I have to draw this blade on you again, Captain Grist, it'll be the last thing you see,' Frey replied.

They retreated to the antechamber, where Crake began gathering up his equipment and moving it down to the room with the sphere.

Frey didn't help. Instead he took his lantern and went and stood in the passageway outside the antechamber. He needed a little air, or as much air as he could get in this place.

Frey leaned against the chill metal wall and listened to his heart slow. Damn, he'd been frightened. Hadn't shown it, but he'd felt it inside. There was something about Grist. He'd caught a glimpse of the man under the grins and the laughter and the backslapping, and it had scared him. Something black and furious and maniacal.

He hadn't forgotten Gimble's fate either, the careless way Grist's bosun abandoned a wounded crewmate to die. A captain's nature was reflected in his crew, Frey reckoned, and that didn't speak well of Grist. Partnering up with him seemed like less and less of a good idea.

But he was committed now. And to be fair, Grist hadn't done anything Frey wouldn't have done himself, if he were in Grist's boots. So what if he'd kept some secrets to himself? A lie by omission was barely a lie at all, really. At least Frey had figured it out in time.

Maybe they could still come out of this rich. But he'd have to keep a close eye on Grist. That was for certain.

You don't know nothin' about me, Grist had said. That, at least, was the truth.

He thought about heading off to search for Silo and Jez, but decided against it in the end. No sense everybody getting lost. If they weren't back by the time Crake was done, they'd all search together. In the meantime, he daydreamed about the kinds of things he could spend all that money on. This time, he promised himself, he wouldn't fritter it away. He'd do something worthwhile. No blowing it on cards and booze and women.

Maybe he'd build an orphanage. After all, he'd have money to burn. Might ease his conscience a little. It'd go some way to making amends for a squandered life, anyway. Besides, a man could do pretty much what he wanted, as long as he could say he'd built an orphanage. You could shoot someone and it'd be okay. What kind of monster would hang a man who'd built an orphanage? A man who'd helped out all those little kiddies?

Presently he heard footsteps, and saw lanterns. Silo and Jez, back from their travels. He had no idea why Jez had wandered off, and he didn't care to ask. Jez looked a little shaken, but they both appeared unharmed.

'Everything alright?' he asked.

'Fine,' said Jez. 'Just went for a look around.'

'Find anything exciting?'

'A few things,' she said. 'Did Crake get through the door?'

Frey noted the rapid change of subject, but he was happy to let it pass for now. 'Yeah. It was some daemonism thing. Apparently Manes are daemons. Did you know that?'

Jez went white. 'No . . .' she said. She swallowed. 'No, Cap'n. I didn't.'

'Are you alright? You look like—'

He was cut off by the sharp sound of gunfire.

Eleven

Gunfire – The Beast-Men Of Kurg – Death Or Glory –
Frey's Mathematics – A Debt Soon Repaid

Frey ran through the antechamber, towards the room where the metal sphere rested on its pedestal. Grist, Crattle and Hodd were coming the other way, faces underlit by their lanterns.

'We heard shots . . .' Crattle began.

'The lookouts,' Frey said. 'Trouble outside.' He pushed past them, into the room where Crake was working. Tuning rods were arranged all around the sphere, linked by cables to the resonator. Crake was squatting in front of it, scribbling down readings in a notebook.

'Tell me that wasn't gunfire,' he murmured.

'Get moving. We need to get back to the others.'

'I'm not leaving my equipment!' Crake protested. 'There's no way I could afford to—'

'Alright! Gather it up! I'll send Silo down to help you.'

On cue, Silo appeared in the doorway. 'Cap'n.'

Frey was wrongfooted by Silo's unusually fine sense of timing. 'Erm . . . Help Crake,' he said.

'Cap'n,' replied Silo, brandishing the packs they'd brought the equipment in. Crake began frantically disconnecting everything. Grist loomed into the already crowded room.

'Is that thing safe or not?' he demanded, pointing at the sphere.

'I don't know!' Crake said. 'I haven't had time! It takes tests, procedures, careful study—'

Grist reached past him and snatched up the sphere.

'However,' Crake continued, 'a reckless disregard for one's own life will do just as well.'

There was another volley of gunshots from outside, snapping through the silent, empty dreadnought.

'Pack up your junk and catch us up!' Frey snapped at Crake. He ran out of the room, with Grist and Crattle hard on his heels. Grist had the sphere under his arm, which Frey wasn't happy about, but now wasn't the time for arguments. He'd make damned sure he didn't let the captain out of his sight, though.

They found Jez sitting by the doorway, a distant look in her eyes. Shell-shocked. Frey didn't have time to wonder what was wrong with her. He hauled her up. 'On your feet, Jez. You alright to shoot a gun?'

She shook herself and focused on him. Her face firmed. 'Yes, Cap'n.'

'Come on, then.'

They backtracked through the dreadnought. The gunfire intensified as they approached the breach where they'd entered. Finally they saw daylight ahead. There, crouching among their abandoned packs in the cover of a bulkhead, was Tarworth. He was using the rifle that had been his crutch to fire out into the undergrowth. Frey reached him first. Tarworth looked up, and his eyes were afraid, but he said nothing.

Frey peered out around the ragged edge of the rip in the dreadnought's hull. Beyond was the forest, steeped in weak daylight. It was alive with movement. Leaves rustled. Half-glimpsed figures rushed this way and that. A few dozen metres ahead of him, he could see the ridge they'd clambered down to get to the floor of the defile. That was their only way out, as far as he knew. The other three sides were sheer.

The undergrowth heaved and Pinn and Malvery burst out of it. They raced towards him, firing wildly over their shoulders and yelling. A spear followed them and buried itself in the ground centimetres from the doctor's foot.

'This way!' Frey cried. He drew Gimble's revolvers and fired covering shots into the undergrowth, aiming at nothing.

'Where do you think we're bloody running to?' Malvery howled back.

They bundled in through the breach and flung themselves into cover, just as Jez, Grist and the others caught up with Frey.

'Where's Ucke?' Grist demanded of his crewman.

'He was out there,' Tarworth said. 'I don't—'

'He's done for,' Malvery panted. 'They got us by surprise. He was the first one. Didn't stand a chance.'

They clustered on either side of the breach, looking out, seeking targets. It wasn't easy. They never stayed visible for long.

'There!' Jez cried.

Frey caught a brief sight of one of their attackers as it loped through the undergrowth. It looked almost like a man, but it must have been seven feet tall, thickly built and covered in black, shaggy hair. It wore beads and was wearing some kind of crude armour, made of hide or leather. In one hand it carried a carved wooden club, decorated with painted symbols and bands of colour; in the other was a spear.

'The beast-men of Kurg,' Hodd breathed, rather unnecessarily.

'Thanks, Hodd,' Frey replied sarcastically, reloading his revolvers. 'I wasn't sure for a minute there.'

'We saw some smaller ones,' said Malvery. 'Ugly little things. Red fur instead of brown.'

'Those,' sniffed Hodd, with a disdainful look at Frey, 'are the females.'

'*Those* are the native women?' Pinn cried, with the unique anguish of someone whose dreams have just been violently shattered. 'What happened to the sex-crazed tribes of warrior women?'

'Oh, they're rumoured to live in the northern tundra,' said Hodd. 'Actually, there's quite an interesting story I once heard—'

'Will you two shut it?' Frey cried. 'I'm trying to think of a way out of this!'

'Think hard, Cap'n. They've cut us off,' Jez muttered. She took a potshot at something moving in the undergrowth. 'We're trapped in the defile. More of 'em moving up all the time.'

'Where?'

'Over there.' She pointed out into the forest. There was a meaty impact, and she pulled her hand back with an arrow sticking through the palm. Frey stared at her.

'Ow,' she murmured. She went faint, staggered back and sat down heavily. Malvery went to attend to her just as Silo and Crake came running up the passageway, their packs loaded with Crake's gear.

'What's going on?' Crake demanded of the group in general.

'Beast-men!' said Hodd. 'They appear to have the advantage over us.'

'Can't *you* do something, Crake?' Pinn asked. 'You're a daemonist, aren't you? Make them die or something. Shoot fireballs!'

'Daemonism, you bloody dullard, is a science and an art!' Crake declared indignantly. 'I'm not some two-bit stage magician. If you want to make them dead, use your gun. It's what it's there for.'

'Fat lot of good *you* are, then,' Pinn muttered.

Frey shook his head in exasperation. Pinn never failed to get a rise out of Crake, even when he was in his blackest humours. He was pleased that his crew were just about capable of working together as a unit nowadays; he just wished they could do it without all the bitching and bickering. But then, he supposed, they wouldn't be his crew.

'Malvery?' he called. 'How's Jez?'

'She's okay, Cap'n. Won't be playing the piano for a while, though. Now grit your teeth, Jez, that arrow's gotta come out.'

'Why does it have to come ouaa*aaaAAARRGH!!*'

'There, now. That wasn't so bad.'

Jez was still whimpering as Malvery applied the bandages. Grist hunkered up next to Frey. 'We can't let 'em shut us in,' he said. 'If we don't move now, there'll be too many of 'em.'

'There's probably *already* too many of them.'

'Well, then there'll be even more,' said Grist. 'We can't stay here. Might be this breach is the only way in and out of this dreadnought, but might be there are others. We don't know 'em, but maybe the beast-men do. They could get in behind us.'

Frey chewed his lip. 'You're talking about a death-or-glory break for freedom, aren't you?'

'Might be I am.'

'I hate those.'

'Done many?'

'Not lately.'

'Don't worry.' Grist laid a heavy hand on Frey's shoulder. 'I've done a few. They always work out.'

'Well, 'course they do,' said Frey. 'If they hadn't, you wouldn't be here to talk about it.'

Grist chewed over the logic of that. 'You want to live for ever or somethin'?'

'I told you. Yes.'

'Sirs,' said Hodd, breaking into their debate. 'Might I make a suggestion?'

'What is it?' Frey asked impatiently. But he lost all interest in a response the moment he saw a shaggy figure running up the passageway behind Hodd, a spear raised in its hand.

He reacted instinctively, lunging towards Hodd and shoving him out of the way, aiming with his other hand. He squeezed the trigger too late to stop the beast-man releasing the spear, but he saw it coming and pulled his shoulder back just in time to avoid being impaled. The spear flew past them all and clattered harmlessly down the passageway. The beast-man staggered, dropped to one knee, and keeled over.

Lucky shot, thought Frey. *Lucky dodge. Lucky all round, really.*

Hodd was staring at him with awe. 'You saved my—'

'Yeah, yeah. Anyone see any more coming?' He ducked as an arrow from outside flew in through the breach and bounced off the metal wall.

'Can't see any right now,' Malvery replied.

'I hear them,' said Jez. She'd taken on that trance-like, distant look that she got more and more lately. Or it might just have been the shock of getting an arrow pulled out of her hand. 'A dozen or so. They're inside the craft.'

Frey turned to Grist, and saw the captain staring intently at Jez, a frown on his face. 'She's got good ears,' he said quickly. 'Seems like you were right. There *is* another way in. We can't stay here.'

Grist stuck a fresh cigar in his mouth and lit it with a match. 'Death or glory, then?'

Frey sighed. 'I suppose so.'

They spilled from the breach in a disorganised mass, guns pointing everywhere, firing randomly and shouting insults. The rainforest hid their assailants. Arrows thumped into the ground at their feet or hissed through the air, coming from nowhere. They ran headlong towards the enemy, racing for the low ridge which was the only way out of the trap. It was just visible through the trees, a craggy wall three or four times the height of a man. They'd have to climb it, while those bloody beast-men were doing their level best to kill them.

Frey was terrified. Full-frontal assaults were among his least favourite ways to spend a day.

Two revolvers, he thought. *Five chambers each. That's ten bullets. One of them is in that hairy bastard back in the dreadnought. That leaves nine.*

Something moved at the periphery of his vision. He saw a red-furred creature squatting on a tree branch overhead, aiming a bow down at them. It was flat-faced and heavy-browed, with hardly any nose to speak of. It wore a tangle of bone jewellery and a crudely patterned smock. He shot it and it flew backwards off the branch, the arrow going wide.

Eight.

'Hey!'

He glanced over his shoulder. The cry had come from Tarworth, the crewman Pinn had shot in the leg. He was limping after them with his rifle as a crutch, but he was unable to keep up. Frey didn't have the slightest intention of slowing down for him, but he thought Grist and Crattle might have spared a moment to consider their crewman. Apparently not. That wasn't how it worked under Grist's command.

'Hey, wait for me!' Tarworth called, fear giving his voice a touch of hysteria. Two arrows hit him, almost simultaneously. One in the chest, one in the eye. His crutch slipped under him and he went down in a clumsy tumble.

Frey looked away. No time to give a damn. Men died all the time. His concern was protecting his own.

The beast-men came out of the foliage, rushing in with their carved wooden clubs, ready to crack skulls. Frey was crushed amid a chaotic melee. Shotguns roared at close range. Hot blood spattered his face. He saw Silo, pistol in one hand, machete in the other. He swung and split the jaw of a beast-man. Malvery fired wildly and blew off one of their assailant's legs at the knee.

Suddenly the group of defenders surged and Frey found himself out on the edge. One of the creatures was coming at him, a thing out of nightmare, a monstrous pile of muscle, lips skinned back, yellowed teeth like tombstones. Nobody to hide behind now. Frey stuck out both revolvers and fired. The savage crumpled, but its momentum carried it forward into him, knocking him to the ground. He struggled frantically under its weight, its rank stink filling his nostrils. Feet stamped all around, threatening to trample him. With a huge effort, he shoved the dead thing aside, scooped up his revolvers and got to his feet.

Six bullets left.

'Come on, you ugly sons of whores!' Grist cried, sphere tucked under one arm, revolver levelled. Crake was stuffing bullets into the drum of his own weapon, having no doubt wasted the previous five. The daemonist's lack of accuracy was legendary. An arrow whisked past Frey's head and thumped, quivering, into a tree trunk. He ducked, long after it would have done any good.

Seconds passed, and no new attack. A break in the assault. Frey took the initiative before any more arrows came.

'Get going! To the ridge!'

That spurred them. They ran onwards. The beast-men rustled and moved with them, always staying out of sight. Impossible to tell their numbers. Ten? Fifty? Frey saw Malvery empty his shotgun into the foliage in a cloud of shredded leaves and blood.

What have I got us into? Frey thought, not for the first time.

'They're coming up behind us!' Crattle yelled. He was pointing to where the hull of the dreadnought rose over them, partially obscured by the trees. Beast-men were shambling out of the breach. Some of them had taken up the chase, others were investigating the abandoned packs piled at the entrance. Only Silo and Crake were encumbered now, carrying the daemonist's equipment; the rest had left their gear behind in favour of speed.

Frey pushed on towards the rock wall that was their only way out. A red-furred female popped up on top of it, pointing a bow down at them. Even the smaller females were almost two metres tall. They were breastless, and only differed outwardly from the males in the colour of their fur and their slighter build. It snarled and aimed, feral intelligence glittering in its small eyes.

There was a volley of gunshots from behind Frey. The beast-woman jerked and keeled over, arrow tangling in her fingers, unfired.

'Cover me!' Frey cried. 'I'm going up!'

He thrust his pistols into his belt and began to climb. It was only halfway up that he began to consider what in damnation he was doing. There were plenty of other people who could have gone up first. Why did *he* volunteer?

A rush of blood to the head. Swept up in the moment. The kind of stupid bravery that got people killed. But it was too late to back out now.

He got his arms over the top of the ridge and pulled his head and shoulders up. Two beast-men were running along the ridge towards him, clubs in their hands. Faced with a leg-breaking drop if he let go, he chose to go on, straining to lift himself over the edge. If he could get his feet under him in time, if he could get a revolver out—

There was a crackle of gunfire below him. One of the beast-men tumbled. The other came on, unhurt. Frey was still scrambling desperately on to the ridge when the beast-man reached him. He got his knee over and rolled aside just as the club smashed into the ground, centimetres from his head.

He sprang to his feet, but the beast-man was quick. With its other hand, it snatched him up by the throat, lifting him off the ground with effortless strength. Frey choked as rough fingers cut off his air. He kicked uselessly, one hand clawing at the beast-man's hairy wrist. The savage raised its club, ready to smash his skull like an egg.

Two gunshots. The beast-man's face changed from fury to puzzlement. A disturbingly human expression. Then the fingers around Frey's neck loosened, and the beast-man fell. Frey staggered back, one hand going to his throat, the other still holding the revolver he'd pulled from his belt.

Four.

His companions had started climbing up from below, one by one, while the rest held off the beast-men. Frey hid behind a tree near the lip of the ridge. He scanned the undergrowth, ready to defend his position until reinforcements could arrive. He rather hoped that the three savages who lay dead nearby would be all he had to deal with, but, as usual, he was disappointed. A thrashing of leaves warned him as two more males came running out of the forest, bare feet pounding the ground, beads and hide armour flapping around them.

Frey was ready for them this time. He calmly aimed and shot one of them in the head.

Three bullets left.

He shifted his aim to the other, sighted, and pulled the trigger again.

The revolver clicked as the hammer fell on an empty chamber.

There was a moment of cold realisation as the flaw in Frey's maths revealed itself. He had ten bullets in two revolvers, but he hadn't been firing them equally. He'd been favouring the one in his right hand. And now it was out of bullets.

He raised the gun in his left hand but the beast-man was too close. It swung its club down at him. He half-dodged at the last moment and caught a glancing blow on his outstretched forearm, hard enough to numb his hand. His revolver fired uselessly into the ground – *two left* – and dropped from his nerveless fingers.

The beast-man was startled by the noise of the revolver, long enough for Frey to back off a few paces. He sized up his options. The pistol in his right hand was empty, and he needed that hand free so he could draw his cutlass. But it seemed a shame to waste a good weapon, so he flipped it into the air, caught it neatly by the barrel, and sent it spinning towards his attacker. It cracked the beast-man hard on the forehead and flew away into the undergrowth. The beast-man staggered backwards, lost its footing, and plunged off the lip of the ridge.

'Oy!' cried Malvery from below. 'Don't send 'em down to us! We've got enough of our own!' His complaint was followed by a gunshot as he executed the bewildered beast-man somewhere out of sight.

Frey drew his cutlass as another beast-man came growling into sight. It lunged at him, and he let the blade draw his arm into a parry. The blow from the club came hard, jolting his arm. Another blow came, and another. Frey blocked them, but each time his block was weaker. Even with the strength of the sword to aid him, the beast-man's raw power was overwhelming. It attacked in a frenzy, battering at Frey's guard. He tried a counter-thrust, but only opened himself up to a swing that he just barely evaded. Teeth gritted, sweating, he backed off under the fierce rain of blows.

I can't hold it off! he thought, panicking. *I can't . . .*

There was a tremendous boom to his left, and a gory hole was punched through the beast-man's chest, flinging it away. Frey looked over his shoulder and saw Grist clambering awkwardly over the lip of the ridge, lever-action shotgun in one hand, sphere tucked into his elbow, cigar still clamped firmly in his mouth. Frey was astounded that he'd managed to climb at all, carrying all that. Grist picked up the pistol Frey had dropped and held it out to him.

'You owe me one, Cap'n Frey,' he said.

There was a sharp hiss as an arrow slipped through the undergrowth. Frey heard it, swung his arm, and the cutlass did the rest. He cut the shaft in half an instant before it reached Grist's chest, then spun on his heel and flung his cutlass like a spear into the undergrowth. There was an animal shriek, and a beast-woman staggered out into the open, the cutlass buried in its chest. Blood soaked through the coarse fibres of its smock, and it toppled to the earth.

'Not any more,' said Frey, taking the pistol.

Grist gaped, staring down at the halves of the arrow that had bounced harmlessly off his coat. 'How . . . ?'

'It's all in the wrist,' he said. He hurried over to the fallen beast-woman, planted his foot on its shoulder and wrenched the bloody cutlass free with his left hand. He was getting the feeling back in his arm and fingers now. They hurt like buggery, but at least they still worked. He thought about looking for the other pistol, but it was lost in the undergrowth and he didn't fancy seaching for it while surrounded by murderous savages. No great loss, anyway: he was a bad shot with his left hand.

Others were clambering up on to the ridge. Jez, Crattle, Pinn. They took positions on the edge and covered Crake, Hodd, Malvery and Silo as they climbed up after. Frey and Grist watched the forest warily. All had gone suspiciously quiet. They could still hear the beast-men rustling about, but no more arrows were loosed, and no more attacks came.

'You think they've given up?' Frey asked. He popped the drum of his remaining revolver and slid in fresh bullets.

Grist's eyes were grim beneath his bushy brows. 'Might be they're smart enough to know when they've bit off more than they can chew.'

'Let's hope so,' he said, snapping the drum shut. Behind him, Malvery was struggling on to the ridge. The last of them. 'We all here?' he asked.

'All here, Cap'n,' Jez replied, wiping sweaty hair away from her face with an expression of vague amazement. 'Somehow.'

'Mr Hodd!' Frey called. 'Point us in the right direction. Let's get moving before these beast-men decide to have another go at us.'

'That way,' Hodd said, thrusting out a finger without hesitation.

'Right,' said Frey. 'Eyes peeled, weapons ready. Reload if you need to. And if you see anything with more than fifty per cent body hair, shoot it!'

Twelve

The Prognostications Of Doctor Malvery – Old Acquaintances –
A New Light Is Shed On Captain Grist

The rain began again in the night. They trudged through the mud, slipping on roots, cold and soaked to the bone. Any hope of shelter had been left behind with their packs. Though they were hungry and tired, nobody had any thought of stopping. They had no idea if the beast-men were tracking them or not, but Frey didn't want to get caught napping. By unspoken consent they travelled through the night, making their slow, frustrating and occasionally painful way through the near-total dark of the rainforest.

The downpour let up at dawn, and a dull light came over the cloud-shrouded land. By then Frey was utterly miserable: half-drowned, freezing and exhausted. But nothing had killed them in the night, and the worst they'd suffered on their journey were scrapes and bruises, so he reckoned they could count themselves lucky.

We're coming back three men less than when we set out, he thought. *But none of them were mine. That's the important thing. I brought them all back alive.*

Grist was plodding along tiredly ahead of him, following in Hodd's footsteps. Frey eyed the strange metal sphere cradled under his arm. He hadn't let it go for a moment, not even when the beast-men attacked.

What are we gonna do about that? he wondered. He didn't trust Grist not to pull a doublecross. Didn't feel at all easy about letting him hold on to that thing. There'd be another confrontation before all of this was over. He wondered if he'd come out of it so well the second time.

They reached the landing site in the early morning. There was a general exclamation of relief as they spied the gunwale of the *Storm Dog* rising over the treetops, and a round of congratulations for Hodd, who'd guided them expertly by night to get them back to safety. The mood became suddenly buoyant. They'd made it. Even if they weren't exactly carrying chests of booty, they still felt like they'd conquered the savage island. Frey's crew would be glad just to get back to somewhere they could get a good meal and a mug of grog.

The trees thinned out and they walked into the barren clearing where their aircraft stood. The sounds of the awakening rainforest filled the air, and they could hear the distant bellow of the waterfall that fell from the mountains, but otherwise all was quiet. The cargo ramps of their craft were closed, and there was not a sign of another living being. They came to a stop, sensing something amiss.

'Maybe it's earlier than we thought?' Crake suggested, consulting his pocket watch. 'Nobody up yet?'

'Something ain't right,' Malvery rumbled. 'Feel it in my pods.'

'In your *pods*?' Pinn asked.

Malvery clasped his crotch with one hand. 'My pods are shrinking,' said Malvery. 'Trying to hide, ain't they? Sure sign of trouble.'

'Sure sign of you being a bloody fruitcake,' Pinn muttered. 'The day I take advice from your bollocks is the day I—'

'Go back to your fairytale sweetheart?' Crake finished for him, rather maliciously.

'Hey!' Pinn cried, but Malvery's guffaw drowned him out.

Frey was getting a bad feeling about this whole situation. It got worse when he heard the crunch of a shotgun being primed behind him. Malvery's laughter died away to a quizzical and rather worried chuckle.

'Everyone stay right where you are,' said a voice. 'Keep your hands away from them pistols!' He heard footsteps on the stony ground. Men coming from the trees behind them.

His heart sank. He should have seen it coming. Should have known Grist would try and pull something.

'Throw your weapons on the ground, all of you!' ordered the voice.

'You just told us to keep our hands away from them!' Frey said. 'Make up your mind.'

It wasn't a smart thing to do, but Frey was frustrated and he couldn't curb his mouth in time. He was rewarded with a shotgun butt to the back of his head, which sent him to his knees, skull pulsing with white agony.

'Anyone else want to be clever?'

Frey spat bitterly and blinked to try and clear his vision. He pulled out his pistol and tossed it away.

I should have seen it coming. Should never have trusted that bastard. Not even for a moment.

But when he looked up, he saw Grist throwing his own weapon on the ground, his face dark as a thundercloud.

Not him? Then who?

Frey got back to his feet, his hands in the air, and faced the newcomers. There were six he could see, and several more stepping into the clearing from the other side. They must have encircled the aircraft and lain in wait. Hard-faced men who looked like they knew their business. The foremost – the one who'd almost brained him with a shotgun butt – was a hulking bruiser with a face like a bag of spanners. A man behind him was fumbling with a flare gun, which he raised and fired into the sky.

'Where's my crew?' Grist snarled.

'Trussed up safe, Cap'n Grist. Don't you worry,' said Spanners.

'And mine?' Frey asked.

Spanners gave him a look. 'Still in the *Ketty Jay*, far as I know. She ain't goin' anywhere, and nobody's stupid enough to try gettin' inside with that golem waitin'. Don't intend on tanglin' with *that* beast twice.'

Twice? Frey thought. *Who are these people?*

Then he heard the rumbling of engines overhead. He looked up to see the prow of a frigate gliding into sight from behind the peak of a nearby mountain. His heart had already sunk into his stomach; now it felt like it was trying to make its way down his leg with the intention of tunnelling through his foot and heading underground.

He knew that frigate. That black, scarred monster, built like an ocean liner, her deck laden with weaponry.

Trinica Dracken's craft: the *Delirium Trigger*.

He watched the shuttle descend from the frigate with a deep sense of trepidation. *She* would be on it, of course. The woman he'd loved, once, back when they were both young and didn't know any better. The woman he'd deserted on their wedding day. The woman who'd tried to kill herself in her grief and only succeeded in killing the baby in her womb. *His* baby.

But that was a long time ago. Before she became one of the most feared pirates in Vardia. Before she robbed him of a fortune outside Retribution Falls.

Before she changed into something else.

They waited at gunpoint, surrounded by armed men. Their own guns had been unloaded and left in a heap a short distance away, along with their blades and other weaponry. Frey's cutlass rested on top of the heap; assorted knives, machetes, clubs and a set of knuckle-dusters were scattered around it.

A cold wind blew across the landing site. Frey tried not to shiver in his wet clothes. He clamped his jaw, which was threatening to tremble. He wouldn't show any weakness. Not to her.

The shuttle touched down, and a ramp opened to let the passengers out. His stomach was a painful knot of anticipation. Damn it, how did that woman do this to him? Half of him hated her, the other half craved seeing her again. It had been more than a year since he'd last laid eyes on her, while she was depriving him of a hard-won chest of ducats that could have made him a rich man.

He'd imagined a reunion many times since, in many different ways. But always in circumstances more favourable than this.

Then he saw her. She stepped off the shuttle, her bosun by her side. Slender, dressed head to toe in black. Chalk-white skin, short blond hair hacked into clumps. Red lips, garishly painted. She wore contact lenses to blacken her irises, making her pupils seem wide as coins. Everything about her was calculated to unsettle. She dressed like Death's bride, or perhaps his whore, and people called her both.

The very sight of her made him angry. He couldn't help it. How could she bury her beauty under this horrifying façade? Her very existence was a blasphemy against the girl who lived in his memory. His idealised portrait of perfect romance. The love that might have been.

How could she do that to him?

'Trinica Dracken,' Grist muttered. 'I heard of her.'

'Yeah,' said Frey. 'Me, too.'

He recognised her bosun from their last meeting. A squat man, with matted black hair that hung untidily around a swarthy, simian face. His skin was puckered in a patch over his cheek and throat, a burn scar, visible above the collar of his shirt. Frey tried to keep his eyes on the bosun as they approached, so he wouldn't have to look at Trinica. But his gaze kept going back to her, and eventually he gave in to it.

She stopped in front of them and looked them over. Her black eyes lingered a moment on Frey before passing by with scarcely a glimmer of recognition or greeting. Then she looked at Spanners.

'This is all they had on 'em,' he said, holding out the metal sphere.

'Then that's what we came for,' Trinica said. 'Mr Crund?'

Her bosun took the sphere from Spanners. Grist glowered and seethed at the sight. Frey fancied he could feel the heat of the rage coming off him.

'Captain Grist, Captain Frey,' said Trinica, nodding at both of them. 'It's been a pleasure.'

And with that, she turned and walked away. Crund departed with her. The armed men who'd surrounded them backed off towards the shuttle, keeping their weapons trained on the captives.

Frey stared after her. Stunned.

That was it? That was *all?* No 'Long time, Darian?' Not even the banter of old adversaries? He'd waited a year to see her again and that was all she gave him?

She'd robbed him doubly this time. It wasn't just that she'd taken the sphere from them; it was that she'd done it with such a shattering disregard for his feelings. He'd thought about her ever since their last meeting, reliving that final smile she'd given him. A smile that came from the old Trinica, the briefest glimpse of the young woman he'd loved. He believed in that smile. He'd convinced himself that young woman was still there, buried under the heartless criminal she'd become. He'd fantasised about meeting her again, teasing out that smile once more.

But she, apparently, hadn't given him a moment's consideration.

They stood in silence as the shuttle rejoined the frigate. Nobody was quite sure what to say. They watched as the *Delirium Trigger* lit its thrusters and slid out of sight over the mountains.

'I really hate that bitch,' Frey muttered.

'How did she know?' Grist snarled. There was danger in his tone, like the ominous rumblings that precede an earthquake. His face was red; he was almost choking with rage. 'How did she find us? How did she *know?*' He turned and faced the group. *'Which one of you told her?'*

Frey was intimidated enough to take an unconscious step back, but Malvery was uncowed. 'Calm down, mate,' he said. 'We've not been out of your sight since you came to us with the job. It's hardly gonna be one of us.'

Hodd raised a quivering hand. 'Remember that I, ah, approached several people before I came across your good self, Captain Grist. It's entirely possible that—'

He got no further. Grist gave a bellow of rage, and punched him in the face with appalling force. Hodd squealed as he fell to the ground, holding his bloody mouth, eyes wide with fear and distress. Grist stamped over to the heap of weapons, scooped up a machete, and stamped back towards Hodd, who'd got to his knees and was making incoherent shrieking noises through his hands.

'Here, wait a minute . . .' said Malvery, but his protest was half-hearted. None of them really thought he'd do it. Not until he swung the machete with all his might and buried it in the side of Hodd's neck.

Time stopped for Frey. The shock of the moment froze them all where they were. Hodd gaped blankly.

Then he coughed, and a flood of red spilled from his throat and over his lips. His hand came up and felt for the grip of the machete, as if trying to work out what it was. He made a feeble attempt to pull it free, but his hand slipped on the blood that had already coated the handle. It squirted from the wound in grotesque pulses.

His eyes had that terrible look in them. A look Frey had seen many times before. The look of a man who couldn't quite believe his time was up.

He keeled over sideways and was still.

Grist stared down at the explorer, his chest heaving. Nobody said a word. They watched him carefully, waiting to see what he'd do next.

'We're gonna get the sphere back,' he said eventually. 'We're gonna get it back, you hear? Your crew and mine. We'll track that woman down and we'll have what's ours and more besides. *Nobody* steals from Harvin Grist.' He took a breath, straightened, and looked over at Frey. 'You in, or not?'

Frey looked back at him. Trying to judge the depth of the mania in Grist's eyes. His first appraisal of the man had been seriously off. There was a blackness at his core that Frey didn't like at all.

To give up his shot at a fortune was no easy thing. This was the second time Trinica had stolen from him, and that was hard to take. But even so, he could have walked away. He was getting in over his head, and he knew it. Might as well play with dynamite as have a partner like Grist.

But she'd scarcely acknowledged him. That was what burned. All this time, all that had passed between them, and he meant less than nothing to her. He felt snubbed and humiliated, and he wanted to make her pay for that. He wanted revenge. She'd never walk all over him again.

'I get Hodd's five per cent,' he said, motioning toward the dead man.

Grist snorted in disgust. 'Fifty-fifty it is, you bloodsuckin' bastard,' he said. He turned his back and walked off towards the *Storm Dog*. Crattle followed him.

'Another mission ends in resounding success, then,' Malvery said sarcastically. He headed for the *Ketty Jay*. The others drifted away after him, all except Jez, who was eyeing the corpse of Hodd.

'You sure about this?' she said doubtfully.

'No,' said Frey. 'But we're doing it anyway.'

Jez nodded to herself. 'Right you are, Cap'n,' she said. Then she, too, walked off towards the *Ketty Jay*, and Frey was left alone.

Thirteen

The Butcher's Block – Pinn Gets A Letter –
Advice From A Drunkard

Marlen's Hook stood between the Blackendraft ash flats and the Scourfoot Desert, an outpost of humanity in the most lifeless of places. To the west were the Hookhollows, their sharp tips peeping over the edge of the high Eastern Plateau. Restless volcanoes hidden among the mountain peaks filled the sky with a grimy haze which was carried on to the plateau by the prevailing winds. The land was gloomy and bleared.

The port was built on a blunt lump of black rock that thrust dramatically upward from the ash-crusted earth. The heart of the settlement was on the flat top of the rock, where there was a landing pad for aircraft. It was the only place in Marlen's Hook that had anything recognisable as streets.

Jez stood at Frey's shoulder as he brought the *Ketty Jay* in towards the landing pad. She'd been to Marlen's Hook twice since joining Frey's crew, and she never looked forward to returning. The place was a lawless den of thieves and cut-throats. The Coalition Navy ignored it because it was so remote from civilisation, and because the ash in the air clogged up engines and lungs alike. Just being here was bad for your health.

She turned her eyes to the horizon, where the day was burning down in shades of pink and yellow and purple. *Still*, she thought, *at least it makes for a dramatic sunset.*

Outside the central mass of the town, shanty dwellings had gathered in clots. Tents and lean-tos crowded for space. Buildings clung to the sloped flanks of the rock wherever they could, forming a rickety maze of plank walkways and chiselled stairs. Shadows stretched long fingers eastward, or pooled in the hollows.

The *Storm Dog* was ahead of them and below, descending towards the port. Powerful beam lamps shone up from the landing pad, cutting through the murk, guiding her in. The *Ketty Jay* followed, her outflyers trailing behind.

'Well,' said Frey. 'It may not be pretty, but if anyone knows where Dracken might be found, they'll be down there somewhere.'

'Let's hope so, Cap'n,' Jez said neutrally. Frey was just talking to fill up the silence. She could tell he was full of doubts, just as she was. The atmosphere on the return journey from Kurg had been strained. The crew had retreated to their quarters or occupied themselves with solitary tasks. Hodd's murder had sobered them. Nobody missed the explorer, but nobody thought he deserved what he got, and they were all wary of Grist now. They didn't like throwing their lot in with someone like that. They'd rather give up on this whole thing.

But the Cap'n had decided otherwise. He'd got the bit between his teeth, and he wasn't going to stop. Jez wished she knew what was going on in his head. He'd been different ever since Grist had turned up. The old Frey would have known when to retreat. He would have folded his hand and got out while they still could. But something had lit a fire under him. There was a kind of doggedness in his manner that she hadn't seen since they got tangled up in the Retribution Falls affair. She sensed they'd be following this through to the end.

But if Grist was a dangerous ally, then Dracken was an even more dangerous enemy. Her involvement was unlikely to be a coincidence. There was more to this than a simple treasure hunt. She just hoped the Cap'n knew what he was doing.

Meanwhile, Jez had preoccupations of her own. Now that the shock had worn off, she'd had time to process everything she learned aboard the dreadnought. Foremost among them was this: Manes were daemons. Daemons that took over the bodies of men and women.

She had a daemon inside her.

The thought was horrifying. Ever since she'd first realised she was dead, she'd thought of the Mane part of her as an infection, a disease that she must resist if she wanted to retain her humanity. But now it was different. Now she was *possessed*. The enemy was intelligent, and it was within her. Not some mindless force of transformation, but a malicious invader that knew her thoughts and plotted her overthrow.

She held up her hand in front of her and stared at it. The arrow wound she'd sustained on Kurg had already closed up. There was no trace of a scar, and her fingers worked fine. Once her ability to heal rapidly had seemed a useful side effect of her condition; now it was just more evidence of the dreadful entity within her.

Her skin no longer felt like her own. She was violated. Somehow, she had to expel the invader.

This can't go on, she thought.

For years she'd lived in fear of herself, hiding from her fellow humans, afraid to make friends or to stay in one place. She'd tried to resist the creeping influence of the Manes, hoping to drive it back by willpower alone. She'd told herself that she would have been consumed long ago if not for that.

Maybe that was true, maybe not. But the influence grew, nevertheless. Her trances came more easily and frequently now.

She hadn't been winning. She'd just slowed the speed at which she lost.

Something's got to be done, she thought. *And soon.*

The Butcher's Block stood on a grubby thoroughfare, sandwiched between a pawnshop and a whorehouse. It was a patched-up mess of wind-blasted sheet metal and flapping tarp. The façade leaned outward as if the whole building was about to tip drunkenly into the street. Lamp-posts, made filthy by the insidious ash in the air, glowed in the dark. Most passers-by wore goggles and face masks; those who didn't had red-rimmed eyes and racking coughs.

Inside, smoke replaced ash as the pollutant of choice. The tables and stools were as mismatched as the clientele. An electric iron candelabra hung from the ceiling, buzzing. The rattling of an oil-powered generator could be heard through the outside wall.

Frey pushed in through the door, unwrapping the scarf from around his face. Pinn, Malvery and Crake followed, hacking and spluttering. None of the worn-looking patrons paid them any attention.

'Someone get me a drink!' Malvery rasped. 'My mouth tastes like a fireplace.'

'Darian Frey!' called the bartender, seeing them come in. 'Rot and damn! How are you?'

Frey walked over and shook his hand. His name was Ollian Rusk, and he was the proprietor. Huge, fat, permanently sweaty and bald as an egg. He kept a shotgun on a rack over the armour-plated bar, to distract attention from the bigger one he kept hidden underneath it.

'How's things in the ashtray of the world, Rusk?' Frey grinned.

'Getting by, getting by. Some drinks for your boys?'

'Reckon so. What do you recommend?'

'Beer's best, if you want to wash the atmosphere off your tongue.'

'Beer, then.'

'Coming up.'

Frey eyed the room, searching for familiar faces as Rusk poured the drinks. A lot of people came and went in Marlen's Hook. Every lowlife Frey had ever met – and he'd met quite a few – passed through here at one time or another. But tonight he was out of luck.

'Quiet lately,' said Rusk, divining his thoughts. 'Navy have come around sticking their noses in. Once word gets about, people don't want to come here so much.'

'Is nothing sacred?' Frey commiserated.

'Navy's jumpy. All these stories about colonies vanishing in New Vardia. Then there's those rumours that the Sammies found aerium, down where Murthia used to be. Everyone's paranoid they're kitting themselves up with a new Navy. Not to mention the Awakeners getting pissy 'cause the Archduke is trying to cut them down to size.' He laid the beers on the bar. 'The higher-ups think there might be conspiracies afoot. Looking for spies and such, I imagine. Turbulent times, friend.'

Malvery, Pinn and Crake snatched up their beers and downed them thirstily. Pinn burped and slammed his empty glass back on the bar.

'Three more, I suppose,' said Frey, whose own mug was only halfway to his lips.

Rusk poured the beers. Halfway through, he suddenly raised a finger and said, 'I forgot. I've got mail for you.'

'Bring it out,' said Frey. 'Let's have a look.'

The Butcher's Block was one of a dozen mail drops Frey had all over Vardia. It was a system used by many freebooters, who tended to have no fixed address. This way, they could be contacted through the underworld without a lengthy search. Some liked to have mail sent to a post office where they could collect it, but Frey distrusted post offices. Returning to the same spot frequently made him too easy to find, and some of the packages he received were suspect, to say the least. Employing bartenders and shopkeepers as unofficial mail drops carried the risk of theft, but usually the need to maintain a reputation kept them honest. Ollian Rusk handled more mail than some post offices did, because he was as trustworthy as they came.

Rusk went into a back room and emerged with a bundle of six letters wrapped in string.

'What do I owe you?'

'One bit and two for the letters. I'll run you a tab for the drinks.'

'Obliged,' he said, as he took them. The sight of the first letter made him groan.

'Bad news, Cap'n?' Malvery asked. 'You haven't even opened it yet.'

'No, it's nothing,' said Frey.

Malvery looked at him expectantly.

'Alright, it's from Amalicia,' he said. 'I recognise the handwriting. I've had a lot of letters from her lately.'

'Amalicia Thade?' Crake asked. 'The young lady you, er, *rescued* from the Awakeners by getting her father killed?'

'Hey, he got *himself* killed!' Frey protested. 'And yes, her.'

'What's she after?' Malvery asked.

Frey squirmed.

'Come on!' the doctor cried, joshing him. 'You might as well tell us. You'll get no peace till you do.'

'Well, she might have somehow got the impression that I was in love with her.'

'Might she?' Malvery asked with a grin. 'And who gave her that idea?'

'I never bloody thought she was going to get out of that hermitage!' Frey said. In fact, he hadn't really thought about the consequences at all. He rarely did when he was making promises to women. The idea that he might have to fulfil them one day rarely crossed his mind, as long as he got what he wanted right then.

'Isn't she the head of the Thade dynasty now?' Crake asked. 'Powerful woman.'

'And filthy rich, too,' said Malvery. 'Not a bad catch, Cap'n. Can't think what she sees in you.'

'I expect it's my rugged charm and roguish demeanour.'

'Must be.'

Frey undid the string and flicked through the rest of the letters. 'There's one here for you, Pinn.'

'For me?' Pinn asked in surprise.

'Oh, that's right,' said Rusk. 'It didn't have your name on, Frey, but it was addressed to the *Ketty Jay*, so . . .'

Frey handed the letter to Pinn, who tore it open.

'And who's writing to *you*?' Malvery demanded, descending on Pinn like a slightly inebriated vulture.

'I don't know till I read it, do I?' Pinn said, shrugging him off. He squinted at the letter, concentrating hard, mouthing the words as he processed them. Pinn could just about read and write, although it required a bit of effort. After a few lines his face cleared and a huge smile split his chubby face.

'It's from my sweetheart Lisinda!'

Malvery choked on his beer and sprayed it all over the back of Frey's neck.

'She says . . . she says . . .' Pinn began, then realised he hadn't read that far and went back to the letter. Slowly his smile faded.

'What's the matter?' asked Frey, mopping himself angrily with his scarf. 'What does she say?'

Pinn looked up at them, and his eyes were bewildered and shocked. His expression was one of profound distress.

'She says she's getting married.'

After they left the Butcher's Block, they toured the bars of Marlen's Hook, looking for information about Dracken and the *Delirium Trigger*. Rusk hadn't been wrong: the port was noticably quieter than usual. Frey complained that many of the familiar faces were absent. It was bad luck that the Navy had come visiting recently.

Crake trudged along, uninterested in the chase. He was rather annoyed that they kept shifting venue, wasting valuable drinking time by wandering the filthy streets. But for once Frey's mind was on the job, not on the booze. He led them here and there, chatting to barmen and interrogating drunks.

Pinn hung about looking glum. He'd barely said a word since reading the letter from his sweetheart, and nobody spoke to him about it. No one was quite sure how to deal with his stunned grief.

Malvery looked particularly awkward. Presumably he was feeling guilty because of all the times he'd said that Lisinda didn't exist.

Privately, Crake sneered at Pinn. His own stupidity had put him in this position. He'd abandoned Lisinda years ago for some absurd quest for glory, and he deserved what he got. If she'd finally woken up and dumped him, well, Crake couldn't really have cared less. Pinn's pain was laughable in comparison to Crake's.

Besides, he wasn't sure if Pinn was even smart enough to feel pain in the way other humans did. It was more like separating animal companions in a zoo, and watching one of them pine for the other.

Eventually, Pinn put them all out of their misery and wandered off back to the *Ketty Jay*. The mood lightened immediately, though not by much. Crake had been hoping for a raucous night, ending in oblivion, but Frey was too preoccupied and Malvery had something on his mind.

Well, at least there was the booze. He didn't need much more than that.

At one point, they bumped into Grist, Crattle and a few men from the *Storm Dog* in the street. Grist seemed to be having a similarly frustrating time. Crake, nicely smashed by this point, allowed himself a bitter smile. Good. He'd come to despise Grist, and was quite scared of him. No matter how much Crake had wanted to plunge a machete into Hodd's neck himself, it was inexcusable that Grist had lost control like that. What was a man if he didn't have control? Nothing better than those savages from Kurg.

Let Dracken disappear without trace, he thought. *She outwitted us. Move on.*

When they got to a bar, Crake and Malvery were largely left to their own devices while Frey went to work charming the clientele. They took their drinks to a corner and set to work on them. Conversation was minimal. Malvery kept on glancing at him, as if he was about to speak, and then didn't.

'What?' Crake asked irritably.

'Nothing,' said Malvery.

It was the eighth or ninth bar they'd visited, and they were both unsteady on their feet, when Malvery broached the subject he'd been working up to all night.

'Know how long I've been an alcoholic?' he asked.

Crake picked up their bottle of rum and filled Malvery's mug, narrowly avoiding igniting the sleeve of his coat on the candle that sat in the centre of the table.

'Oh, you're not an alcoholic,' Crake said. 'You just like a drink.'

Malvery barked a laugh. 'No, mate. Whatever way you cut it, I'm an alcoholic. Five years now.'

Crake didn't quite know what to say. 'How's that going?' he managed eventually.

Malvery grinned. 'Suits me, actually. I don't mind a bit.'

'Hmm.'

They both drank from their mugs. Crake had a suspicion that something more was coming, but he wasn't going to be the one to prompt it.

'Listen,' said Malvery. He leaned forward. His green-lensed glasses sat askew on his broad nose, and droplets of rum hung from his big white moustache.

Crake waited. When Malvery still hadn't said anything after several seconds, he said, 'Um . . .'

Malvery held one thick finger in the air to silence him. 'Remember . . .' he said. 'Remember I told you what I did?'

There was only one thing he could be referring to. Several years ago, he'd operated on a friend while drunk, and killed him. It had cost him his livelihood, his wife, and everything he had.

'I remember,' said Crake.

Malvery's eyes drifted out of focus. 'I always thought . . . things could've gone two ways that day,' he said. Suddenly he snatched up the bottle of rum and held it between them. 'See, I could've said, "Oi, mate, you know who killed your friend? That bottle in your hand! Get rid of it!" And I'd have gone clean and sober. That would've been the sensible thing to do.' He put the bottle down. 'But instead I just drank more. Wanted to. I wanted to block it out. To forget.'

Crake was watching the mesmerising play of candlelight in the curve of the bottle. 'That, I understand,' he said.

Malvery wiped his moustache with the back of his hand. 'Let me tell you. Doesn't work.' He tapped the bottle with a finger. 'This bottle ain't gonna forgive you, Crake. You've got to do that yourself.'

Crake's eyes went to Malvery's. 'Some things can't be forgiven,' he said.

'Then they can't be forgotten, either,' Malvery replied.

'I suppose not,' Crake conceded.

Malvery sat back in his chair. 'So you can't forgive yourself and you can't forget. Fine. Now what?'

Crake was confused by that, and irritated by the turn of the conversation. 'There *is* no "now what",' he said.

''Course there is,' said Malvery. 'You just keep on living, don't you?'

Crake shrugged.

'Look, mate. It was you that persuaded me to pick up a scalpel again, after all those years. We saved Silo, between us. Remember that?'

'Of course I do.'

'Now I ain't never going to be the surgeon I once was, and I've still got a liver blacker than pickled shit, but I know how to save a life. Maybe I've got ten years left, maybe just one, but maybe in that time I can save someone else. Maybe you.'

'What's your point? That you figured out how to be a doctor again? Malvery, you're still drinking.'

'It's far too late for me,' he said. 'Besides, I'm a damn good alcoholic.' He swigged his rum to prove the point, then wagged a finger at Crake. 'But I ain't nobody's role model. Why'd you wanna go this way?'

'I'm not your bloody apprentice, Malvery,' Crake said. 'This isn't about you.'

But Malvery wasn't about to be put off. 'You're a smart feller. Careful. Polite. You think things through. But lately, mate, you've been getting nasty when you drink. And that's not you.'

This was ridiculous. Crake felt like he was being preached at, and it made him angry. 'So what's the diagnosis, doc?' he said, his voice dripping with scorn. 'How do you propose to cure me?'

'I faced my daemons, mate. You made me. Now you gotta face yours.'

'What do you know about my daemons?' Crake sneered.

Malvery shrugged. 'Not much, not much. But I know you've got 'em, and they're big ugly bastards at that. Otherwise you wouldn't be spending half your life in a bottle.'

'More than half,' Crake said, refilling his mug. 'So what?'

Malvery studied him for a moment. 'How'd it feel, when you fixed that door for us?'

'What do you mean?'

'The door in the dreadnought. The one you popped open.'

Crake thought about that. 'It felt good,' he said. 'I felt useful.'

'You like all that daemonist stuff, don't you?'

'I wouldn't be a daemonist if I didn't,' Crake replied. He ran his fingers through his scruffy blond hair. 'Obsession comes with the territory. Once you've seen the other side . . .' he trailed away.

'And how much have you done, these last couple of months?'

'Excuse me?'

'How much *daemonism*, mate? New stuff, I mean. Testing your boundaries, learning your craft, all of that.'

'I don't see what you're driving at.'

Malvery leaned forward on his elbows. 'I see the stuff you've made. Frey's cutlass, your gold tooth, those little ear thingies the pilots wear, that skeleton key you've got. Some of those things are real damn clever.'

'Thank you.'

'Now how many of them did you make in the last six months?'

Crake opened his mouth to reply, then shut it again.

'I expect you've been all tied up in research, trying out some new method or something, ain't you?' Malvery prompted. 'Maybe you're working on something really special?'

Crake glared at him. Malvery sat back and folded his arms. Point made.

Crake took a resentful swallow from his mug. Being called an alcoholic was easy enough to take, but he didn't like having his commitment to the Art questioned. And yet, he couldn't deny Malvery had a point. He didn't have any excuses. He'd stopped practising daemonism almost entirely of late. The thrill of it, the allure of new discoveries, had disappeared.

For a while, he'd rather enjoyed the challenge of working aboard the *Ketty Jay*. Being without a sanctum forced him to think of creative ways to get the best out of his portable, sub-standard equipment. But as the weeks passed there were fewer and fewer hours in the day when he was clear-headed enough to study the formulae he needed. He seemed to be always hungover or drunk, and it became a huge effort to turn his brain to the complex problems of daemonism. Easier to leave it until the next day. He told himself he'd do some work then. But the next day was the same as the last, and somehow it just never happened.

He looked at the bottle on the table. It was the first time it had occurred to him that his drinking was affecting his Art. Without that forbidden knowledge to set him apart he was just another layabout aristocrat, no better than Hodd. The idea appalled him. He considered himself better than that. Yet the evidence indicated otherwise.

Then an idea occurred to him. A drunken, stupid, furious idea born out of frustration at being faced with his own inadequacies. Something he never would have dared consider when he was sober. But he was keen to prove Malvery wrong, keen to show the doctor – and himself – that he was still worth something. He was more than a privileged idler with a hobby; he was extraordinary. So he said it aloud, and once said, he was committed.

'I think I know a way we can find that sphere.'

'How?'

'I'm going to ask a daemon.'

Fourteen

An Unexpected Visit –
Crake's Request – The Summoning

C rake raised his hand to knock on the door, hesitated, and let it fall. He looked both ways up the winding, lamplit alley. Narrow, elegant, three-storey dwellings were crammed shoulder-to-shoulder along the cobbled path. The air was fresh with the salt tang of the sea. There were voices coming from beyond the end of the alley, but nobody he could see. It was an innocuous, out-of-the-way house that he'd come to, and that was exactly how its owner liked it.

Crake turned up the collar of his greatcoat and raised his hand again, knuckles bunched to rap on the wood. His skin was clammy and his palms were damp. Everything felt closed-in and unreal, as if seen through a camera lens. The taste of whisky still lingered in his mouth. His heart skipped a beat now and then. It was a distressing new development that he'd noticed lately, usually when he was hung-over.

I shouldn't have come here.

He thought about making up an excuse. He could rejoin the crew in the morning and tell them he'd tried and failed. No harm done. Maybe it was better they didn't find Dracken anyway.

But he wouldn't lie like some common scoundrel to his friends. That would be too much of an injury to his pride.

Pride? A failed daemonist, drinking himself numb? Where's the pride in that?

Self-disgust spurred him on. He knocked on the door.

'You told them you'd do this,' he murmured to himself. 'What's a man, if he doesn't do what he says he will?'

He heard footsteps, and the door was opened to reveal a short, round man in a brocaded jacket, wearing a pince-nez. He was bald on

124

top of his head, but a thin fringe of grey hair fell to his collar. His eyes bulged at the sight of Crake.

'Rot and damnation, will you get out of sight!' he snapped. He grabbed Crake by the arm and yanked him inside, then looked both ways up the alley and shut the door.

'A pleasure to see you too, Plome,' said Crake, smoothing out his coat and admiring the hallway. 'How have you been?'

'You can't keep turning up on my doorstep like this!' Plome spluttered. 'There are procedures for this sort of thing! A letter, a clandestine rendezvous, disguises! Be more circumspect, won't you?'

'Noted, Plome,' said Crake. 'But I'm here now, and nobody saw me. Will you please relax?'

Plome produced a frilled handkerchief and mopped his brow. 'I'm running for the House of Chancellors, you know,' he said.

'I didn't,' Crake replied. 'Congratulations.'

Plome harumphed and flounced into the sitting room. 'The slightest whiff of scandal, do you understand? The slightest whiff could ruin me.'

Crake followed him in. The sitting room, like the hallway, was panelled in dark wood and hung with portraits. Two armchairs sat to either side of an unlit fireplace, with a lacquered side table between them. Plome went to the liquor cabinet and pulled the stopper from a crystal decanter.

'I'm sorry,' said Crake. 'I wouldn't have come if I wasn't in desperate need.'

Plome poured two glasses of brandy and held one out to Crake. He'd intended to resist the temptation of alcohol – he'd need a clear head for the night's work – but his resistance crumbled at the sight of it. A clear head was no good without steady nerves, after all, and he didn't want to risk causing offence by refusing. He took a sip, and felt a bloom of warmth and well-being.

'As you see, we have electricity in Tarlock Cove at last,' said Plome, indicating the light fixtures. 'And a great improvement it is too.'

Crake made an admiring noise. It wasn't news to him; he'd seen it mentioned in a sidebar in the broadsheets months ago. He wouldn't have come otherwise.

Last time he'd visited, Tarlock Cove had run exclusively on gas. The portable generators that provided many remote settlements with electricity had been outlawed. They were too noisy for a picturesque coastal town, and they put out unpleasant fumes. Instead, the town's founders had built a small, quiet power plant, and now charged the residents for their supply. It was the way it was done in the cities, and it was rapidly spreading to smaller settlements as the technology became cheaper.

Crake was all for progress in that regard. He needed a steady flow of electricity for what he had in mind, and using a generator would be risky. Generators broke down too easily.

Plome settled himself in an armchair with a nervous glance at the windows to make sure the blinds were secure. Crake sat in the other, the brandy glass cupped in his hand.

'So you're to be a politician?' Crake prompted.

'I hope so,' said Plome. 'I have the support of the Tarlocks, and they have been most thorough in introducing me to other aristocracy in the Duchy. I'm the horse they're backing, so to speak. The incumbent has proposed some unpopular motions to the House and all indications are that he's on his way out.' He took a sip. 'I stand in good stead, but it's still two months to the ballot.'

'Isn't it dangerous to put yourself in the public eye like that? I thought you were trying to keep out of sight?'

'A calculated risk,' said Plome. 'I hope to obtain enough leverage to quieten anyone who might discover my less socially acceptable activities. At the very least, I should escape the gallows if I'm caught.' His tone changed, became wary and grave. 'They say things about you, Crake. What you did. Why you're on the run from the Shacklemores.'

Crake looked at his reflection in the lapping surface of his brandy. He swirled the liquid to break it up. 'It didn't happen the way they say.'

Plome shook his head. 'Spit and blood, Crake. If it happened at all . . .'

'It wasn't me!' said Crake sharply. 'At least . . . it was my body doing it, but I wasn't there. You understand? I reached too far, Plome. A procedure got out of control.'

Plome left his seat and paced the room in agitation. Crake stared at the fireplace. What would come next? Accusations? Recriminations? Would he be thrown out? It would be less than he deserved. At least then he wouldn't have to go through with this ill-advised plan of his.

Plome returned holding the crystal decanter. He topped up Crake's glass and his own, then put the decanter down between them and sat.

'I don't have the words,' he said. He shook his head. 'The price we pay for our calling is sometimes . . . terrible. Terrible.'

Crake swallowed as his throat tightened at the unexpected sympathy.

'What do you need?'

'I need to use your sanctum.'

Plome studied him. 'You want to use the echo chamber, don't you?'

Crake held his gaze.

'I've never dared use it,' Plome confessed. There was a tremor of excitement in his voice.

'I've used one,' said Crake. His tone left Plome in no doubt as to the result.

'After what happened, you still want to try again?'

'I'll get it right this time.'

'What if you don't?'

'I'll get it right,' Crake said firmly.

Plome mopped his brow and licked his lips nervously. 'I want to be there.'

'No. It's far too—'

'I insist!' he said, his voice shrill. 'It's my sanctum!'

His small eyes shone with fervour. Crake knew that look. He'd worn it himself once. Plome might maintain the façade of a businessman and a politician, but like Crake he was a daemonist first and foremost. The secrets of the other side were an addiction. Crake suspected that the tragedy attached to his name, far from appalling Plome, had actually increased his respect for his guest. Crake had been blooded in a way that Plome hadn't. He'd made a terrible sacrifice to the Art, and he was still coming back for more.

Plome admired him. The thought made Crake feel even worse.

'You'll handle the second line of defence,' Crake said. 'If it gets past me, we can't let it out of the sanctum.'

Plome nodded eagerly and sprang out of his chair. 'Shall we get started, then?'

'One more thing,' said Crake. 'Do you have a gun?'

Plome frowned. 'I do. Why?'

'I want you armed.'

'Armed? Whatever for?'

Crake stood up and walked past Plome towards the door. 'Because if things go wrong, I want you to shoot me.'

Plome's sanctum lay underneath his house, in a hidden basement accessible through a daemon-thralled door which employed a strong mental suggestion to turn away casual snoopers. It was well organised and laid out like a laboratory. Electric bulbs hummed behind their shades. Complex chemical apparatus stood on a workbench near a chalkboard covered with scribbled formulae. Shelves were loaded with forbidden books. Resonators and modulators were fixed to frames and trolleys. The equipment here was the best: bigger and more powerful than the portable gear Crake used. Plome was not short of cash, and not afraid to spend it on his passion.

A globular brass cage had once dominated the room, but now it had been relegated to the corner along with a few portable oil lanterns. The new prize piece stood in the centre, amid a mass of heavy cables. The echo chamber. Crake felt his stomach tighten at the sight.

It looked like a bathysphere: a ball of riveted metal, two metres in diameter, with a single porthole in a door on one side. It stood on a low plinth, braced by struts. Cables were plugged into it all over its surface.

Crake stared at the porthole, and the darkness within.

You could still turn back. Tell them you couldn't do it. They'd understand.

But back to what kind of life? What would he be to his crew, after this? Dead weight? Someone to be pitied and tolerated? No, he'd had enough of that from his family, when he was a younger man. He'd borne it from them because he didn't like or respect them. But he couldn't bear it from Frey, or Jez, or Malvery.

He refused to be pathetic. Better to be dead.

He set to work. He checked the cables to the echo chamber, making sure everything was plugged in properly. After that, he familiarised himself with the control console, which differed in small ways to the one he knew. Lastly, he pulled over a resonator and connected it to a sequence of inputs on the echo chamber.

Plome was occupied with his own preparations, constructing a three-tiered defence of oscillation spheres, pulse pods and resonator masts. Crake approved of his thoroughness, but privately he wasn't at all sure that any conventional methods could contain a daemon capable of breaking out of an echo chamber.

Crake was studying formulae from a book when Plome came over to him, mopping his brow. 'Boning up on echo theory, eh?' he asked nervously. 'I thought you knew all about that stuff?'

'I do.' Crake snapped the book shut. He'd just needed something to stop his anxiety getting the better of him. He had it all by heart anyway. Not that it had done him much good last time. 'I'll assume this place is soundproofed? Things will get loud.'

'Oh yes. Daemons thralled to the walls and ceiling. We could have an orchestra down here and you wouldn't hear it in the sitting room.'

'Good,' said Crake. He'd used similar methods himself, in the wine cellar where he'd built his own sanctum.

'Shall we, then?'

'Activate the perimeter,' Crake told him. 'And whatever happens, stay out there. There's no telling what might come through.'

Plome nodded. 'Good luck, Crake,' he said. He scurried away a few steps, then stopped and looked over his shoulder. 'For what it's worth, you're a braver man than I.'

He retreated to the edge of the sanctum, where he'd connected up a series of control consoles to manage the defences. Crake felt a low vibration build in the air around him. Gradually a high-pitched whine slipped in, just at the edge of hearing. Soon the air was alive to his finely honed senses, a mass of sonic whorls and eddies. The invisible discord would confuse, repel or destroy any daemon that ventured outside the echo chamber.

At least, that was the idea. But the idea was based on the weak, dim daemons that could be snared using conventional methods of daemonism. Echo theory gave access to the deeper realms, where dreadful beings lay. Creatures of craft and cunning. Whether or not they were susceptible to the crude science of their human adversaries depended on the strength of the daemon.

Not for the first time, Crake wondered if he could have done this another way. Maybe he could have created a tracking device, like Frey's ring, that would lead them to the sphere? He could have done that using simpler, less dangerous techniques that he was comfortable with.

But no, it wouldn't have worked. He'd have needed the sphere with him, so he could bind an identical daemon to both tracker and target in the same procedure. And if he had the sphere with him, there'd be precious little point looking for it. Perhaps, with time, he could have refined his methods and come up with a way to do it. But that was time they didn't have. So there was only one option left: to find a daemon smart enough to ask. And to be smart enough himself to get an answer from it.

But there was another reason, too. It came from a bloody-minded, angry, stubborn place inside him. He *wanted* to face the echo chamber again, because he was damned if he'd be afraid of it any more.

'Ready,' said Plome.

Crake went to the resonator that was attached to the echo chamber. He tuned it carefully, according to the readings he'd scribbled down in the dreadnought. He'd noted the frequencies given out by the sphere while he was trying to determine if it was dangerous or not. Those frequencies formed a unique fingerprint that could be used to identify it.

'Ready,' Crake agreed. He threw a switch on the side of the console. A bass hum came from the echo chamber, growing louder as it powered up.

Crake closed his eyes. That sound. Just like last time. The feeling of retracing his steps towards disaster was inescapable. He knew what lay at the end of this path.

Her.

Slowly he started to turn the dials, seeking frequencies. He'd calculated and memorised the range he intended to search in. It was a space where, historically, there had been several notable successes and relatively few disasters. The knowledge did little to reassure him. He'd played it safe last time, too, and look how things turned out.

No, he reminded himself. *That was your fault. You found a monster and you didn't let it go. You wanted to be a pioneer.*

He worked the dials, beginning at the upper and lower ends of the range and narrowing in. He closed his eyes and tried to relax. It wouldn't be any of the five conventional senses that told him when he found a daemon.

The sudden, oppressive sense of being watched came upon him. The kind of feeling a mouse must get when it knows it's been spotted by a cat.

Each daemon was like a vast, complex chord, with primary and secondary notes. If he could match those notes, he had the anchors he could use to drag it into phase with his world.

The room felt darker and colder suddenly. His skin prickled.

That was it. He'd found its range, its highest and lowest frequencies. He opened his eyes and looked at the control console.

It was enormous.

'You've found something?' Plome called from the other side of the sanctum.

Crake stared at the dials for a moment. *Could you do this? Could you bring it through? With Plome here as witness? Spit and blood, how they'd talk about that one in the secret journals.*

He caught himself. Hadn't he learned anything? Didn't he know where unrestrained ambition would get him?

'It's nothing,' he said, and reset the dials. He wouldn't make the same mistake this time.

He began again. Daemons fluctuated, shifting pitch and bandwidth all the time, and they were frustratingly tricky to pin down. It was another half hour before he found one that stayed still long enough for him to catch it. This one was smaller, occupying the higher end. He penned it in with interference frequencies, preventing it from escaping into the subsonics, and then set about identifying its primary resonances. It began to struggle, but Crake was persistant, and each time he nailed one of the notes in the chord it had a little less wriggle room.

Acrid sweat trickled from beneath his hairline as he worked. Lost in his work, he forgot himself and where he was, his mind focused entirely on the task. A smile tugged at the corner of his mouth.

'You're not getting away,' he murmured. 'Not from Grayther Crake.'

An atmosphere of unreality had descended on the sanctum. An indefinable feeling of strangeness. The mind knew something was wrong but couldn't quite work out what. The presence of a being from the aether disturbed the senses on a subconscious level.

Something pounded on the inside of the echo chamber, making Crake jump.

'By the Allsoul,' Plome gasped. 'Something's here.'

Crake held his hand out to Plome to shut him up. He checked his dials again, zeroing in on the last of the frequencies he'd identified. He couldn't risk it slipping away or getting free.

Another ringing metal impact. Crake wiped sweat from his eyes and turned a dial by a fraction of a centimetre.

Got you.

There was a flurry of pounding on the inside of the metal sphere. Crake reached for a lever and threw it, blasting the interior of the echo chamber with a muddle of conflicting frequencies boosted to incredible volume. The daemon wailed in agony and confusion, a high, thin shriek that made Plome clap his hands over his ears.

Crake returned the lever to its original position, and the tumult ended.

'I know you can hear me,' he said sternly, addressing the daemon in the chamber. 'Behave.'

There was no sound from the daemon.

He flipped a switch to turn on the resonator. It filled the echo chamber with the frequencies he'd recorded when he was studying the metal sphere. 'I'm searching for this,' he said. 'You will tell me where I can find it.'

Crake waited. The echo chamber sat there, humming. The control panel was on the side of the chamber, and he couldn't see the porthole from where he stood. He felt a powerful urge to go round and peer inside, but he also remembered what had happened last time he did that. Glimpsing a daemon could send a man out of his mind.

Careful, he thought. *Get the job done. You can indulge your curiosity afterwards.*

A sudden, loud impact on the inside of the chamber, hard enough to dent it. A feral, blood-chilling roar. Crake threw the lever, and the roar turned to a squeal. He kept up the torture for longer this time.

'You will damn well do as you're told!' he snarled through gritted teeth.

He pulled the lever back, and the squeal faded. For a time, there was only the hum of the echo chamber and the mass of semi-audible frequencies thrown out by Plome's perimeter defence. Crake could feel his heart skipping, and hear the breath in his ears.

Then there was another sound. A moist clicking, coming from within the chamber. Half-drawn breaths, quick, desperate gasps.

Crake went cold. He'd heard that sound before.

Throw the lever. Throw the lever and blast that thing back to the aether.

But he didn't. He *needed* to see. A terrible curiosity drew him. It couldn't be what he thought it was. It was just a trick. It had to be. But he needed to prove that to himself.

He stepped away from the controls and moved around to the front of the echo chamber. Plome was watching him breathlessly from the edge of the room, where he crouched by his own array of control panels.

That sound. That wet, rattling clutch for breath. It couldn't be.

He looked through the porthole.

There was a little girl in the chamber. She was lying on her back, head tilted, staring out at him with an expression of terrified incomprehension. There was blood in her hair, blood on her lips; her white dress was sodden. It welled from slashes down her arms, across her collarbone and scalp. She drew a short, clicking gasp, dragging air into punctured lungs.

His niece.

An involuntary cry of anguish tore from his throat. A flood of sudden weakness threatened to make him faint. He stumbled back from the chamber, vision blurring with tears, then staggered sideways and tripped against one of the thick cables plugged into the echo chamber. There was an fizz and a bright shower of sparks as the cable plug was tugged halfway out of its socket. The sight alarmed him enough to shake him out of his horrified state. He lunged towards it, seized the cable with both hands, and plunged it back into the socket.

There was a snap of wild electricity, and the lights in the sanctum went out.

'Crake!' Plome cried. 'Crake! What's going on?'

It was pitch black, and the temperature had plunged to below freezing. Crake listened to his own frightened breathing, to reassure himself he was still there. He fumbled in the pocket of his coat for matches. He always had matches somewhere on him, for those rare times when he felt the need to smoke.

'Crake!'

'Stay there!' he called. 'Don't leave the controls! That's what it wants!'

Suddenly he remembered the oil lanterns he'd seen in the corner of the room. He lit a match. It illuminated little more than his hands, the steam of his breath, and the curve of the echo chamber. The darkness was thick and unnatural.

'Crake! Crake, speak to me, damn it!'

'I said man the controls!' he shouted.

'Crake!' Plome's voice was distant now, fading. 'Crake, say something!'

'Stay where you are!' Crake yelled. But he heard nothing more.

He walked carefully around the echo chamber and headed across the sanctum in what he hoped was the right direction. He lit a new match from his old one, afraid to let the dark close in for even a moment. The flame seemed unnaturally feeble. He listened, but heard only the sounds of his own terror.

His foot bumped against something, and he leaned down. A tarnished lantern. He grabbed it, and put his match to the wick. The flame caught and swelled, and drove the darkness back. Crake let out a shuddering breath, then stood up and came face to face with Bess.

His hand flew to his chest at the sight of the great metal golem. *This can't be right! She can't be here!* But when several moments passed and she still hadn't moved, he realised something was different about her. He peered inside her face-grille and saw no light within. She wasn't there. It was only the armoured suit, vacant and immobile. Cables ran from it into the darkness. Back towards the echo chamber.

Just like the night I made that suit come to life.

He turned away from the suit and raised his lantern higher. The light shone on stone pillars, and hinted at arches high above. Crake knew this place. It had been a vast wine cellar, before he made it his own. This was his sanctum. Here, he'd created the sword Frey carried, and the gold tooth in his mouth. Here, he'd created a golem. And here, he'd committed the crime that had destroyed his old life for ever.

This is the daemon's doing, he thought. *It's playing with me.* But it felt no less real for that.

Shivering with the cold, he moved back towards the echo chamber.

The room was silent. Even the electrical hum of the chamber had quieted. The tap of his boots rang through the freezing cellar.

What's it waiting for? What does it want?

He stepped around the front of the echo chamber. The door, the seal that kept the daemon inside, hung ajar.

Crake reached out and pulled the door open. He steeled his nerve and shone his light inside.

The chamber was empty.

He heard wet, clicking breaths coming from beyond the range of his lantern.

No, he thought to himself. *Please not that. Don't make me see her again.*

He became aware of a dripping sound, and looked down. In his hand was a letter knife with the crest of his university on the hilt. His hand and the knife were covered in blood. It dripped from the blade on to the stone floor.

He cried out in pain and flung the blade down. Something scraped in the darkness behind him. He spun around, but saw nothing.

'Curse you!' he shouted. 'You are *not* that daemon!'

Not the one that made him do what he did. Not the one that made him stab his niece seventeen times with a letter knife.

Then, a voice from the blackness. His niece's voice.

'Why'd you put me in there, Uncle Grayther?'

Crake looked around, teeth gritted, desperately seeking the source of the voice. He knew it to be a trick, but tears welled in his eyes anyway. He couldn't help it.

'Why'd you put me in there?' the haunting voice asked again. There was a groan of metal, and the armoured suit tipped forward with a crash, cables snapping free as it fell.

'You're not her! How dare you pretend you are!' he cried.

But despite what his mind knew, his senses told him otherwise. That was Bess's voice, who he'd put into an echo chamber while she was dying, and whose essence he'd transferred into an armoured suit. But the process had been crude and hurried and was way beyond his abilities; she hadn't come through it whole. What was left was a simple creature, more like a pet than the little girl he knew. A daily reminder of his crime.

'I'm so lonely, Uncle,' came her voice again. 'I'm so lonely and it'll never end.'

'You rot-hearted bastard!' Crake shrieked into the dark. 'I loved her!'

'It's so hard to think in here, Uncle. What did you do to me?'

Crake choked back a sob.

'You should've let me die,' she said.

'I loved you! I love you!' he protested.

'How could you?' came the whisper, from right by his ear. He swung around in alarm.

She was there, reaching towards him, sodden red, open wounds pulsing with blood. But the look in her eyes was pleading.

'How could you?'

He screamed, and the light from his lantern went out.

Hysterical, weeping breathlessly, he fumbled for his matches again, but in his haste to light them he dropped them on the floor. He went down on his knees, searching. At any moment he expected to feel the dreadful touch of the bloodied apparition. But then his fingers found the matchbox, and he managed to steady his trembling hands long enough to strike one. He touched the tiny flame to the wick of his lantern, and light returned to the freezing room.

There was no sign of Bess. But there, lying next to him like an accusation, was the letter knife.

He put the lantern on the floor. Sobs racked him, each one like a punch in the chest. He stayed on his knees. He wasn't sure he had the strength to stand any more.

'I thought I could control it,' he gasped between sobs. 'You weren't supposed to be there.'

'Sssh,' came the disembodied voice. 'You know what you have to do.'

'I couldn't let you die.'

'Sssh.'

His fingers closed around the hilt of the knife. A sense of peace filled him at its touch. Yes, it would be so simple, wouldn't it? An end to the constant, grinding agony of memory.

'You've suffered enough, Uncle. It's time to rest.'

Time to rest. He liked that. She'd given him her blessing, hadn't she? And he was so very tired.

He put the blade to his neck, angling it under the curve of his jaw. One swift cut in the right place, and he could sleep. He couldn't remember the last time he'd slept well.

'Now push!' hissed the voice from the darkness. 'Push! Push!'

He felt a trickle of blood running down his throat, and realised he'd already broken the skin. He was already that far along; why not go a little further?

He took a breath, steadied his hand for the final thrust.

'Goodbye, Uncle,' said the voice.

And Crake stopped. Goodbye, indeed. With that one quick cut, he'd be leaving her. He'd be at rest. But Bess wouldn't.

And who'd save her then?

He took the blade from his throat. It fell from his hands, ringing as it hit the stone floor.

Rest. Peace. He didn't deserve it.

He got to his feet. From the dark, there was only silence.

The daemon that made him stab his niece had left him alive for a reason. It wanted him to suffer for his arrogance in meddling with forces he didn't fully understand. To spend day after day in torment. In trying to avoid his sentence, Crake had unwittingly made it worse. By refusing to let her die he'd condemned them both to an eternity of misery. He'd only served two years, but it had almost broken him.

Yet now there was a chance of release, he couldn't take it. Not while Bess was still alive. Bess needed him, and she was his responsibility.

He'd spent three months as a drunken vagrant before he pulled himself together and found the *Ketty Jay*. Life on board had brought a window of clarity, but once the whole Retribution Falls affair was done he'd begun sliding back again. Blocking out the pain instead of tackling it. He'd always *meant* to do something about Bess, but somehow it had never happened. He was too afraid of the possibility of failure. Too scared to leave the relative comfort of the crew to strike out on his own. He knew, one way or another, that this was a task for him alone, and that frightened him.

But now it came to it, now he had the chance to give up his burden of grief, he found that he couldn't. He'd never atone for what he'd done, but he couldn't turn his back on it either. So there was only one other option. He had to face up to it, and *fix* it.

The thought lit a flame in his breast. This was his burden and he'd

bear it. Suicide was the coward's way out. And Grayther Crake was
no coward.

'Look what you did to me, Uncle,' whispered the voice. Crake
turned, and saw her. Lying there, just as he'd found her that day, with
that same look of incomprehension and betrayal on her face. Blood-
soaked, gasping, paralysed by shock.

The sight brought fresh tears to his eyes. His lip trembled and he
teetered on the edge of hysteria again. But he heaved in a shuddering
breath, and he made himself look.

'Yes,' he whispered. 'Yes, I did that.'

He walked over to her, picked her up, and held her against him.
The sodden, slight, ragged weight of her. She squirmed in his arms,
trying to push him off her, but he was too strong and wouldn't let her
go. Warm blood slicked his neck and hands.

'Don't worry,' he murmured. 'Uncle Grayther will make it better. I
promise I'll make it better, somehow.'

She began to squeal and shriek, thrashing in his grip. She pummelled and scratched at him. But he held her tight, tears streaming
down his face, as the bloody child fought against him. The pain
meant nothing to him now. He could take everything and more, as
long as he didn't stop holding her.

Her screams reached a deafening crescendo, and then the darkness
erupted into chaos.

'Crake!'

It was Plome. The child in Crake's arms was gone. An unnatural
wind was blasting through the sanctum, a hurricane, sending apparatus crashing past him in the dark. There was a terrible roaring,
and the sound of something pounding against metal.

He snatched up his lantern before it could be blown away. On the
floor was a sharp length of steel, tipped with blood. His blood. A
moment after he saw it, it was caught by the wind, skidded along the
floor and out of sight.

He looked for Plome, and saw him, on the other side of the room.
He was struggling with his control panels, lit by the faint glow from
the gauges. Desperately trying to keep up the perimeter defences.

'The chamber!' Plome yelled, pointing.

Crake staggered into the wind, towards the chamber. It was rocking
against its struts, dented by the inhuman pummelling from the

creature within. The door was still firmly closed. The daemon bellowed as Crake stumbled past the porthole, and he caught a glimpse of a thrashing muddle of eyes and teeth in the lanternlight. Then he was at the control panel. Fumbling fingers found a lever. He threw it.

The daemon screeched as it was bombarded with agonising frequencies. Crake leaned against the lever, his eyes closed, wishing ever greater pain on the monster in the chamber. For what it had done to him, for what it had shown him, he wanted to tear it apart. If he leaned on this lever for long enough, it would be shredded to pieces, dashed by the flux.

He wanted that. He wanted it so badly. But he had a job to do. He had people relying on him. So he took hold of the lever, and he pulled it back. The wind dropped, and there was silence. Several of the electric lights came back on, flickering and crackling uneasily.

Crake brushed sweat-damp hair back from his forehead, panting.

'Are you alright?' Plome asked, from where he knelt by his controls.

'I'm alive,' he said. 'You?'

'Yes, yes, quite unharmed,' he said, his voice wavering. He brandished the pistol he'd brought at Crake's request. 'No need to shoot you, then?' he joked weakly.

'I should think not,' said Crake. He threw the lever again, out of spite, and listened to the daemon shriek for a few more seconds before he turned it off. Then he walked round the echo chamber, and stood in front of the porthole, looking in.

'Now,' he said to the daemon. 'Let's begin again, shall we?'

Fifteen

Pinn, Lost In Thought – Jez Takes A Walk –
A Fortress – Frey Has A Plan

Artis Pinn lay on his bunk, fingers laced behind his head, and stared at the metal ceiling. It was possible to see shapes in the ancient grime, if you looked hard enough. But today he wasn't playing his usual game. Today, he was thinking.

The quarters he shared with Harkins were narrow, cluttered and dirty. He had the top bunk, due to Harkins' unfortunate tendency to spasm out of bed several times a night. A square vent high up on one wall let in cool air from outside, wafting away the stench of unwashed bedding. There was a small storage cupboard crammed with their meagre possessions, but space for little else. The *Ketty Jay* wasn't built for luxury.

Pinn had lain there for hours now, trying to make sense of things. He didn't know what this empty, listless sensation was, but he didn't like it much. He didn't want to get up. Didn't want to sleep. Didn't want to do anything, actually. The thought of flying his Skylance failed to excite him. Even the prospect of booze had lost its charm, and he'd often said that when that day came, he'd eat a bullet. But he didn't feel much like shooting himself, either.

Lisinda, he thought. *My sweetheart is marrying another man.*

Was it even possible? He wasn't sure. After all, she'd said she loved him. Hadn't that meant anything to her? It had certainly meant something to him. It had inspired him to be a hero. It made him want to be a better man. It even made him want to stop cheating on her, although the gap between the desire and the reality was vast indeed.

How could she do it?

A sudden thought struck him, that hadn't occurred until now, even after hours of contemplation. If she was marrying another man, that

140

must mean she'd been fooling around with him for at least a couple of months. Maybe longer. A flood of rage swept through him, and he gritted his teeth. How he'd like to get his hands round that other bloke's throat! Messing with another man's woman! Didn't he know she was taken? She'd already made her choice. Hadn't she said she loved him?

But killing her husband-to-be would surely make Lisinda a bit sad. He'd never do anything to make her cry, and yet honour demanded he stamp his rival's face into the ground. How to solve a problem like that? It was all very confusing. He wished he had half the Cap'n's brains. The Cap'n would have known what to do.

No matter how he turned it over in his head, he couldn't conceive how Lisinda would want to marry anyone else. It just wasn't possible. She must be an innocent victim in all this, somehow. Her heart had been swayed by some sleazy charmer from out of town. Women couldn't help themselves sometimes, that was just a fact. She couldn't be blamed. She was powerless to resist his influence.

Or maybe she was being forced into it. Yes, that was it! She'd said in her letter that she was very happy, but that clearly couldn't be true. Not when her heart was with her absent hero.

His blood boiled at the thought. His Lisinda, married off to some scheming aristocrat three times her age! The kind of man who coveted her beauty because he was too old to win her by fair means. He'd bought her like an ornament to wear on his arm, no doubt.

What if she'd been kidnapped? What if the letter was her coded cry for help? She must have known he'd never believe she would leave him. It was too ridiculous. Had her kidnapper allowed her to send this letter, thinking it innocent? Had she cleverly concealed a message within the message?

He pulled the letter out from under his pillow and began frantically scanning it, searching for codes or clues. Halfway through, he froze as another possibility occurred to him.

Could it be that this was all a plan by some love rival? Perhaps *they* had written the letter, hoping that Pinn would come racing home prematurely. Then Lisinda would see that he hadn't yet become the strong, honourable and, most importantly, *rich* man he'd promised he'd be. She'd turn away from him then, disappointed. Right into the arms of another.

He studied the letter furiously, searching for signs of forgery. What did Lisinda's handwriting look like, anyway? She'd never written him a letter before. Neither of them were much for reading or writing. Eventually he gave up. He'd never recognise a forgery if he didn't know the genuine article.

It all made his head hurt. What did the letter *mean*? And what was this strange, aching feeling in his guts, this heaviness in his limbs, this lack of appetite? He supposed that all this thinking was making him ill.

He heard a noise by the door and stuffed the letter back under the pillow just as Harkins peeped in. He was carrying a large butterfly net. His eyes roamed the room nervously.

'Pinn. Er . . . you wouldn't happen to . . . I mean, have you seen the cat?'

Harkins' eyes widened as he saw that the grille had been taken off the air vent and was lying on the floor. No matter how many times he fixed it back, Pinn always took it off again, complaining that it made the room stuffy. It also allowed Slag to creep into the room and suffocate Harkins, which was part of the fun.

'You took the grille off,' Harkins accused.

'Yeah,' said Pinn.

Harkin's lip quivered. A determined look crept into his gaze. Pinn could see him visibly plucking up his courage. Allsoul's balls, was the twitchy old freak actually going to try to stand up to him?

'Now you listen!' Harkins said sternly. 'I've had enough of this! This is my room as much as yours, and I—'

'Piss off, Harkins, I'm thinking,' Pinn snapped.

Harkins flinched at the tone of his voice and scurried out. Pinn sighed, settled himself back on his bunk and stared at the ceiling again.

Lisinda. Sweetheart. What are you trying to say to me?

Jez clambered up the ladder to the upper gantry of the engine room, trying not to spill the mug of coffee in her hand. The engine assembly was quiet, but it still radiated a faint warmth. A sleeping monster of pipes and black iron.

Silo had a panel off and was poking around with a screwdriver. She squatted down next to him and put the coffee by his side.

'Made it just short of lethal, the way you like it.'

He grunted in thanks and kept poking.

'How's it going?' she asked, trying to peer past him.

'Same as before,' he said. 'Can't do nothin' without the parts. She could hold up for weeks. She could give out any minute. No tellin'.' He found something loose and tightened it. 'You thought about what I said?'

Jez remembered their surprising conversation in the rainforest of Kurg. 'I have. I am.'

'Talked to Crake?'

'Not yet,' she said. It seemed hard to find the right moment. 'You know he hasn't had a drink since last night?'

'He tell you that?'

'I can smell it on him.'

'Huh.'

Sensing that nothing else would be forthcoming, Jez ducked away and headed back down the ladder. The truth was, she'd been thinking a lot about Crake of late. She was becoming more and more convinced that he was the only one who could help her. Who better to deal with a daemon than a daemonist?

But it wasn't quite as simple as just walking up and asking. There had always been a distance between them. Crake seemed to resent her a little for being the one he'd confessed his crime to. Jez, for her part, had found it hard to entirely forgive him for what he'd done. Then there had been the drinking, and his gradual deterioration of late. He'd become bitter and unapproachable.

Jez was never the kind who was comfortable opening up to others. She was afraid they might one day use her vulnerabilities against her. And she was still afraid of what would happen if she admitted the whole truth about her condition. What if Crake reacted with fear and panic? What if he felt he had to tell the Cap'n? No matter how much the crew liked her or how useful she was, having a Mane on board would make anyone nervous. She could be shunned and ejected from the *Ketty Jay*, and she couldn't face that. She couldn't go back to that life of wandering, moving from crew to crew, never putting down roots.

But she had a daemon inside her. And the longer it stayed the more power it would have over her. Sooner or later she'd be forced to take action. Even if it cost her her place on the *Ketty Jay*.

She went out into the passageway. She could see Malvery through the open door of the infirmary, asleep on the surgical table, snoring. Ahead of her, Harkins was stalking down the corridor on tiptoe, a butterfly net in his hand. He flushed beetroot red as he saw her.

'Jez! Um . . . I . . . you see, I picked this up in Tarlock Cove and I . . . er . . .'

'I don't think I want to know,' said Jez.

'Right. Hm. Yes. Probably best.'

She went down to the cargo hold and outside. The *Ketty Jay* sat in a grassy mountain dell, high up in the Splinters. A broken, bald peak thrust up ahead of her. Frey and Crake were somewhere on the other side, with Grist and his bosun. Scouting out the location that Crake's daemon had identified, the place where Grist's mysterious sphere was being kept. Nearby was the *Storm Dog*. A few of Grist's crew lounged about, enjoying the bright, cool morning. Jez walked past them, towards the trees that fringed the dell.

She still had deep misgivings about this whole affair, but she was loyal to her Cap'n. He'd given her a home, and she had a way to go before she paid him back for that, even if she'd already saved his life more than once. She felt included here, and needed.

Just as she'd felt when that Mane was trying to turn her, on that snowy night in Yortland. The moment when she'd seen into their world, and felt the connections between them.

She understood why that crew on the crashed Mane craft had lain down and died. She'd only had a taste of what could have been. Having that, living with it and then giving it up would have been unthinkably terrible. A mutilation of the senses.

And yet they did it anyway. They made that choice. So maybe they're individuals, rather than slaves to a collective mind. Maybe I wouldn't lose myself if I joined them.

Dangerous thinking. A temptation like that would be too easy to give in to. It was no easy thing to resist the call, day after day, night after night. The need to belong had always been a part of her. And no one belonged like a Mane did.

Jez had spent her whole life looking for her place. For as long as she could remember, she'd been unable to fit in. She'd always had friends, but somehow it never seemed like the friendships she read about in books. She liked them, and they liked her, and it went no deeper. If she never saw them again, she wouldn't have shed a tear. Nobody said so, but she knew they felt the same about her.

Her childhood was spent watching her companions with secret envy. She was always the last to be involved. The cog in the gears that didn't quite mesh.

When she was a little older, she began to blame her father. Him and his obsession with trying to improve her position in life. He was a craftbuilder, an artisan, more respected than the peasantry but still a world away from the scholars, officials and aristocrats.

Once he'd been content with his lot; but after the sickness took her mother, he changed. Suddenly, a craftbuilder's life wasn't good enough for his daughter any more. He forced her to study when she wasn't helping him in the workshop. He saved up for a tutor who'd knock the common edges off her accent. By the time Jez reached the age where she just wanted to be the same as everyone else, she was already different in a thousand little ways.

Her apologetic displays of knowledge intimidated her friends. She found herself frustrated by their lack of ambition. Her horizons had been expanded through literature, but theirs hadn't, and she couldn't understand how they could think so small. They were still friends, as they'd always been; but no matter how she tried, she was faintly alien to them now.

There was no help among the educated, either. They spotted her immediately, and despised her as a try-hard attempting to rise above her station. A few small friendships blossomed, but they could only survive in isolation, and circumstances eventually put an end to them.

She hardened herself to rejection. She embarked on adolescent romances, and found them as unsatisfying as her friendships had been. She always broke them off before her partner could.

Her father talked of university, but it was his dream and not hers. Someone like her didn't get into places like that. And even if she did, she'd never escape her birth. It would be just another round of being on the outside. So when the time came, she broke her father's heart and went off to see the world in the little A-18 he'd built for her sixteenth birthday. Out there, she'd find her place. Or if not, at least she'd be alone on her own terms.

Funny, how things turned out.

She walked out of sight of the men in the dell and picked her way through the trees to a likely looking rock, where she sat down. There, she pulled out a book and opened it. The writing was all circles and arcs. It still smelled of the captain's cabin in the dreadnought.

The patterns made no sense to her, but she stared at them anyway.

'Awakeners,' said Crake. 'I hate Awakeners.'

Frey wasn't too fond of them himself. It was the Awakeners that had been behind the attempt to frame him and his crew for the murder of the Archduke's eldest son. And now, if Crake's daemon was to be believed, they were behind the theft of Grist's mysterious power source.

He shifted uncomfortably on the ridge and angled the spyglass down at the Awakener's compound. It was a collection of grand buildings, the size of a small town, with the look of a sprawling university or an ancient library complex. A high wall surrounded it, studded with guard posts, overlooked by a clock tower that rose from the central quad. It sat on a bare island in the midst of a deep blue lake that ran the length of the valley. Next to it was a landing pad, upon which several aircraft sat dormant. Hovering at anchor over the lake was the dirty black bulk of the *Delirium Trigger*, spoiling the sense of idyll entirely.

Frey felt a surge of irritation and anger. What was Trinica doing, working for the Awakeners again? Hadn't she learned her lesson last time, after the whole debacle with Duke Grephen? She was probably already under sentence of treason because of that little affair. But she just had to get involved, didn't she? She had to get in his way. Just to spite him.

There was a bigger question here than Trinica's involvement, however. What interest did the Awakeners have in a crashed Mane aircraft? Why had they sent anyone at all?

He scanned the outer wall. Sentinels walked there, armed with rifles. They wore grey, high-collared cassocks and carried twinned daggers in their belts. On their breasts was the Cipher, the emblem of their faith, a tangled design of small, linked circles.

146

Huge lamps like lighthouses had been built on every corner, no doubt powered by generators inside the compound. Approaching unseen across the lake and the barren island would be impossible, whether by day or night.

Grist lay next to him, smoking angrily. 'You see a way in?'

'There isn't a way in,' Frey said.

'There's always a way in,' Grist replied.

Frey put down the spyglass. 'Well, I don't much fancy assaulting a heavily fortified compound with a handful of men, if that's what you're thinking. Might as well shoot each other now, save everyone a bit of time.'

'Can't we sneak inside?' suggested Crattle, raising his head to look over his captain at Frey.

'Even if we could, which we probably can't, what happens then?' Frey asked. 'Follow the arrows to the treasure? Look how big that place is. We'd need days to search it.'

'In disguise, then?' Crattle persisted.

'You'd be caught,' said Crake, who lay on Frey's other side. 'Without even a basic knowledge of the Cryptonomicon, they'd identify you as a fraud before the end of your first conversation.'

Frey looked over at the daemonist. He certainly seemed brighter and sharper today than he had been of late. Frey had found him awake early, polishing Bess while Silo patched up rust spots on her armour and fixed broken rings in her chain mail. And Frey had to admit, Crake had stepped up when it came to do his part. He had no idea what the daemonist had gone through to find the whereabouts of the sphere, but he was sure it hadn't been easy.

Grist took a puff on his cigar and scowled. His good cheer had been almost entirely absent since Trinica had robbed them. Without it, he was an unpleasant man to be around.

'So if we can't get in, what do we do now?'

Frey rolled his shoulders, which were getting stiff from lying there. 'Now, we find out what the Awakeners are up to, why they're interested in the sphere at all, and why they went to the trouble of hiring a pirate to get it instead of doing it themselves. Once we know that, we'll have a better idea of how to get our hands on it.'

'And how d'you propose to do that?' Grist asked.

'I'm gonna do my best not to *propose* at all,' Frey said grimly.

Crake caught on. 'Amalicia Thade,' he said with a grin.
Frey had the look of a man facing a firing squad. 'Amalicia Thade.'
There was a long, grave and meaningful pause before Grist said:
'Who?'

Sixteen

Amalicia Thade – A Warm Welcome –
Invitations – How The Rich Live

The Thade estate sprawled across the forested hills, an island of carefully maintained paradise. Raked paths meandered round well-tended lawns and willow-fringed lakes, past fountains and gazebos built in pre-Revolution style. Statues of monarchs and dukes stood on plinths. A glassy arboretum was perched on a hilltop. Next to it was a hunting lodge and an observatory with the lens of a huge brass telescope poking through a slit in the dome. At the centre of the grounds, a vast manse sat foursquare and impressive, with walls of robin's-egg blue, tall windows and alabaster eaves.

Frey lounged in the back of the open-top motorised carriage, and let the sun warm his skin. This far south, springtime felt like summer. A manservant sat on the driver's bench up front, gripping the steering wheel as if it was something unfamiliar. He was dressed in a stiff uniform of white and cream, and doing his best not to sweat and ruin it.

Frey ran his knuckles over the leather of the seat and looked out at the estate as they puttered up the drive. All of this was Amalicia's. And this place was only a fraction of her holdings. He knew the Thade family was rich, but he hadn't quite imagined the scale of it.

Not bad. Not bad at all.

What would their reunion be like, he wondered? He had to admit to a certain amount of trepidation. After all, he'd been indirectly responsible for the death of her father. But then Amalicia had been rather keen on getting him hanged anyway. She hated him for cloistering her in an Awakener hermitage. That was also Frey's fault, since he'd been the one who deflowered her, but Frey wasn't about to take the blame for her father's prudishness.

Gallian Thade's death made Amalicia the head of the Thade

dynasty and the inheritor of all that he saw before him and more. But still, girls were apt to get cranky when you got their dads shot by the Century Knights. He just hoped she was in the mood to look on the bright side.

The carriage pulled up in front of the house where half a dozen manservants were lined up outside the grand double doors. As he was dismounting, the doors were thrown open and Amalicia walked through.

He caught his breath as he saw her. She was more dazzling than he remembered. She must have been twenty-three by now, or thereabouts, but she seemed unaccountably mature for her age. More the elegant young lady and less the frisky, fiery girl. Her long black hair had been cut short to show off her neck. She wore riding boots, hip-hugging trousers and a silk blouse. There were hints of silver at her throat and wrist.

'Darian,' she said with a smile, as she descended the steps. Frey managed to get down from the carriage without falling. He gawked at her, dazzled. *This* was the woman he'd forgotten about, the woman he'd left behind in an Awakener hermitage without a second thought? *This* was the one whose letters he'd been ignoring? What was *wrong* with him?

She presented her hand. He stared at it for a few moments before realising what he was supposed to do, then raised it to his lips and kissed it.

'Come inside, please,' she said.

He followed, dazed, wrongfooted by the change in her. She was confident where before she'd been arrogant. Assured where she'd been spoiled. She'd grown to suit her new role quickly and well.

The entrance hall was colossal, with a curving staircase of polished stone. Thin pillars drew the eye to the arched moulding on the ceiling. Valuable urns rested on pedestals with the casual precariousness only found in houses that didn't have dogs or children in them.

A manservant stood by the doors to a drawing room. He opened them and Amalicia led Frey through into a beautiful room with gold-chased panelling and a fireplace that would embarrass a duke. Settees and divans were arranged near a side table of sweetmeats and refreshments. A servant was pouring tea as they entered.

Amalicia clapped her hands. 'Leave us,' she said. 'Darian and I have a lot of catching up to do.' The servant scurried out, and the handsome manservant pushed the doors closed. As he did so, Frey caught his gaze. The manservant winced in sympathy, and then the doors clicked shut.

Frey didn't like that wince. He had a dreadful premonition of what was coming. He turned around to see Amalicia advancing on him with terrible purpose, her serene, aristocratic smile turned to an ugly snarl. 'Now wait a mi—' he began, but he was interrupted by the heel of her riding boot connecting with his jaw hard enough to send him tumbling over the back of a settee.

He was still seeing stars as she pulled him up by the collar of his shirt. Where was the pretty, cultured lady of a moment ago? Surely she couldn't be this rabid harpy, drawing back a bunched fist to drive into his eye socket?

'*Where . . . were . . . you?*' she screeched, punctuating each word with a savage strike to the face. '*Where . . . were . . . you?*'

'Will you let me explain?' he spluttered. A couple of his teeth felt loose.

'No! You always do that! You explain, and I stop being mad, and I forgive you and then you leave me again! You're a liar, Darian. A damned liar!'

'I never lied to you!' he lied.

She stared at him, open-mouthed, and then kicked him between the legs. 'Don't you dare try and weasel out of this one! Don't you dare!'

He barely heard her words. They seemed to come from a great distance away, floating through a fog of perfect agony. There was a strange, sad void in his lower belly, a grey pall of aching misery, as if his guts were attending the funeral of his reproductive system.

'Why weren't you there when I got out of that hermitage, Frey?' she demanded. 'Where was my dashing buccaneer lover waiting to sweep me off my feet? What about all those things you said?'

Frey tried to protest that she wouldn't have got out of there at all if not for him, but the only noise that emerged was a shrill whimper at a pitch audible only to bats.

'Not a word! For a year!' Amalicia shrieked. 'Don't even pretend you didn't get my letters, Frey! I sent them everywhere!'

Frey held up a hand and swallowed against a hard lump in his throat that may or may not have been one of his own testicles. 'I thought . . .' he croaked. 'I thought . . .'

'Thought what? Thought I'd forgotten your promise? Thought I'd forgotten that you said you'd marry me?'

Technically, Frey had done no such thing, but he thought it unwise to argue the point, given his present situation. 'I thought . . . you'd reject me.'

'You thought *what*?'

He caught his breath. The ache in his groin was a little less unbearable now, enough that he could manage a coherent sentence. 'I thought I wasn't good enough for you.'

'Oh, that's just rubbish!' Amalicia scoffed. 'What an excuse!'

'Look around you!' he said, swinging out an arm. 'You see? Look at what you have! You're a lady. Sure, you loved me when your father was alive. What better way to piss off Daddy than by hitching up with some lowlife freebooter, right? But the game's changed now. Daddy's gone. We dreamed of running away, but now there's nothing to run away from. What do you need me for, when you have all this?'

Amalicia looked shocked. 'It was *never* about that!'

But she was already on the back foot, and Frey kept pushing. 'Don't you think I know what would have happened next? The society balls, the dinner parties, mixing with the rich and powerful? How long would it have been before I embarrassed you? How long before you got bored of me and found someone who knew how to eat soup without slurping?'

'Darian, that's not true,' she protested, but it came out weak and unconvincing. She'd been so busy being angry and lovesick that it had probably never occurred to her until now.

'It *is* true, and you know it,' he said, getting delicately to his feet with the help of a nearby chair. He felt himself to be sure everything was still where it was supposed to be.

Amalicia stamped huffily over to the windows, frustrated at having her righteous wrath blunted. She crossed her arms and stared out over the lawns of her estate. Regrouping. After a moment she whirled and came back. 'So you just decided it was over?' she snapped. 'You just left without a word?'

'No,' he said. 'I always meant to come back to you. But not as some filthy pirate. I wanted to come back as a man worthy of a lady like you. I wanted to come back rich and respectable. But I failed you, Amalicia. I failed.'

The Pinn Defence. Neat, deadly, and virtually impossible to refute. Nothing cut a girl's legs out from under her like a noble justification of an apparently ignoble act. The angrier they were, the worse they felt when you sprang the trap.

Tears shimmered in his eyes, more from the pain in his pods than sorrow, but that didn't matter to Amalicia. Her anger blew out like a candle.

'You didn't think you were *worthy* of me?' she asked, and he knew by the tone of her voice that she'd forgiven him right then. It was that *I-can't-believe-how-sweet-you-are-you-delightful-thing* kind of tone that, in Frey's experience, was generally employed in response to a thoughtful and unexpected present, or one of his rare displays of tenderness.

'I've tried to go straight, tried to make my fortune by honourable means,' he said. 'I could start a business, maybe buy some land. But . . .'

'Spit and blood, Darian. All this time you've been thinking I wouldn't want you?'

Frey held his aching jaw. He could feel a bruise forming where her heel had caught him. 'You mean you do?' he asked, with the expression of a man who hardly dared to hope.

'Of course I do, Darian! Why do you think I was writing to you all this time?'

'After everything I've done, you still want me?'

'Yes!' she laughed. She took his rather damaged face in her hands and gazed up into his eyes. 'Yes! I never stopped wanting you.'

'Oh, Amalicia!' he hammed. 'I've been a fool! A damned fool!'

The melodrama was lost on her. 'Darian!' she swooned, and she kissed him with such brutal passion that he feared she'd end up swallowing one of his loosened teeth.

'Come on,' she said eagerly, as soon as they'd surfaced for breath. She tugged him towards a door. 'The bedroom's this way.'

Frey clutched at his pulverised groin. 'I'm not sure I can . . .'

'Darian,' she said, with an unmistakable warning in her voice.

Frey took a steadying breath. 'Alright,' he said. 'I suppose I'll manage.'

*

It took a while to entice his traumatised equipment into action, but once he got going, he managed a passable performance. Amalicia didn't seem to mind that he was sub-par. She detonated with a scream that had Frey hurriedly clamping a hand over her mouth in case the household guards should burst in and shoot him.

Later, they lay in bed together. She was curled up against him, he on his back, looking up at the ceiling. 'What are you thinking about?' she asked him.

'Nothing,' he replied.

What he was thinking was how fine it was to lie here in an expensive bed with a beautiful young woman beside him. They could lie here all night and all day, if they wanted. And the next night, and the next. He'd never have to go back to his mouldy bunk on the *Ketty Jay*, with that threadbare hammock hanging over his head, always threatening to snap and crush him beneath an avalanche of luggage. How would it be, to live this way?

That was what he was thinking, but he said none of it.

She stirred against him and raised her head. 'Why did you come back?' she murmured.

'I came back for you.'

'Darian,' she said, the word a gentle threat. 'Why now? And don't tell me it's because you couldn't stand to be without me a moment longer.'

Frey had been about to say exactly that. He had to think a moment. Eventually, too drugged by post-coital lethargy to come up with anything clever, he told her the truth. 'I need your help.'

She tensed in his arms.

'Wait, hear me out,' he said. 'I found a way to get rich. Really rich. I wanted to be worthy of you, remember?'

'I remember,' she said suspiciously. Now that the first chaos of passion had settled, she was getting sceptical.

'Thing is, I can't do it without your help.'

'You need money, then,' she guessed, icing up.

Yes. Always. 'No!' he said. 'What do you take me for?'

'I don't know, Darian. I don't know what to think.' Now she was sullen and resentful. Frey was already having trouble keeping up with her moods. He remembered why he kept leaving her. A familiar irritation crept into his thoughts, but he kept it from his voice. 'I'm trying to get something. Something very valuable that the Awakeners have.'

'Ah.'

'Your father was a great friend of the Awakeners, of course. I sort of assumed you still have connections with them, even if you don't like them much. So I wondered if—'

'What do you need?' she interrupted.

'This . . . thing. It's a metal sphere. Very valuable. They have it inside a compound up in the Splinters. Place is like a fortress. I need a way to get in, or a way to get it out.'

'A sphere,' she repeated. 'Valuable.'

'Yes.'

'I don't suppose I want to know any more than that.'

'Good policy. If it makes you feel better, it's rightfully mine. Well, mine and my colleagues, anyway. They stole it from us. We want to steal it back.'

'And once you have it, you'll be rich?'

'Astronomically so, apparently.'

'And then you'll think yourself worthy of me?'

'Absolutely.'

She rolled over in bed, facing away from him. She managed to convey her sadness and disappointment through the set of her bare shoulders, though Frey couldn't work out how.

'I'll see what I can do,' she said.

They had breakfast on the south terrace in the morning, overlooking a calm lake edged by drowsily nodding trees. The sun was strong, for they'd slept in till past midday, and Amalicia was all smiles again. Frey enjoyed himself immensely. Etiquette made him awkward, but being waited on hand and foot was an experience he didn't think he'd ever get tired of.

'A man could get used to this,' he murmured, as he took his third glass of sparkling breakfast wine. Amalicia gave him a sideways glance and said nothing.

Later in the afternoon, they walked in the gardens, among the flowerbeds and the arbours. Frey wasn't much for plant life, but he was feeling quite grand today and more than a little buzzed from the wine. The presence of a beautiful woman who plainly adored him wasn't exactly unwelcome, either.

They'd been ambling around for some time when a manservant approached and whispered something in Amalicia's ear. She smiled and nodded.

'Plotting something?' Frey asked, watching the manservant retreat down the path.

'Actually, yes,' she said. 'I've secured us invitations to a soirée in Lapin.'

'A party?' Frey exclaimed. 'What did you go and do that for?'

'Because that's where you'll find out what you want to know.'

Frey scratched the back of his neck. The thought of a society party made him uneasy. Give him a good old life-threatening gunfight anyday. At least there, if someone was wittier than you, you could just shoot them in the face.

'It's a very exclusive soirée,' said Amalicia. Frey felt his nerves tighten another notch. 'Among the guests will be three Interpreters and a Grand Oracle.'

'Three whos and a what now?'

'High-ranking Awakeners, Darian,' she explained patiently. 'There are only four Grand Oracles in all of Vardia, and they are second in power only to the Lord High Cryptographer himself.'

'And you think they might know something about the sphere?'

'I'm sure you can get something useful out of them. You're a resourceful sort.'

'That I am,' he said. 'But do you think they'll even talk to me? I mean, look at me. They have handkerchiefs that cost more than my entire wardrobe.'

Amalicia gave him an up-and-down appraisal. 'Yes, we'll have to tidy you up a bit. But I shouldn't worry. They'll accept you as long as you're with me. And you'll find that the great and good are a lot less formal in these small, private gatherings than they are in public. We aristocrats get up to all kinds of things when the commoners aren't looking.' She smiled to show she was joking. Sort of.

'I'm not very good with polite conversation,' said Frey. 'It's more Crake's thing.'

'Don't fret, my darling. I have a scheme in mind. You see, there's always a games room at these little affairs. And this particular Grand Oracle is very fond of Rake.'

Frey's eyes lit up. 'Rake, you say?'

'Sit him down at a table, ply him with drink, lose some hands to him. He'll be your best friend in no time.'

Frey chewed his lip. 'I could do that. I'd still feel better if Crake came too, though. Another pair of ears in the room. He's an aristocrat; he wouldn't embarrass you.'

Amalicia tutted. 'Very well. I'll see it's done. But he'd better behave himself, Darian, or I shall be very put out.'

'Don't use his real name on the invitation.'

Amalicia rolled her eyes. 'Such reputable company you keep. I'll say he's your cousin. How's that?'

They walked for a little while.

'Why are you helping me, Amalicia?' Frey asked at length.

'Because I love you, of course,' she replied.

'Not because you want to get back at the Awakeners for all that time you spent in the hermitage?'

A wicked smile touched the edge of her lips. 'What kind of petty, vengeful woman do you take me for?' she asked with exaggerated innocence. 'The soirée is in a week. Until then, you're mine.'

Frey was allowed a brief visit back to the *Ketty Jay* to explain things to his crew and to tell Grist what was happening. Grist was enraged at the delay, but there was little he could do about it. He'd left some of his own men keeping watch on the compound where the sphere was hidden, in case the Awakeners moved it, but Frey thought it a futile exercise. Aircraft probably came and went all the time, and there was no telling if any of them were carrying the sphere, and no chance of following them anyway. Even small aircraft would be spotted in open sky and chased off.

His duty to his crew done, Frey returned to Amalicia. The days that followed were slow and luxurious. He spent the majority of them in bed, occasionally rising to enjoy exquisite meals or to wander the grounds of the Thade estate in the sun. On the second day Crake visited, and they were fitted for new clothes and seen to by a barber. When their transformation was complete, they looked a strikingly handsome and sophisticated pair. Frey spent the evening resisting the urge to preen.

Amalicia, for her part, was sweetness itself. Gone were the rapid and occasionally violent mood swings he remembered. She was attentive, considerate and sexually voracious. Frey had a wonderful time in her company, and he basked in the attention she lavished on him.

'You still want to run away, Amalicia?' he asked at one point. 'Still want to go slumming round Vardia in a battered old aircraft with a bunch of inept alcoholics for company?'

The sun fell on one side of her face as she sipped her glass of wine, and she looked devastatingly serene. 'No,' she said. 'Do you?'

It was a question Frey spent a lot of time pondering, during those heady days. What was there for him back on the *Ketty Jay*? Sure, he had friends, and that was worth something. But was it worth the endless toil, the frustration, the danger? How much further would his luck take him before he caught a bullet somewhere vital, or his craft got shot down?

Sooner or later, a man had to stop wandering and plant his flag. Wouldn't this be a fine place to do it?

She'd marry you, if you asked her. You know she would. She's loved you all this time.

But even thinking it made him restless. How long before he got bored? Bored of her, bored of all of this? The fine food and quality booze were undoubtedly attractive, but there were only so many gardens a man could wander. Sleeping on silk sheets with a pretty young woman was all well and good, but what about after a month? A year? A decade?

Amalicia, for her part, was obviously on her best behaviour. He knew what she was doing. Seducing him with her lifestyle. Intoxicating him with the dream of aristocracy. *Think what your life could be, Frey,* she was saying. *Why carry on with this foolish scheme of riches? I have all the riches you'll ever need.*

With money like hers, he could do whatever he wanted. He could build a dozen orphanages. He could make a mark, something to leave behind that said: *Here was Frey. He might not have been perfect, but at least his life meant half a shit.*

But already he felt caged.

Damn it, what was *wrong* with him? This was exactly what he thought he wanted. It was everything he'd decided he needed to fill the yawning chasm that had opened up inside him. And yet now that it was within his grasp, he didn't want it.

It took five days of living in luxury with a perfect woman to make up his mind. After the soirée, he was leaving.

Seventeen

High Society – 'We Do Meet In The Strangest Places' –
Parlour Games – A Winning Smile

The soirée was hosted by the Duke of Lapin's third cousin, Aberham Race, and held at his townhouse in the duchy's capital. Unlike the Archduke and his wife, Race was a devout supporter of the Awakeners, and not afraid to show it. He used these soirées to drum up support for the organisation, which was suffering under progressively harsher edicts passed down against it by the Archduke. Frey thought that punishment was only fair, really, since the Awakeners were behind the murder of the Archduke's son the winter before last.

Politics had always depressed him, so he only paid cursory attention to Amalicia's explanations as they rattled along the cobbled avenues in the back of a motorised carriage. Crake sat opposite Frey and Amalicia, looking slick and composed. Frey had known him so long that it was easy to forget he was born to the aristocracy. His accent had become so familiar that Frey didn't notice it any more. But seeing him dressed up this way, listening to his polite banter with Amalicia, Frey was reminded of the vast difference in the circumstances of their birth. Amalicia seemed rather charmed by him, despite her initial reservations. She viewed all Frey's companions with mistrust, as if she held them responsible for her lover's long absences.

The townhouse stood in a tree-lined avenue facing a lamplit park. They pulled up outside and a doorman showed them in. A manservant led them upstairs into a series of large drawing-rooms, where the soirée was already well underway.

Frey had to resist the urge to stare. There were glittering chandeliers, gold ceiling roses and embroidered drapes. A glass swan presided over a table of canapés, none of which Frey recognised as food. Bizarre sculptures, apparently designed to intimidate the uneducated, threatened him from their pedestals.

The guests were no less magnificent and alien. The men wore jackets stitched with gold and silver thread; the ladies wore gowns and jewels and glittering headpieces. Frey felt suddenly and completely out of his depth. He was outnumbered here. What did he have in common with these people? Did they even speak the same language he did?

'You look a little grey, Cap'n,' Crake said, with a hint of amusement in his voice.

'Don't call me that,' Frey replied. 'You're my cousin, remember?'

'I remember, dear cousin,' Crake smirked. Frey had the unpleasant feeling that the daemonist was enjoying his discomfort.

A manservant approached with a tray full of glasses of bubbling wine. They all took one.

'Stay sharp tonight,' Frey reminded Crake, indicating the drink in his hand. 'We've got a job to do.'

'Oh, don't worry about me,' said Crake. He glanced off to Frey's right and muttered, 'Incoming.'

A portly, middle-aged woman was making her way across the room towards them. The wrinkles in her sun-beaten face were buried under a thick plaster of make-up. 'Amalicia Thade,' she said. 'So glad you could come.'

'I wouldn't think of missing it,' Amalicia smiled. She turned to Frey and Crake, offering introductions. 'This is Lady Marilla Race, our hostess. Lady Marilla, may I introduce Darian Frey, my fiancé.'

Frey choked on his mouthful of wine and bubbles foamed out of his nose.

'Dear me,' said Crake, handing Frey a handkerchief. 'That wine can be tickly on a dry throat, can't it, cousin?' He bowed gallantly to Lady Race. 'My name is Damen Morcutt, of the Marduk Morcutts. It's an honour to attend one of your soirées. Really, quite the highlight of my year so far. May I be bold enough to beg the pleasure of your company for a short while? I'm keen to hear all about Jadney and his exploits in the Navy. I hear he's become quite the young officer.'

'My little Jadney?' Lady Race cooed, as Crake led her off. 'Why, I'd be delighted!'

Frey wiped his face with the handkerchief and looked at Amalicia. 'He's good at this.'

'Pull yourself together,' Amalicia said through gritted teeth. 'What was that all about? Choking in public. Honestly! Can't you behave?'

'Fiancé?' Frey asked. 'When were you going to tell me?'

'You wouldn't have got in the door otherwise. Now keep up. That's Chancellor Previn and his wife Marticia. We're going over there. Try to control yourself this time.'

The next hour was a particularly unpleasant one for Frey. It seemed that he met more people during that tortuous sixty minutes than he had in the preceding thirty-one years of his life, and none of them liked him. Somehow everything he said came out wrong. His attempts at wit fell flat. He did his best to follow what they were saying, but it all seemed so damned inconsequential. Marriages, scandals, investment opportunities. Who'd said what about who. Even the men gossiped like old women. Frey tried to come up with something intelligent to contribute, but all he got were blank stares or mildly condescending comments. Amalicia's fixed smile was beginning to crack and wobble at the edges, her patience wearing thinner with every blunder.

Eventually Frey had had enough. He excused himself as best he could and went to locate Crake.

He was surprised to find the daemonist in conversation with a familiar face, and an extremely attractive one at that. It was Samandra Bree, one of the Century Knights, the Archduke's elite hundred. She looked very different without her ever-present tricorn hat, her battered coat and twin shotguns. Instead, she was dressed in a sleek gown of red and black, her dark hair gathered in a ponytail.

'Darian Frey, I declare,' she said as he approached. 'We do meet in the strangest places. As I recall, last time I saw you, you had a noose round your neck.' She looked around the room. 'You've come up in the world.'

'I think I'd rather be hung at this point,' Frey said miserably.

'High society not treating you well?' Crake inquired.

'How do you *talk* to these people?' Frey asked in exasperation. 'It's like the moment I open my mouth, they're looking down on me.'

'Yes, they'll do that,' said Crake. 'The trick is not to try and engage them on their level. They'll spot a fake. Just be yourself.'

'It's not that easy.'

'Sure it is,' said Samandra. 'Tell me, what do you *really* think of 'em? Honestly, now.'

Frey gave her a suspicious look. 'You're not an aristocrat, are you?'

'Me? No. Daddy was a Militiaman. Wanted me to follow in his footsteps, but they plucked me out of training school when I eight and sent me to the Knight's Academy.'

'You don't seem out of place here, though.'

'Well, after they got done teaching me to put a bullet between someone's eyes at a hundred yards, they taught me a little etiquette. The Archduke likes some of his Knights to be the public face, you know? That's why my partner ain't here.' She put her hand to her mouth. '*Isn't* here, I mean.'

'Colden Grudge?'

'Yeah. Poor Colden. Put him in a place like this and he'd auto-cannon half the room.'

'Now *he* sounds like the kind of feller I could get on with,' said Frey. 'Speaking of which, we're not still under sentence of death or any-thing, are we? Never did get to collect those pardons for that whole misunderstanding about the Archduke's son.'

Samandra waved it away. 'Drave took care of it. You're in the clear.'

'Oh, good. I was just thinking how nice it was to meet you again. I'd hate to have to flee for my life.'

'And I'd hate to have to kill you. You seem a decent sort.'

Crake laughed nervously. 'Might I ask what a representative of the Archduke is doing here, at a soirée thrown in support of the Awakeners?'

Samandra looked skyward. 'Good question. I have to be the least popular girl in the room right now. The Archduke wants someone here to remind them we're watching. So here I am.' She nudged Frey. 'You never answered my question. What do you think of the com-pany here?'

'I think they're a bunch of pompous, stuffed-arse idiots and their conversation is boring as watching shit crust over.'

'And how long do you think they'd last in our world? Out there, where the rest of us live?'

Frey grinned. 'Most of 'em would get killed in the first bar they walked into.'

'There you go. Now stop thinking they're better than you, 'cause they ain't. I mean, *aren't*.' She rolled her eyes. 'All them etiquette lessons. Waste of good shooting time.'

'I *like* the way you talk,' Crake murmured into his glass, but nobody heard him.

'Y'know, Samandra, you're right,' said Frey. He was feeling considerably better. 'Who do these rich folk think they are? They're not better than me!' He looked at Crake, then down at the drink in his hand. 'Stay sharp, remember?'

'Stop fretting, Cap'n,' Crake said. 'It's under control.'

Samandra slapped Frey on the shoulder. 'Go out there and get 'em.'

Frey headed back to Amalicia, and met her coming the other way, a look of urgency on her face.

'Where've you been?' she asked. Then, without waiting for an answer, she slipped her arm through his and motioned towards a pudgy man on the other side of the room, who looked rather lost. 'That's the Grand Oracle. Now's our chance.' She propelled him towards their target. 'Just smile a lot, and I'll do the rest.'

The Grand Oracle didn't look particularly grand to Frey. He was a balding, worried-looking man with weak eyes hidden behind a thick pair of spectacles. Frey had imagined him dressed in expensive robes, but instead he wore a long jacket of deep blue velvet, parted down the middle by the thrust of his belly. The emblem of the Cipher was tattooed on his forehead, declaring his faith to everyone.

'Grand Oracle Pomfrey,' said Amalicia. 'Please allow me to introduce my fiancé, Darian Frey.'

Frey winced inwardly. He'd heard that word many times over the last hour, but it still came as an unpleasant surprise, like being cudgelled by a mugger.

'Amalicia Thade!' exclaimed the Grand Oracle. 'My, how you've grown!' He shook Frey's hand. 'You're a fortunate man, sir. Congratulations to you both.' Then he turned to Amalicia and became grave. 'Terrible, about your father, my dear. He was a great friend to the Allsoul.'

'As I will be, Grand Oracle,' said Amalicia. ' You know, of course, that I was in training to be a Speaker before tragedy called me away to fulfil my duty to my family.'

Frey raised an eyebrow. As he recalled, she'd been dragged kicking and screaming to that hermitage.

'Quite so, quite so,' said Pomfrey. 'I do hope you can lend your influence against the Archduke and that poisonous wife of his. Do you know, they're attempting to force us to shut down our operations in the cities? Planning regulations or some such rubbish. As if they didn't know they'd be severely cutting our income by doing so.'

'Those of faith will simply travel to the countryside to seek the wisdom of the Allsoul,' Amalicia said, with the blithe confidence of someone who didn't give a toss either way.

'I hope you're right, child,' he said glumly. He looked at Frey. 'And you, young man. What is it that you do?'

'I'm in merchandise,' he said. 'Cargo.'

'Ah, you own a shipping line?'

'Indeed I do,' said Frey, accidentally putting on a posh accent as he did so. Amalicia kicked him in the ankle.

'And how are you finding the party?'

Frey leaned in, shielding his mouth with his hand in a parody of conspiracy. 'To tell you the truth, Grand Oracle, I feel like the Ace of Skulls in a hand of Quad Ladies.'

The Grand Oracle's eyes creased in amusement. 'I had that very hand only last week. Four Ladies and I turned over the Ace of Skulls. Lost everything. I was sick as a dog. You play Rake?'

'Oh, I'm just an eager amateur.'

'Perhaps you'd care for a hand or two in the parlour? If the lady wouldn't mind, of course?'

'Darling?' Frey inquired sweetly.

'Please, go ahead. You menfolk must have your games,' said Amalicia. She gave Frey a kiss on the cheek and whispered, 'Nicely done,' in his ear. Then she drifted off across the room in search of other conversation.

Frey walked into the parlour with the Grand Oracle. It was a small, cosy room with high windows looking out over the square. The air was rich with the scent of cigars. Several tables had been laid out, some for cards and some for other traditional parlour games like

Peepers and Whizzbang. All of them were occupied, but Frey spied a game of Rake in the corner with a few seats free.

'I imagine having the Allsoul on your side must be a bit of an advantage in cards,' Frey commented, as they made their way to the table.

The Grand Oracle smiled. 'If only I were allowed to abuse my talent so. Are you of our faith?'

'My parents brought me up to worship only cold, hard currency,' Frey lied. 'I've always felt there had to be more to life than that, but . . .' He shrugged. 'Maybe I never found the right teacher.'

'Hmm,' said the Oracle. 'Or perhaps you are not aware of what the Awakeners can do for you. Through us, the Allsoul's favour may be begged to know the future, and even to change it. A great asset in business.'

'I'd heard it was possible, but I never understood how.'

They took seats at the table, returning the nods of the other players as they settled themselves.

'The patterns of the air, the turning of water in a bucket, the arrangement of a shuffled deck – all these are part of the Allsoul's pattern. Nothing is random. There is nothing it does not touch. But through the Cryptonomicon, we have the wisdom to interpret these signs as the voice of the Allsoul. And those with especial skill can arrange signs to speak to the Allsoul itself, and be understood.'

'Amazing,' said Frey, as he emptied out a purse of money that he'd borrowed from Amalicia. 'The arrangement of a shuffled deck is part of the Allsoul's language?'

'Indeed it is,' Pomfrey smiled.

Frey whistled. 'I think I'm about to lose a horrible amount of money, Grand Oracle.'

Pomfrey chuckled as the cards were dealt. 'The Allsoul's will be done.'

Four hours later, they were still at it. By then only Frey and the Oracle were left at the table. Frey had been carefully eliminating all the other participants and then losing his winnings to Pomfrey. The standard of play was shocking. Manipulating the game was no trouble at all for someone like Frey, who'd spent a sizable fraction of his life in Rake dens.

Early on, Frey had snagged a manservant and told him to bring a bottle of rum. He'd been aggressively filling everyone's glass ever since, especially the Grand Oracle's. Pomfrey was long past the point of refusing as he topped him up again.

'I have a Run!' he declared, showing his hand triumphantly.

Frey looked. A Run was five cards of any suit in numerical sequence, without a break. Pomfrey had 3, 4, 6, 7 and 8.

'So you do,' Frey smiled, shaking his head in mock disbelief. He pushed the pile of money, gathered from the other players, towards the Grand Oracle. 'You really do have the Allsoul on your side.'

'Ha!'

Frey dealt the cards again, then caught sight of Crake and surreptitiously motioned him over. Crake ignored him. He was still talking with Samandra Bree. In fact, he hadn't left her side all night. Frey tried again, more vigorously. Crake pretended not to see him, until Frey's flailing became so pronounced that he was in danger of toppling off his chair.

'What are you doing?' asked the Grand Oracle, blearily.

'I have a friend I'd like you to meet,' said Frey, as a sullen Crake joined them at the table. 'Damen Morcutt, this is Grand Oracle Pomfrey.'

Pomfrey was too interested in his cards to manage more than a quick hello. Crake looked over his shoulder for Samandra, but she'd already disappeared. He was looking distinctly unsteady.

'Had a few, have we?' Frey whispered, with a suppressed threat in his voice.

'I was enjoying the company of a beautiful woman,' Crake slurred.

'I told you to stay sharp.'

'I *am* sharp.'

'You'd better be.' He looked around to be sure nobody was nearby, but the parlour was largely empty now. Pomfrey was studying his cards with an expression of fierce concentration, the tip of his tongue poking out the side of his mouth.

'Grand Oracle, my friend here has something to show you.'

Crake went white. 'Not here!' he whispered. 'What if it goes wrong?'

'He's drunk. It'll be fine,' Frey assured him under his breath. 'Grand Oracle!'

Pomfrey looked up, startled to find himself at a card table. 'What? Er, oh, yes. Sorry. Pardon me.'

'I said, my friend has something to show you,' Frey repeated. 'A quite remarkable gold tooth he has.'

Crake glared at his captain, then turned his attention to Pomfrey and grinned his best grin.

'Oh,' said Pomfrey, not impressed in the slightest.

'Why don't you have a closer look?' Frey urged.

'Spit and blood, Mr Frey, you are acting awfully strange all of a—' Pomfrey trailed off as he caught sight of his reflection in Crake's smile. 'My,' he said. 'That is a very nice tooth.'

Crake kept grinning as the Grand Oracle's eyes glazed further, slipping from drunken to mesmerised.

'Now,' said Frey. 'I've got a couple of questions.'

They left the table soon afterwards. Crake felt faintly nauseous from using his daemon-thralled tooth while drunk. Before he left, he made sure that Pomfrey remembered nothing of what had been said. Frey scooped up the money on the table for good measure, since the Grand Oracle would be in no state to recall whether he won or lost in the morning. After that, they found Amalicia and made their exit.

Crake was wounded to note that Samandra Bree had left too, without saying goodbye. He hoped he hadn't said anything foolish to her. He couldn't remember most of the last hour or so of their conversation. Rot and damnation! He'd never meant to drink so much, but he'd got carried away in her company.

She was just so bloody *charming*, that was the problem. The lively twinkle in her eyes, that mischievous mouth of hers. He didn't mind admitting he was quite taken by her. It had been a long while since he'd had any interest in the fairer sex. He wasn't sure if it was the drink or the memory of Samandra that was making him dizzy as he sat in the back of the motorised carriage, heading for the private landing pad where the guests' aircraft waited.

The sight of Frey sitting opposite soured his thoughts. He was angry at being pulled away from Samandra and missing his chance to say goodbye. He was doubly angry that Frey had made him use his gold tooth in a place like that. If the Grand Oracle hadn't been so drunk, he might have realised what was being done to him. A daemonist, unmasked in the midst of a house full of Awakeners? He'd have been hung for sure.

The Cap'n was losing perspective. That sphere had come to mean more to him than just the prospect of a fortune. He was chasing something else, and chasing it hard. But Crake wasn't sure if even Frey knew what that something was.

Eighteen

Slag's Ambush – The Great Outdoors –
A Stealthy Exit – Frey's Chivalry Is Tested

The rooms and corridors of the *Ketty Jay* were the domain of the lumbering, strange-smelling entities that Slag deigned to share his aircraft with. He suffered their presence when it suited him, but usually he avoided them, preferring to remain in his own kingdom, the maze of vents and pipes and maintenance crawlways that ran behind the walls of the aircraft. He was the terror of the rats and mice that bred there, and he ruled with a red claw.

Tonight, he had bigger prey in mind.

The room was in darkness. On the top bunk, the fat one was snoring hard enough to inhale his blankets. Below him, the scrawny one lay quite still, breathing deep and slow.

Slag watched them lazily from the vent high up on the wall, his paws crossed before him. Sometimes there was a barrier here, a grille that prevented him getting through, but not this time. That was good. The rats had been hiding too well lately. He was bored, and in the mood to torment his plaything.

He'd been watching for some time now. Usually he wouldn't trouble to be so careful, but something was amiss. He sensed it, even if he didn't know what it was.

Perhaps it was the odd behaviour of the scrawny one that was perturbing him.

Slag had got used to bullying Harkins. He sensed the fear coming off him, and fear meant weakness. Slag hated weakness, and was determined to punish it wherever he found it. But Harkins had been acting differently of late. Poking round the cargo hold with that metal beast clanking along behind him. Creeping through the *Ketty Jay* with a net.

Slag was supposed to be the hunter, not the hunted. This prey seemed to have got confused about his role. It was Slag's job to remind him.

Slag slipped warily out of the vent on to the top of a storage cupboard. From there, he dropped down on to an iron-bound trunk, and then to the floor. He sniffed the air suspiciously. His instincts still insisted that things weren't quite right, but he didn't understand why. There was no danger from the snoring fat one, with whom he shared a mutual disdain. Harkins was asleep and helpless. Everything looked normal enough.

Maybe it was because his prey wasn't twitching and muttering as much as he usually did. But his eyes were closed, and his breathing deep, so Slag hopped up on to the bed.

Some of these odd beings slept heavily. Not like a cat at all. Slag could thump about the room as much as he liked and nobody would notice him. But it still took technique to clamber on to a face without waking its owner. Slag was massive, old and scarred from a thousand fights, but despite his hefty frame he was a master of the art of stealth.

He slipped along the bunk towards Harkins' head. He could smell the stale breath of his enemy, feel the air brushing past his sensitive whiskers. He slowed, examined the terrain, picked out the best method of approach. When he was ready, he made his move.

Suddenly the ground surged underneath him. As if the bed itself had snapped shut like a set of jaws. He tensed to bolt, but a white sack enveloped him first, tangling his paws and blinding him. He thrashed, but he couldn't get a proper grip to run, and he felt himself lifted into the air. He tumbled on to his back, upside down, helpless, constrained. He hissed and spat and writhed in fury, but the sack had him trapped.

'Ha!' Harkins cried. 'Ha! Thought I was asleep, didn't you! Well, I fooled you!'

It was a gabble of meaningless sounds to Slag. He was shaken all about in his awful white prison. He twisted and turned, trying to right himself. Nobody did this to him! Nobody! Least of all that filthy fearful prey-thing!

'How do you like *that*, eh? I'll show you!'

'Will you shut your damn meat-hole?' moaned Pinn, who'd been awakened by the commotion.

'I got him! I got the cat!'

'Great,' said Pinn irritably. 'Throw it in a river or something. Scabby little bag of stink.'

'Throw it in the river? That's a good idea, Pinn! A good idea!'

'Happy to help. Now bugger off.'

Slag's flailing had got one of his claws hooked into the fabric of the sack. He struggled to free his paw, but instead succeeded in using it as an anchor to twist himself round into an upright position at the bottom of the sack. Now with his paws beneath him, he tugged. The fabric tore, but his paw remained trapped by a loop of stubborn thread. He pulled again, and this time a longer tear appeared.

'Erm,' said Harkins.

There was a creaking of bedsprings. Pinn rolling over to look down on the scene. 'I hope you didn't think your pillowcase was going to hold a cat that size, did you?'

Slag's claw pulled free, but he'd sighted freedom and attacked the rent, slashing and shredding. The scrawny one squealed, and the sack suddenly, terrifyingly, plunged downward as it was released. Slag hit the floor in a heap, but now at least he'd found the ground, and it would take more than a fall like that to hurt him. With the sack settling around him, he oriented himself, picked himself up and thrashed his way out of the neck of the pillowcase.

'Uh-oh,' said Pinn gleefully. 'He's mad now.'

Harkins was struggling with the door, trying to slide it open. The fear was coming off him now, that familiar smell. Harkins was many times his size, but Slag would have attacked anything at this point, even the oily monster that lived in the hold. He was berserk with rage.

His whole life, he'd been top of the food chain. He'd had vicious fights with enormous rats, but he'd never been beaten and never backed down. And he'd certainly never been manhandled in such a way. What had been done to him was too much to bear. It demanded bloody revenge.

He launched himself at Harkins' calf and sank his claws through his trousers. Harkins squealed in agony, swatting at him, but Slag clambered up his legs, arse and back, his claws cutting through cloth and hooking into flesh. Harkins was desperately trying to reach behind himself as he stumbled through the open door. His arms occupied with the cat, he tripped and went head-first into the metal wall of the corridor beyond. Slag jumped free as his victim crumpled to the floor, wailing and clutching his head. Pinn was helpless with laughter in his bunk.

Harkins tried to scramble away, but Slag wasn't about to let him. This wasn't finished until his prey was no longer moving. He sprang at Harkins' face. Harkins got his hands up in time to protect his eyes, but Slag sank yellow fangs into his fingers instead.

Harkins screamed, scrambling to his feet, desperately trying to shake off the cat. Slag was having none of that. He hung from Harkins' hand by his teeth, scrabbling for purchase with his claws. Harkins trilled an operatic wail, eyes wide as he stared in horror at the black, furry mass attached to him. Then his hand clamped around Slag's belly and tore him away, along with a chunk of finger. Slag found himself lobbed down the corridor towards the engine room, the taste of blood in his mouth. A seasoned warrior, he flipped in the air, landed on his feet, and charged back for more.

Harkins was running away down the corridor, his wounded hand clutched to his chest. Just then the female, Jez, stepped out of her quarters, holding a pistol.

'Harkins! Hey, are you alright?'

Harkins let out an incoherent blubber of terror and pushed past her, heading for the cargo stairs. Slag skidded to a halt. The female was standing between him and his prey. He hated this one. She made him afraid. The mere sight of her was enough to get his hackles up. She was *wrong*. Not natural. Unknown.

'Will you quit tormenting him?' she snapped at Slag. Slag just hissed at her. After a moment, she shrugged and went back into her quarters. 'I give up. I've got my own problems.'

As soon as the door to her quarters was shut, Slag raced down into the cargo hold. Harkins had reached the lever that activated the ramp. As Slag came thumping down the steps, he pulled it. Hydraulics whined as the ramp began to open. Harkins looked over his shoulder and saw the cat approaching.

'Stay away from me!' Harkins shrieked, pressing himself up against the bulkhead of the *Ketty Jay* as if he could melt through it. 'Get . . . just get away!'

He bolted for the gap that was opening at the end of the cargo ramp. Slag ran to intercept, but at the last moment Harkins threw himself down and rolled sideways, slipping out through the gap. There was a short squeal and a heavy thump as he hit the ground.

Slag went to the edge of the ramp and looked down. Harkins was getting painfully to his feet a couple of metres below, staggering away across the grass. He went a short distance, stopped, and turned back.

The ramp bumped on to the ground. Beyond was tarmac. Slag sniffed it distrustfully, then recoiled a step. He glared at Harkins.

'Ah!' Harkins gloated, bloody but defiant. 'Can't come out, can you? Think you're so special! Try and get me out here on the landing pad!'

Slag didn't understand the words, but something in Harkins' manner told him he was being taunted. He didn't like that one bit.

He peered out from the cargo ramp. Beyond it, everything was unfamiliar. The hard comfort of grimy metal and oil was replaced with strange textures and smells. Air so fresh that it felt like it was barely there at all. Frightening shapes loomed in the brightly lit darkness, big things with wings and fat bodies, like colossal metal flies. Behind them were sinister dwellings, their windows glowing.

Overhead, Slag could see the night sky to either side of the *Ketty Jay*'s tail assembly. It was black and speckled with strange lights. Something told him that there wasn't any roof up there. What kept the lights from falling down?

The world outside was too big, too overwhelming. But still, there was his enemy, his punishment incomplete. He was dancing around and pulling faces now.

Slag focused all his concentration on Harkins. The way he did when he stalked rats. The world didn't exist. There was only him, and his prey.

He took a step forward. And another. His paw touched the tarmac.

Harkins yelped, turned tail and ran as fast as his legs could carry him, away into the night.

Slag left the paw where it was until Harkins was out of sight, then drew it back. He sat on his haunches and began to groom himself, one eye on the landing pad. A satisfactory encounter, all in all. His dominance had been asserted. No need to venture out there, not when he was master of his own domain. What he had was quite enough.

Pleased, he settled down to guard the entrance. Let that scrawny one try and come back tonight. Slag would show him what a real predator could do.

'Get up.'

Crake surfaced into awareness, found it unbearably terrible, and sank back towards sleep again.

'Crake! Get up!'

Someone shook him. His eyes fluttered open. A dark bedroom, plush and unfamiliar. Frey stood next to him, hand on his shoulder. Dawn light crept in through the curtains.

His face felt swollen and greasy with night sweats. His lips were sticky and the corner of his mouth was caked with something foul. He felt like he'd been shat whole from the dirty arse of some pestilent herd animal.

'Please go away, Cap'n,' he croaked. 'If I'm not unconscious in thirty seconds I may very well die. I mean it.'

'Get dressed,' said Frey. 'We're getting out of here.'

Crake lifted himself up on his elbows and turned his head with some difficulty. The bones in his neck had apparently rusted together in the night. Frey was dressed, clad in his familiar grubby garb, pistols and cutlass stuffed through his belt.

'You're not serious?' Crake pleaded.

Frey checked his pocket watch. 'Jez is bringing the *Ketty Jay* to meet us at four o'clock on the edge of the estate.'

'When did you arrange that?'

'A week ago, when I came back to see you lot. Thought I might want to make a quick exit after the soirée. Turns out I do.'

Crake sat up, rubbing his aching neck. 'If you put half as much effort into planning your robberies as you do sneaking away from your lovers, we'd all be rich by now.'

Frey didn't have the patience to discuss it. 'Look, Crake, it's almost four. If you don't get moving, I'll leave you behind. You can explain my absence to Amalicia.'

'No thanks!' Crake said, suddenly finding his motivation. He hauled himself out of bed and began pulling his clothes on over his undergarments, pausing only to prevent himself from being sick.

Frey glanced around uneasily. 'Hurry up, will you? I don't think my pods could survive the kicking if she catches me running out on her.'

'I must say, Cap'n, this doesn't rank amongst the most spectacularly brave things you've done.'

'I'm just not big on histrionics,' he explained. 'Don't like to see a woman cry.'

'But you're okay with *making* them cry?'

'Hey, I don't *make* anyone do anything. They *choose* to cry. Can't help it if they think I'm something I'm not.'

'You really are quite a shit, aren't you?'

'Why? Because I cut out the unpleasant stuff? One day she'll thank me for not dragging this out.'

'Oh, you're doing this for her? Very noble. I should have realised.' He pulled on his boots. 'I'm ready.'

They headed out of the bedroom and into the cool, shadowy corridors of the manse. The house was silent, the servants asleep. Crake did his best to creep along behind Frey, but his hangover and lack of sleep made him feel like his head was underwater. He had the unpleasant sensation that nothing was quite real. His brain and his body had become estranged and were only cooperating by a gentleman's agreement.

They sneaked downstairs to the entrance hall, beneath the disapproving gaze of the portraits that hung above the staircase. The hall seemed cavernous in the early morning quiet. The tiny tapping of their boots created echoes.

They'd reached the front door when they heard the unmistakable click of a pistol hammer being primed.

'Stop there.'

Amalicia stepped out from a curtained alcove. She was wearing a long nightgown, and was barefoot. A revolver was in her hand, trained on Frey. Her expression was dark.

'Ah,' said Frey. 'Listen, I know how this looks, but—'

'Don't,' she snapped. She crossed the space between them, never taking the gun from him. It trembled in her hand. 'I knew you'd be coming this way when I woke up and you weren't in bed,' she said. 'Leaving without a word. Isn't that your style?'

'Put the gun down, hmm?' Frey said nervously.

'So you can run off again?' she asked. 'I don't think so.'

'If you're trying to stop him running off, shooting him probably isn't the best way to do it,' Crake pointed out, in what he hoped was a reasonable manner.

Amalicia thought about that for a moment, then shifted her aim towards Crake. 'You're right,' she said. 'I'll shoot *you* instead.'

Crake dearly wished he'd kept his mouth shut.

'Amalicia, come on,' said Frey, holding up his hands as if placating a wild animal. 'Let's talk about this.'

She shook her head, her lip quivering and tears in her eyes. Dangerously close to hysteria. 'No more lies, Darian.' She tossed her hair and composed herself. 'It's become clear to me that you aren't in your right mind.'

'*I'm* not in my right mind? Who's got the gun?'

'I know there's something in you that makes you run away. I offer you all this, all my riches, and you still want to go back to your flea-bitten, raggedy life. But I understand, Darian. You can't help it. You're scared. Scared of love.'

'Scared,' said Frey flatly. 'Of love.'

'Cap'n . . .' Crake warned. He rather hoped Frey wasn't thinking of getting confrontational while there was a pistol pointed at his chest.

'I know it's frightening,' Amalicia said, suddenly sympathetic. 'It's scary to open your heart to another. To leave yourself vulnerable, to let others in. It's alright to admit it, Darian.'

Frey just looked embarrassed. 'Really, you've got this all wrong.'

'Of course you deny it! You don't even see it yourself. My poor orphan. *I* won't desert you.'

'What does my being an orphan have to do with any of this?' Frey cried.

She gave him a pitying gaze, moist with compassion. 'You don't know what's best for you, my love. So you're going to stay here. I'll show you there's nothing to be scared of.'

'You're kidnapping me?' Frey said, aghast.

'For your own good.'

Frey took a steadying breath and tried a new tack. 'Listen,' he said. 'Let me tell you what I learned at the party last night. This sphere – the sphere that will make me rich, remember – they're moving it by air to another location. This evening, at dusk. It'll be under heavy guard, but with the *Storm Dog* on our side, we can take it. We know the route and we'll set an ambush. It's our best and only chance.' He checked his pocket watch again. '*That's* why we're sneaking off. I didn't want to worry you. As soon as we're done, I'll be straight back. I promise.'

'Is that true?' Amalicia asked Crake. He nodded frantically. *All except the last part, anyway.*

She evidently didn't believe him. 'Oh, Darian,' she said, with an indulgent tut. 'You will use every trick in the book, won't you? But you don't fool me. You're staying here.'

Frey gave a little scream of frustration. 'I *can't* stay here,' he said 'This is too important!'

'More important than love?'

'Yes!' he replied, without an instant's pause.

'You see?' said Amalicia. 'You're not thinking clearly. You're scared. Who in their right mind would take money over love?'

'Oh, for shit's sake,' Frey said, exasperated. He pulled a pistol from his belt and pointed it at her head. 'Just drop the damn gun.'

Amalicia went white and stared at him in surprise. Then an uncertain smile spread across her lips. 'You wouldn't shoot me,' she said.

'I'm a pirate, Amalicia. You think I haven't shot women in cold blood before?'

Crake hadn't thought so until now, but suddenly he wasn't sure. Amalicia was even more worried by the suggestion. She hadn't seen this side of Frey. The hard, uncaring, brutal side. She didn't move, perhaps expecting him to drop the act at any moment. But Frey's expression was like stone.

He cocked his pistol. 'Gun down, Amalicia. This isn't a game. That's a member of my crew you're threatening. I'm not asking a third time.'

Amalicia's eyes welled with tears at the tone of his voice. An expression of shock settled on her face as she realised he was serious. She looked like a child stunned by an undeserved reprimand.

'Darian,' she whispered. 'You couldn't.'

He closed one eye and sighted down the barrel towards her forehead.

She looked from one man to the other, and then she lowered her weapon. Crake breathed a low, whistling sigh of relief and took the gun from her hand. She slumped to the floor, her legs gone weak.

'How could you do this?' she asked, head hung. 'I love you.'

Frey shoved his pistol back in his belt. 'I never asked you to.' He walked to the front door, pulled it open, and went out into the dawn light. Crake cast one last, apologetic look at Amalicia and followed him.

'You don't know how to love, Darian Frey!' she shrieked after them, as they hurried down the drive towards their rendezvous. *'You don't know how to love!'*

Nineteen

The Flashpan – A Flight Through The Storm –
Dead Reckoning – Unexpected Resistance

'Quite a storm,' Frey said.

Jez's reply was drowned out by a clap of thunder loud enough to rattle the brass-and-chrome fixtures of the *Ketty Jay*'s cockpit.

Frey held his nose and blew through it till his ears popped. 'Say again?'

'I said, I've seen worse,' Jez told him. 'You've never flown the Flashpan before?'

'Can't say I've had the pleasure.' Frey was trying to peer through the lashing rain that assaulted his craft. It was almost pitch black out there. Thick clouds cloaked the glow of the moon. They were flying without lights. 'I can't see for buggery, Jez.'

'Then they can't see us, either. I thought that was the point?'

'Just tell me if I'm going to fly into anything.'

'Will do, Cap'n.'

Frey wasn't enjoying himself one bit. People avoided the Flashpan for a reason. It was an area of boggy moorland that sat at high altitude just east of the Splinters and north of the Vardenwood. Innocuous enough, except for the near-constant storms that raged here. Some unlucky trick of the geography, apparently. Something to do with warm, moist air from the south mixing with freezing air coming the other way. Jez had explained it to him, but he hadn't listened very hard. He'd been too busy shitting himself at the prospect of the battle to come.

They were going up against the *Delirium Trigger*.

By the time Frey and Crake had got back from the Thade estate, they were already cutting it fine if they hoped to intercept Dracken and the barque she was escorting. Frey held a hasty discussion with

Grist, and they headed off immediately afterwards. Their plan wasn't the tactical masterpiece Frey would have preferred, but it would have to do. They didn't have anything better.

The *Storm Dog* was a beast of an aircraft, but even so, Frey wasn't sure she could go toe-to-toe with the *Delirium Trigger*. What they needed was the element of surprise. Not easy when their targets would be flying across open grassland.

But if it was at night, in the middle of a terrific storm? It was possible to sneak up on them that way. But first they had to find them.

The problem was, the aircraft they were searching for would be running without lights. Nobody flew the Flashpan unless they didn't want to be found. According to the Grand Oracle, the Awakeners' lives were being made miserable by the Navy lately. Archduke's orders, no doubt. Awakener craft were boarded and searched wherever they were encountered. It wasn't that the Navy expected to find anything; it was just to piss them off. But the Awakeners couldn't risk their precious Mane sphere being found by the Navy, so they were sneaking across the Flashpan at night. In the dark and rain, they were all but invisible.

Not to Jez, though. If anyone could spot them, Jez could.

While she scanned the horizon, Frey concentrated on maintaining course and keeping a safe altitude. The wind jostled the *Ketty Jay* about, making her groan and rumble. He was flying by his instruments, since vision was almost zero except when a flash of lightning lit up the land. He kept a wary eye on the rock masses that hulked out of the moors below him, half-expecting one of them to loom up into his path.

To calm his nerves, he ran over what he'd learned from the Grand Oracle, hoping to get one step ahead of the game. Pomfrey had been forthcoming about the details of how the Awakeners intended to transport the sphere, but Frey had been left frustrated in other areas. When he asked the Grand Oracle what the Awakeners intended to do with the power source from a Mane dreadnought, Pomfrey had only looked confused.

Frey had prompted him. Were they planning to sell it? Perhaps they wanted to make a deal with the Archduke, a trade in return for freedom from further persecution? Or did they have designs on building an invincible fleet of their own?

The Grand Oracle had seemed mystified. 'What power source?'

At that moment, several people had entered the parlour, and Crake had been forced to wrap it up quickly, commanding the Grand Oracle to remember nothing of the conversation.

But Frey remembered.

What power source?

Grist had lied to him. It wasn't a power source at all. So what exactly *was* it?

Whatever that son of a bitch was up to, he still wasn't being straight with Frey. And Frey was damned if he'd be mucked around like that.

Once they located their targets, it would be the *Storm Dog*'s job to deal with the *Delirium Trigger*. The *Ketty Jay* was far too small to handle her. Instead, she'd go after the Awakener barque, to capture its cargo. The Mane sphere.

As soon as they had that, Frey was going to run for it. Forget Grist and his secrets. Whatever that thing was, Frey was having it, and Grist could go hang. He'd work out later what to do with it.

Some things are worth riskin' everythin' for, Grist had said. But what was it he was after? What was worth that much?

'Doc!' he called through the cockpit door. 'Are they still with us?'

'Wait a sec!' Malvery called back from the gunnery cupola. There was a flash of lightning and a tearing sound overhead. '*Storm Dog*'s right on our tail, Cap'n!'

Frey stared out into the night. The cockpit lights had been doused, except for dim night-flying bulbs on the dash to illuminate the instruments. Another flash of lightning showed him the Firecrow and Skylance, flying some distance below them, as Frey had instructed. A lightning strike wouldn't affect the *Ketty Jay* or the *Storm Dog*, but smaller craft had a tendency to explode that way. The *Storm Dog*'s outflyers were safely stashed in a hangar in her belly, but that wasn't an option on the *Ketty Jay*, which was less than a tenth her size. Instead, he used his craft to shelter his pilots as best he could, hoping it would soak up the lightning.

'Harkins. Pinn. Everything alright?' he asked.

'Darker than a miner's arsehole down here,' came Pinn's reply through his earcuff. 'Otherwise, fine.'

Jez had suggested that they might give an earcuff to Grist, to better coordinate the attack, but Frey had flatly refused. The earcuffs were a secret that only the crew of the *Ketty Jay* shared. A little stroke of genius from Crake. It gave them an advantage that other crews didn't have. He wasn't sharing that with an untrustworthy bastard like Grist.

He hunched forward in his seat, searching the darkness. 'Where are you, Trinica?' he muttered. 'Where'd you go?'

Trinica. In among all his other problems, there was Trinica. Why did *she* need to get involved? Why did it have to be *her* who robbed him on Kurg? If it had been anybody else he might have given up, cut his losses and parted company with Grist. But he couldn't take the humiliation, not from her.

He found himself thinking of this operation more and more in terms of Trinica. It was *her* he was beating. Maybe he couldn't take her on himself, but it was *his* plan, his effort that had set up the ambush. It would be him that ended up with the prize. Maybe the *Storm Dog* would shoot her down, or maybe she'd shoot down Grist. As long as they kept each other busy for long enough, he couldn't care less. But he'd like to see the look on her face when she realised who'd done her over.

'Cap'n,' said Jez. She craned forward and narrowed her eyes. 'Contact.'

Frey sat up. 'You see them?'

Jez looked for a few more moments. 'Bearing two-eighty-five, heading across us to the east.'

Frey thumped the dash in excitement. 'Alright, we're on!' he announced. 'Harkins, Pinn, hit the deck. Stay low, and listen to Jez for course corrections. We're heading up into the clouds.'

'Can we *shoot* at them this time, Cap'n?' Pinn asked. He was still sore about their last encounter, when they were bested by yokels flying mail planes and cropdusters.

'Unless you can think of some other way of blowing them out of the sky.' Frey replied.

Pinn whooped. 'Watch out, boys! It's dyin' time!' he yelled. Frey presumed he was addressing the enemy.

'Crazy idiot,' Harkins said under his breath, loud enough for everyone to hear.

'Meow,' said Pinn.

'Shut up! You shut your fat yap!' Harkins snapped. Dumb as Pinn was, he was very accurate when it came to hitting a nerve.

'*Both* of you shut up,' said Frey. 'I want you coming back alive. Remember, as soon as we've got the sphere on board, you break off and fly like your tails are on fire. We'll meet up at Osken's Bar in Westport. Got it?'

'Got it, Cap'n,' said Harkins.

'Meow,' said Pinn.

'That's it!' Harkins shrieked. 'I've had just about enough from you, you, you ignorant piece of—'

Frey pulled his earcuff off and tossed it on to the dash. He pinched the bridge of his nose, where his headache had focused. He didn't need this on top of a hangover and a sleepless night.

'Taking us up,' he said. He fed more aerium into the tanks and the *Ketty Jay* rose towards the clouds. 'Doc! Tell me if we lose the *Storm Dog*, okay?'

'Right-o!' came the reply. Frey heard the unmistakable sound of a bottle being swigged.

'Are you drinking up there, Doc?'

'There's a quarter-inch of windglass between me and five crillion volts of lightning, Cap'n. You'll forgive me if I take a nip, eh?'

Frey thought that was fair enough, so he kept quiet. As long as Malvery could still shoot straight. He wasn't exactly a crack shot with an autocannon, but Crake was worse, and Frey couldn't spare anyone else. Silo needed to concentrate on keeping the engine running. He still didn't have the parts he needed to fix it properly, so he was forced to do the best he could with what he had.

The black clouds swallowed them up. Once they were far enough in, Frey flicked on the tail-lights to give the *Storm Dog* something to follow. Jez went back to her charts and began plotting the trajectory of their targets based on their speed and direction. Frey found it rather impressive that she'd divined that information from many kloms away on a dark, rainy night, but he was used to being impressed by Jez. He took it for granted nowadays.

'Adjust to two-seventy,' she said. Frey did so. Winds shoved the *Ketty Jay* this way and that. Frey bullied her back on course. He dumped some aerium to lend them weight and stability. Lightning flickered, muffled by the clouds. Thunder detonated all around them.

Frey gripped the flight stick, shoulders tense, and trusted to Jez to get them where they were going.

'Two points to starboard,' Jez said.

Frey adjusted. An odd feeling of unreality had settled on him. Flying through this black churn of wind and rain and flickering light, the air charged and taut, he could almost believe that he'd slipped into another world entirely. He picked up the earcuff from the dash and clipped it back on. Suddenly, he needed to be connected to something familiar, something outside the storm.

'Anyone see anything?' he asked Harkins and Pinn.

'No, Cap'n,' said Harkins, who was in a sulk.

'Me, neither,' said Pinn.

'Keep your eyes peeled,' Frey advised. 'You won't see them till you're right on top of them.'

'*What was that?*' Pinn cried suddenly. Frey jumped in alarm.

'What? What?' Harkins was already panicking.

'Something went flying past me in the dark,' Pinn said. 'Missed me by a *whisker*.'

It took Harkins a long moment to get it. 'You rancid bastard, Pinn!'

'Meow,' Pinn said.

Harkins erupted in a barrage of incoherent swear words. Frey looked over his shoulder at Jez and grinned. Jez shook her head in despair.

The *Ketty Jay* was battered and flung in every direction, but she'd ridden out plenty of storms before. Frey kept her under control, dealing with the jinks and dips with practised skill. Malvery yelled periodic reports, to the effect that the *Storm Dog* was keeping pace with them. Jez offered course corrections now and again.

Frey tried to concentrate on the journey, not the destination. His nerves were jangling, and not just from the electricity in the atmosphere. Pinn was the only one among them looking forward to the prospect of a dogfight. Anyone with any sense was scared silly.

'I see 'em!' Pinn cried suddenly. 'Dead ahead!'

'He's right!' Harkins said. Their differences were immediately forgotten. 'I saw them . . . er . . . in a flash! Of lightning!'

'Dead ahead, Cap'n,' said Jez. Frey thought he detected a slight edge of self-satisfaction in her voice. 'Three kloms, I make it.'

'Nice work,' said Frey. Jez had put them right on top of their enemy, plotting their course by dead reckoning, based on a glance from kloms away. The woman was phenomenal.

Now it was his turn. He killed the *Ketty Jay*'s tail-lights: a signal to the *Storm Dog*.

'Brace yourselves, everyone!' he yelled. 'Dive! Dive! Dive!'

Black clouds flurried at the windglass as the *Ketty Jay* dove through the clouds. Frey sat hunched over the flight stick, heart thumping in his ears. The cockpit rattled and shook all around him. An unfamiliar and distressing whine had developed in the engines, but it was too late to worry about that now. Too late to do anything but press forward.

The clouds tattered and fluttered away, and there below were the rolling moors of the Flashpan, lit by a stunning blast of lightning. The *Delirium Trigger* was beneath and ahead of them, huge and black and terrible, its deck and flanks spiky with cannons. Frey felt a little bit of sick jump into his throat at the sight. It was shadowing a double-hulled barque, several times the size of the *Ketty Jay* but still dwarfed by its escort.

'*Storm Dog*'s breaking through the cloud behind us, Cap'n!' Malvery yelled from the cupola. 'If I were you I'd get out of the way!'

Good advice, thought Frey. He rolled the *Ketty Jay* to starboard, swooping out of the *Storm Dog*'s line of fire, and angled towards the barque. His guns couldn't scratch a frigate like the *Delirium Trigger*, but they could certainly put a few holes in the Awakener craft.

'Open fire!' he called to Malvery. With exquisite timing, the *Storm Dog* picked that moment to unleash her battery of cannons in a deafening barrage.

The *Delirium Trigger* was taken completely by surprise. A chain of explosions ripped across her hull and deck, blooms of flame lighting her up against the rain and the dark. The force was enough to knock her off course and she went yawing and tipping to port. Frey grinned savagely as he imagined the panic and shock belowdecks. Surrounded by open terrain, when they thought they were all but invisible, they must have believed themselves safe from ambush. But Frey had proved otherwise.

Didn't see that one coming, did you, Trinica?

The *Storm Dog* thundered past the *Ketty Jay* as Frey went to take care of his own target. Grist was moving into position between the *Delirium Trigger* and the barque, to block her off and give Frey time to

186

work. The *Delirium Trigger* would have her cannons in action in moments. She was wounded but far from finished.

The barque was slower to react to the attack. It continued on its course as if oblivious, widening the gap between itself and its escort. It was long and thin, the stern end boxy and stout with stubby fins sticking out to either side to serve as mounts for her ailerons. The foremost two-thirds of the craft was split along its length, giving it the look of a twin-bladed bayonet. A Dakkadian bayonet, like the one Frey had taken in the guts back in Samarla. The memory made Frey's stomach cramp unpleasantly.

He craned forward to see through the rain on the windglass, his finger hovering over the trigger on the flight stick. The barque was a design he'd never come across, and he had nowhere to aim. Not that it bothered Malvery, who was blasting away on the autocannon with reckless abandon.

'Jez!' he snapped urgently. 'You ever seen this kind of craft before?'

'It's a Kedson Harbinger, Cap'n.'

'Any idea where the aerium tanks are?'

'Two on each side, port and starboard. One about ten metres back from the bow, one beneath the ailerons.'

'I could kiss you.'

'I'd rather you didn't. Allsoul only knows where that mouth's been.'

The barque loomed closer. It still hadn't showed any sign of reacting to the surprise attack. Slow crew, badly trained. That was good. They weren't pirates and they weren't Navy. What did Awakeners know about aerial combat?

Frey heard a bellow of cannon to port, and the night was lit by fire: the *Storm Dog* and the *Delirium Trigger* were engaging each other in earnest. He ignored them, hoping he was beneath their notice. In this visibility, with all that was going on, the *Delirium Trigger* probably didn't even know the *Ketty Jay* was there.

He adjusted his approach, aiming his machine guns for the aerium tanks on the barque's stern end. Shoot out the aerium tanks, and the craft would lose buoyancy and sink. Once they brought it down, it would be easy pickings.

'Steady,' he muttered to himself. 'Steady.'

A stutter of lightning lit up his target.

Not yet . . . not yet . . .

He pressed down on his guns, and at the same moment, the night exploded.

It was like being swatted by a giant. The *Ketty Jay* was thrown sideways, machine guns raking wildly along the flank of the barque. Frey was flung about in his seat and Jez almost fell out of hers. Pipes shrieked and burst out in the corridor, spraying gas and fluid everywhere. There was the sound of shattering glass and Malvery came tumbling down the ladder that led to the cupola. He crashed in a heap at the bottom, accompanied by a squall of wind and rain.

Frey had just about enough sense to pull the *Ketty Jay* aside in time to avoid ramming the side of the barque. They shot past on the aft side, passing through the backwash of the engines. The *Ketty Jay* was lifted and blasted aside, rolling crazily, engines coughing as they threatened to stall.

Don't die on me, girl! Frey begged his aircraft as he wrestled to stop her flipping entirely. Jez hung on to her seat for dear life. Malvery was sent skidding down the corridor on his back, bellowing like a bewildered walrus. Frey could hear distant machine guns, and saw tracer fire gliding past him in the night from the direction of the barque. A moment later, a dozen sharp, punching impacts echoed through the *Ketty Jay*.

'You never told me the damn thing was armed!' Frey screamed at Jez.

'I didn't think I needed to!' she screamed back. 'I thought you'd be expecting a little resistance!'

'Well, you thought wrong!'

'Well, you're an idiot!' she replied. Then, respectfully, 'Cap'n.'

By now Frey had fought the *Ketty Jay* level, and the engines were settling down. They raced away from the barque and the *Delirium Trigger*, slipping safely out of range. Frey's hands were trembling. A freezing hurricane was blowing through the cockpit from the corridor. The cupola was smashed, and rain from outside lashed the passageway.

'Doc! Are you alright?' Frey called through the door of the cockpit.

Malvery was piled against the engine room door in a position that had to be painful. 'Just about, Cap'n,' he wheezed.

'Damage report,' Frey ordered.

'Cuts and bruises. Bashed my knee pretty bad. I've felt better.'

'Not *you*. The aircraft.'

'Oh. Right-o,' said Malvery. 'I'll ask Silo, shall I?'

'Would you?'

Malvery untangled himself and headed into the engine room while Frey turned the *Ketty Jay*.

'*Delirium Trigger*'s putting out her fighters, Cap'n,' said Pinn in his ear. '*Storm Dog* too.'

'Get in there,' said Frey. 'Make sure none of them come after me.' He turned to look at Jez, who was arranging herself in her seat again. 'Okay. This time we do it right.'

The aerial battlefield swung into sight as he brought the *Ketty Jay* around for a second run at the barque. The *Delirium Trigger* and *Storm Dog* glided past each other in different directions, slow leviathans, their cannon batteries flashing. Gouts of yellow flame erupted from their hulls; slabs of armour buckled and wheeled away into the storm. The *Delirium Trigger*'s outflyers – Norbury Equalisers, fast and deadly – were spraying from her hangars, emerging to meet the *Storm Dog*'s ragtag squadron of heavier fighter craft. Lightning flickered and thunder shattered the air.

Frey couldn't see Harkins or Pinn in the mix. They'd be waiting for their moment to dart in and hit the Equalisers. Satisfied that the *Delirium Trigger* and her outflyers were fully occupied, Frey turned his attention back to the barque.

The Awakeners, foolishly, were making a run for it. Perhaps frightened by the sudden appearance of the *Storm Dog*, they'd boosted their thrusters and opened up distance between themselves and the *Delirium Trigger*. Maybe they believed they could lose themselves in the storm and escape, leaving their escort behind. But all it did was rob them of their best defence.

Frey closed in on them. This time, he took an evasive pattern, rolling and diving as he approached. A blast of artillery rattled the *Ketty Jay*, but it didn't come close enough to trouble them. The heavy machine guns fared little better. Tracer fire slipped out of the dark from the turrets on the back of the barque, but it waved about wildly and never got a fix. Now that he was moving around instead of coming in straight, they couldn't draw a bead on him.

'Engines weren't hit, Cap'n!' Malvery shouted from down the passageway. 'Rot knows where we took the bullets, but if you can't feel it in the controls then Silo says not to worry. We probably won't know until we explode.'

Frey barely heard him. He was focused only on his target.

Gunfire came at him from several turrets, but he slipped between it. He headed for the aerium tank at the end of the barque's port prong. With the autocannon out of commission, he only had the nose-mounted machine guns to work with. The trick was to graze the tank, causing a slow leak that would force the pilot to land the craft. But Frey was angry and shaken up, and not in the mood to be subtle. He squeezed the trigger hard, and kept it down. His machine guns didn't so much graze the tank as rip it apart.

The *Ketty Jay* dove underneath the barque as it vented a pungent cloud of aerium gas. Frey smelt it on the cold wind that whipped around the cockpit and blew his hair against his face. The barque slid through the sky overhead, metal groaning as it tilted. The sudden weight on its port side was pulling it down.

Malvery stumbled into the cockpit, holding on to his glasses with one hand. 'Silo says go easy! Don't tax the engines too much!'

'She'll hold,' Frey said, through gritted teeth. 'Shut the door.'

Malvery hauled the door to the cockpit shut, closing out the wind from outside. Sporadic machine-gun fire followed the *Ketty Jay* as Frey pulled her around for another pass. The battle between the frigates was in full swing. Their fleets were dogfighting in the space between and around them. Frey caught flickering glimpses of combat, punctuated by occasional explosions that pushed back the blackness for a moment. He heard Pinn's whoops in his ear, and Harkins' cowardly gibbering. They were still in one piece, then. He took heart from that.

The barque was in trouble. It was still moving at full speed, kloms away from its escort, but it couldn't pull itself level and was flying aslant. At this distance, there would be no help from the *Delirium Trigger*. Its guns were having trouble aiming at anything as the pilot fought to correct the uneven weight of the twin hulls. Tracer fire burned away in all directions, but the artillery cannon had gone silent. Its operator knew that accuracy was impossible until the craft was under control, and had decided not to waste the ammo.

'Got you now, you son of a bitch,' Frey murmured. He raced in, heedless of the gunfire, aiming for the starboard bow tank. A small voice of caution told him that he was supposed to be bringing this craft down gently, but he'd been scared by the barque's surprise attack and he wanted it out of commission, fast. He closed in and yawed to starboard, his machine guns clattering as they punched holes all along the barque's hull. His touch was lighter this time, but not by much.

Frey couldn't see the gas that spewed from the rupture, but he could see the effect. The barque's bow tilted downwards, the push of its thrusters driving it towards the ground. The pilot fought to compensate, but to no avail. The craft was too big and too clumsy.

The pilot airbraked as much as they could on the way down. Somehow they got the bow almost level, so it came in low and flat, like a skimmed stone. Lightened by all the aerium in its stern tanks, the impact wasn't as hard as its size would suggest, but it was still catastrophic. It hit the ground with a wail of metal, ploughing through the soft earth, rending a trench across the moors. Its double bow buckled and split. One of the prongs snapped off altogether. Its underside came away in shreds. An explosion tore through its flank, sending girders and armour plate wheeling through the night.

Finally, after what seemed an age, it came to a halt in the shadow of a rocky outcrop. Crippled, wrecked, but mostly whole.

Malvery whistled. 'Nice one, Cap'n!' he exclaimed, amazed by the scale of the destruction.

'I'm just glad he left enough of it for us to rob,' Jez said.

'I brought it down, didn't I?' Frey said. He looked at Malvery. 'Go get Crake and Silo and tool up. We're boarding that thing. I want that sphere.'

'Right-o,' said Malvery. He made for the door, but Frey stopped him.

'Oh, Malvery? One more thing. Tell Crake to wake up Bess. We're gonna need her good and angry.'

Twenty

Manoeuvres In The Dark – Pinn Is Distracted –
A Dreadful Opponent – Jez, And Yet Not Jez

P inn was having a rare old time.

He swooped and rolled and plunged, laughing maniacally. He sprayed tracer fire into the night, chasing half-seen phantoms through the rain. He yelled with joy whenever thunder boomed around him.

Visibility was terrible. The other fighters were flying well below full speed, afraid of a mid-air collision. Pinn concluded, therefore, that they were all pussies. He screamed through the skies at a speed that bordered on suicidal. Pinn was a man who lived without fear of death, because he was too dim to imagine it. For him, this was a happy hunting ground.

The fighters orbited their massive parent craft, which were locked in a deadly slugfest. Cannons blazed along their flanks. Turrets boomed and heavy machine guns tracked targets through the sky. Tactics had been all but abandoned as the two leviathans blasted chunks out of each other. It was all about who was the toughest, who could load and fire the fastest, who had the biggest guns. But the *Storm Dog*'s surprise attack had put the *Delirium Trigger* on the back foot, and she was fighting for her survival.

Something shot out in front of Pinn, right to left, slashing through the storm. Too fast to see whether it was an ally or an enemy, but he felt the cockpit shudder as it passed. It had been mere metres from taking the nose off his aircraft and sending them both to a fiery grave.

He banked hard and set off in pursuit. Before him was only rain and darkness, but he knew that craft had to be out there somewhere. Then, a burst of machine guns, and his target was lit in the muzzle flash of its own weapon. He saw the telltale shape of a Norbury Equaliser: a rounded, bulbous bow end; straight wings, clipped at the end; a lean, narrow profile with a kinked back. Pinn grinned at the sight. He opened up the throttle and closed in.

Another craft raced past, close enough to make the Skylance shimmy in the turbulence. In this storm and at this speed, by the time he saw something in his path it would be far too late to evade. If he was going to hit something, he'd hit it. No point worrying, then. Pinn ignored the danger and concentrated on his target.

Tracer fire floated eerily through the blackness ahead of him. Some invisible conflict in the storm. For every blazing bullet he could see, there were five, just as deadly, that he couldn't. Harkins used to talk about them all the time, those unseen bullets in tracer fire. *They* were the ones that would get you, he said. But Pinn preferred to believe that if you couldn't see them, they weren't there.

He spotted his target as it fired again, and lined up on its tail. Harkins was yammering something in his ear, but he wasn't paying any attention. He'd learned to tune out his fellow outflyer's near-constant state of panic in a firefight. Instead he flexed his finger over the trigger on his flight stick and waited for the right moment.

'Here it comes, you son of a bitch,' he muttered.

Lightning flashed and thunder roared. Pinn squeezed the trigger, but the Equaliser banked suddenly. The pilot had spotted him in the lightning flash. Bullets tore through the air around the Equaliser, smacking into its rear end. It dodged away, trailing smoke from its thruster. Pinn shot past, banked hard, came back around; but by then his target had disappeared.

'Did I get him?' he said to himself, searching the storm. 'Did I get him?'

In the distance, there was a dull explosion, and an aircraft was consumed by flames, heading earthwards like a meteor. His quarry, or someone else's? He didn't know. He'd claim it anyway, but it would have been nice to be sure.

Pinn had become detached from the fray, so he turned the Skylance back towards it, seeking new targets. The *Storm Dog* and the *Delirium Trigger* fought at the heart of the battlefield, high above the moors, flashing monsters of iron and steel. The smaller fighters hung close by, preying on each other.

His eyes flickered over the instrument panel on his dash, then settled on the ferrotype of Lisinda that hung from it. It was dangling and spinning on its chain, showing her face in teasing glimpses. He saddened at the sight of her. For a short time, lost in the thrill of combat, he'd forgotten the empty ache in his guts, the sad, grey feeling that had settled on him lately. But one glimpse was enough to bring it all back.

What was she doing now? There was no date on that letter, no telling when it was sent. A month ago? Three? Was her new husband already enjoying her, this imposter who'd taken his place? Was she with him now, all creamy thighs and soft breasts, surging blankets and sighs? He'd never known her that way. She was too sacred, too pure to be sullied by anyone but a hero. But this newcomer had tricked her somehow, maybe even *forced* her into yielding to him.

The thought made him furious. He was no longer sad; he was consumed by a bitter, savage anger that flooded through his veins like molten metal.

'What's that weird grinding sound?' Harkins queried in his ear.

Pinn unclenched his teeth and gave a terrible howl of rage. Harkins squealed in fright. A flash of lightning lit up the battlefield, and a crack of thunder rocked the Skylance. Pinn saw aircraft swooping in the distance. He felt a deep need to avenge himself on the whole world. Those Equaliser bastards would be a good start.

The Skylance's engines shrieked as he flew at reckless speed towards the aircraft. Lightning, muzzle flashes and tracer fire drew him towards an Equaliser that was heading away from him. He gave chase, hoping to catch the pilot unawares, hoping to blast his sorry arse out of the sky before he even knew what was happening.

Then suddenly the air was full of bullets. Tracer fire, flitting all around his craft. Sharp impacts as his hull and wings were hit. Pinn looked frantically over his shoulder, yelled in alarm as the saw an Equaliser hanging on his tail, and rolled out of the way.

'Pinn? Are you alright?' It was the Cap'n, but Pinn didn't have time for a chat right now.

'I think . . . I mean, Cap'n, it sounds like he's gone crazy!' Harkins opined.

'Pinn? Have you gone crazy?'

'Will you both bloody shut up?' Pinn cried. 'I've got an Equaliser on my tail!'

'Get over there and help him out!' Frey ordered Harkins.

'Where?'

'Near the frigates!' Pinn shouted. He banked hard, but the Equaliser stuck to him like glue. Just ahead, a bolt of lightning struck the *Storm Dog*, fizzing off her black hull. The *Storm Dog* shrugged it off and kept firing.

He heard the chatter of his pursuer's guns, but this time he was ready for it and he dodged. Another spray came out of nowhere; he barely pulled away in time. He twisted his neck, searching for the source. *Another* Equaliser, coming in high at seven o'clock. Pinn swore. Two of them, ganging up. Their cowardice infuriated him.

'Alright, shitwads,' he snarled. 'I'll give you a chase.'

He broke hard to starboard, slipping out of the way of another volley of machine-gun fire. He'd caught a couple of hits, but the Skylance was still handling well. The *Storm Dog* and *Delirium Trigger* slid into view in front of him. He boosted the thrusters and arrowed towards them.

The sudden jump in speed threw his pursuers for a few seconds. They forgot about shooting at him while they concentrated on catching up. Pinn considered engaging the Skylance's racing afterburners, leaving them all choking on his fumes, but that would mean abandoning the fight and the *Ketty Jay*. In the mood he was in, he wasn't about to do that. He wanted to kill someone first.

By the time the Equalisers had got back within firing range, the frigates loomed large before them. They were flying alongside each other, lumbering through the black sky, cannons blasting. The space between them was a mess of artillery fire and bullets. Pinn headed straight for it.

The Equalisers opened up on him. He swung left, left again, then dived, making himself a hard target. The frigates swelled as he neared them. An alley of death between them, their blasted metal flanks the walls. Turrets on the *Delirium Trigger* had swivelled to track him: he heard autocannons kicking in.

Go!

He rolled hard and kept rolling, corkscrewing wildly through the deadly mesh of gunfire. Explosions rattled the Skylance, knocking him off course, jerking him about in his seat. It was only a few seconds, but it seemed to stretch out for ever. He pulled the Skylance level and rammed the thrusters to maximum, racing straight along the length of the frigates and out of the alley, whooping all the way.

He craned around in his seat in time to see one of his pursuers ripped to pieces in the crossfire. He couldn't see the other. Maybe that one hadn't been stupid enough to follow him in. Either way—

Machine guns. A rain of tracer fire from above. Pinn's head snapped up. An Equaliser, coming in from directly overhead. The Skylance was laid out flat beneath it, the whole craft presented as a target, with Pinn totally exposed in his cockpit. Rookie mistake. The Equaliser couldn't miss. Pinn's heart sank.

Then the Equaliser erupted in a blast of oily fire, spinning away in a dozen separate pieces, fading to invisibility in the storm. Harkins' Firecrow sped across the sky in the opposite direction to Pinn.

'Pinn! Did he get you?'

Pinn slumped back in his seat. 'No. He didn't get me.'

'You let him come in from above!' Harkins snapped, sounding unaccountably outraged. 'You could have been killed! Pay attention! What's wrong with you?'

'I don't know,' Pinn murmured, gazing at the ferrotype of Lisinda hanging from his dash. 'I don't know.'

Crake's palms were clammy and chill. The revolver in his hand felt like it weighed twice as much as usual. His heart skipped and tripped, little irregular bumps and flutters in his chest. He felt dried out and sick, and he was dog-tired from lack of sleep. On top of all that, he was probably going to get himself shot sometime in the next few minutes.

Not for the first time, Crake wondered how a man like himself, a man of good education, breeding and prospects, had ended up this way.

The cargo ramp was opening, squealing gently on its hydraulics. Cold wind blew in, stirring his hair and clothes. Tarpaulins flapped on the crates stacked nearby. Between the booming of the thunder and the shudder of lightning, there was the quieter sound of distant cannon fire and machine guns.

Silo, Jez and Malvery were keyed up, fidgeting with anticipation. Frey was loading his revolver, his cutlass dangling from his belt. He'd taken out his earcuff, unable to stand listening to Harkins and Pinn babble any longer. Jez would be their contact with the pilots.

Bess stood next to Crake, shifting restlessly. She smelt of old leather and machine grease. A thrumming noise came from her chest, a sign of tension and unease. She knew what was coming. He laid a hand on her mailed elbow to calm her.

I'll fix you, Bess, he thought. *I'll make this better somehow. For now, we have to get through this.*

He just hoped she wouldn't get hurt. Even though he knew she was all but invulnerable to anything short of high explosives, he hated himself every time he allowed her to be sent into battle. But how could he explain his reluctance to the Cap'n without also confessing his crime? To the rest of the crew, Bess was just a dumb lump of metal. Only Jez knew the truth.

I'll be with you, he told the golem silently. *Don't worry.*

The ramp thumped down. Frey raised his pistol in the air, looked back at his crew and yelled, 'Board 'em!'

They ran down the ramp and out. Wind and rain assaulted them. The hardy moor grass whipped around their legs. A dozen kloms away, the flashing of cannons and the slow lines of tracer fire lit up the *Storm Dog* and the *Delirium Trigger*, caught in their own private war. Lightning flickered, scarring jagged paths through the night. The air was charged with it.

Before them, like some vast, slain creature of the deep, was the crumpled hulk of the Awakener barque. They were close enough now to see the name painted along the buckled hull: *All Our Yesterdays*. Smoke leaked from vents near its stern end. It lay in a trench that stretched away out of sight, the earth rucked up in piles all around it.

'The entrance will be over there,' said Jez, pointing. Jez, the craftbuilder's daughter. She knew her aircraft better than any of them.

They sallied across the gap between the aircraft and located the door that Jez had promised. There was no sign of anybody coming out of the *All Our Yesterdays*. The door had been bent and twisted in the impact, and was half-buried by the banked-up soil. Bess dug it out with her hands, took hold of the edge, and tore it off.

Frey peered inside. 'We don't want any trouble!' he yelled. 'Put down your weapons, and you won't be—'

He was interrupted by a volley of gunfire, and jumped back sharply. 'Well, I tried,' he said with a shrug. 'Get 'em, Bess.'

Bess roared and charged in through the door. There was a brief salvo of bullets, dissolving into screams and cries of alarm.

'Let's get in there,' Frey said, motioning to his crew. Then he plunged through the door, firing his revolver. The others piled in after him. Crake was not ashamed to be last.

Inside, it was chaos. Crake found himself in an assembly area, with a high ceiling and a gantry that ran around the edge of the chamber. The roof had split in the crash, shedding debris from the room above on to the floor. Cables hung in thick clusters like vines; exposed girders were bent and snapped off; cracked pipes leaked and hissed. A thin, poisonous pall of smoke hazed the air. Emergency lights provided a sinister twilight.

Hiding among the ruination were Sentinels, wearing grey, high-collared cassocks and carrying rifles. The Sentinels were Awakeners who didn't have the talent or the intelligence to become Speakers – those who preached and practised the Awakeners' craft – so they expressed their faith in other ways, by taking up weapons in defence of their organisation. Crake thought them mindless, brainwashed fools, but he supposed a bullet from a fool's gun hurt just as much as any other, so he kept his head down and ran for cover.

Bullets clipped through the air, but nobody was shooting at him: all attention was on Bess. The Sentinels scurried away or took frightened potshots from a distance as she ploughed into the room. Bullets bounced from her scratched and pitted armour, but some penetrated the soft parts at her joints, which only enraged her. She hefted a huge girder and lobbed it at her tormentors, mangling two Sentinels who were making a break for safety. The act of picking it up revealed a third Sentinel, who'd been hiding behind it. He was crouched in a ball, head in his arms, trembling. Bess looked down at him with a quizzical purr and booted him across the chamber.

Crake winced. He didn't like seeing her this way. She was a child, and she had a child's way with violence: thoughtless, gleeful, malevolent. Her good nature turned so easily to viciousness.

Frey and Silo scampered across the room, sniping at the retreating Sentinels. Crake stuck close to Jez and Malvery, who provided covering fire. They moved between the debris, keeping low. Crake squeezed off a shot now and then, without much expectation of hitting anything. Occasional bullets came their way, but the resistance from the Sentinels had crumbled quickly at the sight of the golem, and they were too busy running to put up much of a fight.

Bess lunged among them like a cat in a flock of pigeons, snatching up those she could. She was quick and terrible when angry. Crake saw her grab one man by the head, clamping her massive fingers round his skull and picking him up off the ground. She shook him like a doll and then, satisfied he was broken, she flung his corpse at his panicked fellows.

Frey whistled. 'This way!' he cried, beckoning them towards a doorway that led into a wide corridor.

'Why *that* way?' Malvery asked as they hurried over.

Frey looked lost for an answer. 'Just because,' he offered at length. 'Crake, call your golem, eh? She's had her fun.'

'Bess! Come on!' Crake shouted. Bess came pounding eagerly through the debris. He patted her on the shoulder and pointed up the corridor. She lumbered off, and they followed.

The smoke was thicker in the corridors, and it was hard to see more than a few dozen metres. Crake's eyes stung and he wanted to cough. Figures stumbled through the gloom ahead of them, calling out for help, asking questions, shouting orders. They fled at the sight of Bess.

The crew of the *All Our Yesterdays* was in disarray. The Awakeners didn't have the martial discipline of the Navy, or combat instincts of pirates and freebooters. They were scholars and preachers, who relied on their Sentinels for protection. This was not a craft intended for battle, and hardly anyone carried weapons or knew how to use them.

A short way along the corridor they came across a wounded man lying against the wall. He was small and bald, wearing glasses with one lens cracked. Blood leaked from a gash in his forehead, staining his collar. He wore a white cassock with red piping, the uniform of a Speaker, the Awakeners' rank and file.

Frey crouched down in front of him. The man looked up at him, dazed.

'You're carrying a special cargo,' said Frey. 'Where is it?'

The Awakener focused, and his eyes hardened as he realised who they were. 'I'll never talk. The Allsoul will protect m—'

Frey pistol-whipped him round the head with shocking speed. The man fell on his side, wailing and blubbering, holding his aching skull.

'Not doing a very good job so far,' said Frey. 'You think the Allsoul will protect you from a bullet in the ear?'

'It's that way!' the Awakener cried, pointing up the corridor.

Frey grabbed him by the collar and pulled him upright. 'Take us,' he said. He shoved the little man towards Malvery. 'Watch him, Doc.'

Malvery grinned and waved his shotgun. 'Don't think of running, now,' he advised his prisoner. Then he poked the barrel into his back. 'Lead on, mate.'

They went deeper into the craft, following their guide as he stumbled through the smoke. He was holding his head as if it would burst. People ran this way and that in the dim emergency lighting, arms over their mouths, coughing into their sleeves. Crake heard the murmur of distant flame, and once they heard an explosion that made the whole craft shiver.

The people they encountered were occupied with fighting small fires or attempting to escape. Some wandered, blank-faced and shell-shocked, through the ruination. Occasionally a Sentinel was brave or idiotic enough to stand up to the invaders, but they were gunned down in short order or pulverised by Bess.

Crake stepped over their corpses, and those of others killed in the crash. Their eyes were wide and they stared at nothing. He dry-heaved at the sight. He'd seen dead men before, but he was too delicate to take it right now. He just wanted this whole affair to be over so he could find a bed and sink into oblivion.

The smoke got worse as they went on, and soon everyone was coughing except Jez. The crackle and snap of a fire was clearly audible now, and they could feel the stifling heat of it.

Frey stopped up ahead, at a corner where a corridor branched off from theirs. He peered round and held up a hand. 'Trouble,' he warned.

Crake caught him up and looked round the corner. Through the murk, he could just about make out the obstruction. The corridor was choked with torn metal and the floor had buckled upward, forming a jumbled barricade.

'I can't see anything,' Crake said.

'When you've been shot at as often as I have, you get used to assuming the worst,' said Frey. 'They'll be waiting for us.'

Crake wiped his tearing eyes, and as he did so he thought he saw someone moving behind the barricade. But when he looked again, he wasn't sure.

Frey went to their prisoner. 'Is there another way round?' he demanded.

'This is the only way,' said the Awakener. 'It's in a room at the end of that corridor.' Frey grabbed him by the collar and glared at him, searching for a lie. 'I swear by the Allsoul!' he cried, his voice high and fearful.

Crake took sour pleasure in seeing the prisoner cringe. He hated Awakeners even more than he hated overprivileged layabouts like Hodd. Them and their ridiculous faith, based on the thoroughly insane ramblings of the last king of Vardia. It would be comical if it weren't for the fact that half of the population believed in their rubbish. It was the Awakeners who championed the persecution of daemonists. Many good men and women had been hanged because of them.

Frey shoved the man away, having evidently decided he was telling the truth. 'Get out of here,' he said. The prisoner needed no second invitation.

Jez looked around the corner at the barricade, then back at her captain. 'Full frontal assault?' she suggested cheerily.

Frey sighed. 'Why not?' He slapped Bess on the shoulder. 'You first, old girl.'

Bess thundered off with a roar. Bullets and screams greeted her as she piled into the barricade like a battering ram.

'That's stirred 'em up,' Malvery grinned.

'You have to admit, she's effective,' Frey said, loading his revolver.

'Are we going to help her at all?' Jez asked.

Frey snapped the drum closed. 'Let her mop up a bit first.' He counted off a few seconds, listening to the wails of Bess's unfortunate victims. 'Now.'

They ran for the barricade, cloaked by the smoke. Crake stayed low, slipping along the side of the wide corridor, mouth dry and throat tight. He was worse than useless in a firefight, but he couldn't leave Bess to do it alone.

Bess was already over the barricade by the time Frey and the others reached it. They scrambled between the twisted girders and plates of ripped metal, shooting at anyone the golem had missed. Crake heard more guns on the other side. He came across a man who'd been impaled by Bess, a spike through his guts, still horribly alive. Silo pushed past and put him out of his misery with a shotgun.

He saw Jez, aiming and firing up the barricade through the smoke. A figure at the top jerked like a marionette and fell backwards. Bess was roaring somewhere out of sight, and men shrieked and swore. Blood pounded in Crake's head. He saw a figure scrambling along the barricade, aimed, and almost fired before Silo grabbed his hand and pushed it down.

'It's the Doc,' he grunted, and then headed up the slope.

Crake squinted, and saw that Silo was right. He slumped against a girder, overwhelmed with relief. *Stupid! Stupid!* He'd almost shot a friend.

Then he saw a movement, behind them, someone hiding in the rubble that they'd passed. He was squatting, his eye to a rifle, aiming upslope.

Crake couldn't see well enough to know who it was, but the rifle gave them away. None of his companions carried rifles. He thrust out his arm with a yell and emptied his revolver in their general direction. The Sentinel flinched as bullets sparked off the barricade all around him. Then, rather surprised at finding himself unhurt, he switched his aim towards Crake.

A shotgun blast, deafeningly close to Crake's ear. The Sentinel flailed and disappeared.

Silo emerged through the murk, eyes bright in his narrow, beak-nosed face. He gave Crake a strange look, then grabbed him by the arm and propelled him up the slope to the crest.

Beyond the barricade was another barricade. The corridor had compressed like a concertina, leaving a narrow, junk-strewn battlefield between. Corpses lay here and there. Bess was busy making more. Frey, Malvery and Jez hid among the debris, picking off the Sentinels as they fled from the golem's wrath. Beyond the second barricade, the red glow of flames could be seen. Thick black smoke roiled along the ceiling.

Silo pushed Crake down as bullets came their way, and they began to creep through the forest of tangled metal. The heat and smoke at the crest were too much to stand for more than a few seconds. Crake tried to shoot at a fleeing Sentinel, but his gun clicked empty. He found a sheltered spot and fumbled some more bullets into the drum while Silo blasted away.

Then, all at once, the fear hit.

It came from nowhere, overwhelming, clawing at his throat, robbing him of breath. It was thick enough that it seemed like a physical weight, crushing him to the floor. He wanted to scream and run, but he couldn't move. He stared this way and that, eyes wide and desperate, filled with primal dread. To his right, he saw that Silo had been similarly affected. He was huddled down like a rabbit in the shadow of a hawk.

What's happening to us?

The makeshift battlefield had gone silent. Crake folded trembling fingers round the edge of his shelter and peered out.

There was a figure standing on the crest of the second set of battlements, backlit by the restless glow of the fire. It was cloaked, hooded and masked, dressed head to toe in close-fitting black leather. Crake felt his stomach knot into a ball at the sight.

An Imperator. One of the Awakeners' deadly elite. Men who could read your thoughts, who could scour a mind clean with their terrible gaze. The ultimate inquisitors.

Spit and blood. We're all dead meat.

The Imperator came walking unhurriedly down the slope of the barricade. The Sentinels were all gone now, dead at the hands of Bess or her allies, but the Imperator was not troubled at being outnumbered. No one dared to raise a gun to him. They were all afflicted with the same awful fear.

He was heading for the spot where Frey hid. Crake saw his captain go scrambling away on his hands and knees, shaking his head, begging incoherently. The Imperator drew a long black knife from his belt and walked relentlessly onward.

There was a screech of metal, and Crake's gaze went to Bess, who was pulling aside a girder that was in her way. She was not crippled by fear like the rest of them, it seemed, but only bewildered by the sudden end to the violence. Seeing the Imperator advancing on Frey, she went lumbering in to attack.

The Imperator held up a dismissive hand. Bess froze, mid-stride, and toppled over with a crash. She didn't move again.

The sight was like a punch in the chest to Crake. He wanted to scream her name, but no noise would come. What had been done to her? Why wasn't she moving? Had she been put to sleep, the way he put her to sleep with his thralled whistle? Or had she been extinguished, like a candle? The thought that he might forever lose the chance to save his niece, to atone for his crime – it was more than he could possibly suffer. If that was the case, he'd rather die now.

The Imperator turned his black gaze to Frey, pinning him like an insect. Frey rolled over on his back, whimpering. The Imperator put his boot to Frey's chest and shoved him down. He leaned over his victim, knife raised.

A gunshot made Crake jump. The Imperator staggered sideways, clutching his shoulder. Another, knocking the black-clad figure back further.

Jez, getting to her feet, pistol in her hand. Jez, and yet not Jez. There was a strange look to her now. Her usually pale face had gone paler still. Her hair hung lank, eyes dark, lips skinned back over her teeth, a snarl on her face. Something animal in the way she moved, slightly crouched. Feral.

The Imperator straightened. The bullets hadn't harmed him. Jez pulled the trigger again, but the gun was empty. She tossed it aside, and as she did so, she *flickered*. One moment she was there, the next she was half a metre to her left, and the next she was back again. Quick enough to be a trick of the eye. But Crake saw it.

I knew it, he thought. *I knew it all along.*

The Imperator's grip on Crake's mind had weakened. The paranoia, the nameless horror, receded to bearable levels. In some distant, rational part of his mind, he found he *recognised* this feeling of horror that the Imperator inspired. In a strange way, it was familiar to him. He'd come across it before, to a lesser degree, in his experiments. It was the feeling of being close to something *wrong*. The body's instinctive reaction to something not of this world.

What manner of man is this?

The Imperator backed away from Jez, blade in his hand. Frey scrambled off gratefully to cringe in a new hiding place. Jez prowled closer to the Imperator, her gaze fixed on him. Nothing physical had changed about her, but her *aspect* was different. Where once there had been a petite woman in a baggy jumpsuit, now there was something fearful. Something inhuman, alien. A creature that wore the shape of their navigator.

The Imperator was intimidated by her, his dark grandeur diminished. He readied his blade as she moved closer. Then, when she was close enough, he lunged.

Jez flickered. Suddenly, she seemed to be in three places at once: before him, beside him, behind him, flitting from one position to the next in the time it took to blink an eye. The Imperator's thrust hit nothing; Jez sprang on to him from his left, hands clutching the masked head. Her weight took him down to the ground. She smashed his skull twice against the floor, the second time accompanied by a grotesque crack. Then she tore his head off.

The effect was immediate. It was as if Crake had been gripped by an invisible hand, squeezing his chest, and now it had been released. He gasped like a drowning man reaching the surface. Next to him, Silo was experiencing similar relief.

It had an effect on Jez, too. She stood up and staggered backwards, the Imperator's head dangling from one hand. There was an expression of bewilderment on her face, a look of shock and fear. No longer was she the feral thing they'd seen a moment ago. Now she was small, and scared. She stumbled for a few moments, and then her eyes rolled back and she fell to the ground.

Crake hung on to a girder, letting the strength seep back into his body. The choking smoke and murk was getting thicker by the moment, but he breathed it anyway, and coughed. It was worth it, to be alive.

Frey and Malvery were getting to their feet. They approached Jez carefully, as though she were a dangerous beast that might spring up and lunge at them. Already they were afraid of her. They'd seen the other side of their navigator, and nothing would ever be the same after that.

Damn it, Jez, he thought. *Sooner or later they had to find out. But I wish they hadn't seen you this way. I wish you'd told them first.*

Then his thoughts went to Bess, lying motionless on the battlefield, and he scrambled to his feet to help her.

Twenty-One

A Retreat – Uncertainties – The Interpreter –
Frey Stands His Ground – Down To Earth

'Get him off me! Get him off my tail!'

A chatter of machine guns, and the night was full of tracer fire, ripping past Harkins' cockpit. He banked and dived, squealing all the way, and by some miracle he didn't catch any of it.

'Will you shut your meat-hole, Harkins?' said the voice in his ear. 'I can't bloody think with you shrieking like a pansy.'

Pinn. How he hated Pinn. Of all the men and women and small furry animals that mocked and humiliated him, Pinn was the worst. Well, except for the cat. He'd rather have Pinn than the cat.

'What's there to think about? Just shoot him!' Harkins cried. He twisted in his seat, trying to locate his pursuer.

There was no sign. Hard to see anything in a storm like this. The Equaliser was probably somewhere in his blind spot, anyway. He went into a steep climb and rolled to starboard. A smattering of bullets chased after him through the rain.

'Pinn? Pinn? Stop scratching your fat arse and help me!'

There was a dull boom, and the windglass of his cockpit lit up with reflected flame. He looked behind him and saw the unfurling flower of a mid-air explosion, yellow against the night. The Skylance went spinning past, its pilot whooping in triumph.

'That's five for me!' Pinn said. 'How many have *you* got, eh?'

Harkins slumped back in his seat and mopped his face with his sleeve. His heart was kicking against his thin ribs and his gorge had risen dangerously high.

'Three, I think,' he said weakly.

'Hah!'

He couldn't care less how many he'd shot down. All he cared about was that he was still breathing. His life was a miserable affair for the most part, scurrying through the shadows of other men, ignored or derided by everyone. But all the same, he clung to it with a fierce grip. Death was even scarier than life was.

Lightning flickered, illuminating the moors beneath. Harkins scanned the sky for potential threats. All he could see was the motley of aircraft that formed the *Storm Dog*'s squadron of outflyers.

'The *Delirium Trigger*'s pulling out!' Pinn yelled suddenly. 'Look! Dracken's running, that pasty-faced chickenshit bitch!'

Harkins banked to bring the frigates into view and saw that Pinn was right. The *Delirium Trigger* had broken off from the *Storm Dog* and was rising towards the clouds. The other was making no attempt to pursue. Both craft were battered and blasted, leaking smoke and flame. The Equalisers were scattering across the plain, racing away in different directions, no doubt to rendezvous at some pre-arranged location.

Harkins gave a broad smile at the sight. The battle was over! He'd made it through!

'Cap'n!' he said. 'Cap'n, did you hear that?' There was no reply. 'Jez?' he inquired tentatively, his voice softening.

'Jez? Jez?' Pinn mimicked in a simper. 'They're not listening. Must've taken out their earcuffs. Probably sick of hearing a grown man squeal.'

Harkins bit his lip. *Don't rise to it. That's what he wants.* But it still hurt.

Once, he'd been a Navy pilot, and his nerve had been as strong as anyone's. What if Jez had met him then, uniformed and proud? He'd always been awkward and highly strung, never quite at ease in his own skin, but he'd been more of a man back then. At least until his comrades started dying in the Aerium Wars. Until he'd been shot down that first time, and then twice more. Until the miraculous escapes began to add up.

If Harkins had been an optimist, he might have thought himself a lucky man. He'd survived dozens of dogfights and got out of scrapes that left his companions dead in his wake. But he was no optimist. Instead, he fretted about how much luck he could possibly have left, and when it was finally going to run out.

Not tonight, though. Not tonight.

Flying was all he knew how to do, but if he had his way, he'd never fight again. All he wanted was an aircraft of his own, and the wide blue sky to fly in. Just to soar for ever. There would be no one to make him feel small. Just him and the sun and the air. He wouldn't ask for anything more.

Well, maybe *one* thing more. Maybe someone to share it with. Someone he trusted to be kind to him.

Jez, he thought. *I wonder what she's doing now?*

'Jez?' said Frey tentatively.

She wasn't moving. She lay on the ground next to the decapitated corpse of the Imperator, face down, her hair across her cheek. Frey crept up to her and gave her a poke with the toe of his boot.

'She's not going to bite you, Cap'n,' said Malvery, in the tone of someone who didn't much fancy finding out the truth of that statement for himself.

'How do you know?' Frey asked. 'You saw what happened! She ripped the Imperator's head off with her bare damn hands! One moment she was there, the next she was somewhere else! What *was* that?'

'That was Jez, and she saved our lives,' said Silo. 'Ain't the first time, neither.'

'That,' said Frey, pointing at her, '*wasn't* Jez.'

'Ain't the time nor the place, Cap'n,' said Silo. He picked up the navigator's limp body and slung her over his shoulder like a sack of potatoes. 'Let's get done here and go.'

But Frey couldn't shake the memory of her, feral and snarling, that terrifying look in her eyes. That wasn't anyone he recognised. She'd *changed*.

Crake was at Bess's side. The golem was stirring, to Crake's evident relief. He was tearing up, and not just from the smoke. Well, at least they hadn't lost anyone. At least there was that.

But could he ever look at Jez in the same way again? Would he be able to fly, knowing she was at the navigator's station behind him?

The Imperator's head lay a short distance away. The smooth mask had come loose, and was hanging off. Frey walked over to it. 'Keep an eye out for any more Sentinels,' he told his crew.

'Cap'n,' said Malvery, a warning in his voice.

'I've dealt with these Imperator bastards before,' Frey said, as if that was an explanation. The truth was, he was angry. This was the second time he'd been unmanned by an Imperator, forced to cower in fear like a whipped dog. He wanted to see the face under the mask. Somehow, he thought it would lessen his fear of them.

He was wrong. When he pushed the mask aside with the barrel of his revolver, the face beneath was enough to make him recoil with a shout. The cheeks and eyes were sunken, irises yellow like a bird of prey. The mouth was stretched open as if in a scream, showing sharp, uneven teeth in receding gums. White, dry skin; the septum of the nose rotted away. It looked like something you'd uncover in a grave.

'Blimey,' said Malvery. 'Someone needs to eat their greens.'

Frey screwed up his face in disgust and looked closer. A stump of a tongue, cut out at the root, showed between cracked lips. There was only a spotting of blood on the floor, despite the brutal nature of the Imperator's death.

'That,' said Frey, 'is not natural.' He turned away and looked at Jez, who was hanging over Silo's shoulder. 'Can anyone enlighten me as to what in buggery just happened to my navigator, by the way?'

'She's a Mane,' said Crake, coughing. 'Partly, anyway. I suppose she wasn't fully infected.'

'You *knew*?'

'I guessed. Not long after she first came on board. No heartbeat, no need to eat, all of that. There've been other half-Manes, you know. They've come up in daemonist texts. Like I told you, there's always been a school of thought that said Manes were daemons. And really, what other explanation was there?'

'I was trying not to think about it too much, to be honest,' Frey said. 'I didn't think she was a *Mane*, though.'

'Because you lot don't know anything about them, outside of the drunken tales you hear in bars.'

'Fair comment,' said Malvery. 'We are a pretty thick bunch, all in all.'

'You're supposed to be a doctor,' Frey accused. 'That makes you smart.'

Malvery shrugged. 'I bring up the average. It still ain't great.'

'You do have Pinn on board,' Crake pointed out.

Frey waved his hands. 'Alright, alright! We'll sort this whole bloody mess out later. Malvery, you're with me. Crake, stay with Silo and

Bess. Make sure nobody comes up behind us. Let's get what we came for and hoof it before Grist gets wind that we're planning to rob him.'

Beyond the barricade were scattered heaps of debris, and beyond them the corridor was aflame. Slicks of inflammable fluid sent up hazy curtains of black, foul-smelling smoke. Frey could dimly make out a doorway through the debris, uncomfortably close to the fire.

'You think that's where our sphere is?' Malvery coughed.

'One way to find out,' said Frey. He hurried through the steaming debris, his arm over his face to shield him from the heat. By the time he got to the doorway, it was too painful to be cautious, so he just ran right in and hoped nobody would shoot him.

The heat lessened to a tolerable degree once he was inside. It was a small store room, with shelves of chests and rolls of documents that were getting dangerously close to bursting into flame. A large lockbox in the centre stood open and empty.

Malvery hurried in after him, swearing as his moustache singed. He looked around the room, then grabbed Frey's arm and turned him.

'Wakey wakey, eh, Cap'n?' he said, pointing.

There was an elderly man huddled in the corner of the room, propped against the wall. Frey hadn't seen him. He was wearing Awakener robes, but they were not the white of the Speakers or the grey of the Sentinels, but crimson. That made him an Interpreter, according to Crake. Only one level below the Grand Oracles in the Awakeners' organisation. An important man, then.

A long brown beard tumbled over his chest, almost concealing the sphere he held in his bony hands. Blood ran from his nose and stained his lips. His eyes focused in and out uncertainly beneath the Cipher tattooed on his brow.

'Doesn't look good for him, Cap'n,' Malvery murmured. 'Probably got knocked around in the crash. Broke something inside him.'

'How did . . . ?' the old man said. 'The Imperator . . .'

Frey crouched down in front of him, arms crossed over his knees, looking him over. He tutted. 'You shouldn't play with daemons, you know.'

The Interpreter's eyes widened. Enough to tell Frey that Crake's theory was right. Frey put his hand out expectantly. 'I believe you have something of mine.'

The old man clutched the sphere closer to his body. His gaze became baleful. 'How dare you? Damn thieves!'

'You stole it first,' Frey said.

'You don't know . . .' the Interpreter began, then dissolved into violent coughing. Something rattled inside him with every breath. Blood glistened on his beard. 'You don't know what . . .'

'Alright, alright,' said Frey, holding up his hands. 'Easy, old man.'

'You're meddling with forces you don't understand!' he snarled.

'That?' asked Frey, looking at the sphere. 'I understand a lot of people want it. That makes it valuable.'

'It's more than valuable, you fool! Do you know what would happen if it fell into the wrong hands?'

'Far as I'm concerned, it's already in the wrong hands,' said Frey. He grabbed the sphere and pulled it out of the Interpreter's feeble grip. The old man spluttered in outrage, and then he began to cough again, more violently than before.

'Hey!' said Frey, backing off. 'Calm down, eh? You're not in great shape there. Think of your health, or something.'

'Thousands . . .' the old man said, clawing at Frey's trouser leg. 'Thousands will die!'

Frey didn't like the sound of that at all. 'What does *that* mean?' he demanded.

The Interpreter had gone red in the face, his eyes bulging like they were going to pop out of his head. His coughs had become long, painful wheezes, horrible to hear.

Frey grabbed him by the shoulder and shook him. 'Hey! Hey! What did you mean, *thousands will die*? What *is* the sphere?'

'Thousands . . .' the Interpreter whispered. Then he gave one last, rattling breath and slumped to the floor.

Frey let out a little scream of frustration through gritted teeth. Malvery squatted down, felt for a pulse, lifted up the Interpreter's head and looked into his eyes. Then he let the head drop unceremoniously to the floor with a dull thud.

'Dead,' Malvery said.

'Oh, really?' Frey snapped. 'Is that your professional opinion?'

'Don't get ratty with me. I'm just doing my job.'

'Couldn't the old bastard have hung on for a few more sentences before he croaked?'

Malvery slapped him on the shoulder. 'Tough luck, Cap'n. We got what we came for, at least. Let's get going. All this smoke can't be good for us.'

Frey stared at the body of the Interpreter, hearing his final words over and over again. *Thousands will die.*

He had the unpleasant feeling that they'd drifted far, far out of their depth.

When they got outside, the *Storm Dog* was waiting for them.

She'd put down on the moors, a short distance from the *All Our Yesterdays*. She was scarred and battered, bearing signs of heavy cannon damage. Her crew were busy rounding up the evacuating Awakeners, who were surrendering without much resistance now that the *Delirium Trigger* had abandoned them. The prisoners stood in a loose group under guard, miserable and sodden in the rain.

Frey cursed at the sight of Grist, who was striding towards them with a few of his men. He'd hoped Trinica would keep Grist busy long enough for him to make a break for it with the sphere. In fact, he'd rather hoped they'd blow each other out of the sky. He belatedly realised that he should have kept his earcuff in, so Harkins and Pinn could keep him informed. He'd been relying on Jez to relay information, but she was in no state to relay anything right now.

They scrambled down the earthen bank that had piled up around the *All Our Yesterdays* and met Grist at the bottom. He was accompanied by Crattle and two others that Frey didn't recognise.

'Cap'n Frey!' Grist grinned, showing yellow teeth around the stub of a cigar. The rain had extinguished it, but he kept it in his mouth anyway. 'Pleased to see you're well.'

'Likewise,' Frey lied. 'You took care of the *Delirium Trigger*?'

'She turned tail and ran,' Grist declared proudly. He gestured at Jez, who was slung over Silo's shoulder. 'One of yours down, eh?'

'She'll live,' said Frey.

'I'll wager she will,' said Grist. 'I bet she heals real quick, don't she?' He walked over to Silo and picked up one of Jez's limp and dangling hands. 'After all, she took an arrow through this palm not two weeks past, and it's good as new.'

Frey didn't like the knowing tone in his voice.

'It'd be terrible to lose someone who reads the wind as well as she does,' Grist said. 'She put us right on top of the *Delirium Trigger*, flying blind. That's something special.'

'She's a talented woman,' said Frey.

Grist held her wrist for a moment, then turned to Frey with an expression of mock surprise. 'Why, Cap'n. She don't have a pulse. I reckon she's dead!'

Frey had had enough. 'We're taking her to the infirmary.' He tried to leave, but Grist blocked him with a calloused and smoke-yellowed hand.

'Whoa, there, Cap'n. Aren't you forgettin' somethin'?' His gaze drifted to the sphere, cradled in Frey's arm. He had that hungry look again.

'I'll hold on to this,' said Frey. 'Just until we sell it. Fifty-fifty, remember, *partner?*'

Crattle and the other men raised their pistols.

'Oh, I don't think it's gonna work that way,' said Grist.

Bess growled and stirred, but Crattle's pistol was trained on Crake. He primed the hammer with a click. 'Tell your beast if it makes a move, you'll have a chestful of lead,' the bosun said.

'She gets it,' said Crake, holding up his hands. 'Don't you, Bess?' Bess subsided with a rustle of leather and chain mail. A sinister sing-song echoed up from deep within her. It sounded like a threat.

Frey stared at Grist hard. He'd seen it coming. Seen it coming, and been unable to do a damned thing about it. His men were hopelessly outnumbered by the *Storm Dog*'s crew. He should never have got tangled up with this man. He should have listened to sense and turned his back after Grist killed Hodd.

'What is the sphere?' he asked. 'What is it, really?'

Grist just grinned. 'It's mine,' he said. He held out his hand. When Frey was still reluctant to give it up, he said, 'Wouldn't be wise to make me ask again.'

Frey offered him the sphere, bitterly. That little ball of black metal, its surface marked with swirling curves and arcs of silver. The cause of all his trouble. He'd gone through so much to get that thing, and then to reclaim it, and he still didn't know what it was.

Do you know what would happen if it fell into the wrong hands?
Thousands will die.

Grist took it. Lightning flickered and thunder boomed. He narrowed his eyes and looked at Frey, rain dripping from his heavy brow. Then he pulled out his pistol from his belt and levelled it at Frey.

'A smart man don't leave his enemies behind to take revenge,' he said.

Frey thumbed at Bess. 'A smart man would realise that us being alive is the only thing stopping that eight-foot monster from putting her arm down your throat and pulling your guts out through your mouth.'

Grist looked Bess up and down. 'Aye. You make a good point.' He motioned towards Jez with the barrel of his gun. 'But we'll be takin' your navigator, if you don't mind.'

'What do you want *her* for?' Frey asked, then remembered to add, 'Besides, she's dead.'

'I think we both know that she ain't as dead as she seems, Cap'n Frey,' said Grist. 'Don't we?'

How does he know that? Frey thought. But he never got the chance to ask. There was a short shriek of incoming artillery, and then a terrific blast, big enough to light up the night and make Frey stumble with the concussion.

'The *Delirium Trigger*!' someone shouted. 'She's back!'

Grist swore loudly. 'That mad bloody whore! Don't she know when she's beaten?'

The crew of the *Storm Dog* fled back towards their craft as the *Delirium Trigger* sank through the clouds, her remaining guns firing at the grounded *Storm Dog*. Geysers of soil rained down on the scattering Awakeners. The earth shivered with the force of the detonations.

'Your navvie!' Grist said, snarling. He was no longer quite so jovial as he thrust his pistol at Silo. 'Give her over. Now!'

Silo just stared at him and made no attempt to move.

'You got what you came for,' Frey said. Grist took a step towards her, but Frey put his hand on his chest to stop him. Grist stared at the hand, and then at Frey, in amazement.

'Dead or alive, she's one of my crew, Grist. You're not having her.'

Grist was almost quivering with fury. 'Cap'n!' said his bosun. 'There's no time!'

Grist looked over at Bess, then back at Frey. There was raw hatred in his gaze. 'You thank your stars for that tin guardian of yours,' he growled, and then he turned and ran for his craft. Crattle backed off a few steps, keeping them covered with his gun, and then he ran too.

Frey briefly thought about chasing after them, or at least shooting Grist in the back, but it was foolish. There were two dozen of the *Storm Dog*'s men running towards their craft. No way his crew could get through a firefight like that without one of them dying, not even with Bess on their side.

'Back to the *Ketty Jay*!' he said. They sprinted through the long grass towards their aircraft. Rain lashed at their faces. Pounding concussions came from all around them. The *Storm Dog* was returning fire on the *Delirium Trigger*, but it was an easy target until it got into the air. A hole was blasted in its keel as the *Delirium Trigger* scored a direct hit.

Frey dug his silver earcuff out of his pocket and clipped it to his ear.

'—oody Equalisers coming from everywhere!' Pinn was yelling. 'Sons of bitches doubled back and the *Storm Dog*'s outflyers are all docked up inside her!'

'Harkins! Pinn!'

'Cap'n!' said Harkins, perilously close to hysteria. 'We've been . . . that is . . . I mean . . . Where've you *been*? Is Jez okay?'

'Listen up!' Frey snapped. 'Hightail it, both of you. You won't last two minutes against that many Equalisers.'

'You sure?' asked Pinn.

'Yes! Get to the rendezvous! We'll be right behind you.'

'See you later, then.'

By the time they reached the *Ketty Jay*, the *Storm Dog* was rising from the ground, thrusters already lit to push her forward. The *Delirium Trigger* was coming in fast, guns blazing. All the artillery was focused on the *Storm Dog*. The *Ketty Jay* was either unnoticed or considered unimportant. Either was fine with Frey.

He raced up the cargo ramp and headed for the cockpit. Malvery came panting along behind him while the rest of them bundled into the hold. The craft rocked with the force of nearby explosions as he flung himself into the pilot's seat, punched in the ignition code and boosted the aerium engines to maximum. She rose on her struts with the usual chorus of groans and squeaks, and lifted herself off the ground.

Malvery hurried into the cockpit, red-faced and sweating. 'Anything I can do?'

'Just hold on tight!' Frey said. Malvery clung to the doorframe and squeezed his eyes shut as Frey shoved the thrusters to maximum.

Nothing happened. Frey tried again. Still nothing. The *Ketty Jay* was gliding upward into the storm, but she had no way to push herself forward. The thrusters wouldn't light. The engines had finally broken down on him.

Malvery opened one eye. 'Did we escape?' he asked.

'Silo!' Frey yelled. 'Get up here!'

But it was too late. The cockpit flooded with blinding whiteness. Three Equalisers hove into view, their machine guns trained on him, lights shining.

'I think they've got us covered, Cap'n,' said Malvery.

'I think so too,' said Frey. He vented aerium until the *Ketty Jay* was heavier than air again. She stopped rising and began to sink gently to the ground.

In the distance he could see the *Storm Dog* lumbering away towards the rumbling clouds. The *Delirium Trigger* was harrying her the whole way, but it wasn't enough to stop her. He watched the *Storm Dog* disappear into the storm. With her went the sphere he'd worked so hard to obtain. Stolen from him. Again.

'Bugger,' said Malvery.

'Bugger,' Frey agreed, and they came down to earth with a bump.

Twenty-Two

Captive – Best Of Enemies –
Jez Awakes – Crake's Announcement

'Darian, Darian, Darian,' said Trinica Dracken, as if to a way-ward child. 'What am I going to do with you?'

She was wearing a slight, contemplative smile. Lightning flickered outside: sharp shadows lunged across her ghost-white face.

Frey leaned back in his chair and took an idle survey of her cabin. Brass and dark wood. Electric lights, set low. A bookcase with novels and manuals and maps. Foreign titles were mixed in among them. Trinica had been schooled in Samarlan and Thacian from a young age. The advantages of a privileged upbringing, Frey supposed.

'You could start by giving me back all the money you stole from me outside Retribution Falls,' he suggested. Then he grinned. 'On second thoughts, keep it. It'll just about cover the damage to your aircraft.'

Trinica sat behind her desk, next to a cracked window of reinforced windglass. The cabin had been tidied and cleaned before his arrival – Trinica liked to be neat – but she couldn't disguise all the evidence of the pounding the *Delirium Trigger* had taken. Outside in the corridor there were the sounds of running feet, and the air smelled of burnt oil.

'You shouldn't have robbed me,' said Frey. 'I let you off the first time, on account of our previous good feeling towards each other. But twice? Not a chance.'

She gave a derisive snort. 'Yes, Darian. Grist has run off with your treasure and your crew is languishing in my brig. You've certainly come out on top this time.'

'You didn't do so well yourself.'

'I'll survive.'

'So will I.'

'Ah, but that's *my* decision now, isn't it?' she said. Her black eyes hardened. 'You've inconvenienced me greatly.'

Frey made a *do-I-look-like-I-care* face. 'I didn't ask you to get involved. Actually, I seem to recall *I* had the sphere first.'

'You've cost me men and fighter craft. *Good* men, some of them.'

'Oh, piss off with your threats, Trinica,' Frey snapped. He was suddenly irritated at her. Just the sight of her wound him up. 'What would *you* have done? You robbed me *again*.'

'I rather expected you to chalk it up to experience and move on,' she said.

'Well, you expected wrong,' he said sullenly. 'I thought you'd have learned by now: you don't know me half as well as you think you do.'

He tapped his fingers on the arm of his seat. Impatient, agitated. It was hard to keep his cool around her. She had a way of making him lose his temper. It frustrated him. He could be the soul of charm around other women, but her mere presence was enough to have him behaving like a surly adolescent.

'I wish you'd scrape that shit off your face,' he said at length. 'You always had great skin.'

Trinica made a distracted noise of agreement. 'I did take very good care of myself, back then. You remember my dressing table, I'm sure. Groaning under the weight of my cosmetics.'

'You'd spend an hour making yourself look like you weren't wearing make-up.'

'It's easy to become obsessed with the unimportant, when nothing you do means anything.'

Frey made a sweeping gesture to indicate the *Delirium Trigger*. 'And this does?'

'Oh yes. The power of life and death. I'm *very* important to you right now.'

Frey couldn't argue with that, but he didn't like to concede the point. He was still bitter about the way she'd snubbed him back on Kurg.

Trinica was watching the rain pouring down the outside of the window. The storm had eased and the sky had lightened a fraction. It was nearing dawn. Frey had spent hours in the brig, awaiting an audience. The second night he'd had without sleep. He needed a big dose of Shine and a day-long nap.

'The Awakeners are baying for your blood,' she said. 'They're not at all happy about what you did to their aircraft. I gather your golem notched up quite a bodycount in there.'

Frey shrugged, picking at the arm of his seat with a fingernail. 'I gave them a chance to surrender,' he said. Then he looked up. 'What are you doing working for the Awakeners again? Don't tell me you're starting to believe that junk about the Allsoul?'

Trinica laughed: a cold, humourless cascade. 'Please, Darian. Me, a warrior of the Allsoul? It was money. Just money. They pay extraordinarily well for someone reliable and discreet. And they were very impressed with the work I did for Duke Grephen on their behalf.'

'As I recall, that didn't work out too well for Grephen.'

Trinica tilted her head, staring at him curiously, as if she'd only just noticed him. 'He paid me to catch you. I caught you. What happened afterwards was no concern of mine.'

Frey didn't want to hash out the past any more than he had to. 'So the Awakeners hired you again. Presumably so they wouldn't get their hands dirty?'

'They were very keen that their involvement was known to nobody except me.'

'What's their interest in the sphere?'

'I didn't ask,' she said.

Frey waited expectantly. When she said nothing more, he prompted her. 'Come on. You must know something. Indulge my curiosity. It's not like it makes any difference now.'

Trinica considered that for a moment, and evidently decided he was right. 'They told me an explorer named Hodd had approached one of their faithful, a rich patron called Jethin Mame. He came begging money for an expedition to Kurg to find a crashed aircraft. Mame sent him away, but eventually it was mentioned to someone important at a party somewhere, and the Awakeners suddenly became interested.'

'Enter Trinica,' said Frey.

'I admit, I didn't think much of it. Sounded like a fool's errand to me, and they were only offering to pay on delivery. I didn't think I'd find anything, so I wasn't prepared to waste my time.'

'What changed your mind?'

'You, my dear Darian,' she said. 'The Awakeners had their spies hard at work. By the time they contacted me, they'd already heard of Grist. They knew Hodd was with him, and they knew he'd been asking about for you.'

'And you just couldn't resist.'

'I do like to be a torment,' she admitted. 'And it really was very easy. Hodd had told Mame where the landing site was. When I arrived, you were already there. So I thought I'd wait and let you do the work.'

Frey had to restrain himself from picking a book off the shelf and flinging it at her. A heavy one, with sharp corners.

'Haven't you had enough of revenge yet?' he asked.

'Not while you're alive,' she said. 'Speaking of which: give me one reason why I shouldn't kill you.'

Frey recognised that line. He'd asked her that very same question in Mortengrace, Duke Grephen's stronghold, with a sword at her throat. Part of him wished he'd done her in then, but another part – some absurd, ridiculous part – was glad he hadn't.

Damn, he hated her. But damn, how he loved to do it.

He sat back in his chair and folded his arms. 'We both know you won't kill me. There's no point to it. The sphere is gone. You've already been paid for its delivery, I assume. So where's the profit?' He raised an eyebrow. 'Besides, you'd miss me.'

Trinica laughed, and it was genuine this time. Frey knew the difference. This one made him feel warm. 'You're remarkably sure of yourself these days,' she said. 'And what about my men who were killed? The damage you've done?'

'It's all in the game, Trinica,' he said. 'You don't get to be a terror of the skies without taking a few knocks. You know that; don't pretend you don't. Besides, it was mostly Grist, if you think about it.'

'No doubt you had a hand in it.'

'No doubt I did. Tell you what: forget killing me for a minute. I've a proposition.'

Trinica raised an eyebrow. 'A proposition? And such a strong bargaining position you have. I can hardly wait.'

Frey took a mental deep breath. It was a proposition, alright. A plan that Frey had formulated during those few hours he'd spent in the *Delirium Trigger*'s brig. Usually, he'd discuss his ideas with his crew, but this one he kept to himself. He knew what they'd say. He could see a hundred ways in which it was a bad idea. And yet, he'd been itching to tell Trinica ever since he'd walked into her cabin. It had taken an effort to stop himself blurting it out the moment he sat down.

She's a snake, Darian. Just remember that. It doesn't matter what you once had. The way she was at Kurg, that shows how much she thinks of you. She'll turn on you if you let her.

'The way I see it, we have no reason to fight. But we do have a common enemy. And he has something we both want.'

Lightning flashed and slow thunder rolled outside. Trinica leaned forward over her desk. She made a cradle with her knitted fingers and rested her chin in it. 'Darian,' she said, amused. 'You're surely not suggesting we join forces? After all we've done to each other?'

'You and me,' said Frey. 'We'll find Grist and get that sphere back.'

'And why would I want to do that, if I've already been paid for retrieving it?'

'Because you're the dreaded pirate Trinica Dracken, and Grist just gave you a lashing like you haven't had in years. Your crew will talk. The moment this craft gets into dock, everyone's going to know how the *Storm Dog* beat you.'

The slightest flicker of anger passed over Trinica's face.

Gotcha, he thought.

'I make it a month at least before the *Delirium Trigger*'s up and ready for a fight again, even at the best workshops in the land,' Frey said. 'Grist's trail will be cold by then. But the *Ketty Jay* can be running in a matter of hours. Soon as we get some new windglass for the cupola and Silo gets his hands on that bloody engine.' He paused for a moment to let that sink in. 'The *Ketty Jay* can't take on the *Storm Dog*. But the *Delirium Trigger* can. And with me on your side, next time it'll be *you* who has the element of surprise.'

She watched him carefully, sizing him up. Her contact lenses made her irises black, turning her pupils huge. An illusion calculated to intimidate and unsettle. But Frey knew what colour her eyes were, underneath.

'You'll never find him without me,' he said. 'And I'll never beat him without you. I know the man and you don't. I need your contacts, you need my aircraft. If we pool our resources, if we get going right away . . . well, we might just catch that son of a bitch.'

Trinica unfolded, lounging back into her chair, spreading across it.

Her mannerisms were different to the girl Frey remembered. Odder. Her moods slipped from playful to maudlin to angry. One minute she was mumming horror, the next she was genuinely wrathful. A powerful leader, a cruel killer, then a child. Fractured states of mind, reflections in a broken mirror.

He knew that something must have cracked inside her at some point. Had it been when he jilted her on their wedding day? After her failed suicide attempt? After she lost their baby? Or in the years of horror that followed, as a brutalised concubine on board various pirate craft? No way of knowing. But he'd set her on that road. It hurt him to think of it.

'You're suggesting that I travel with you on the *Ketty Jay*?' asked Trinica.

'Just until the *Delirium Trigger* is fixed.'

'Darian, do you really think you're being wise?'

'When have I ever been wise?'

It was true that he had his doubts about whether they could stand each other for several weeks, but he was certain of one thing. He needed her. Whatever his feelings, or hers, this was too important.

Thousands will die.

'Do you know what that sphere does?' he asked.

'No,' she said. 'If anyone does, it would be a high-ranking Awakener. But thanks to your elegant work in bringing their aircraft down, all the high-ranking Awakeners on the *All Our Yesterdays* are dead.'

'One of them wasn't,' said Frey. 'He told me something. "Thousands will die," he said. I'm not certain what that sphere is, but it came from a Mane dreadnought, so I'm pretty sure it's gonna end up being bad news. I'm also sure that Grist knows exactly what it is, and he's planning to use it, or to sell it to someone who will.'

'You think it's a weapon?'

'Maybe.'

'And you intend to prevent him using it.'

'Yes!'

Trinica got out of her seat and stretched. 'There I was thinking you wanted to sell it and make a fortune. How civic-minded you've become.'

'This isn't the time for your bloody sarcasm!' Frey snapped. 'That bastard made mugs of us both, and I owe him for that. But if he unleashes whatever power is in that sphere, if it does what I think it might . . . Well, I played my part in making that happen. So I'll play my part in stopping it.'

Trinica looked surprised. Then her expression softened, and just for an instant, he recognised the face of the woman he'd known.

'You're right, Darian,' she said. She lowered her gaze. 'It seems I really don't know you half as well as I thought.'

Frey was wrong-footed by the sudden capitulation in her voice. He wasn't used to submissiveness from her. But the moment passed, and when she spoke again she was crisp and sharp.

'Alright,' she said. 'Your aerium engines still work, I noticed. Float your craft and we'll tow you to dock. I'll leave my bosun in charge of the repairs to the *Delirium Trigger* and come with you. We have an understanding?'

'We do,' said Frey. He got to his feet and held out his hand. She came out from behind her desk and took it. Her grip was cool.

'This is an alliance of necessity,' she said firmly. 'Nothing more. When this is over, we are enemies again.'

'Best of enemies,' Frey said with a grin.

A wry smile touched the corner of her painted lips. 'Best of enemies,' she agreed.

When Jez came back to consciousness, she found herself in the *Ketty Jay*'s tiny infirmary, lying on the surgical table. She recognised the grubby ceiling and the smell of rum in the air. Malvery was there, standing next to her. Silo sat in the corner.

She was still wearing her jumpsuit. Malvery hadn't attempted to treat her. There was nothing he could do to help. They'd simply put her here and waited to see what happened.

The doctor peered at her over his green-lensed glasses. 'You alright?'

She gave a small nod and stayed where she was, staring at the ceiling.

'Hmm,' said Malvery. He made a show of looking about for something, then patted her awkwardly on the arm and left.

He's scared of me now. And so he should be.

Jez listened to the room, and to Silo's breathing. The *Ketty Jay* was airborne, but the engines were quiet. They were being towed, then.

Presumably by the *Storm Dog*. Apparently, the Cap'n's plan to abscond with the sphere hadn't gone entirely as hoped. She didn't really care.

She felt achingly, horribly lonely. Lonelier than she'd ever felt in her life. She'd been there, among the Manes. She'd shared them. And now they'd gone again. It was like she'd awoken from a dream of happy crowds to find herself abandoned on an endless sea.

She remembered everything that had happened. The Imperator's terrible influence, how she'd quailed and cowered with the rest of them. She'd been pressed to the floor by the weight of his presence. Then, the trance. Surging up and overwhelming her. Her enfeebled human mind had been incapable of resisting or controlling it. It took her eagerly, a mad beast finally uncaged. And everything became different.

That feeling. The *power* of it. She'd been more than just flesh and blood then. Her small body had become the sum of thousands. The world had gone dim and yet been stark with detail. She saw the curl of the smoke along the roof and she could track its pattern. She smelt the terror of her companions. She felt the savage joy of the Manes, her invisible brothers and sisters behind the Wrack, as they welcomed her among them. And she heard the mad voice of the Imperator, a thrashing mess of harmonics tearing into her consciousness.

She had to extinguish it.

The urge to rid herself of her opponent was primal, unquestionable. She used her gun at first – a human weapon, which proved ineffective. Then she went in with hands and teeth.

Strong. Fast. Terrible.

With the death of the Imperator, her humanity had rallied and driven the Mane part of her into retreat. But the pain of loss it brought was unbearable. The sense of inclusion, the warmth of the Manes, all of it had disappeared. Better that she'd never known it at all, than to have it and then be shut out.

She was thrown back to the world she'd always known. Except that now her crew knew what she was. They'd seen it. And she was ashamed and frightened.

'Say something,' she murmured.

Silo got up from his chair and walked over to her. She turned her head to look at him. So hard to read a Murthian's expressions. Was it just Silo, or was it a trait of their kind? Perhaps generations of slavery had taught them never to show their real selves. Jez had learned that lesson on her own, and look where it got her. She was sick of the secrecy. They all put so much effort into being alone.

'Damn your silence,' she said. 'Tell me what you're thinking, for once. You talked to me in Kurg. Why not now?'

'That was then,' said Silo. 'Words don't never do justice to a man's thoughts. What you care 'bout mine?'

'Because I counted you as my friend, Silo. I want to know if you still are.'

'That ain't changed. Whatever you be, that ain't changed.'

'Then what has?'

Silo didn't answer. Instead, he said, 'Remember what I told you, back in the rainforest?'

'You said it wasn't any good trying to ignore your bad side. You have to face it down. Master it. Make it a part of you.'

A calloused hand slipped over hers and tightened. Jez felt tears gathering.

'Now you know,' he said, sadly. 'Now you know.'

Evening found Crake and his captain leaning on a wooden railing, wrapped in furs, their breath steaming the air. The sun was setting in the west, throwing a bleak light over the tundra. The great plain was depressingly barren. Only the hardiest of shrubs and grasses grew in the frozen earth, in the lee of the stony hillocks that rumpled the landscape. A spiteful wind nipped at their faces. Even in spring, a mere hundred kloms or so north of the border, Yortland was bitterly cold.

From their vantage point – a path set into the hillside – they had a good view of the docks below. The main landing pad was cluttered with ugly, blockish aircraft. Flying bricks, Jez liked to call them: she didn't have a high opinion of Yort design. Nearby, in the workshop area, sat other craft in various states of disrepair. Two colossal hangars dominated the scene, their arched metal roofs patched with unthawed snow. The *Delirium Trigger*, battered and blasted, was slowly easing herself into one of them. Crake watched as she was swallowed up, then turned to Frey and said:

'I'm leaving.'

Frey stared down at the docks, his face grim. He didn't speak for a long time. 'You coming back?' he said eventually.

'I hope so. When I've done what I need to do. I'd intended to stay on long enough to help you get hold of that sphere – I thought it the honourable thing – but now, well . . .'

'You can't put it off for ever, right?' The wind blew black strands of hair around Frey's face. 'No telling when, or if, we'll find that bastard.'

Crake nodded.

'Something's been eating at you a long time,' Frey said. 'Ever since you came aboard, you've been on the run.'

Yes. From the Shacklemores. From myself.

'Some things . . .' Crake began. He knew that Frey didn't require an explanation, but he felt compelled to try. 'Some things, a man can't live with on his conscience. I thought I could keep ahead of it, you see? Keep on the move.'

'I get it, Crake. We all get it. That's why you were such a good fit for us.'

Crake was grateful for his understanding. Frey wasn't the kind who asked questions. A man's past was his own on the *Ketty Jay*.

Mostly, he reflected, that was a good thing. On Frey's crew, your only judge was yourself. But the conspiracy of silence had its downside. How could you be sure who was your friend and who wasn't, when they'd never seen the worst of you? When the secrets came out, who'd stand by your side?

What would happen to Jez, now? Could they forgive her for what she was?

And what if they found out about *his* crimes?

He couldn't face that. It was time to stop procrastinating. He'd made a promise to Bess. He'd atone for what he'd done. He'd find a way, somehow, to bring her back.

He looked out past the docks at the city beyond. Iktak was not a pretty sight. Its black stone buildings were bunkers against the cold. Most of it had been built underground, as all Yort settlements were. White ghosts of steam rose from the massive pipes that crawled across the landscape. Industrial chimneys smoked like restless volcanoes. A joyless place, more like a vast refinery than a place for people to live. A city of factories, waiting for winter's return. Without its cloak of snow to hide it, it was brown and bare and miserable.

'I'll be taking Bess,' he said.

'Thought you would,' said Frey. 'What'll you do with her? You can't have her walking around.'

'I'll put her to sleep, box her up, have her delivered to where I'm going.'

'Mind if I ask where that is? In case I need to find you?'

Crake took a slip of paper from his pocket, and handed it to Frey. He opened it and read the address.

'Tarlock Cove? Don't you have a friend there?'

'That's him. Plome. I'll be there some of the time. If not, I'll leave word for you. I'll be travelling a lot.'

'Travelling?'

'I have a few visits to make.'

A half-dozen, actually. Six names and addresses, given to him by Plome. Six people who, between them, could lay their hands on the best daemonic texts in the land.

I expect you've been all tied up in research, trying some new method or something, ain't you? Malvery had asked him once. *Maybe working on something really special?*

The doctor's voice had been sarcastic then. Pushing him, making him look at himself and what he'd become. It was an alcoholic's warning to a man he saw heading down the same route. And it had worked. Spit and blood, it had really worked. Crake was going to miss having a friend like Malvery. He was going to miss all of them, except Pinn.

But it couldn't be helped. Because now he *was* working on something really special. He was going to learn how to reverse what he'd done to his niece. He was going to bring her back to life. *Real* life, not the half-life she led inside a suit of armour. From that dim-witted thing that was more like a pet than a human, he'd extract the little girl inside, and restore her. Somehow.

If it sounded like madness, so be it. If he had no idea where to start, then he'd find a place. Whatever it took, there *had* to be a way.

He'd had a long talk with Plome, after their brush with the daemon in his sanctum. The politician was frankly in awe of him by then. Plome was the kind of daemonist who dabbled but never dared too much. Crake represented the man he wished he could be, if only he had the courage. Seeing him master the monster in the echo chamber had made him something of a hero in Plome's eyes.

Crake took advantage of that. He explained his plan. And he secured Plome's promise that he could make use of the politician's sanctum to conduct his experiments in.

'Hang the risks!' Plome had said, flushed with the excitement of their recent encounter. 'I'd be honoured, Crake! Honoured!'

Crake and Frey stood together for a time, neither quite knowing how to end it. Finally, Crake spoke up.

'I need money.'

'Oh?' Frey replied neutrally.

'Plome's agreed to help me out, but it won't be enough. What I'm up to . . . it's expensive business.' He looked over at his captain. 'I believe I played some part in obtaining all that money from Grand Oracle Pomfrey at the Rake table.'

'I'd have won it from him anyway, fair and square,' Frey said stiffly.

'Possibly,' said Crake. 'Or maybe he'd have got up and left with his winnings, too drunk to play on. We'll never know.'

He hated himself for asking. No matter how valid his claim to those ducats, he still felt like a beggar.

'Alright,' Frey said, not without a little bitterness. 'I've already had to shell out for new windglass for the autocannon cupola, but you can take half of what's left. Rot knows, you've earned it in your time on my crew.' He jabbed Crake in the chest with his finger. 'Don't you breathe a word to the others though, or they'll be on me like vultures.'

'I won't,' said Crake.

'Hey, why don't you take the compass?' Frey suggested suddenly. He lifted his hand, to show the silver ring on his little finger. 'It's your device, after all. That way you can come find us, if you change your mind. Just follow the compass back to me.'

Crake smiled. He'd made the ring and compass almost as a joke. Two daemons thralled together, one always pointing toward the other. It was so absurdly simple in comparison to what he'd be attempting.

'And who'll track you down next time you go missing in a Rake den, or in some woman's bed?' he said. 'Better the others keep hold of that.'

Frey looked crestfallen. 'Alright,' he said. 'That's sensible, I suppose.'

'It's just . . . it's something I have to do. I don't know how long it'll take, but . . .'

'I know.'

'I'll leave word at all of your mail drops when I'm finished.'

'Do that.'

Frey had closed up. Crake had hurt him.

'Thank you, Cap'n,' Crake said eventually, as if that would salve his feelings.

'Frey,' he said. 'It's just Frey, now.'

There was something terrible and final in that. Crake suddenly wanted to take it all back, to stay on the *Ketty Jay* with the people he cared about. He wanted to ask for their help, to have them share in his mission. But he couldn't. It would mean telling them what he'd done. Like Jez, he was going to hold on to his secret to the end.

They walked back down the path towards the docks. Despite the warmth of his furs, Crake felt as cold as he'd ever been in his life.

Twenty-Three

Hawk Point – The Whispermonger –
A Curious Alliance – Grist As A Boy

'Another day, another rat-hole,' said Frey with forced cheeriness, as he brought the *Ketty Jay* in over Hawk Point.

The settlement below had a blank, starved look to it. It was crushed into a mountain pass, deep in the Splinters, blanched by the hot spring sun. Carefully laid rows of buildings betrayed its orderly origins, but it had long since turned ramshackle. Brown strips of withered flowerbeds rotted on the main street. Slates had gone missing from the roofs. Though the town centre still had a ghost of its former pride, the outskirts had decayed into shanties.

Frey had never been here before, but he'd seen its like a hundred times. Another dying outpost, founded on high hopes and promises of freedom, only to end up violence-ridden and destitute. Honest traders came here to escape the cities and the crushing grip of the Guilds, but without Guild bribes the Ducal militia paid it no attention, and soon the criminals took over. Before long, the dreams of the first settlers had fallen into ruin, and they abandoned their failed town to try again elsewhere.

The Coalition Navy traditionally showed little interest in out-of-the-way, insignificant places like Hawk Point. Which made the presence of one of their frigates all the more unusual.

'What are *they* doing here?' Trinica muttered. She was standing at Frey's shoulder, one hand on the back of the pilot's seat. Jez sat at the navigator's station, behind him. Individually, they made Frey uneasy; together, it was all he could do not to jump whenever one of them spoke.

'Still a wanted woman, Trinica?' he asked.

'Of course. Quite a bounty on my head, last I heard. Though I think they have other matters to worry about right now.'

'You mean all that about the Sammies arming up in the south?'

'Amongst other things.'

'Like their mortal enemies, the Awakeners, trying to steal some terrible doomsday weapon that could possibly destroy vast swathes of Vardia?' Frey suggested.

Trinica ignored the jab. 'I'd be surprised if they knew about that at all.' She watched the frigate turning slowly in the air above the town. Its thrusters glowed, and moments later they heard a low roar that rattled the cockpit.

'Looks like they're heading off,' said Frey.

Trinica tutted. 'I hope they haven't disturbed my contact. He'll be far less agreeable if he's agitated. Not that he's *usually* very agreeable.'

'Are you sure this feller's any good?' Frey asked.

'The best. When I need information, he's the first one I go to.'

'Really? I know lots of whispermongers, and I never heard of Osric Smult.'

'You wouldn't have,' said Trinica, and left it at that. Frey felt his hackles rising at the slight edge of disdain in her voice.

Calm down, he thought. *Don't let her know that she gets to you.*

'Wind from the north, Cap'n,' said Jez from behind him. 'You'll get some heavy push on the way in.'

Frey made a grunt of acknowledgement. Jez had been subdued ever since she emerged from the infirmary. She went about her job quietly and with her head down, saying only the bare minimum to fulfil her duties. Frey, for his part, was fine with that. He didn't want to tackle the question of Jez right now. He had enough on his plate.

The problem was, he felt betrayed. A Mane, a damned *Mane*, here on his aircraft! He'd been hearing tales of those sky-ghouls since he was old enough to fly. He'd never have hired Jez if she'd told him about her condition in advance. Not that he'd have done differently in her shoes, but that was hardly the point.

The point was, she let him care about her. She didn't tell him, and she let him care about her, and then he found out. That was the betrayal.

Not only was she the best navigator he ever had, and utterly invaluable, but he *liked* her. She was a friend. She was, in fact, Frey's *only* female friend. For the rest, friendship was just an inconvenient stage on the way to sex. But he'd felt almost brotherly towards Jez.

Largely it was because she wasn't up to his standards as far as women went, but it was also because he respected her. There weren't many women Frey respected, but Jez was one of them.

He knew there was something off about her, of course he did. But he'd never thought . . . well, not *this*.

Now he was repulsed by her, and afraid, and guilty for feeling that way. He knew she was the same old Jez, but at the same time she wasn't, and that confused him and made him angry and frustrated. He was mad at her for that.

Why did she have to screw everything up by being a Mane?

The tension was scarcely less outside the cockpit. Morale was low throughout the crew. Like him, everyone was nervous around Jez. They didn't quite know what to make of her since they'd seen her rip the head off an Imperator with her bare hands.

There were other problems, too. The departure of Crake and Bess had left a hole bigger than anyone would have thought. Malvery missed the daemonist most of all: he was gloomily drinking himself stupid. Meanwhile Harkins had taken to sleeping in the cockpit of his Firecrow, and hardly set foot on the *Ketty Jay*. Whenever he did, Slag emerged to drive him off. Silo kept his own counsel, as ever, but Pinn was becoming a handful. He'd been depressed ever since he got that letter from his sweetheart, but he became downright mutinous at the news that Trinica Dracken would be travelling with them. It took all of Frey's powers of coercion, and a few good old-fashioned threats, before he'd consent to go anywhere with a woman he loathed.

Pinn's opinion of Dracken was shared by the rest of the crew, although none of them were as vocal as he was. Even Frey had decided he didn't much want her on board. It had seemed a good idea at the time, but having her here destroyed the one safe haven he had in his life. When he was flying the *Ketty Jay* he could pretend that he was a mighty captain, free to find adventure wherever it lay. A lord of the skies! But Trinica's presence punctured all his illusions. Reflected in those black, black eyes, he saw himself as she must: captain of a heap of junk, leader of a miserable crew, a man who'd made nothing of himself.

'Are your engines supposed to make that sound?' she inquired, as Frey lowered the *Ketty Jay* towards the small, crowded landing pad.

'Didn't have time to get them fixed in Iktak, did I?' he said. 'Speed is of the essence, and all that. It would've taken a couple of weeks to get the parts.' *Not that I could have afforded them, anyway*, he added mentally.

'You must have a fine engineer, then,' Trinica remarked.

He couldn't work out whether the compliment was snide or genuine, but it didn't matter in the end. Just by being here, she made him feel like a failure.

What was he even doing? Chasing after some artefact with no clear idea of what it was or what it did? It wasn't as if he could sell the thing, even if he did get his hands on it. Frey didn't have the most sensitive conscience, but he still balked at the idea of delivering a super-weapon into the hands of the highest bidder. His dreams of a fortune had gone up in smoke, yet he went on anyway. Just like one of those idiots he saw at the Rake tables. The ones who lost everything while waiting for their luck to change.

Was he doing it to get back at Grist? Perhaps. Perhaps it was just because he was tired of being stepped on by everyone, not least the woman standing next to him. Or perhaps . . . perhaps he just *needed* this.

What will I leave behind? The question that had been plaguing him ever since he'd almost died while being chased by a bunch of over-persistent yokels. Well, if he could avoid leaving thousands of corpses behind, that would be good. Mass murder was a legacy he could do without.

Damn the reasons. Damn it all. He wasn't failing this time. That was all there was to it.

The town hall was one of the oldest structures in Hawk Point. It was a grand building, stony and solid, dating from a time when Hawk Point was young and full of optimism. It had been designed as the heart of the settlement, the place from which the founders would put all their plans into practice. Plans for a just and honest outpost, where a man would get a fair wage for a fair day's work, and people were decent to one another.

That had been a long time ago. Those plans were forgotten, the people who made them dead or departed. The streets stank in the heat. The gutters were choked with rubbish that the sewers coughed up when the rains came. Mould streaked the post office walls. The schoolhouse windows were all smashed. The town hall itself was surrounded by a spiked barricade and watched by armed guards.

'This Smult feller,' said Frey, as they made their way up the street. 'He can't be doing too well for himself if he lives in a dump like this.'

'You always did judge by appearances, Darian,' Trinica said.

'What of it? Most of the time it's a pretty good indicator.'

She tutted. 'And I thought you were sharper than that. People only show you what they want you to see. Haven't you learned that by now?'

Frey looked her over with a raised eyebrow. Her deathly pallor, her butchered hair. 'I've picked up some hints,' he said. She scowled at him.

People watched them from doorways and alleyways. Mostly men and a few women, their gazes hungry or hostile. This wasn't a place for strangers. Frey kept his hands near his cutlass and pistols. Trinica didn't show the slightest sign of being intimidated.

'We're safe enough,' Trinica said. 'Everyone here knows who I am. Nobody will bother us.'

Frey was scarcely reassured. He'd wanted to bring some men along for protection, but Trinica had forbidden it. Smult wouldn't respond well to that, and he might well be on edge already after the Coalition Navy's visit.

Frey wasn't sure who he'd have brought, anyway. Malvery? Too drunk. Harkins? Too cowardly. Pinn? He could barely haul himself out of bed nowadays. Silo was liable to inspire aggravation; Murthians weren't too popular in Vardia, having fought on the wrong side of the Aerium Wars. That left Jez, who may or may not turn into a raging daemon and tear his head off at an inconvenient moment.

Crake and Bess? Gone. Gone to take care of some business of their own.

He missed them. Difficult as it was to admit, he admired Crake. He respected the daemonist's smarts, his education, his way of putting things. Crake was a good sort, and those were hard to find in the world Frey lived in.

He could understand Crake's need to deal with whatever was troubling him. The damage it was doing to him was obvious. These past few months Frey had watched the daemonist hollowing out in front of his eyes. But he wished they hadn't had to leave.

The crew of the *Ketty Jay* were a finely balanced group. Individually, each man and woman was a mess, but together, somehow, they'd found a way to work. The loss of two of their number had thrown everything out of kilter, and the whole operation was beginning to feel like it was in danger of falling apart.

That scared him. Once, he'd only cared for his aircraft, and his crew had meant less than nothing. Now, he had no idea what he'd do without them.

They approached the barricade surrounding the town hall. The guards on the gate recognised Trinica. It was hard not to. There wasn't a pirate or a criminal in Vardia who hadn't heard of the white-faced woman with the black outfit and blacker eyes. Her legend went before her.

'I'm here to see Smult,' she said, and they let her in. They barely glanced at Frey. They assumed that the tattered-looking man following in her wake was her bosun, or a general dogsbody from her crew. It didn't do Frey's pride much good.

A gun-wielding thug met them at the door. He looked Trinica over, dismissed Frey with a snort, collected their weapons and escorted them inside.

Inside, the town hall was a cross between a junk shop and a treasure trove. The stone corridors were piled high with artefacts and antiques. Strange sculptures and paintings were heaped up in the foyer, peeping out from behind velvet drapes. The sheer variety of objects was bewildering. There were boxes of guns, elaborate game boards with crystal pieces, a section of the chassis from a mechanical carriage, a curving broadsword of foreign design.

'Vases from Thace, armour from Yortland, perfume and necklaces from Samarla,' Trinica murmured as they walked through a narrow aisle between mountains of clutter.

'Bet he doesn't have a mysterious sphere from Kurg,' said Frey, rather childishly.

'Neither do we,' Trinica said. 'That's why we're here, remember?'

'Your man's quite a collector, though,' Frey murmured, looking around in wonderment. 'This stuff must be worth a fortune.'

'No doubt,' said Trinica. 'If you can sift out the valuable bits from the junk.'

'What's the point of all this? He's not showing it off. Does he sell it?'

'Not that I know of,' said Trinica. 'He just likes to have them.'

Frey shook his head. All that wealth, just lying around. Some people weren't meant to be rich. When it was his turn, he intended to do a better job of it.

They were shown in to a dim room, draped in fabrics and stacked with artefacts. There were mannequins and chests of drawers, side tables and mirrors. Stuffed animals glared from the shadows with glassy eyes. The room was stifling and close. Despite the heat of the day, the boiler had to be running hard.

At a table in the corner was Osric Smult. He was sitting on an antique chair, his entire attention focused on the jigsaw before him. Two bored-looking bodyguards were staring vacantly into space as Frey and Trinica were led in. Spotting her, they shook themselves and woke up a little.

'Trinica Dracken,' said Smult, without raising his head. 'Ain't you a sight?'

Frey presumed that was meant as irony, because if Smult had any eyes at all, he certainly couldn't see through them.

Smult was a wiry, tall man, dressed in a faded shirt, trousers and boots, and he wore a wide-brimmed hat. Beneath his clothes, every inch of exposed skin was covered in bandages. Rusty patches of dried pus and blood seeped through here and there. His face was similarly bound, and his eyes wrapped tight. The only gaps were for his mouth, and small holes for the ears and nostrils. Glimpses of the red and blistered skin around his lips indicated some kind of disease that Frey would rather not know about. He looked up at them and smiled horribly, revealing yellowed teeth and breath that smelt of sweet rot, even from across the room.

'Osric Smult,' she said. 'How's your jigsaw?'

'Fine, fine. Man's gotta have a hobby, huh?'

Frey was unable to stop himself. 'How do you, er . . . how do you do a jigsaw when you can't see?'

Smult picked up a piece, turned it round in his hand, running his bandaged fingertips over the edge.

'Don't need to see it to make it fit,' he said. 'And who're you, sir?'

'Darian Frey, captain of the *Ketty Jay*,' Frey said, doing his best to make it sound more impressive than it was.

Smult tilted his head, interested. 'Strange company you're keepin', Miss Dracken,' he said. 'Real strange, considerin'.'

Considering what? thought Frey. *How much does he know?*

'These are strange times,' Trinica said neutrally.

'They are,' Smult agreed. 'I expect you saw the Navy leave?'

'We did. Might I ask what they were after?'

'Spies,' said Smult.

'Spies?'

Smult was feeling around the ragged interior of his jigsaw, searching for a place to put the piece in his hand. 'Do you remember our beloved Earl Hengar?' he asked.

Frey went pale. He remembered Hengar rather well, since he'd accidentally killed him when he accidentally blew up the *Ace of Skulls*, accidentally. It was an accident, though.

'What does the Archduke's son have to do with it?' said Trinica.

'Well, we all know he was dallying with the Samarlan ambassador's daughter, don't we? Rumour has it that lovestruck young men sometimes say silly things. Unguarded things, the kind that a member of the Archduke's family really shouldn't say. Especially not to a woman who'd have been his mortal enemy only a few years before.' Smult scratched at his cheek. New bloodstains seeped through the bandages. Frey tried hard not to notice. 'Apparently, he said a lot of them.'

'He was leaking secrets to the Sammies?'

'Maybe. That's what the Navy think, anyway, though they'd never say as much. Probably Hengar reckoned it was all over and everyone was friends again. He always was a brainless boy. That's why the people loved him. He appealed on their level.' He lifted up his head and turned his face towards Frey. An ugly leer spread across his lips. 'Whoever killed him did us all a favour.'

Frey attempted to look nonchalant, then stopped when he realised it was useless against a blind man. Hengar's death had been widely reported as the result of a catastrophic engine malfunction. Only a few people knew Frey had been involved in it, and he wasn't keen on advertising the fact. Smult's grin made him distinctly uncomfortable.

'Anyways,' Smult said at length. 'Seems like the Sammies suddenly know more than they should about certain things. Navy came by to see if I could help them with their investigations.'

'And could you?' Trinica asked.

'Oh yes,' he said. 'But I didn't. I don't work for Navy, whatever the price. A man needs principles.' He pressed the jigsaw piece into place, and it fitted with a click. Then he sat back in his chair, as if well satisfied with his achievement. 'So,' he said. 'To business. You'll be looking for Harvin Grist, then?'

If Trinica was as surprised as Frey was, she didn't show it. 'News travels fast,' she said.

'I make it my business to be the first to know,' said Smult. 'That's why I charge what I charge.'

'And you know where he is?'

'Not yet. But I have my eyes and ears out there. It won't be long. In the meantime, I can point you in the right direction.'

Trinica produced a bag of coins from some concealed pocket in her clothing. Frey hadn't even known she was carrying any. She held it up and jingled it. Smult tilted his head, listening.

'Why don't you tell me what you *do* know?' Trinica suggested. 'And I'll come back with more when you find him.'

Smult nodded at his bodyguard, who took the bag from Trinica and opened it up. Frey stared at it enviously. It galled him that Trinica could throw money around like that when he had barely enough to keep the *Ketty Jay* in the air. But he was damned if he'd ask her for any. That would be too much to take.

The bodyguard whispered in Smult's ear, then put the bag on the table next to him. Smult nodded and waved him away.

'Harvin Grist,' said Smult. 'Here's what I know. Born in White-rock, north of Marduk. Cold up there. His father was a scholar. Maurin Grist. Mother died of some kind of wasting disease; Grist watched her go. Long, drawn-out affair. Quite traumatised the boy, if I understand correct.' Smult's tongue, rough with boils, slipped out to lick at dry lips. 'Maurin moved them to Bestwark soon after. Had a position at the university. Went on to become a big name there.'

Frey opened his mouth to ask what his father had to do with anything, but Trinica silenced him with a glare. Frey rolled his eyes and settled back on his heels. He had the feeling that Smult was showing off the fact that he had all this information to hand.

Just tell us where to look for him!

'By all accounts, the boy didn't get much attention,' Smult continued. 'Maurin was wrapped up in his work. Distant sort. Young Harvin was an outstandin' student, sportsman, all of that. The pride of his school. But Daddy didn't notice. In fact, the only time Daddy noticed him was when he was misbehavin'. So he misbehaved. And he kept on misbehavin'. Went off the rails, I believe is the term.'

Trinica was listening closely. She seemed to be finding some value in this tale that Frey was obviously missing.

'So he's smart? Educated?' she inquired.

'Smart, yes. Educated, to a point.'

'What then?'

'He left. Dropped out of school, ran away with some friends of his. They signed on with a freight captain and never looked back. He moved from place to place, crew to crew, all the usual. He talks like a pirate, but he's cleverer than he looks. He saved what money he had, put it places where it'd grow. Made deals and investments. Picked the right crews, made big scores, took the money and moved on. Sooner or later he got the scratch together for a craft of his own. That's when he started running narcotics.'

Despite his impatience, Frey was becoming interested. It was strange to hear the details of Grist's past laid out like this. Curious to think that the grizzled, cigar-smoking bully had once been young. A boy who had watched his mother slowly decay, in painful degrees, before his eyes. A young man clamouring for a distant father's attention.

'I imagine he made a lot of money,' Trinica suggested.

Smult nodded. 'He did. Worked the north coast, up in Marduk and Yortland. He'd fly through the fogs, when other pilots wouldn't dare for fear of the Manes. With the profits, he bought bigger craft. Had quite a few to his name at one point. Then he sold 'em all off and bought that Cloudhammer he flies about in now. Didn't have much fear of the Navy after that. The *Storm Dog*'s big enough to go one-on-one against most Navy craft.' He turned his blind gaze towards Trinica. 'Big enough to take on the *Delirium Trigger*, so I hear.'

There was something deeply unpleasant in his tone, but Frey couldn't pin it down. Was he gloating? Was there a warning there? A threat? He saw Trinica stiffen slightly.

'And now?' she asked.

'Of late, he's picked up odd habits. His haunt's in the north, see. But since the spring before last, he suddenly started turnin' up wherever the Manes have been.'

'The Manes?'

'They come and go quick,' said Smult. 'Take what they want and kill the rest. Nobody knows when or where they're gonna strike, so nobody can do a thing about it. But whenever they do, you can bet that Grist'll be there. The same day, or the day after. He comes running when the Manes kill. Asking questions. "What happened? Where'd they come from? Which way'd they go?"' He scratched at his ribs. 'Make of that what you want.'

'And you think that's where he is? In the north?'

'That's what I think. Up in Marduk and Yortland. Up in the snows.'

'That's a lot of territory,' Trinica said. 'Can you be a little more specific?'

'Can't work miracles, Miss Dracken,' he said. 'I'm fast, but I ain't *that* fast. Grist's kept his head down for a long time now. But I'll find him. You could come back in a week or so.' He picked up another piece of jigsaw and began feeling around for a place to put it. 'Wouldn't advise it, though.'

'What does *that* mean?' Frey asked, who was a little tired of being left out of the nuances of this conversation.

'Means your ladyfriend took a big chance, comin' here,' Smult said. The shadow of his wide-brimmed hat fell across his face as he turned back to his jigsaw. 'Walking around in the open, her craft and crew hundreds of kloms away, with just you for protection? Or perhaps she believes her reputation alone is enough to make men fear her? Foolish attitude, if you ask me. The bounty that's on her head, someone might be tempted to take a risk.'

Frey's eyes flickered over the bodyguards. They'd sensed the change in the air, and were ready with their guns. He wished he hadn't given his weapons in at the door now.

Trinica's expression was hard. 'You wouldn't touch me,' she said to Smult. 'You're a whispermonger. You don't take sides, and you don't get involved. If word got out, you'd be ruined.'

Smult cackled. 'You reckon me right, Miss Dracken. That bounty ain't worth a chicken's arse to me. But I can't speak for them out there.' He thumbed over his shoulder, in the vague direction of the outside. 'Might be there's people waitin' for you. People who heard you were comin' to Hawk Point in the company of some shabby, no-account bunch who couldn't be trusted to tie their own bootlaces.'

'Hey!' Frey cried. 'I can tie my damn bootlaces just fine!'

Trinica ignored him. 'You sold them the information,' she said coldly. 'You knew I'd be looking for Grist, and you knew I'd come to you first.'

'You said it yourself,' Smult grinned. 'I'm a whispermonger. I don't take sides. Not even yours.'

'This is dogshit!' Frey said. 'If they knew we were here, they'd have jumped us the moment we left the landing pad.'

Smult tapped the bag of coins of the table in front of him. 'I asked 'em not to. I hate to waste a profit.'

'How much for you to tell us where they'll be waiting?' Trinica said.

Smult smiled to himself, and clicked another piece of his jigsaw into place.

Twenty-Four

Double-Dealing –
Spindle Street – A Surprise

The back streets of Hawk Point could scarcely be called streets at all. They were a shanty of lean-tos and hovels that had crowded together without pattern or purpose. The gaps between dwellings were little more than baked mud tracks strewn with old litter. The wind that blew across the mountains couldn't find a way into the maze, leaving the air ripe and stale. The inhabitants – old dogs and half-starved cut-throats – stuck to the shadows and sweltered.

Frey kept a wary eye on the shanty dwellers, who watched him warily in return. They were desperate people, ignorant and unskilled, mostly descended from the serfs that the Dukes freed when they deposed King Andreal of Glane. They came to the cities in an attempt to escape the poverty of the countryside, only to find they were unable to afford Guild fees and therefore couldn't work. Eventually, they ended up in the settlements and outposts, scratching a living as black-market dock-hands or petty thieves. Able-bodied men found themselves recruited as pirates. Women were taken on as cleaners, if they were lucky. Children were often sold off to the mines.

They had a bad lot, all in all. But desperate people tended to do desperate things, so Frey's hand was never far from his pistol.

Smult had been good enough to return their weapons after he'd taken Trinica for all the money she had. He'd given them detailed information about where their enemies lay in ambush for them, and told them how to avoid the traps. So now they were on their way back to the *Ketty Jay*, taking a route through the outskirts that circled the settlement. Scurrying like rats, hoping to stay unnoticed.

Frey had to admire the whispermonger's gall. Selling out Trinica,

242

then selling out the people he'd sold her out to. Trinica, however, was not at all amused. She was incandescent with suppressed rage.

He took the silver earcuff from his pocket and clipped it on. 'Jez? Can you hear me?'

'Cap'n.' She sounded faintly surprised. Perhaps she hadn't expected him to speak to her.

'There's two men with rifles covering the landing pad. One in the north-east corner on the roof of the dock master's office. The other one on the roof of the warehouse to the north-west. They won't be watching out for you; they're waiting for us. Think you and Silo can take care of them?'

'Of course, Cap'n,' she said. 'Are you in trouble?'

'When aren't I?' he replied, and took off the earcuff.

Trinica was glowering at him. 'You can speak to your crew with that? That's a good trick.'

'I'm just full of 'em,' Frey said with a wink. He was unaccountably light of heart, despite their predicament. Perhaps because, for once, Trinica was getting screwed over rather than him. She didn't seem to like the taste of her own medicine very much.

She snorted in disgust, and turned away, concentrating on the route. Frey followed her, faintly amused. He knew exactly why she was so mad. You didn't get to the point of marrying someone without having a little insight into their character. And he had to admit, despite the threat to his own life, he was rather enjoying her discomfort.

She'd miscalculated. She'd got so used to being the dread pirate queen that she'd started to believe her own legend. She thought she was untouchable, even without the *Delirium Trigger* and her crew to back her up. She'd fashioned an image for herself, one that struck fear into the hearts of men, but she'd worn it for so long that she'd come to believe it was a shield.

Today, she'd been rudely reminded that it wasn't. That white make-up, her butchered blond hair, her black eyes and black attire: it was no protection without her men and her aircraft. Worse, it made her a target. Underneath the ghoulish exterior she was still a woman, flesh and blood. She'd die from a bullet or a knife like any other. Perhaps she'd forgotten that, until now.

She'd been made vulnerable. And what was more, it had happened in front of Frey. She hated that.

'That bastard,' she was muttering through gritted teeth, as they dodged between shacks of discarded metal and peeling wood. 'That rotting whore-son bastard.'

'Ah, look on the bright side,' said Frey. 'At least he gave us a way out.'

'This is your fault!' she snapped, turning on him. 'Do you have any idea what you've done? He'd never have dared to do this before.'

'Before I showed you up and the *Delirium Trigger* got beaten?' Frey suggested maliciously.

Her eyes blazed, and for a moment, Frey thought she would hit him. She was trembling with rage. He belatedly realised that this wasn't the time to be needling her. It had gone beyond a joke.

'Hey,' he said, turning serious. 'It's not so bad. We'll get out of Hawk Point, find Grist, make him pay. You get your revenge, your reputation is restored. Hang his head off the prow of the *Delirium Trigger* if you like.'

Trinica nodded at that, making a hissing noise through her teeth.

'But until that time,' he said, 'you're going to have to watch out. Every drunk with a knife, every dealer looking for an angle, everyone with a grudge against you, they're all going to be lining up to take their chance. They're going to see that Trinica Dracken's been brought down and they're going to take their shot at you while they can.'

'I can look after myself, Darian,' she snapped.

'Can you?' he asked. 'Can you shoot? Can you fight?'

'I can shoot,' she said, showing him the revolvers in her belt.

'Can you shoot *well?*'

She glared at him, and he had his answer. Trinica wasn't a fighter. She'd got to where she was by guile, manipulation and sheer ruthlessness. She wasn't physical enough to compete in the brutal world of pirates. She'd used others to protect her and fight in her place. Smart people stayed out of gunfights.

There was no crew to hide behind now, no one to issue orders to. Here, she was out of her element, and it scared her. She hid it behind a wall of frost and rage – perhaps she even hid it from herself that way – but none of that fooled Frey.

He'd not seen her scared for a long time. Not since before their aborted marriage, before he ran out on her. More than a decade had passed and they were both different people now, but the feelings that came to him were the same as if it had been yesterday. He felt protective. He actually wanted to hold her in his arms. But that would be the grossest insult to her, the final humiliation, and she'd never allow it.

'Come on,' he said gently. 'Once you get the *Trigger* fixed, you can come back here and bomb the shit out of this whole town. How's that?'

'I just might do that,' Trinica said darkly. 'I just might.'

But until then, Frey thought, *I'll look out for you.*

Their route took them the long way round the settlement, and navigation wasn't easy. A few times Frey had to stop and ask for directions. Usually they wanted money in return, but Frey had a gun, which cut through the tiresome process of haggling. Once they were established as dangerous, the shanty dwellers left them alone. They weren't interested in trouble.

The shanty petered out into a mess of run-down alleys that smelled of old fish and tanneries. Frey got his bearings by shinning up a drainpipe until he could see over the rooftops to where aircraft were taking off from the landing pad. Not far, by the looks of it.

Trinica stuck close to him as he led the way through the alleys. She probably didn't notice she was doing it, but Frey did. It warmed his ego to think of himself as her guardian. For some reason it made him feel a bit better about things.

They came out of the alleys on to something that resembled a street. It was narrow and grubby, but it bore signs of being a thoroughfare, and the buildings on either side didn't look in immediate danger of collapse. That was an improvement on much of the town.

'Spindle Street,' said Trinica, pointing at a faded sign high up on one of the walls.

Spindle Street. Smult had mentioned it. *When you come out of the shanties, look for Spindle Street. Follow it to the landing pad.*

The landing pad, and the *Ketty Jay*, and then out of this dump for ever. Frey had a long list of places he never wanted to return to, for one reason or another. Hawk Point had qualified before he'd even landed.

There were a few people about, bartering at stalls or chatting in doorways. 'Just act normal,' he said to Trinica, and they walked out of the alley and down the street.

Frey could feel the glances of the townsfolk as they headed towards the landing pad, but they were left alone. If Smult was right, the men who lay in wait were behind them by now. Only the gunmen at the landing pad were left, as insurance in case they should slip past the others. Jez and Silo should have taken care of them.

Better check, he thought, reaching into his pocket for his earcuff. He was just clipping it to his ear when there was a flurry of movement to his left. An elderly woman was pushed aside as a pair of gunmen came running out of an alleyway, shotguns held at waist height, trained on Frey and Trinica. He heard footfalls behind him and yelps of surprise from the scattering townsfolk. He turned and saw a third man, moving up from behind with a pistol aimed.

'Weapons on the ground! Real slow!' barked the first of the gunmen, a heavyset man with a bushy beard that hung down over his chest.

Trinica looked at Frey, as if expecting him to do something about it. But Frey just shrugged at her. *Some guardian I am. That didn't last long.*

'Do it,' he said. He threw his revolvers on the ground before him. His cutlass followed. Then he raised his hands.

Trinica was still staring at him, an expression of frustrated disappointment on her face. As if she couldn't understand why he'd given up so easily. As if she'd expected him to fight three men that had the drop on them.

Who does she think I am? he thought angrily. *I'm not one of the Century bloody Knights.*

But he couldn't hold her gaze, so he turned his head away. After a few moments, he heard her guns clatter down on top of his.

'Bounty's ours, boys!' crowed the second gunman, a long-faced fellow in a dirty shirt, with braces holding up his trousers. 'Trinica bleedin' Dracken!'

'I told you!' said the third one, who'd moved nearer now. He was the youngest of the three, barely old enough to grow a decent stubble on his cheeks. 'Cost us every shillie we had, but she'll be worth it.'

The heavyset man was looking Trinica over. 'Aye. The Navy'll pay us back five times over. You was right; Smult was good as his word.'

Frey felt Trinica tense at the sound of his name. Smult. He'd sold them out twice over. Bleeding all sides for as much money as he could get.

'Your friend Smult,' said Frey under his breath, 'is quite a piece of shit.'

'If we ever get out of this,' said Trinica, 'I'm going to teach him the meaning of suffering.'

'Oh, I shouldn't worry about that. You take out the two in front, I'll handle the one behind me.'

'What?' said Trinica. 'How can I—'

But he wasn't talking to her. He was talking to Jez and Silo.

Gunshots. The heavyset man and his long-faced companion wheeled and jerked, eyes wide in shock. Frey was already moving as they fell, turning to face the man behind him. As he did so, he held out his arm, and his cutlass leaped from the ground of its own accord. He felt it slap into his palm just as his opponent raised his pistol and fired at his chest from a distance of two metres. The blade jerked in his hand; the bullet sparked off the metal. His attacker had only a moment to stare in disbelief before Frey cut his hand off at the wrist and beheaded him on the return stroke.

Three corpses slumped to the ground together. Frey turned to Trinica, raised an eyebrow at her, and then walked away towards Jez and Silo. The look of amazement on her face was priceless.

Jez and Silo hurried up to him from the direction of the landing pad. 'Everything okay, Cap'n?' Jez asked.

'It is now,' he said. 'Should I ask how you found me?'

Jez brandished Crake's compass. 'Followed the needle. We came looking for you after we dealt with the men on the roof. Thought you might need a hand.'

Frey held his hand up before him and studied the ring on his little finger. 'I keep forgetting about this thing.'

'I take it things didn't go so well with the whispermonger?'

'We've got enough to be going on with,' said Frey. He spotted Trinica walking over to them and added, 'If Trinica asks, I planned this whole crafty counter-ambush all along.'

'Right you are, Cap'n,' said Jez. Her eyes roamed his face

uncertainly. Neither knew quite how to behave around the other. Frey felt that he was supposed to be mad at her, but it didn't feel right after what had just happened. And yet, when he looked at her, he still saw something he was afraid of.

'Thanks,' he said awkwardly. Then he looked at Silo, where he was on safer ground. 'Both of you.'

'Um,' said Jez. 'You're welcome.'

Then he walked off down the road, heading for the *Ketty Jay*. With every footstep, his good humour grew, and by the time she came into sight he was positively brimming with confidence. Smult might have tried to get one over on them, but they'd slipped the trap. And however he'd done it, he'd saved Trinica, and now she owed him. A pretty satisfactory day, all in all.

On the cargo ramp, he paused and looked back over the blasted, ramshackle settlement towards the town hall.

'Now who can't tie their bootlaces, you scabby son of a bitch?' he muttered under his breath. And with that, he headed to the cockpit for take-off.

Twenty-Five

Among The Civilised –
Kraylock's Revelations – Frey Joins The Dots

Bestwark University was one of the oldest and most prestigious
seats of learning in all of Vardia. It had existed for over a
thousand years. Kings and queens, dukes and earls had studied there. Great advances in science, medicine, and avionics had been
made behind its enormous sandstone walls. Its shadowy studies and
echoing halls had played host to conversation and debate between the
greatest philosophers, artists and mathematicians in history. The very
air was heavy with knowledge.

Frey sat at a table in the university café, rustled his broadsheet, and
did his best to look educated.

The café was built into one side of a large, grassy quad. Tall, square
windows looked out over a stone veranda laid with tables and chairs.
It was a sunny day, and most of the tables were occupied, but Frey
had snagged one near the edge where he could watch the students
going to and from their classes. They hurried along the flagged
pathways between the trees and ornamental pools, chatting amongst
themselves, their faces alight with a kind of enthusiasm that Frey
hadn't seen in years. Young men and women, brimming with dreams
and possibilities. Young men and women who hadn't yet been let out
into the world, all their protection stripped from them, and left to fend
for themselves.

Just you wait, Frey thought. *You wouldn't smile like that if you knew.*

But for all his silent, smug warnings, he was jealous. They reminded him of when he was their age, when he thought the way they
did. He'd imagined himself as a dashing freebooter, or a rich and
famous explorer like Crewen or Skale, the men who discovered and
mapped New Vardia. He remembered that first couple of years with

Trinica, when he'd believed he was the luckiest man alive, and he'd been unable to imagine any obstacle they couldn't overcome together.

Sometimes he wished he could be that naïve again.

He sipped his coffee and made a show of studying his broadsheet, just for effect. He was acutely aware that he didn't belong here. He couldn't shake the suspicion that he'd only been permitted to enter by mistake and that he'd be escorted out at any moment. Even the waitress who served him the coffee had given him a frankly insulting once-over. Although she might have just been eyeing him up. Frey's instincts were all off in this place. Academia intimidated him.

There was plenty of drama in today's broadsheet. The big news was that the Archduke had announced that his wife was pregnant. The country was in raptures, apparently. Celebrations planned in the cities, and all of that.

An heir, to replace poor dead Earl Hengar. That was bad news for the Awakeners. The Archduke and his wife were staunch opponents of the organisation, and even more so since Hengar's death. The Awakeners had had a hand in that, even if they'd never been held to account for it. They might have hoped the Archduke would die childless, to pass the reins of power to a more sympathetic member of the family. But that hope was now extinguished.

The other news also concerned the Awakeners. A vote was to be taken in the House of Chancellors on a new proposition to ban Awakener activity in the cities. Just the thing that Grand Oracle Pomfrey had been complaining about, shortly before Frey robbed him at the card tables. Frey suspected it had been timed to ride the wave of public support in the wake of the Archduke's announcement. The Archduke didn't actually need the approval of the House to pass any laws, but there were a lot of people out there who'd get angry about the Archduke messing with their religion. The House was the voice of the people, traditionally, even if it was only the aristocracy who got much of a say in it. Their support would make things much easier.

Strange times, he thought. But times had been strange since the Aerium Wars began. Frey didn't trouble himself with the big picture too much. Let the world take care of itself, and he'd do the same. That was his usual philosophy, anyway. Yet, somehow, here he was at Bestwark University, waiting to meet a colleague of Grist's father. All in the name of chasing down that Mane sphere before Grist did anything too terrible with it. And where was the profit in that?

Nowhere. Except that maybe he'd be able to sleep at night, knowing he'd at least tried to prevent a disaster he'd had a hand in causing.

Smult's information had given them a few leads, even if the scumbag had subsequently sold them down the river. Grist was likely on the northern coast somewhere. That was the best place to start asking after him. But before they went flying about, freezing their pods off in the arctic air, Frey wanted to have a word with Daddy. See if he could narrow the search a bit.

So they'd flown over to Bestwark. Trinica had composed a polite letter of introduction. They didn't want to alarm Grist's father, so they pretended to be scholars, interested in discussing his research. She gave false names, just to be safe.

They'd had the letter delivered to the university. The next day, they received a reply from a man called Professor Kraylock, inviting them to meet him. Trinica was surprised at the speed of the response, but neither of them were of a mind to question their luck.

Trinica had disappeared from the *Ketty Jay* early that morning, to 'make some preparations'. She left word that she'd meet Frey at the university café. So Frey went alone, rather nervously. The gate guard had his name on a list, and he was allowed through. He made his way in, and settled there to wait, feeling slightly cowed by the whole experience.

He looked around for Trinica, saw no one, and returned to hiding behind his broadsheet. His eye fell on an article which caught his interest. The Meteorologist's Guild in Thesk was predicting a resurgence in the Storm Belt, the vicious weather system that ran across the Ordic Abyssal and separated the continent of Pandraca from the islands on the far side of the planet. The Aviator's Guild feared that New Vardia and Jagos could become even more isolated if aircraft were forced to take the eastern route instead. That would involve circumnavigating almost two-thirds of the globe, and it was prohibitively fuel-expensive, not to mention dangerous.

'Anything interesting?' It was Trinica's voice. He closed the broadsheet and looked up at her. And kept on looking.

'Darian, you're staring,' she said. A gentle admonishment. Her expression was a little awkward, uncertain, embarrassed. Not exactly the emotions he'd associate with Trinica Dracken, pirate captain.

But he couldn't help it. Whoever this was in front of him, it was not the woman he'd last seen on the *Ketty Jay*.

She'd transformed herself. The chalk-white pallor and vulgar red lipstick had gone. She wore only the slightest hint of make-up now. Her hair, that had been butchered as if with a blunt knife, had been cut into a short, fashionable style. The black contact lenses had disappeared. Her eyes were green, the way he remembered them. She was wearing a light, summery dress that exposed her pale collar-bones.

It was like the past come to life. A vision of the woman he'd loved all that time ago. Oh, there were differences: ten years had passed, after all. Tiny lines at the corners of her eyes. Her face a little leaner than before, cheekbones a fraction sharper. And her hair was different, of course. But none of that was anything to him. Damn, his heart was actually beating harder at the sight of her.

'Are you alright?' she asked. 'You seem a little out of sorts.' There was a smile in her tone. She was flattered by his reaction, even if she didn't want to be.

'You . . .' Frey fought for something witty to say. 'You clean up pretty well,' he managed.

'Seemed foolish to advertise myself, given the circumstances,' she said. She sat down with practised elegance. 'Osric Smult taught me a lesson I won't soon forget. I have you to thank that I'm still alive to learn from it.'

The waitress who had served Frey drifted over to the table. Frey was grateful for the chance to gather his wits as they ordered more coffee and some pastries.

'I missed breakfast,' Trinica confessed with a smile.

Even her manner was different. Not so hard, not so cruel. That outer layer of her disguise had been scraped away. Neither of them were quite certain what lay beneath it.

She leaned back in her chair and looked out over the quad. Watching the students, as he had done. 'I would have gone to a place like this,' she said. 'Bestwark or Hoben or Galmury. I was a good student, you know. And with my family's money, well . . .' She let the sentence drift. 'I wonder what things would have been like, then.'

'At least you would have got in,' said Frey. 'Orphan boy like me, no family name . . . I wouldn't have got within fifty kloms of this place, no matter how well I did.'

Trinica laughed. 'You hated studying. You told me so.'

'Well, maybe if I'd have thought I might get to university, I'd have had more of a crack at this "learning" thing,' said Frey, making quotation marks with his fingers.

'You can't blame everything on the circumstances of your birth, Darian,' she said. 'Besides, you didn't do badly for a poor orphan boy. You were a hair's breadth from marrying into a fortune, I recall.'

Frey watched her for signs of an accusation, but she wasn't making one. She seemed in a good mood, in fact. She closed her eyes and lifted her face to the sun. The first time she'd felt it on her bare skin in years, perhaps. Frey found himself worrying that she might burn.

You're worrying? About her? You should worry about yourself!

The voice of reason. He reminded himself not to be beguiled. Just because she'd changed her appearance, it didn't make her any more trustworthy.

The waitress arrived with their drinks and a plate of pastries. Trinica took one and bit into it. Frey realised that he'd never seen her eat while she was aboard the *Ketty Jay*. She'd taken her meals in her room, perhaps aware that her presence was poisoning the atmosphere in the mess. She had a fussy, precise way of eating that Frey had always found sort of adorable.

He ate a pastry himself. For a short while, they didn't speak. Absurdly, Frey began to feel comfortable. Like they'd known each other for ever. Like it was no big thing that they were sitting together in the grounds of an ancient university eating pastries on a sunny day. The whole situation was bizarre in its normality.

'Trinica, do you ever question what you're doing?' he said.

She peered suspiciously at the pastry in her hand. 'Should I?'

'No, I mean, do you ever wonder if you're on the right road?'

'My road chose me, rather than the other way around.'

'But, I mean . . . You're rich, right? Even without your family. You could sell your craft, retire. Do anything you wanted.'

She laughed a little laugh. 'Like what? Keep bees? Potter about my manse looking at the flowers?'

'You could read. You always liked to read.'

Trinica gave him a look that was midway between indulgent and patronising. 'I rather think it's you we're talking about here, not me.'

She was right. It had begun as an idle thought, but it had always been heading somewhere. He knitted his fingers behind his head, trying to think of a way to explain the empty, directionless feeling he'd had ever since this whole affair began.

'Let me guess,' said Trinica. 'You're looking for something, but you don't know what it is.'

He was amazed that she'd summed it up so neatly. 'How'd you know?'

'Because you've been saying the same thing since you were seventeen.'

Frey looked blank. 'Have I?'

'Yes!' she said. 'When I met you, you were flying for my father. You'd mortgaged yourself to the eyeballs to afford a second-hand rust bucket called the *Ketty Jay*, but you were regretting it already, because you'd decided you wanted to join the Navy and fly a frigate.'

Frey did dimly recall wanting to join the Navy at some point, but it seemed unimaginable now.

'Then you decided you were in love with me, and you wanted to be with me for ever, and we all know how that turned out.'

Again, there was no hurt or accusation in the tone. Simple fact. He was a little offended that she could talk about it so lightly.

'I *did* join the Navy!' he said, suddenly remembering. 'Second Aerium War, flying cargo to the front.'

'You didn't *join the Navy*,' she said. 'You flew a lot of insanely dangerous freelance missions with the intention of getting yourself killed. And when you almost did, you *blamed* the Navy and you've hated them ever since.'

She had him there. He tried to think of a rejoinder and couldn't.

'Sorry, Darian. I don't mean to rake over old coals. I'm just making a point. You don't know what you want. You never have.'

Frey thought of Amalicia Thade, how he'd run away from a life of luxury with a beautiful woman. 'Things just seem so much better in theory than in practice. I even wanted to be a pirate for a while, like a *real* pirate. But it turns out I'm just not that cold-blooded. No offence.'

'None taken,' she said, sipping at her coffee.

'I suppose, at some point, you just have to make a choice and stick to it,' he said, unconvincingly. 'Make the best of things.'

'So they say.'

'Hardly seems fair, does it? All that compromise. Never quite getting what you dreamed of.'

'No one gets what they dream of, Darian. That's why they call them dreams.'

'You think so?'

'Even if you get everything you ever wanted, it's rarely all it's cracked up to be. The rich are as unhappy and screwed-up as the poor. Just in a different way.' She looked down into the black surface of her coffee. 'You can't get away from yourself.'

'What does *that* mean?'

'Well, wherever you go, whatever you do, you're still *you*. You can change your surroundings, start a new life, but you'll always fall into the same old patterns, make the same kind of friends, commit the same mistakes. The thing you need to change is yourself.'

'What's wrong with *me*?' Frey protested indignantly.

'I'm speaking generally. The thing a *person* has to change is themselves.'

'Like you did?'

'Like I did.'

'And you're happier?'

'No,' she said. 'But I'm alive.'

She gave him a sad sort of smile. Frey was overwhelmed by a surge of affection. That smile made him want to sweep her up in his arms, to protect her from all harm, to erase the damage of the past somehow.

'I forgot what it was like, talking to you,' he said. 'I mean, really talking, without all the threats and recriminations and stuff.'

'We have a lot to recriminate about,' she said.

He opened his mouth to speak, to say something complimentary, something to express his feelings, even in a small way. But she'd already detected the change in him. She'd seen the tenderness in his eyes and heard the softening of his voice.

'Darian, don't,' she said quietly.

So he didn't. The feeling curled up and died in the heat of

bitterness and embarrassment. He got to his feet and threw some money on the table.

'Let's go see this professor, then,' he said.

Trinica nodded wordlessly, left her coffee, and followed him.

Professor Kraylock was a small, thin, elderly man, with a tidy white moustache and a bald head speckled with liver spots. Little round glasses perched on a nose purpled with broken veins: the sign of a man who enjoyed his hard liquor. He was dwarfed by his chair and a colossal desk of walnut and leather. Sunlight beamed through two tall, arched windows behind him, edging him in dazzling light and casting his face into shadow. Blazing dust motes hung in the air around him.

Frey and Trinica sat on the other side of the desk. Trinica and the professor were talking and laughing. Preamble stuff: greetings, inquiries about each other's health, that kind of thing. Frey had stayed largely silent. He wasn't good making small talk with educated folk.

Trinica was, though. She chatted pleasantly with Kraylock, asking him about his studies and the affairs of the university, commenting on some rare sculpture he had in an alcove. This was the Trinica he remembered. The Trinica who would charm the socks off her father's guests at some swanky dinner function. The Trinica who you could talk to for hours, because she made you feel that everything you said was fascinating and important.

Frey's eyes roamed the study, idly wondering if there was anything worth stealing. There was a lot of potentially valuable junk here. A brass orrery, an ornamental spyglass. Furniture that looked older than the planet. And books. Lots of books.

Frey distrusted books. He had a sneaking suspicion that most people only bought them to make themselves seem impressive. He couldn't possibly imagine anyone reading so many massive, boring tomes. Had Kraylock *really* ploughed through every one of the forty volumes of the *Encyclopaedia Vardia*? Or the whole of *Abric's Discourses on The Nature of Mankind*? He doubted it.

'I do appreciate you taking the time to speak with us,' Trinica was saying. 'But could I ask why Professor Grist wasn't able to meet us himself?'

'Because he's dead,' Kraylock replied. 'In fact, I was rather surprised you didn't know that yourself. It's been almost two years now.'

Great, thought Frey. *Just great.*

Trinica looked appropriately bewildered. 'I'm sorry. We didn't know.'

'You didn't, hmm? Your letter said you were interested in discussing his research. What research, exactly, were you interested in discussing?'

It was obvious by his tone that the game was up before it had begun. He didn't believe their cover story for a moment. Trinica was still searching for a response when Frey leaned forward. 'Look,' he said. 'We're not students. We're searching for Professor Grist's son, Harvin. He's stolen something from us and we want it back. Well, actually the Awakeners stole it first, but that's by the by. We were hoping to talk to his dad and get an idea where he was. But his dad's dead, so . . .' He spread his hands. 'Sorry to have wasted your time.'

He was getting out of his chair when Kraylock spoke. 'The Awakeners, you said. They stole something from you?'

'Right.'

'May I hazard a guess as to what it was?'

'If you like.'

'Something to do with the Manes?'

Frey became suddenly interested again. 'That's quite a guess.'

Kraylock motioned at him with one thin hand. 'Sit down.'

Frey did so. Kraylock regarded them both from behind his glasses. 'Do you intend to kill him? Harvin, I mean?'

Trinica leaned forward, her face solemn. 'He has a Mane artefact that could be extremely dangerous. We believe he intends to use it to cause harm to a lot of people. We're trying to stop him. But first we need to find him.'

Kraylock studied them, searching for a lie, finding none. Eventually he sighed. 'That boy,' he said. 'He was nothing but heartache for Maurin. I always knew he'd come to a bad end.'

'Can you tell us about Maurin Grist?' Trinica said. 'What was his field of research?'

Kraylock blinked. 'Isn't it obvious? Manes. He was foremost authority on Manes in Vardia. Perhaps the world.'

Frey and Trinica exchanged a glance.

'We were friends for thirty years,' he said. 'We spoke often about his research. He believed the Manes' condition was a result of daemonic possession. That is nothing new, of course. It is a theory that has been widely discussed in the scientific community. But his unique idea concerned the nature of the daemon itself. Do you know what a symbiote is?'

Trinica gave the answer. Frey suspected it was more for his sake than anything else. 'It's an entity that bonds with another entity for the mutual benefit of both.'

'Exactly. The daemon doesn't consume or destroy its host. Maurin had assembled witness testimonies from survivors of Mane raids. He—'

'Hang on,' said Frey. 'I though Manes didn't leave survivors? I heard they hunt down everyone. They say there's no point hiding from them; they even get you inside locked rooms.'

Kraylock snorted, irritated at being interrupted. 'It's true there have been cases where Manes have got into apparently impossible places. When the bodies are found, the doors are still locked from the inside. No one knows how the Manes do it. But no, they don't hunt down everyone. There have been plenty of survivors over the years.' He glared at Frey. 'May I continue?'

'Sorry,' said Frey meekly. He was having flashbacks to his days in the orphanage, when he'd be chewed out by teachers for interrupting in class.

'Anyway, Maurin saw evidence of free will, decision-making, even arguments and disagreements. In the past, it was popularly supposed that they were mindless puppets, all under the control of a single guiding force – the daemon. It was the only way we could make sense of the way they acted.'

'How's that?' Frey asked.

'Well, for example, their manner is savage and they are never heard to speak. But during a raid they will all retreat together back to their dreadnoughts, without any signal being seen or heard. That, we thought, was evidence of control. They build and fly aircraft of their own, using technologies that even we don't understand. But they seemed so bestial, we had to believe that some other intelligence was responsible for that.'

'And Maurin thought otherwise?' Trinica prompted.

'He came to believe that the Manes were not being *controlled* at all. Instead, they were communicating silently. Speaking without words. He deduced from the evidence that each Mane always knew where the other Manes were, even if they could not see or hear them. From this, he decided that they were connected in some way. The daemon forges that connection between its host bodies. But it does not control them. You've heard the story, perhaps, of the boy whose father came home a Mane?'

'I know it,' said Frey. 'It was thirty years later, but his father hadn't aged a day. The boy killed him.'

'Yes. The tale is true. But before the boy killed him, the father tried to reason with him. Father to son. Tried to persuade him to become a Mane. Spoke of brotherhood and belonging. The Navy has records of the son's story.'

There was a moment's silence while they digested that.

'So why do they look like they do?' Frey asked. When Trinica raised an eyebrow at him, he rolled his eyes. 'Yes, yes, I judge by appearances.'

'It may be supposed that the daemon wreaks some physical change. Maurin never knew why. It differs from Mane to Mane. But there are certain advantages to having longer teeth, specialised vision, and so on. The daemon protects itself by enhancing its host.'

'Enhancing? By making them ugly?'

'They have no need to mate, as far as we can tell. They reproduce by converting other humans. Infecting them, like a virus. So why would they need to look pretty?'

Frey shrugged. 'I dunno. Just because.'

'Maurin theorised that mind-speech means that facial expressions and verbal communication become redundant. Perhaps they lose the finer facets of communication while keeping the more primal, animalistic ones, like snarling.'

Frey thought of Jez, back on board the *Ketty Jay*. What about her? Would she lose the power of speech? Was she part of this . . . connection that Kraylock was talking about? What if she was speaking to the Manes, even now? Feeding them information from all over Vardia while they waited eagerly to invade? How could he be sure where her loyalties lay?

'What happened to Maurin?' he asked.

The professor looked momentarily uncomfortable. The sun went behind a cloud, and the light from the windows dimmed. Kraylock seemed frail in his huge chair.

'He just died. There was no reason. His heart.' He rapped the desk with his knuckles. 'Stopped.'

His manner was too casual. Frey wasn't fooled. 'But you think there's more to it, don't you?'

Kraylock met his gaze steadily.

'The Awakeners,' Frey said. It had been the mention of the Awakeners that had got Kraylock talking in the first place. And from the Awakeners, Kraylock had guessed their business concerned the Manes. 'You think the Awakeners killed him.'

'An Imperator,' Trinica said, catching on. 'His heart stopped, just like that.' She nodded to herself. 'Sounds like something they'd do. But why?'

Kraylock didn't reply for a moment. Debating whether or not to say anything. Then he sighed wearily and spoke.

'His latest paper was going to be . . . controversial. He was drawing parallels between the Manes and the Awakeners. Specifically, the Imperators.'

'Parallels?' Trinica asked.

'He thought the Manes and the Imperators were essentially similar,' Kraylock said. 'Human hosts possessed by daemonic entities. The nature of the daemon is different, but the process is the same.'

Frey was amazed. 'You're saying that the Awakeners have been employing daemons? The same Awakeners who denounce daemonism and hang daemonists wherever they're found?'

'So he believed. The Manes and Imperators are both shrouded in secrecy and myth, but based on what truths he could obtain, he concluded that the Imperators were human hosts, presumably chosen from the ranks of the most faithful, who had been *joined* with a daemon to grant them extraordinary abilities. The Awakeners had always explained the Imperators' powers as evidence of the might of the Allsoul. Gifts from their deity to the loyal. But Maurin didn't hold with any of that. He wanted a scientific answer.'

'And he could prove it?'

'He had compelling research. He believed he had traced the origin of the Manes to its source, for one thing.'

'Where?'

'I don't know exactly. Somewhere in the north, near the coast. Marduk, I believe. Beneath the snows.'

'What happened there?'

'Approximately one hundred and fifteen years ago, a group of eminent daemonists assembled there. Maurin had letters detailing their plans. He even had the location, though, as I say, he never told me exactly. They came together to attempt a grand summoning. Something huge, something never before attempted.' He took off his glasses and cleaned them with a rag from the table. 'Something that went terribly wrong.'

'And the first of the Manes appeared soon after,' Trinica said.

Kraylock nodded. 'Those daemonists were the first of the Manes. Whatever they unleashed infected them. After that, they were the ones who spread the condition.'

Frey was getting impatient. 'So what does this have to do with—'

'The Awakeners?' Kraylock said. 'Because Maurin believed they knew about it. At the time they were aggressively attacking other religions. Any threat to their superiority was being wiped out. All the old gods were dying.'

'Not so immortal after all, eh?' Frey said, but his comment was ignored.

'There were survivors of that first disaster,' Kraylock continued. 'At least two. Maurin had letters, hinting at the tragedy that had occurred. They went into hiding, but then they disappeared. Maurin thought the Awakeners took them.'

'Why did he think that?'

'Because five years later, the first of the Imperators appeared.'

Frey and Trinica worked it out at the same time.

'So, the Awakeners heard what the daemonists were up to,' Trinica said. 'When it failed, they kidnapped the survivors—'

'—refined the process—' Frey continued.

'—and used it themselves, yes,' Kraylock finished. 'Infecting their most faithful subjects with symbiote daemons.'

Frey whistled, impressed by the scale of their hypocrisy.

'But they could never admit to employing daemonism,' Kraylock went on. 'The Lord High Cryptographer had already issued an edict condemning it as heresy. So they painted the Imperators as evidence

Chris Wooding

of the superiority of their faith, and used them to root out and destroy other faiths. Daemonists in particular. They were extraordinarily effective. Their rivals were soon scattered or eliminated entirely.'

'The Awakeners want to control all daemonism in Vardia,' Trinica said.

'Exactly. Daemonists are capable of *genuine* miracles. The Allsoul can't compete with that. So the Awakeners discredited their competition while claiming its achievements as their own.'

'Crake always said the Awakeners were more like a business than a religion,' Frey commented. Now he understood why the Awakeners were so interested in rumours of a crashed Mane dreadnought. They didn't want anyone getting hold of what was on board. The Awakeners knew the Manes were daemons, and daemonism was *their* thing. If there was any daemonic treasure to be had, they wanted control of it.

'So what happened to all this evidence?' said Trinica.

'Gone,' said Kraylock. 'That is what leads me to suspect foul play in his murder. That, and the subject of his paper.'

Frey frowned. 'When did you say he died again?'

'Two years ago.'

Frey snapped his fingers at Trinica. 'And when did Smult say Grist suddenly started taking an interest in the Manes?'

'Don't snap your fingers at me,' said Trinica. 'He said the spring before last.'

'Yes. Two years ago.'

Frey watched Trinica make the deduction in her head. 'What if Maurin *suspected* he was going to be killed?'

Frey grinned. 'What if he made a copy of his research and sent it to someone nobody would suspect?'

Excitement was dawning on Trinica's face. Frey was feeling so damn clever, he barely knew what to do with himself.

'He sent his notes to his son!' Frey said. 'That's how Grist knew about the sphere. That's how he knew to bring a daemonist to unlock the door. That's how he got access to Navy reports. It was all in his father's notes.'

'You think they might not have been lost?' Kraylock said in amazement. 'You have to get them back! That research, in the right hands . . . it could be the end of the Awakeners!' He sat back in his chair and blew out a breath, as if unable to believe what he'd just said.

262

'The end of the Awakeners,' he said, more quietly. 'If the Archduke got hold of that . . . if the House of Chancellors knew about it . . . Why, the Awakeners have been using daemonists for more than a century! Spit and blood, that would be something. Maurin would laugh at that from his grave.' His eyes were alight. 'You must get me those notes!'

Frey got to his feet. Trinica rose with him. 'First we have to find Grist,' he said. 'North coast of Marduk. Sounds like a good place to start.' He shook Kraylock's hand vigorously. 'Thanks for your help, Professor.'

'The notes!' Kraylock said as they walked out. 'Don't forget the notes!'

Trinica gave Frey a sideways glance as they walked out of the door. 'I'm impressed, Captain Frey,' she said wryly. 'And that's the second time in three days. What's become of you?'

Frey was more than a little impressed himself. 'Stick around,' he said. 'There's more where that came from.'

Twenty-Six

The Hospital – Crake's Progress – The Deal

The hospital stood on a hill on the edge of town. It was an old building with many windows, some of them lit to fend off the night. Sills crumbled at the edges; panes were cracked here and there; the walls were weathered and mossy. The darkness hid the worst of the dilapidation, but not enough of it.

Crake gazed bleakly at the scene from the back seat of the motorised carriage. The cab driver was hunched over on the bench up front, his shoulders squared and a cap pulled down hard over his head, as if he was driving through a thunderstorm. But the night was warm and still. Apart from the rattle of the engine, it was eerily quiet.

A long, curving gravel drive led away from the walled perimeter and the iron gates that squeaked with rust. The grounds that it passed through were badly kept: the grass was long, the trees overgrown and shaggy. The carriage pulled up outside the hospital. Crake checked his pocket watch – *right on time* – and got out.

'Wait for me here, please,' he said to the driver. 'I shan't be long.'

The driver touched his cap in response, then returned to his previous position and stayed there, unmoving, like some dormant automaton from a science-fiction novel. The man made Crake uneasy. He didn't like the driver's silence, his stillness, the stoic way he went about his job. On another day, it wouldn't have bothered him, but lately he found such small oddities hard to bear. Little things made him angry without reason. Sometimes he'd become over-emotional, and the slightest matter would make him want to weep. Even Plome had commented on it, and taken to avoiding him whenever it was decently possible to do so. Crake, for his part, passed most of his time in the sanctum beneath Plome's house. The longer he stayed there, the less inclined he was to deal with the world outside.

But sometimes sacrifices were necessary.

Crake paused for a moment, to arrange himself and marshal his courage. He was heavily bundled up, despite the lack of a chill in the air, and he clutched his coat tightly around him as he entered the hospital reception area. It was brown and dull and smelled faintly of bleach, but it was clean and orderly, which eased Crake's nerves a fraction. He'd always taken comfort in the signs of an efficient civilisation. Banks, theatres and high-class restaurants were a balm to the chaos in his life. At least this place, despite its seedy reputation, looked organised.

It was quiet at this time of night. A middle-aged nurse sat behind the reception desk, talking to a doctor. Both looked up as he entered.

'Visiting hours are over, I'm afraid,' said the nurse, once she'd established that he was not obviously maimed in any way. Her tone was sharp, calculated to persuade the listener that there was no point in arguing.

Crake tried anyway. 'Yes, I'm . . . er . . . I'm afraid I couldn't get here any earlier. It's my uncle Merin. He's very sick, I understand.'

'I'm sorry, but—' the nurse began, but the doctor overrode her.

'You must be Mardrew,' he said, walking over to shake Crake's hand. 'He said you were coming. He's very keen to see you.' The doctor turned to the nurse. 'It's alright, I'll take him through.'

The nurse shook her head and went back to her paperwork. 'Don't know why we bother having visiting hours at all,' she muttered sourly.

'This way, please,' said the doctor, showing Crake through a swing door. He was a short, thin man in his early thirties, with black hair oiled back close to his scalp and a small, tidy moustache. Crake followed him down a corridor until they were out of earshot of the nurse.

'You have the money?' the doctor asked him.

'Yes,' said Crake. And after that, nothing more was said.

So simple. They were past the nurse and in before Crake had time to think twice. A good thing, too. He felt sure that his deeply in-grained fear of authority would have got the better of him if he'd been forced to stand there and wait. He'd have crumbled under the nurse's gaze and turned back. But the doctor was in the reception, just as Crake's contact said he'd be. All Crake had to do was ask for his uncle Merin. The whole thing had gone like clockwork.

So why did he feel more scared than before?

They came across a sign indicating the way to the wards, but the doctor ignored it and went the other way down the corridor. The hospital was sterile and hushed. Nurses padded by, wheeling trollies. Janitors mopped the floors. They passed a hurrying doctor, who exchanged a quick word of greeting with Crake's escort. At any moment, Crake expected someone to challenge him. Surely they could sense he was on forbidden business? Surely it was obvious in his quick, roving gaze and his petrified expression?

But nobody took any notice.

Presently, they came to an door marked simply: ACCESS. The doctor checked to make sure nobody was in sight, then pushed it open and led Crake through.

There was a tight, dim stairwell beyond. They went down one level and through a metal door into another corridor.

The atmosphere here was less savoury than the floor above. The walls were grimy, and there were bits of litter in the corners. Electric lights buzzed overhead, their surfaces smeared with oily thumbprints. There was no smell of disinfectant here, only a hint of mould. It was chilly, and Crake was glad of his coat.

I shouldn't be doing this, he thought to himself. The closer they got to their destination, the more sick and terrified he felt. It hadn't seemed real until he'd got through reception. He'd half-expected to be turned away. But the act of tricking the nurse had committed him. Even though he'd done nothing illegal yet, he felt that it was too late to back out. He looked around nervously, seeking an escape and finding none.

The doctor walked ahead of him, his polished shoes tapping on the stone floor. Leading him on, silently. They both knew why he was here. Crake despised him for being a witness to his shame.

How had it come to this? He'd set out with such high hopes, such optimism. He'd met with men who traded in daemonist texts and held fascinating conversations with them about the nature of the Art. He'd acquired rare tomes at great expense and devoured them greedily. For a time he'd felt like he did when he first discovered daemonism at university. He was a repository, ready to be filled with knowledge. In a few short weeks he'd learned more than he had in the last few years.

But his joy hadn't lasted. He bought book after book but none had contained what he needed. He'd hoped to find a method to extract Bess from the metal suit he'd put her in. If not instructions, then even hints and pointers would have sufficed. But he was disappointed again and again. Plome's credit was not unlimited, and his own money was not sufficient to keep buying valuable, illegal texts. With each book that failed to provide the answers he sought, the stakes got higher, and he found it harder and harder to relax or sleep.

Things had become strained between him and Plome. Crake hated having to beg him for money that he had no realistic prospect of ever paying back. Plome's constant fretting about his state of mind became tiresome. He began to stay down in the sanctum with Bess, and kept himself occupied by teaching her new commands with his whistle. But Bess had picked up on his mood too, and when she was awake she was fidgety and withdrawn. Almost as if she was scared of him. Angrily, he put her to sleep and left her like that; but the sight of the silent, empty armoured suit was like an accusation.

The old feeling started to creep back in. That sense of being trapped. Wherever he turned, he was oppressed. There was nowhere he could get any peace. He became too agitated to study, and that made him more agitated. He ransacked his books with increasing desperation for clues on how to proceed. He bought apparatus and did experiments based on hearsay and rumour. Nothing worked. No one could help him.

But there was Bess, looming hugely in his mind, demanding that he save her.

He refused to fail. And if none of his learned peers had any advice for him, then he'd damn well have to do it himself. His time on the *Ketty Jay* had taught him a little about how to handle the underworld, and it was to the underworld he went. He talked to some people, greased a few palms, and all of it led him here.

Yet, for all that he felt he'd taken matters into his own hands, he never quite felt in control. And now, as he followed in the footsteps of the doctor, he wondered what he'd been thinking.

It's not too late to turn back, he thought. *You don't have to do this.*

But he did. He had to do it for Bess.

The basement level was mostly used for storage and was deserted. They walked a little way and took another set of steps down. The level below was dirtier than the last, and barely lit at all. There was a deep thrumming noise from somewhere nearby: a massive boiler, vibrating through the walls. Despite the boiler's proximity, it was freezing down here, and it stank of something unpleasant that Crake couldn't identify, something dank and cloying and vile. He could hear rats scurrying in the dark.

He began to jump at shadows. Each step took him further into a nightmare. If the cab driver was bad, this was worse. What had he got himself into? Where was this doctor taking him? The clean corridors he'd passed through seemed like a distant memory now. Ahead, a ceiling light flickered, turning itself on and off at random. Crake could barely keep still. He desperately wanted to be gone from this place.

Be strong, he told himself. *Don't fail her.*

The doctor stopped in front of a metal door and unlocked it with a key.

'This is the deal,' he said. 'After we're done here, I lead you out of the front door, past the nurse on reception. I'll meet you at the back entrance at midnight. Half the money on acceptance of the merchandise, half on receipt. Are we understood?'

'Understood,' said Crake. He could barely force the word out through the dread that took hold of him.

'I need hardly remind you to be discreet,' said the doctor.

'No,' he said. 'You needn't.'

The doctor gave him an uncertain look, noticing his distress. He made no comment. Instead, he opened the door and went through. Crake followed.

The room was tiled and white and grubby. Three gurneys were positioned against the far wall, three shapes underneath, covered by white cloths. The doctor passed from one to the other, pulling the cloths away.

Lying there were three little girls, their skin white, eyes staring upward. All of them Bess's age when she died, or thereabouts. Each had a Y-shaped row of stitches, running from shoulders to breastbone to pelvis. So appallingly young and innocent. Crake stared at them, horror constricting his throat. Shame and self-loathing filled him. He reeled and steadied himself against the door frame.

I can't do this, I can't do this, I can't . . .

'Well?' said the doctor, indicating the corpses. 'Which one did you want?'

Twenty-Seven

Meaningful Conversations – Jez Clears The Air –
The Happy Amputee – A New Lead – Departures

Marduk was a cold, bleak and bitter place, even with summer coming on. It was the northernmost of the Nine Duchies, sharing a mountain border to the west with Yortland, which was the only colder place on the continent. Cruel winds blew down from the arctic, off the Poleward Sea. The month of Thresh had begun, heralding the start of the summer, but there was little of summer here.

Frey and Trinica walked along winding, slushy trails. Beyond the nearby buildings, snow-capped mountains rose hard and black. It was not yet dusk, but the peaks had swallowed the sun and the town of Raggen Crag was in twilight.

Neither had spoken for a long time. Wrapped in thick hide coats with furred hoods pulled over their heads, they wandered the paths of Raggen Crag without purpose or intention. It was enough, just to walk.

Lights glowed in the windows of the houses, which had been built in groups, huddled together for warmth. The sound of rumbling industrial boilers could be heard within. The roofs and roads were piled with drifts of dirty snow. Black arctic birds swung overhead, or sat on the heating pipes and puffed up their feathers.

It was a grim and simple settlement, like many others Frey had visited lately. They must have hit twenty-five towns in the last thirty days, and still Grist eluded them. There were sightings, hints – enough evidence to keep them in the chase – but nothing that had brought them closer to their target.

Every day, Frey scoured the broadsheets. But there was no sign of any disaster. No doomsday weapon unleashed.

What was Grist up to? What did he mean to do with the sphere he'd stolen? What was he waiting for?

If Frey was frustrated, his crew were doubly so. They were tired and bored. None of them cared about this mission the way he did. Nobody wanted to be dragged around a miserable duchy like Marduk while summer was wasting in the south. Pinn was almost permanently drunk, and Malvery had taken to joining him. Harkins was hardly ever seen on the *Ketty Jay*; he only came on board for brief visits, and even then he was so skittish that Frey could barely get a sensible word out of him. Silo was his usual self. Jez stayed out of everyone's way. Crake and Bess were gone.

But there was Trinica. At least there was Trinica.

Having Trinica on board hadn't been easy at first. No matter how much they tried to get on, their history always lay between them. The spectre of their unborn child kept them apart. Neither could forgive the other for that. There were so many sharp edges to their conversations.

But they persisted, driven by their common cause. Their encounters with Osric Smult and Professor Kraylock had convinced them that they needed each other, if they wanted to find Grist. In the days that followed, they worked well together. Trinica knew people who wouldn't even open the door to Frey. Frey, in turn, knew lowlifes who were beneath Trinica's notice. Trinica had a way with the high-borns; Frey knew how to butter up drunks. Between them they scoured the inns and drinking houses of the remote northern settlements, plumbing the locals for information.

But there was little information to be had. Grist had disappeared, seemingly without trace.

As time passed, they got used to each other again. The barbed comments came less often. Conversations were no longer loaded with implications. They were no longer walking on eggshells.

More and more, Frey found himself forgetting that they were supposed to be enemies. And it seemed Trinica was forgetting too.

It wasn't all plain sailing. The longer he spent with Trinica, the more he was exposed to her rapid, jagged changes of mood. She was prone to black depressions which made her difficult company. But he learned to ride out her fits of anger and her sullen episodes. Because for every storm there was a period of clear skies and sunlight, where she was suffused with childish joy, or testing him with a wry and wicked wit. For those times, there was little he wouldn't endure.

This evening she was thoughtful, and there was a kind of quiet sadness to her. He wasn't sure where it had come from, but he'd long learned to stop searching for cause and effect where Trinica was concerned. She was a different woman to the one he'd left behind, but now she was free of that ghoulish make-up he could almost believe the last twelve years had never happened.

'I'm worried about your crew,' she said suddenly. They were the first words spoken for half an hour.

He blinked. 'You are?'

'Aren't you?'

He thought about that. *Worried* wasn't exactly the word he'd use. He was aware that the atmosphere aboard the *Ketty Jay* wasn't good, but he'd assumed it would sort itself out without any interference from him.

'It's just this whole Grist thing,' he said. 'Once we catch the bastard, they'll be alright.'

'They won't, Darian. They're coming apart. I know it's mostly my fault, but still—'

'*Your* fault? How's that?'

She gave him a look, her pale face framed by the furred rim of her hood. 'You must see that they hate me.'

Darian plucked at the back of his glove. '*Hate* is a bit strong,' he said. 'If we held a grudge against everyone who'd ever screwed us over, we'd have to leave the country. It's not like we've never been ripped off before.'

'Ah,' she said. 'But I'll bet you never invited the thief on board afterwards, though.'

'That's true. Except once, and that was to kick the shit out of him.'

She sighed, blowing out a plume of steam. Their feet crunched through the thin crust of old snow that lay on the paths. Two townsmen walked past leading a shaggy beast of burden, which was towing a piece of machinery on a cart. Frey had seen several of the creatures over the past month but he still wasn't exactly sure what they were. Something between a cow and a ram, he supposed, but since they came buried under a mass of knotted and tangled fur, it was difficult to tell. All he knew was that they were immensely strong and they stank like a mouldy underwear drawer. He vaguely wondered if they were good to eat.

'Listen,' she said. 'You were never the best at seeing what was in front of you, so I'll explain. Your crew resent me. Not only because I stole from them, but because I'm taking up your time.'

'You think they're *jealous*?' he scoffed. 'Trinica, they're not children.'

'Some of them aren't far off,' she said.

'S'pose you're right at that.'

'Darian, they've lost a friend in Crake. Even I can see that, and I never knew him. At times like that, when things are uncertain and times are bad, a crew looks to its captain for guidance and reassurance. But you're not there. You're with me. They can't understand it, and they don't like it. Darian, do any of them even know we were almost married?'

'No,' he said, uncomfortable. 'I think you're making a bit much of this, though.'

'No, I'm not. I would have said something weeks ago, but I didn't want to tell you how to run your crew.'

'I've done alright so far,' he said. He was on the defensive, and it came out snappy.

'You have. But now you need to do better,' she said. 'Being a captain, it's more than just making good decisions and giving the right orders. It's about trust. You're like the head of a family. They need to trust you, and you need to trust them.'

'They do trust me!' Frey protested. 'Why do you think they've stuck with me?'

'It's a testament to their loyalty that they have,' she said. 'But it won't last forever. You're barely talking to your navigator. For what reason, I can't tell, but it's been going on for a month. The rest of your crew don't really understand why they're being dragged through town after town, because you haven't explained to them why it's important to you. And all of them are feeling the loss of Crake, but their captain doesn't appear to care.'

'I *do* care!'

'But they can't see that.'

Frey didn't like the way this conversation had turned. He knew she was trying to help him, but he still didn't like to be criticised. He bit back a sarcastic comment and tried not to look surly.

When she spoke again, her voice was gentle, cushioning the content. 'You let things fester,' she said. 'It's your way. You're not good at talking about the things that really matter, so you avoid it instead. You wait and hope that everything will turn out well.' She paused, gazing at the ground before her. 'Remember when you left me, Darian?'

'Of course I do,' he said, prickling.

'You were unhappy for so long, weren't you?' Her tone was sad, sympathetic. It confused him. He'd expected an attack.

'I just . . .' he began, but already the words were clogging up. Damn it, he could never say how he felt and make it sound right. 'It was like I was trapped,' he managed at last. 'I was nineteen.'

'You were angry with me for asking you to marry me. For getting pregnant,' she said it matter-of-factly.

'I wanted to be with you,' said Frey awkwardly. 'I just didn't want to marry you. That's a big thing, you know? I was just a boy. I had a thousand things to do with my life.'

'But you didn't *say* that. You didn't say any of it.'

Frey was silent. He remembered how it was, on the day of the wedding. How he'd left it till the last minute, and when there was no other way out, he ran.

'I've thought about that day a lot,' Trinica said, as they trudged down a slope between two clusters of houses. Back towards the tiny landing pad and the *Ketty Jay*. 'I wondered what things would have been like if you'd spoken up earlier. Or if you'd married me anyway, despite your reservations.' She bit her lip, closed her eyes, shook her head. 'I can't see it. Any way you cut it. Wouldn't have worked.'

'I was nineteen,' said Frey quietly. 'So were you.'

'Yes. I was, once.'

The landing pad came into view. The lamp-posts were on. A dozen craft, none bigger than the *Ketty Jay*, rested there. As they approached, they could hear the sound of short, sharp impacts. Jez was there, buried inside a fur-lined coat, chipping ice from the landing struts.

Trinica stopped. Frey stopped with her. 'What?' he asked.

'You should go and talk to her,' Trinica said.

'About what?'

'About whatever's going on between you. I'll walk a little more.'

Frey felt suddenly unwell. 'I don't know what to say,' he protested feebly.

Trinica was firm. 'Anything's better than nothing.'

Frey watched Jez working away in the yellow lamplight. Trinica was right, of course. She was always smarter than he was. She never let him get away with anything. She decimated his excuses. Saw right through him when he tried to weasel out of things. He remembered that about her. She pushed him, always. She wouldn't let him be weak.

You're like the head of a family, she'd said. And that was true. He'd told himself that they were all adults, that they could handle their own problems, but in his heart he'd known that he just didn't want to deal with them himself.

But a captain should lead by example. He couldn't ignore it any longer. He needed to clear the air.

You always let things fester. Well, not this time.

He took a steady breath and began to walk towards Jez. Trinica stayed where she was. After a few steps, he stopped and looked back at her.

'For what it's worth, I'm sorry,' he said. 'Sorry as all damnation for the way it turned out.'

Trinica gave him a forlorn smile. 'Me, too,' she said.

Jez heard the Cap'n coming, but she didn't turn to look. Only when it became clear that he wanted to talk to her did she stop hacking at the ice. But she still didn't meet his eyes. She was angry. She'd been angry for days now.

How easily they turned on her. How many times had she saved their lives? Who among them could claim to be half as useful as she was? She didn't gripe like Pinn or slob around like Malvery. She didn't fall apart like Harkins or desert them like Crake. She deserved her place more than anyone on board.

But none of that counted, because she was a Mane.

At first, she'd been ashamed. Ashamed of her condition, ashamed that they'd seen the bestial side of her that she'd hoped to hide for ever. Ashamed that she'd kept the secret from them. She'd skulked about the *Ketty Jay*, keeping herself to herself. Her only confidant was Silo. When she wasn't in her quarters or about her duties, she was in the engine room. They didn't speak often, but she was content just to be there, to help out where she could. Silo understood.

But shame only lasted so long, and then it began to sour. With every uneasy greeting in the corridor, every hour passed in silence in the cockpit with the captain, her bitterness grew. She was sick of being sorry. She found it pathetic that the crew were all pretending that nothing had happened, and yet they couldn't look her in the eye.

Nobody made any move, whether to make peace or to kick her off the *Ketty Jay*. She waited every day for the axe to fall, but eventually it became apparent that no one was holding it.

Now, as the Cap'n stood next to her, she wondered if the time had finally come.

'Jez?' he said. 'Can we talk?'

She shrugged with an insulting lack of respect. 'Whatever you want.'

'And you can cut out the attitude, Jez, or we're never going to get anywhere.'

He wasn't usually so assertive. It surprised her, but not enough to make her drop the hostility in her tone. 'Where exactly are you trying to get to, Cap'n?' she asked.

He glared at her for a moment, then snorted. 'Forget it,' he said. 'This isn't worth it. Bad idea.'

He turned and began to stalk away from her. But that brief exchange had fired her up. All the pressure in her had just been given a vent. The Cap'n wanted to talk? Well, she'd talk.

'Cap'n!' she snapped.

He stopped and turned around. 'You got something to say?'

'Yeah, Cap'n, I do,' she said. 'I want to tell you I'm rot-damned tired of the way I'm being treated on board this aircraft. I'm tired of being a ghost to all you men just because you're too chickenshit to deal with your feelings. There's a sight too many secrets on the *Ketty Jay*. A little more conversation and a little less ducking the bloody issue would do us all a lot of good.'

She threw the hammer and chisel on the ground and spat after it. Felt good. Felt good to go past the point of caring what the consequences were. She strode up to the Cap'n. She was shorter than him, but so what? It was time he heard how it was.

'I got caught by a Mane,' she said. 'Didn't turn me all the way, but it turned me enough. I'm part Mane, but I'm *still human*. I think like I used to, and I feel like I used to. And I might add that my being a Mane accounts for my frankly phenomenal navigational skills, without which you'd be long dead and your precious craft would be a heap of slag.' She threw her hood back and glared up at him furiously. 'Do you get it, Cap'n? I'm part Mane. You deal with that or you kick me off, but I'm not living like this any more.'

Her words rang out into silence, swallowed by the cold wind that blew through the town. Frey's face was stony and grim.

'What happened on the *All Our Yesterdays*?' he asked.

'I don't know.'

'What if it happens again?'

'I don't know. I can't promise I won't.'

'I have a crew to think about,' he said.

'Yes!' she cried. 'And I'm part of it!' She paced away from him, smoothed her hair back, retied her ponytail. Something she did when she was anxious or upset. 'I'm in trouble, Cap'n,' she said. 'I'm turning. Into what, I don't know. How long it'll take, I don't know. Maybe I'll beat it. Maybe it's unstoppable. But I'm scared. I'm scared I'll lose my mind. And the only person who might have explained any of it to me was Crake, and now he's gone! Because of another damn secret that he couldn't share.'

'I don't think you'll lose your mind,' said Frey.

Her tone made it clear what she thought of his knowledge on the subject. 'You don't? Why not?'

'Because this professor guy told me so. He said the daemon was more like . . . like a sin-boat.'

'Symbiote,' she corrected automatically.

'Yeah, that. And it doesn't take you over or control you or anything. It just . . . well . . . kind of helps you out, I suppose. That and it makes you look like shit.'

She stared at him, aghast. 'You spoke to that professor a *month* ago!'

Frey looked like he wished he hadn't opened his mouth.

'And you didn't *tell* me?' she yelled.

'Things were . . . weird between us,' he mumbled. 'Wasn't sure how to.'

'The way you just did would have been fine!' She slapped the landing strut in frustration. 'Spit and pus, Cap'n! You know what it would have meant to me? To know that?'

'Sorry,' Frey said sheepishly.

She put her face in her hands. Her shoulders heaved with each breath.

'Are you crying?' Frey asked.

'I'm trying to calm down so I don't kill you,' she replied through her fingers.

'Oh.'

She took her hands away, shook her head, blew out a breath. *Under control, Jez. Keep it under control.*

She put her hand on her hip and poked Frey in the chest with a finger. 'I'll tell you what,' she said. 'I'll give you a choice. I quit the *Ketty Jay*. Right here and now.'

Frey looked stricken. 'Wait, you're quitting?'

'Ah! Ah!' she said. 'I'm not done. It seems you have a vacancy for a navigator now. So I offer my services. I'm a navigator. You won't find any better. But I'm also part Mane, with all the things that entails.' She folded her arms and stared at him defiantly. 'Now I've told you, upfront. Either hire me, and we start again from scratch, or don't, and I'll leave right now. But no more of this pussyfoot bullshit.'

Frey stood there in the slowly freezing slush and regarded her thoughtfully. It was impossible to tell what he was thinking. Nothing showed on his face, as if this was a game of Rake and he was considering his hand.

All or nothing. What's it to be?

Then he tutted, and looked up at the sky. 'Who am I kidding? We wouldn't last two days without you. You're the best damn navvie I've ever seen.'

'Because I'm part Mane,' she said. 'Because I can read the wind, and see in the dark. Because I just *know* where things are sometimes. Because I'm part Mane. Say it.'

Frey nodded. 'Okay. Because you're part Mane. And whatever goes along with that. I get it.'

'So,' she said. 'Am I hired?'

Frey grinned. 'You're hired.'

'I want a bigger cut of the profits.'

'What?' Frey was appalled. Jez just stared at him, arms folded, until he threw up his hands.

'Fine! When there's profits to give you, you'll get your cut,' he said. 'If we ever make any.'

Jez felt a grin spreading across her own face. She felt lighter than air. There was a huge sense of release. This whole thing had been building up and building up. Just talking about it made it better. Ironic, really, that it had taken the most silent member of the crew to teach her that.

She held out her hand. 'Thank you, Cap'n. And sorry for keeping it from you. Me being a Mane and all. I won't let you down again.'

He clasped her hand and then, to her surprise, he pulled her into a rough hug. 'Likewise,' he said.

The Happy Amputee was Raggen Crag's classiest bar, which wasn't saying much. It was a grubby, dingy room, lit by blackened bulbs, with tarnished metal fixtures and brass countertops. A broken-down band played on the stage. The locals drank hard liquor and talked in low voices.

Pinn sat at a table in a corner, sweeping a bleary and baleful glare across the room. He was drunk. Mean, stinking drunk. In one meaty hand was the ferrotype of his sweetheart that usually hung from the dash of his Skylance. Malvery sat next to him, hovering on the edge of coma, his eyelids drooping. His round, green glasses sat askew on his nose. Every so often, his head would dip towards the table, and then he'd startle awake briefly before sliding into unconsciousness once again. Several bottles of grog were clustered on the table in front of them.

'Look at 'em,' Pinn snarled.

'Mmf?' Malvery inquired.

'Them!' he said, motioning with his chin. 'The Cap'n and his whore.'

Malvery blinked and tried to focus. Near the bar, Frey and Trinica were deep in conversation with two local men. Tough-looking, ugly sorts.

'Leave 'em alone,' Malvery mumbled. 'Cap'n knows what he's doin'.'

Pinn scowled and took another swig of grog. The Cap'n definitely *didn't* know what he was doing. Palling around with that slut. Oh, she might have cleaned off that ghoul mask that she wore, but Pinn wasn't fooled. She was still a woman. Treacherous as quicksand. Not that Pinn had ever been near quicksand, but he'd definitely heard it was treacherous.

Bewitched, that was what the Cap'n was. What else could it be? What else could explain it? This past month, you hardly ever saw them apart. The Cap'n was all spry as a lark while everyone else sloped around feeling rotten. What was it between them, anyway? Pinn had thought the Cap'n hated her. Pinn had thought they were enemies. Why ask her along?

All Pinn knew was that Trinica had robbed them blind. Twice! Having that bitch on board was rubbing it in everyone's faces. He'd have been rich if not for her. Maybe then he'd have gone back to Lisinda. Maybe then she wouldn't have sent him a letter telling him she was marrying some other man.

He stared at the ferrotype in his hand. Those eyes, that had once gazed at him so adoringly. Even now, they might be gazing that way at someone else. He ground his back teeth together at the thought.

Every day since he'd received that letter had been a torment of indecision. Should he go back to her, to try and pry her from his rival? Or was that exactly what his rival wanted? He needed to do something to prevent the marriage, but he couldn't return yet, poorer than when he'd left. And what if he was already too late? A cold and manly indifference was surely better than coming home to see the gleam of triumph in his rival's eyes.

For a month now, he'd been paralysed. But with each day that passed, matters became a little more urgent. He had to do something. He just didn't know what.

Malvery turned his head with a slow movement, as if he was underwater. He saw Pinn staring at the ferrotype, and snorted.

'Forget her, mate,' he slurred. 'She ain't worth it.'

'Shut your face, Doc. You don't know her.'

'Come on,' said Malvery. 'Be honest. You weren't ever gonna go back to her anyway. Even if she didn't get married.'

'I was!' Pinn snapped. 'When I got—'

'When you got rich, yeah, yeah.' The idiot grin of the truly hammered spread across his face. 'But you ain't never gonna *be* rich, Pinn. Nor 'm I. Nor are any of us.' He aimed a finger at Pinn, squinting down its length as if it was a gun. 'You know that, don'tcha?'

'I,' Pinn declared indignantly, '*love* her.'

'You,' Malvery replied, '*left* her.'

Pinn didn't really understand what the doctor was driving at. He finished his mug of grog and poured some more.

'Look, mate,' said Malvery, slapping him heavily on the shoulder. 'You can't mope about for ever. She's gone. Plenny more fishies in the sea.'

Pinn stared into Lisinda's eyes. 'I don't want fishes,' he said, suddenly forlorn.

The loud scrape of a chair pulled across the floor startled him. He looked up and saw Frey and Trinica sitting down at their table. He spared her a disgusted grimace before turning his attention to the Cap'n.

'We're moving out,' Frey announced. He seemed excited.

'Now?' Malvery groaned.

Frey thumbed at Pinn. 'Soon as he can fly.' He snatched away the remainder of the grog. 'Get some coffee inside you.'

'Hey! I can fly anytime!' Pinn cried. He lunged for the grog, his hand slipped, and he crashed on to the table, scattering the empty bottles everywhere.

Frey waited for the cacophony of smashing glass to subside. 'We'll wait a few hours, eh?' he suggested.

'What's the story, Cap'n?' Malvery asked.

'There's a town called Endurance, not too far from here. Big aerium-mining operation. Those fellers we were talking to just came from there. Apparently, a bunch of Century Knights have turned up. And guess who they're looking for?'

'Grist?'

'Right. Apparently they're asking for this bloke who they think used to be part of his crew. Feller named Almore Roke. They think he's in Endurance.'

Malvery frowned. 'Why are *they* lookin' for Grist?'

'Good question,' said Trinica. 'We don't know. But this man Roke sounds like the best lead we're likely to get.'

'Oh, is that right?' sneered Pinn. 'You calling the shots now?'

Frey gave him a hard look. 'No,' he said. 'I am. Sober up and get yourself back to the *Ketty Jay*. Malvery, see that he does.'

Frey and Trinica got up and left. Pinn waited till they were gone then began mumbling swear words under his breath.

'Don't worry,' said Malvery, who'd perked up a bit. 'Everythin' will be back to normal before you know it. I'll get us some coffee.'

It was almost dawn when Frey flopped into his pilot seat, yawning. He'd managed a couple of hours of sleep before he was roused by Jez. Pinn and Malvery had returned from the bar, and Pinn looked together enough to fly. They probably should have left it till the morning, but Frey was worried they'd miss their opportunity if they did. They needed to get to Endurance as soon as possible.

Jez was already at her station. In the frosty lamplight, he could see Harkins running through pre-flight checks. The pilot had a blanket wrapped around his shoulders, having slept in the cockpit of the Firecrow again. Pinn was clambering into his Skylance nearby.

'Plot us a course for Endurance,' Frey said over his shoulder.

'Did it three hours ago, Cap'n,' she replied.

'Why aren't I surprised?' He stretched and tried to shake off the fuzz of sleep. 'Hey, Jez, you've been hanging about with Silo, right? How's the engine?'

'Holding together. He still needs those parts, you know.'

'Yeah,' said Frey. 'Maybe one day we'll have the money to buy them and the luxury of staying in one place long enough to get them ordered in.'

'We can dream, Cap'n.'

Frey smiled to himself. He'd missed their little interchanges. The cockpit had seemed cold and hollow without them. Maybe there was still the sense that they were trying a little too hard, but that would fade. They'd broken through the barrier. The tension between them was gone.

He felt positive, for the first time in quite a while. Squaring things up with Jez had given him a sense of achievement. One problem fixed. And now they had a solid lead on Grist. At last, something to chase. He was starting to think that things were turning around.

He watched as Pinn settled into his cockpit and flooded the aerium tanks. The Skylance rose gently into the air. Malvery shambled through the doorway of the cockpit and stood there, red-eyed.

'Good work getting him back in one piece,' said Frey. 'I thought you'd be out of it by now.'

'Too much coffee,' Malvery said.

'Malvery, meet our new navigator, Jez,' he said. 'She's part Mane, you know. Don't hold it against her.'

Malvery caught the change in the air and played along. 'Pleased to meet you,' he said. 'I'm Malvery. Resident alcoholic.'

Jez grinned. 'It's an honour to travel in such esteemed company.'

'It is, isn't it?' Malvery said. 'Now, you'd better excuse me. Think I need some grog to take the edge off that coffee.'

Frey was peering through the windglass at the Skylance as it rose. 'You think he might be too drunk to fly?' he asked Malvery idly, as the doctor headed out of the cockpit. 'Maybe we should've waited till—'

He was interrupted by a flash of light and a deafening boom, loud enough to cause Malvery to fall over. Frey cringed back in his seat, blinking rapidly, dazzled. When his vision had cleared, the Skylance was gone.

He snatched up his earcuff and clipped it on. 'Pinn!' he said. 'Pinn, what happened?' But the only reply was Harkins' incoherent gibber. The sudden noise had turned him to jelly.

'Calm down, Harkins!' he snapped. 'What happened? Did you see? Where's Pinn?'

'He . . . ah . . . uuhhh . . . I . . .'

Useless. Frey turned around in his seat. Malvery was just picking himself up off the floor. 'What just happened?'

'Afterburners,' said Jez. 'Pinn hit his afterburners and flew off. You know that craft is rigged for speed.'

'Hit them by accident?'

'I don't think so, Cap'n.'

'But he doesn't know how to get where we're going!'

There was silence for a moment. Realisation dawned on Frey. 'He's not coming, is he?'

'I don't . . . I don't reckon he is,' said Malvery. The doctor was ashen-faced. Perhaps, like Frey, the thought that Pinn would ever leave them was beyond his comprehension. Pinn was too dim and unambitious, and besides, he had nowhere else to go.

They'd misjudged him. The young pilot could take any amount of abuse and mockery and laugh it off with good humour, but the news from his sweetheart had finally proven too much.

No, Frey thought to himself. *It's not that, and you know it. It's Trinica. It's because you brought Trinica on board. You knew he hated her, and you ignored him.*

Frey turned back to the controls, stony-faced. His good mood had withered and died. 'Give me a heading, Jez. I'm taking us up.'

'But what about Pinn?' Harkins wailed in his ear.

'Pinn's gone, Harkins,' said Frey. 'Forget him.'

Twenty-Eight

A Quiet Landing – Worrying Evidence –
An Urchin – Oldrew Sprine

Early morning, and the town of Endurance lurked beneath an anvil-grey sky. Powdery snow sifted down from the clouds, swirling in flurries, dusting the ground.

It was a mean, bare place, crammed into a fold in the mountains, surrounded by hard horizons of dark rock. Simple square buildings crowded in tight, huddled against the bitter north-eastern winds. A short way distant was a mineshaft: the reason for the town's existence. Gargantuan machinery – pumps and elevators and drills – surrounded the entrance. Railway tracks led in and out. Mine carts sat idle. A road led along the mountainside to a refinery at the edge of town. It was a black, sprawling mass of pipes and chimneys, squat and low, a malevolent presence overlooking the drab, slumped houses and joyless streets.

The landing pad was all but deserted, and nobody was around to guide the *Ketty Jay* in. Frey eyed the settlement as he descended. No sign of life. No activity at the mine. The refinery was dormant: no smoke came from its chimneys.

'It's quiet,' he muttered. He left a dramatic pause and then said: 'T—'

'*Too* quiet?' Jez suggested.

'That was *my* line,' Frey said, miffed. He'd always wanted a chance to say it.

'Sorry, Cap'n,' said Jez. Judging by her grin, she wasn't.

He returned his attention to the town below. He didn't like this. Not at all.

'Wake up Malvery, will you?' he said. 'And Silo. Tell them to bring shotguns.'

'What about Captain Dracken?'

He thought about that for a moment. 'Her too,' he said. He wasn't sure how useful she'd be, but she'd never agree to stay behind. 'You'll stay here, with Harkins. Keep in touch with the earcuffs. I've a feeling we might need a quick getaway, and I'll need you to fly the *Ketty Jay* if we do.'

'Cap'n.' She made to leave, but Frey stopped her.

'Wait. Before you go, tell me what you think of those.' He pointed down at the landing pad, where three very unusual aircraft sat. Them, and no others.

'The two on the far side are a Keeley Skywave and a Modderich Grace,' she said. 'Serious luxury craft. And the other's a Tabington Claw. It's the workshop's flagship model, fighter transport, top of the line. It's either escort for the other two or it belongs to some folks who are a sight rougher than the owners of the luxury craft.'

'That's what I thought,' said Frey. 'Alright. Go and wake the others.'

He brought the *Ketty Jay* in and settled her down with a puff of snow. Harkins came sinking through the air to starboard. The pilot had hardly said a word since Pinn's surprise exit. Frey wondered if Harkins was missing their constant bickering. Pinn might have been a torment, but at least he paid attention to his fellow outflyer.

Frey was trying not to think about what Pinn's departure would do to his crew. There was no doubt that Pinn was an idiot, but he was generally an amusing one, and Frey had got used to having him around. Every group needed a scapegoat, and Pinn was the perfect candidate, being too stupid to realise when people were making fun of him. He'd been Malvery's only drinking buddy after Crake had left. Apart from that, he was a fine outflyer, and he'd taken his aircraft with him. After losing Bess and now Pinn, Frey was getting light on muscle.

Damn it! Why did he bolt now? Just when I'd got Jez back on the team.

He was unhappy with how the whole affair had played out. Unhappy with Pinn for leaving without a word. Unhappy with himself for letting it get to that point. He'd always taken Pinn for granted, and now it had come back to bite him. It would be hard to replace him. There weren't many pilots that good who were willing to work for next to nothing.

Well, he'd deal with it as soon as he could. Maybe Malvery knew where Pinn's hometown was, and they could head over there and entice him back. But all that was for later. Right now, he had enough on his plate.

Still, one thing was for sure. With Pinn gone, it was going to be a lot quieter round here.

He looked over his shoulder, checking the cockpit was empty.

'*Too* quiet,' he said aloud, then sank back into his seat with a satisfied smile.

'I heard that, Cap'n!' Jez called from down the corridor.

They assembled outside the *Ketty Jay*, yawning and stamping their boots against the cold. Malvery was still half-drunk, squinting like a newborn puppy in the feeble morning light. Frey adjusted his earcuff.

'You there, Jez?'

'I'm here,' came his navigator's disembodied voice. He looked up and raised a hand. From the cockpit, she raised one in reply.

They headed out into the empty streets of Endurance, their breath steaming in the morning air. Frey rubbed his hands to keep them warm. He wished he could have worn gloves, but gloves and pistol triggers didn't work well together. Trinica stuck close to him. Silo and Malvery flanked them with shotguns.

The town was as silent and deserted as it had seemed from the air. Soft snow gathered in the crevices of worn stone walls. They peered suspiciously down alleys and kept a look out for movement on the rooftops, but the only movement came from the drifting flakes in the air, which settled on the furred fringes of their hoods and melted away.

Maybe it was the lack of sleep, but Frey was finding it hard to stay alert with Trinica next to him. He was worried about bringing her along. He didn't know if she could handle herself in combat, and the only time he'd ever seen her shoot was when she fired a pistol point-blank at his chest, back in Duke Grephen's stronghold the winter before last. But there was another reason, too. He didn't want her getting hurt.

They hadn't gone far from the landing pad when they turned a corner and came across a heap of loose scaffolding and rubble in the middle of the street. They approached it carefully. Upon closer inspection, they saw pieces of broken furniture stuffed in there too. The fabric had been pierced by bullet holes.

'What's this look like to you?' Frey asked the company in general.

'It looks like a barricade,' Trinica replied.

Frey frowned. 'What's been going on here?'

There was a scuffle of movement to his left. Frey turned quickly; his arm snapped out straight, pistol levelled.

Staring at them from the mouth of an alleyway was a boy. Ragged, dirty, no more than thirteen. His eyes widened in fright, and he fled.

'Hey!' Frey cried, breaking into a sprint. He pelted towards the alleyway with Trinica and Silo in pursuit.

'Oh, damnation. Don't make me run!' Malvery complained, accelerating to a boozy waddle in their wake.

The wind whipped along the narrow spaces between the buildings, blowing the powdery snow ahead of it. Frey wiped his eyes, trying to catch sight of his target. There! A clatter of empty petrol containers, somewhere to his right. The boy had tripped over them.

'Hey! I'm not going to hurt you!' he yelled. *Unless I have to run my arse all over town to catch you, that is.*

The boy could shed some light on things, perhaps. Like what had happened to the Century Knights. Like where everybody had gone. Like how to find Almore Roke, Grist's old crewmate.

Frey ran to the corner, and saw another alley, wider than the last, heading between the houses. The overturned petrol containers were still rolling on the stony, frosted ground. At the end was the boy, his mouth in an O, terrified. He was waiting to see if Frey had followed him. When he saw the chase was on, he disappeared round the corner.

'Come back!' Frey called, as he put on an extra burst of speed. 'I just want to talk!'

'Cap'n!' Silo was calling after him. 'Cap'n, wait!'

But Frey couldn't wait. Not if he was going to catch that boy. He rounded the corner and skidded to a halt. The boy was gone. In his place were six men crouched behind an overturned cart, their rifles levelled at him.

Ambush. Frey stared at them in shock.

'Bugger,' he said.

He felt his arm wrenched hard. Silo pulled him sideways just as the rifles opened up. Bullets chipped at the walls and whined through the air. He was yanked back around the corner, out of the line of fire, where he tripped and fell to the ground.

'I seen less obvious traps in my time,' the Murthian said.

Frey ignored him. 'Oi!' he yelled at the gunmen, scrambling to his feet. 'What did I do to deserve *that*?'

'Darian!' Trinica called. He looked to where she was pointing. Another six men had appeared at the other end of the alley, blocking them in. They had rifles too, aimed and ready to fire.

'Whoa! Whoa!' he shouted in alarm, holding up his hands. 'Don't shoot!' He looked around at his companions. 'Guns down, everyone. Let's not make the nice people nervous, eh?'

They laid their weapons on the ground, making no sudden moves. The men approached suspiciously. They were grubby, their faces seamed and lined, and they wore heavy, tatty clothes.

'They ain't mercs,' said one.

'Just 'cos they ain't wearin' the uniform, don't mean they ain't workin' for the company,' argued another.

The first man waved the barrel of his gun towards Trinica. 'Mercs don't use women, far as I know.' He raised his voice, calling to the men around the corner. 'It's alright! We got 'em!'

Frey saw the six men who'd fired on him come swaggering round the corner. 'Anything I can do?' Jez said in his ear. She'd been listening on the *Ketty Jay*.

'Stay put,' he whispered. 'Too many of 'em.'

'No whisperin'!' snapped one of their captors.

Frey decided that they weren't in imminent danger of being killed by someone with an itchy trigger finger, so it was time to get some answers. 'Who *are* you lot, anyway?' he asked.

'We should be askin' *you* that.'

'We're visitors. Looking for someone. Whatever little spat you've got going on here, it's no business of ours.'

'Lookin' for someone? Who?'

'Feller named Almore Roke. You know him?'

There were exclamations of surprise and horror, and a clatter of rifles being primed. Frey stared nervously at the cluster of barrels pointed at his head. 'I take it you do?' he said, his voice small.

'I knew they was in league with Roke!' one of the men said.

'I'm not in league with anybody!' Frey babbled rapidly. 'I'm after a man called Harvin Grist. I heard Roke used to be on his crew. He might know where Grist is. I just want information, that's all! No need for the guns! No need for the guns!'

There was silence as they considered him. Frey was aware that his credibility in Trinica's eyes may well have suffered following his less than manly display, but he decided he'd rather be alive than brave.

'They're mercs!' piped up a high voice. Frey saw the skinny boy that had lured them into the ambush. 'Kill 'em!'

Frey shot him a poisonous glance and wished him a horrible death by venereal disease.

'They *ain't* mercs,' said a grizzled voice from behind them. A middle-aged man was striding forward. He was stout as an oak, with white hair and white stubble on his unshaven cheeks. By the way the others deferred to him, Frey pegged him as their leader. 'We saw 'em fly in, didn't we? You saw their wings. Mercs wouldn't fly a piece o' shit like that.'

Frey bit his tongue. Even though it was a point in his favour, he was tempted to argue out of pride.

'See?' he said, his voice strained. 'Not mercs. Now can I ask what in rotting bastardy is going on here?'

The grizzled man waved at his companions and they stepped back, returning to a state of wary readiness.

'I'll tell you,' he said. 'Name's Oldrew Sprine. Yours?'

'Darian Frey.'

'Right. Now your friend Roke—'

'Not my friend,' Frey interjected quickly.

'—he's the big cheese in these parts. Took his ill-gotten pirate gains and went into a different kind o' piracy. Robbin' the common folk.'

'Sounds like a despicable sort,' Frey commiserated.

Sprine sneered. 'This town is greased wi' the blood, sweat and tears of miners like us. Roke is the company's representative here.'

'The company?'

'Gradmuth Operations.'

'I've heard of them. Big aerium suppliers to the Navy,' Trinica said.

Sprine grunted. ''Cept it's not just the Navy they're supplyin'. It's them pus-arsed Sammies!'

Frey raised an eyebrow. Vards supplying Samarlans? Their old enemies in the south, the same people they'd recently fought two wars against? It didn't sound especially likely.

'Soon as we got word, we was up in arms,' Sprine said. He spat on the ground. 'It's not enough that they pay us barely enough to feed our families. Not enough that they work us harder every day. Now they're makin' traitors of us, too!'

Frey was pleased to note that nobody seemed to want to shoot them any more. He glanced at Trinica, to be sure she was alright. She didn't seem the least bit scared.

'I heard the Century Knights were here?' he asked.

'Aye, they turned up quick-smart, didn't they?' said Sprine. 'Always do, when they're protectin' the rich folk. Don't turn up so fast when it's the miners in trouble. They're holed up in the refinery with Roke and the rest of the company folk.'

'So these mercs . . . they work for Gradmuth Operations?'

'Aye. Paid killers.'

'Well,' said Frey, indicating the dishevelled doctor by his side. 'I think you can see by the state of us that we haven't been paid by anyone in a long time.'

Sprine looked them over. 'Aye. You've a point there.'

Frey fixed his eyes on a point a dozen metres behind Sprine. 'In fact, if we were mercenaries, we'd probably look more like *that*.'

Sprine laughed. 'You don't expect me to fall for tha*aaAARGH?!*' he bellowed, and then pitched forward into Frey as he was shot in the leg.

Pandemonium. The deafening, percussive sound of rifle fire. The air was full of snow and bullets and the stink of gunsmoke.

Malvery heaved Sprine off Frey as the miner fought to untangle his rifle and find a target. The mercenaries, dressed in blue uniforms, were shooting round the corner at the end of the alley. Frey and Malvery went the other way, towards the miners. Malvery dragged his captain towards the wall, as far out of the line of fire as they could go. Hard chips nipped at Frey's cheeks as bullets bounced off the stone.

He cast around desperately for Trinica, and saw her being bundled away by Silo. The miners were in disarray, some of them shooting and others retreating, falling over each other. One lay on the ground, staring upwards, a fanned spatter of red blood on the snow. Everyone was yelling.

Frey and Malvery slid along the wall, pressing themselves close to it. Bullets flew past them in both directions. Some of them thumped into flesh, but thankfully none of it belonged to Frey.

Then they were behind the miners, their heads down, running. The miners were too caught up in their gunfight with the mercs to care about prisoners now. Frey threw himself round the corner after Silo and Trinica, and ran smack into something that felt like a building.

Suddenly, the chaos turned to stillness. Frey blinked. Somehow, he was on his back, gazing at the sky. Snow was floating down to settle on his face. Everything seemed vaguely dreamlike.

There were faces looking down at him. Some he recognised; one he didn't. An ugly face, belonging to a giant. Bearded, beetle-browed, cut from rock. Dimly, Frey came to the conclusion that he'd run head-first into this man's chest.

Everything swam back into focus. The sound of the gun-battle around the corner became loud again. Then another face come into sight, and an altogether more pleasant one. He recognised Samandra Bree, of the Century Knights. Which meant the man he'd run into was her partner, Colden Grudge.

She bent over him, hands on her thighs, her tricorn hat perched on her head.

'Hello, Frey,' she said. 'Fancy meeting you here.'

Twenty-Nine

A Knight's Duty – Signs Of The Underground –
Grissom And Jask – A Stranger – Frey Interrogates

They left the miners and the mercs to fight it out and headed away through the alleys. Bree and Grudge led the way, she with her twin lever-action shotguns, he with his colossal auto-cannon. It was big enough to be mounted on an aircraft, but in his hands it seemed about the right size.

'You're not going to break up the gunfight?' Malvery asked, as the sounds of dying men diminished behind them.

'Not our problem,' rumbled Grudge.

'Not your problem?' Malvery was faintly appalled. 'Then what is?'

'*Our* problem is back in the refinery,' said Samandra.

'That's where we're going now?' Frey asked.

'Yep,' she replied. That suited Frey. If the miners were to be believed, Almore Roke was there.

He drew his cutlass as they hurried through the narrow back ways of Endurance. It made him feel a little better. They'd left all their guns on the ground when they fled, and he felt uncomfortably vulnerable without them.

'I shouldn't worry,' said Samandra. 'The miners might be riled, but they ought to stop short of firing on the Archduke's Knights.'

'Ought to?' Frey asked.

Samandra shrugged. 'Guess you never can tell.'

The snow was coming down thicker now, and settling. Frey glanced over at Trinica, who was sticking close to Silo. The Murthian had pulled her out of the crossfire earlier. He'd done a better job of protecting her than Frey had. Frey suppressed a surge of jealousy.

Just be glad no one got hurt. No one important, anyway.

'I should thank you,' he said to Samandra. 'For coming to collect us. Didn't expect an escort.'

292

'We saw you coming in. Recognised the craft. I wouldn't soon forget the *Ketty Jay*. Not after the shit you pulled at Mortengrace.'

Frey grinned. 'And you just couldn't resist.'

'Actually, it was more 'cause I want to pick your brains about Grist.' She winked. 'And because it'd just break my heart to see that handsome face shot off.'

'Mine, too,' Frey admitted.

He checked on Trinica again. Samandra spotted him. 'She's new,' she said. 'Pretty, too. What's the story?' She nudged him in the ribs.

'Her? Passenger,' said Frey. He hoped that he was offhand enough to discourage her interest. Trinica was under sentence of death for treason, and if the Century Knights realised who she was, it'd all be over for her. Luckily, she was all but unrecognisable without her make-up.

Samandra gave him an insinuating smile, but she didn't pursue the matter.

They came out of the alleys and on to narrow streets. There was more evidence of combat here: bullet holes in the walls, fallen bodies being slowly buried by the snow. Bree and Grudge slipped from corner to corner, covering the angles, each supporting the other. Frey had to admire the seamless way they worked together.

They spotted a group of blue-uniformed mercs ahead, who came sallying out of a side street. They raised their weapons at the sight of the rag-tag group coming their way, but lowered them again as they identified Bree and Grudge. The Knights and their companions were left to pass unhindered.

Now that the distant gunfire had stopped, silence returned to Endurance. The only sound was their boots whispering through the snow, and the clank of Grudge's body armour. Frey found it all a bit eerie.

'Where *is* everybody?' he said.

'That's what worries me,' said Samandra. 'Most of the town disappeared when the trouble began, before we got here. There are little roaming groups fighting skirmishes with the mercs; as to the rest, we ain't got half an idea where they are. But you can be sure they're about somewhere. Probably been rounded up by the Underground, getting ready to make their move.'

'The Underground?'

Samandra indicated a sign daubed in red paint on a nearby wall. An underlined U. Frey had noticed several others on their way, but hadn't thought much of them. 'The Underground. Bunch of militants who say they fight for worker's rights, votes for all freemen, that kind of thing. They've been stirring the locals up good. This place was a powderkeg. Only a matter of time before something set 'em off.'

'So whose side are *you* on?'

'The Archduke's,' she said. 'Like always.' She peered round a corner and waved them on. 'Look, I ain't happy about it. I know how they treat the miners in these parts. I'd rather Roke and his lot were shot. But we're Century Knights. We keep the Archduke's peace. And we can't have businessmen getting offed every time the workers get a bit shirty.'

'Gradmuth Operations must pay a lot of tax, right?'

'That, and they fuel half the Navy.'

'They scratch the Archduke's back, he scratches theirs,' said Frey scornfully. 'And the common man gets screwed.'

'Hey, it's the way of the world,' said Samandra, a harsh edge creeping into her voice. 'You ain't so lily-white yourself, pirate.'

By now, the refinery was visible above the buildings, and the mercenary presence was heavier. They passed a long barricade that had been constructed in the centre of a square, and Frey spotted blue-uniformed men squatting on the rooftops. Eventually they came to the refinery gates, which were set in a high wall and guarded by a dozen men. Frey was finding it hard to see how the miners could possibly be a threat. A ground assault on this place would be suicidal.

The guards let them through, and they crossed a flagged courtyard towards a small metal door in the side of the refinery. The building loomed overhead, massive pipes scoring lines across the grey sky. Samandra held the door open and let the others past. Frey waited with her.

'Can I ask a question?'

'Other than that one?' she replied.

'Why are you looking for Grist?'

Samandra tipped back the brim of her tricorn hat. 'Rumour has it he's made off with a Mane artefact of unknown power.'

'Rumour has it, eh? Where'd you hear that?'

'From your daemonist,' she grinned. 'He's quite a chatty sort when he's drunk.'

Frey groaned. The soirée in Lapin that Amalicia had taken them to. He knew he shouldn't have left Crake alone for so long with Samandra.

'But Grist didn't have it then,' he said. 'The Awakeners did.'

'Yes, he did say the Awakeners had stolen it from you,' she said. 'But when our spies heard the Awakeners recently had a craft downed in the Flashpan, we sort of put two and two together. And when we heard you were looking for Grist all over the North, well . . .'

'Poor old Crake,' said Frey. 'He never stood a chance. Not above using your feminine charms in service of the cause, eh?'

She gave a derisive rasp. 'Me? There ain't much I'm above, when it comes to it. Anyway, he's a sweet feller. The pleasure was all mine. Where is he, anyway?'

'He's gone.'

'Shame. I kinda liked him.'

'Me, too.'

They went inside the refinery. Grudge led them up stone stairways and along tight corridors with smooth walls painted grey-green. It seemed colder in here than outside, and the electric lights did little more than provide contrast for the shadows. Frey guessed they were taking a back way to their destination.

That destination turned out to be a collection of offices and filing rooms, several storeys up. They passed by lamplit desks and shelves of neatly ordered paperwork, emerging at last into a chamber with a long window that took up the whole of one wall. It was divided into squares, and it looked out over the refinery floor, where enormous vats and brooding machinery lay dormant.

Frey guessed this was a common area for the foremen and their staff. Several doors led off from it. A large table took up much of the room. A few mercs were here, idling about or sitting at the table, guns hanging loose in their hands. With them were two men who Frey recognised, even though he'd never met them before.

The first was gaunt and sour-faced, with straggly, grey-white hair. He sat with his boots up on the table. His duster had fallen back to reveal a waistcoat laden with a variety of knives. There were half a dozen sheaths on either side of his ribs, and more inside the duster.

He was rolling a throwing knife through his fingers, flipping it end over end around his knuckles.

The other was more enigmatic. He leaned against one of the doors with his arms folded loosely across his stomach. He was wearing a black coat and a wide-brimmed hat, and he wore a black necktie around his face. All that could be seen of him was a slice of his eyes and forehead, and a fringe of shaggy black hair.

Frey knew them from the broadsheets. Eldrew Grissom and Mordric Jask. Century Knights. Deadly men, both. Grissom had the fastest hands in the game, with knives or pistols alike. Jask was a stone-cold warrior, famously unflappable, a man without fear.

'Everyone, this is Darian Frey and his crew,' said Samandra, as they entered the room. Grissom looked up and grunted. Jask tipped his hat.

'What are you all doing here?' asked Frey.

'Guarding the company men. What else?' Samandra replied.

'Why not just take them out of here?'

'The miners are getting shot down on account of those folks. Marching them through the town might be a provocation hard to take, don't you reckon? We're trying to avoid more bloodshed.'

'So you're gonna sit tight?'

'We sent word to the Navy. They'll be here sooner or later.'

'And you reckon the miners are going to to wait around for that?'

'No,' she said. 'I don't. But I can't see that we got too much choice.'

Jez spoke in his ear. 'The *Ketty Jay*'s small enough to fly over the refinery. Could airlift them out. Or you. Just say the word.'

Frey didn't reply. To do so would be to give away the secret of the earcuffs, and besides, he had a feeling the Century Knights would have thought of that already, and decided against it. There had to be a reason for that.

'Why do I get the impression there's something you aren't telling me?'

Samandra raised an eyebrow. 'Smart feller,' she said. 'Come on.'

She walked over to Jask, who moved out of the way of the door he was guarding. Frey looked inside. Beyond was a room with a desk and some shelves, and little else. Its occupant was sitting on a seat. He raised his head as the door was opened.

He was tall, slim and elegant. His features were narrow and

perfectly proportioned, even beautiful. He wore a coat of exotic silk and tailored clothes of the most exquisite cut.

But none of that was what marked him out. The truly remarkable thing was that his irises were bright yellow, and his skin was black as onyx, a colour so deep that it seemed tinted with dark blue in the dim light.

The truly remarkable thing was that he was a Samarlan.

Jask closed the door. Frey stared at Samandra.

'What in the name of the Allsoul's pendulous bollocks is a Sammie doing here?' he demanded.

'We did wonder the same thing,' she replied. 'Best we can figure—'

'Roke's selling aerium to the Sammies,' finished Grissom. He flipped a knife into the tabletop, where it stuck with a thump. 'Plain as day, not that you can get the bastard to admit it. And we don't have no proof, neither. Yet.'

'We'll hold 'em both till the Navy arrives, then ship 'em off for questioning,' Samandra explained. 'I'm sure our Samarlan friend will have a thing or two worth knowing.'

'There's a Sammie in there?' asked Malvery, who'd drifted over. He'd overheard the conversation, as had everyone else in the room. 'How'd he get here?'

'Just flew in, I imagine.'

'That easy?'

'We're not at war with them any more,' said Samandra. 'It's not illegal for them to be in the country. With all the air traffic, we couldn't stop 'em if we tried. But since they're liable to be lynched the moment they show their faces, they tend to stay at home.'

'Plus,' said Grissom, 'soon as they set foot in Vardia, they're ours.' He smiled a nasty smile.

'Yep,' said Samandra. 'It's sort of policy to pick up any Sammies we find. Just for a friendly chat, y'know? To see what we can glean.'

'You gleaned anything from that feller?' asked Frey, thumbing at the door.

'Not a thing,' said Samandra.

'But then, we haven't really got going on him yet,' added Grissom, spinning a knife in his palm.

'It's got to be something important, though,' said Frey. 'Sammies don't come out into the open much. They've got the Dakkadians to do all their deals and the Murthians for all their dirty work. The whole time I was flying to the front, during the war, I never spotted a Sammie. That's the first one I ever saw outside of a ferrotype.'

'A fact that hasn't escaped our attention,' said Samandra. She looked over his shoulder. 'Is your man alright, by the way?'

Frey followed her gaze to Silo. He was pacing back and forth on the other side of the room, stalking this way and that like a caged animal. His fists clenched and unclenched, eyes focused on something far away. The picture of agitation. Frey had never seen him act that way.

'Hm,' said Frey. 'He doesn't *look* too alright, does he?'

'Not really.'

Frey watched Silo for a few moments, wondering what was up with him.

'Perhaps you should have a word?' Samandra suggested.

'Oh, right. Yes, I will.'

'I'll see about getting you fellers tooled up again. You're not gonna be much use if those miners pull anything and all you've got between you is a cutlass.'

'New guns?' Frey's eyes lit up.

She indicated the mercs that were lolling about. 'Courtesy of the company, of course. They've got enough kit stashed away to supply an army.'

Frey beamed. 'Wouldn't say no. Silo and Malvery prefer shotguns, if you please.'

'Well, alright then.'

Frey went over to Silo while Samandra ordered the mercs to fetch up the weapons. Silo saw him approach. His eyes flashed angrily.

'Hey, hey, calm down,' said Frey. 'What's got into you?'

Silo glared at him, then at the door. Frey realised all of a sudden what was bothering him. He felt a little stupid for not having seen it before. In that room was one of the people who'd enslaved Silo's race for half a millenium. Frey could only imagine what kind of treatment he'd suffered at the hands of the Sammies in his lifetime. Almost certainly he'd lost friends and relatives to them at some point. And now, for the first time since his escape from Samarla, he was in the presence of one of his hated tormentors. No wonder he was keyed up.

Frey had never really thought about Silo's life before they met. As far as he was concerned, the Murthian's history began the day he found Frey dying from a stomach wound inflicted by a Dakkadian bayonet, somewhere in the jungle depths of northern Samarla. He'd nursed Frey back to health, and Frey had flown him out of Samarla and out of slavery. They'd been together ever since, in unspoken and unspeaking companionship. Neither asked anything of the other, and each expected nothing in return. By the act of saving each other's lives they'd forged a bond more subtle than any expression of loyalty.

Frey put his hand on the engineer's shoulder. 'Don't let it get to you, Silo. He's got no power over you here. Not unless you give it to him.'

Silo seemed rather surprised at hearing something wise from his captain's lips. Frey was rather surprised himself. He was on good form today, apparently.

Silo took in a long breath and blew it out. 'You're right. I ain't the 'prisoned one now.' He stepped from one foot to the other. Calmer, but still fidgety. 'Sorry, Cap'n. Brings it back, that's all. Knowing there's one of 'em in there.'

Frey patted his shoulder. 'Hold it together, eh?' he said in what he hoped was an encouraging fashion. He walked away, passing Malvery as he did so.

'Keep an eye on him,' he murmured out of the corner of his mouth.

'Right-o,' said Malvery.

Trinica was looking out of the window that gave a view of the refinery floor. She'd been keeping quiet and out of the way since the Century Knights had first appeared. Frey joined her.

'How're you doing?'

'I'm fine,' she said. 'We should see about speaking to Roke.'

'Better if I do it,' he replied. 'Keep you out of the picture. You're supposed to be a passenger.'

She nodded. 'Do what you can.'

She seemed careless of the presence of the Century Knights. It was as if, without her outfit and her make-up, she really was a different person. An alter ego. One which carried no responsibility for the things done by Trinica Dracken, pirate captain. Given her sometimes fractured state of mind, he wondered if she really *had* separated one from the other. Perhaps, when she put on her disguise of black clothes and white skin, she put on a colder, harder personality with it. It certainly seemed that every day she spent without them, she became more and more like the young woman Frey had once known. Known, and loved. But maybe he was just being fanciful.

He approached Samandra, who was talking with Grissom. She stopped when he came near. 'Something I can help you with, Captain Frey?'

'I want to see Roke.'

'You do, huh? I wondered when you'd get round to asking. No other reason why you'd be in Endurance that I can see.'

'So, can I?'

'I should warn you, he's not been the most talkative of souls.'

'I can be persuasive when I try.'

'I've no doubt. You're welcome to talk with him, but I'll be in there with you. And no rough stuff. He's a powerful man, and we're the Archduke's right hand. Wouldn't do. You understand?'

'Yeah,' said Frey, vaguely disappointed. Getting answers was so much easier when you could boot your victim all over the room. 'I get it.'

She led him down a corridor to another office. The overseers' area was stark and bare, with as much furniture as was necessary to function and little else. He suspected that the real money-makers in the company had plusher offices elsewhere, away from the noise and stink of a refinery in full flow.

Sitting behind a desk, writing a letter, was Almore Roke. He was an erect, imperious-looking man with a close-cropped salt-and-pepper beard. One eyebrow drooped, giving him an expression that suggested permanent suspicion. He wore a neat suit and silver cufflinks.

'Who's this?' he demanded, peering at Frey.

'Captain Darian Frey of the *Ketty Jay*,' Frey replied. He stepped into the room, and Samandra came with him. 'I hear you used to serve on Harvin Grist's crew.'

Roke tossed down his pen and sat back in his chair, arms crossed petulantly. 'This again? What of it?'

'I'm looking for him.'

'So is she,' Roke said, jutting his chin towards Samandra. 'Why should I care?'

Roke's accent was a strange mix between the rough, guttural tones of the commoner, and a crisper, fluting aristocratic lilt. A man born poor, now trying to pass himself off as one of the rich. Frey doubted he was fooling anyone.

'I'm wondering if you have in mind any places he might be,' said Frey. 'Hideouts he once used, familiar haunts, that kind of thing. It's very important that we find him.'

'Is it? Why?'

'Because otherwise he might end up killing a lot of people.'

Samandra stared at him in surprise. 'Excuse me?'

'That device he's got. We reckon the Awakeners know what it is. And they seem to think it could cost thousands of lives.'

'I thought it was a power source?' Samandra said.

'So did we. It's not.'

Roke was watching their exchange with amusement. 'I know where he is,' Roke said. 'His hideout. If he's gone to ground, he's gone there.'

'And?'

'And,' said the businessman, stretching his back, 'I'll tell you after I get an apology from her, and on the condition that my guest and I are released and given safe passage to a port of our choice.'

'Your guest? The Sammie?'

'Vulgar term,' said Roke, with a sneer. 'They're a fascinating people, very cultured. A shame the common man can't forgive what's happened in the past.'

'When did you stop being a *common man*?' Samandra asked.

Roke ignored her jab. 'There's no law against associating with Samarlans, last I heard. Our own Earl Hengar was well known for his dalliances. So why am I treated like a criminal?'

'Because it *is* illegal to sell them aerium, especially since a lot of folk think they're tooling up a navy to have another go at invading us,' said Samandra. 'And that would make you a traitor. Anyway, you'll be given safe passage when the Navy get here. And you'll be released after you've satisfied our curiosity as to why a man high up in an eminent aerium mining company is so chummy with one of our old enemies from the South.'

'That's not good enough,' said Roke.

'Well, it'll have to be.'

Roke rolled his eyes and looked at Frey. 'Your friend here doesn't grasp the basics of negotiation, does she?'

'She does seem an inflexible sort,' Frey agreed.

'Perhaps you're a more reasonable man to deal with?'

'Hey!' snapped Samandra. 'You're dealing with the Century Knights, not him.'

'Then I'm afraid we have nothing more to—'

Roke was interrupted by a rumble that ran through the building, making the walls shudder. Frey listened in alarm as the refinery began to echo with distant groans, shrieks, and eerie wails, as if some enormous metal monster was slowly shaking itself awake.

'The refinery!' Roke exclaimed. 'They've started it up!'

'Who?'

'The workers! Them and their bloody Underground!' Roke sprang out of his chair, agitated. 'They've got inside.' His eyes widened. 'They're going to overload the machines!'

'That sounds like it'll be a bad thing,' Frey observed carefully.

'They'll blow us all to pieces!'

'Right,' said Frey. 'Definitely bad, then.'

Thirty

Insurrectionists – Frey Betrays A Trust –
Foreigners – The Meaning Of Freedom

The window overlooking the refinery floor was crowded with bodies. The besuited officials of Gradmuth Operations had emerged in a panic, alarmed by the noise from below. They jostled for space with the mercs, hoping to see what was going on. Frey pushed through the common room to the window and looked down.

The refinery had come alive. Great rock-chewing machines gnashed their teeth. Vats of viscous liquid had begun to churn. Kilns glowed as they roared into life. There was a furious racket of grinding gears. A thin smoke had begun to rise. Frey saw men running among the equipment, yanking levers, thumping buttons.

'How did they get in?' someone cried.

Gunfire rattled outside. The mercs on the gate were engaging the invaders. Frey doubted the miners and factory workers were stupid enough to try a full-frontal assault. Much more likely, they'd got in behind the defences and were overrunning the refinery compound.

He'd wondered where most of the village had disappeared to. By the sounds of it, they were all here.

Roke pushed in next to him, with Samandra at his shoulder. At the same time, the overhead lamps died. The refinery was already dim – natural light was shut out – but now it was plunged into darkness, lit only by the fiery red of the awakening furnaces. The scampering figures below became daemonic, mischievous imps racing through the bloody glow.

'They're sabotaging the refinery! Those bastard muck-scraping ingrates!' Roke said. 'We have to get out of here!'

'I'm not going down there!' said a bewhiskered and monacled

company man. 'There's dozens of them! With guns! We'll be lynched!'

'Idiot!' Roke said. 'Don't you know what happens if you turn the machines on out of sequence? The kilns will fire up before the coolant starts flowing. The steam pumps will rupture if there's no one to man the valves. This place is going to tear itself apart!'

The company man went white and started to gibber in a manner that reminded Frey of Harkins at his best. 'But . . . but . . . but . . . if they blow up the refinery . . . where will they *work?* What about their *jobs?*'

'Damned Underground insurrectionists!' spluttered one of his fellows. 'Got them so stirred up they don't know which side their bread's buttered!'

The mercs, who'd overheard the news of the imminent disaster, began jostling for the exit.

'Hey! You all stay your damn selves here or I'll shoot your cowardly hides!' Samandra yelled.

There was a boom that made them all jump, and a shower of concrete dust fell from the ceiling. Colden Grudge was standing in the doorway to the common area, his autocannon smoking. Grissom sloped over to stand next to him and shucked back his duster, revealing knives and pistols. Suddenly nobody felt like leaving any more.

'What can we do?' Samandra asked Roke.

'Get us out of here!' he said.

'That's what they want. They'll be waiting for us outside, with overwhelming numbers, and we can't protect all of you. What *else?*'

Roke thought for a moment. 'There's a master override switch. It shuts down the refinery in case of emergency. They won't be able to turn it back on without a code, and only the staff know that. I can show you.'

'Not you,' said Samandra. 'You're staying here. The Navy's going to want a word with you.'

'I'll take you,' volunteered a young man with oiled blond hair in a neat centre-parting. A brave and gallant-looking sort, too young to know what danger was. Probably eager to get the attention of the beautiful Century Knight.

Samandra favoured him with a knee-weakening smile. 'Much

appreciated, sir.' She turned and began calling out orders. 'Grudge, Jask, with me. Grissom, you stay and guard the staff.'

'I'm not babysitting this bunch of—' Grissom began to protest, but Frey cut him off.

'*We'll* stay,' he said.

Samandra looked him over suspiciously. Sizing him up in the red darkness.

'Safer up here. Besides, I'm the only one of my lot that can shoot worth a shit,' he lied. 'And I said I'd look after her.' He thumbed at Trinica.

'The passenger. Right,' said Samandra. She frowned at him. A *you'd better not be up to something* kind of frown. Frey put on his most winning grin.

'Tick-tock, Samandra!' said Grissom, by the door.

'Fine,' she said. 'I can't spare a Knight anyway. Don't even think about going anywhere, though. You'd never make it to your aircraft.'

'Hey,' said Frey, raising his hands. 'Nobody wants to keep me alive more than I do.'

Samandra gave him one last, uncertain look. 'Weapons are on the table,' she said, pointing to the shotguns and pistols that had been brought up by the mercs. 'Good luck.' Then she was heading towards the exit, herding their enthusiastic young guide ahead of her, shouting for the mercs to back them up.

Frey waited till they were gone and said, 'Did you hear that, Jez?'

'Certainly did, Cap'n,' said his navigator, in his ear. 'Meet you on the roof of the refinery in ten minutes?'

'Ten minutes,' he said. He turned to Malvery, who'd scooped up a shotgun and was admiring it. 'Doc, pull that Sammie out of there,' he said, pointing at the door where Jask had stood.

'That's my guest!' Roke protested. 'You'd better not be—'

'I'll make you a deal, Roke,' Frey interrupted him. He picked up a pistol, checked it, and began loading it. *New model. Pristine condition. Very nice.* 'I get you and the Sammie out of here, you tell me where Grist is. Simple, right?'

'Agreed,' said Roke, without hesitation. 'There's a port nearby where I can arrange transport for my guest and I. Take us there and I'll tell you.'

'How do we get to the roof?'

'The roof?' Roke thought for a moment. 'The access door is locked and the head caretaker isn't here. No idea where the key is. We'll have to take the elevator.' He motioned at the window. 'Out there.'

There was a loud bang from below, and several of the window squares shattered. One of the company men toppled backwards, his head and chest a mess of blood and torn skin. The others began to shriek and scramble over each other in an attempt to get away.

'Probably shouldn't be standing next to the window, huh?' Frey muttered to himself, as he pulled Roke aside. Malvery emerged with the Samarlan. Trinica and Silo joined them as the company men hightailed it back to their offices and locked the doors. Silo was glaring with naked hatred at the Samarlan. The very sight of the man inflamed him. The Samarlan returned his gaze with a cool disdain.

Frey took him aside. 'I know, Silo, I know. But we have to find Grist.'

'Grist! Grist!' he snarled. 'What's so important, Cap'n? What you got to prove that's so damn important?'

Frey blinked in surprise. 'I made a mistake, and I'm trying to make it right,' he said.

Silo stared over his shoulder at the Samarlan, nostrils flaring. His fist was clenched and his arm trembled. He looked like he wanted to spring on Roke's 'guest' and beat him bloody.

'Can you deal with it? For me?' Frey asked. 'You don't have to speak to him. Just don't kill him or anything. Please?'

Silo's mouth was pressed tight, as if tasting something bitter. 'I'll do what you ask, Cap'n,' he said. 'But this ain't right. I want you knowin' that. Ain't right.' He hefted his shotgun and pumped the lever-action handle to chamber a round. 'Let's go.'

The refinery floor was like something out of a nightmare. A sea of roaring metal noise punctuated by the shrieking and grinding of gears. Black pistons pumped up and down, shadows lunging against the gory glow of the furnace light. Unoiled mechanisms leaked wisps of acrid smoke. There was a haze in the air that stank of chemicals.

Frey, Trinica, Malvery and Silo hurried down the aisles between the looming machines, weapons ready, alert for danger. Roke and the Samarlan followed, with Roke providing occasional directions. The Samarlan was frustratingly slow; he seemed reluctant to run, and never accelerated above a speedy walk. Malvery was looking distinctly nauseous, still suffering the effects of the previous night. Silo looked like he wanted to murder someone.

They could hear gunshots somewhere ahead of them, and the thumping of Grudge's autocannon. Between the high, echoing roof and the cacophony all around them, it was hard to pick out their location. Frey was as keen to avoid the Century Knights as he was to avoid the armed workers who were sabotaging the refinery. He didn't much want to see the look on Samandra Bree's face when she caught him stealing off with her prisoners.

Frey reached a corner and saw that the coast was clear. He looked back. Once again, the Samarlan was lagging behind, moving with quick steps but not actually breaking into anything that might be described as a jog, let alone a run.

'Will you bleedin' well hurry?' Frey said.

The Samarlan made no effort to do so. Malvery, who was standing nearby, grabbed his arm and pulled him forward with a rough tug. 'Quicken up, eh?'

The Samarlan threw him off angrily, yellow eyes wide in outrage. He began to berate Malvery in his own language: a hissing, harsh tongue that made him sound like a furious snake. Then, realising that Malvery didn't understand him or care, he rounded on Silo, who was standing nearby. He unleashed a tirade, pointing at Malvery and then at Silo. Frey had no idea what was being said, but the Samarlan seemed to be indicating that Silo should have intervened.

Frey had had enough by this point. 'Tell your friend to shut up,' he said to Roke, 'or I'll break his teeth.'

Roke went over and spoke to the Samarlan in his own tongue. Frey looked around anxiously. This was no place for temper tantrums. That Sammie was trying his patience.

The Samarlan calmed, finishing with a few gestures at Silo. Silo hadn't spoken the entire time. He turned away with barely suppressed rage.

'I'm sorry,' said Roke, as he returned. 'He's a Samarlan from the noble caste. They don't run in public. And they certainly don't get touched.'

'They don't *run*?' Frey almost choked in disbelief. 'Has anyone explained to him that he's going to be lynched if he doesn't? Does he even know that everyone who's being shot and killed out there is dying on his account?'

Roke gave Frey an apologetic look. 'Every day since they're born, they're attended to by slaves. They live a life of ridiculous luxury. Manners and etiquette are life and death to someone like him. He won't run. It'd be a terrible indignity. He'd rather die.'

'Would he run faster with my toe up his arse?'

'You get us *both* out, Frey. That's the deal,' Roke reminded him sternly.

Frey rolled his eyes and swore. 'Come on, then.'

They rounded the corner and hurried along a row of vats. Gas flames roared at their bases. Some of them were beginning to bubble. Viscous liquid oozed over the rims and splattered on the floor. The stench made Frey light-headed.

They were halfway along the row when three men ran into view at the far end, carrying shotguns. They were unkempt figures, wearing overalls, their faces lit from below by the gas flames. They paused at the sight of Frey and his group, perhaps thinking that they were on the same side; then one of them raised his shotgun and screamed, *'Sammie!'* Even in the half-light, the Samarlan's skin marked him out immediately.

The moment of hesitation was not shared by Frey and his companions. They got off their first volley before the refinery workers even had a chance to shoot. But their accuracy was less impressive than their speed. The workers, alarmed at finding themselves suddenly under fire, shot wildly in the vague direction of their targets, then threw themselves into cover. Frey's group did the same, squeezing into the gaps between the vats.

The Sammie just stood there in the aisle, back straight, an imperious look on his face. Bullets whined through the air around him. He faced them without fear.

'What in blazing shit is that idiot doing?' Frey cried. Presumably, the Samarlan was too dignified to cram himself into the baking hot blackness with the rest of them. 'Malvery, get him out of there!'

Malvery lunged from hiding, grabbed the Samarlan and pulled him into cover. When he began to hiss again, Malvery whacked his head against the side of a vat. He was too shocked to say anything after that.

Frey checked on Trinica, who was pressed up against him in a not entirely unpleasant fashion, then concentrated on dealing with their attackers. These men weren't gunfighters. They were attempting to use the vats as cover, but when they leaned out to fire, they took far too long to aim. That, and they tended to lean out at roughly regular intervals, letting Frey predict when and where they'd appear so he could line up his shots. Easy pickings.

He clipped one with a bullet in the shoulder, sending him sprawling out into the open where Silo finished him off. Malvery hit another man clean in the face. The last worker was understandably distressed by the sight, and ran away, shouting, *'Sammie! Sammie!'*

Frey breathed a sigh of relief, then yelped as burning hot liquid bubbled up and spilled from the vat overhead, splashing his leg. He danced out into the aisle, beating at himself. The others emerged in a more controlled fashion.

They set off again in a different direction. The Samarlan began snapping at Silo as they went. It was making Frey angry on his friend's behalf. Silo suffered the abuse with a kind of furious submission. He wasn't making any attempt to defend himself while the Samarlan chewed him out.

'What's he saying?' he demanded of Roke.

'He's just confused as to why there's a Murthian here,' Roke replied.

'No, he's not,' said Trinica. 'He's calling your engineer all kinds of names, most of which involve his mother, and he's doing it in the mode they use to talk to slaves and animals.' She listened for a moment. 'Right now he wants to know why Silo didn't try to shield him from the bullets.'

Frey had forgotten that Trinica spoke Samarlan. He was almost as surprised as Roke.

'Er . . .' said Roke. 'You get us both out *unharmed* if you want to know where Grist is,' he reminded Frey.

Frey shook his head and cursed. 'You tell that bastard that we're in Vardia now, and Silo's no slave.' Roke dropped back to do so. Frey went over to Silo, shoving the Samarlan aside on his way. The Samarlan squawked in outrage. Roke did his best to calm him.

Silo was looking at the floor, every muscle tense. Frey thought about putting an arm on his shoulder, then thought better of it. 'Silo . . .'

'Been nine years since anyone spoke to me that way,' Silo said, through gritted teeth. 'Damned if it don't still make me cringe like a dog.'

'Don't listen to him. They're just words. You're free now.'

'If I was free,' said Silo, 'I'd've shot him the moment I laid eyes on him.'

A sudden explosion made them all flinch. A rolling cloud of smoky flame rose up above the machines to their right. More gunfire broke out nearby. They heard Grudge's autocannon once again. The miners and workers would be no match for the Century Knights, but Frey was happy to have someone to draw the heat off while they made for the elevator.

'I've just had a thought,' said Frey. 'What happens to the elevator if they shut down the refinery?'

'It stops working,' said Roke. 'Obviously.'

'Bugger,' said Frey. 'Let's move, people! Time's wasting!'

They came across several more workers as they ran through the factory, but they had an advantage that their enemies didn't. The insurrectionists always paused to be sure they weren't attacking their own; Frey and his companions shot on sight.

'I don't mind saying, Cap'n, I don't feel too great about this,' said Malvery, as he stepped over the corpse of another refinery worker. 'They've got a fair grievance, after all. He really *is* selling to the Sammies. Ain't we fighting on the wrong side?'

'Hey, I'm all for the peaceful exit, Doc. *They're* the ones who want to shoot *us*,' said Frey. 'Far as I'm concerned, we're just getting our retaliation in first.'

'I suppose so,' said Malvery with a sigh. He fired at some kid at the end of the aisle, who threw down his weapon and went scrambling away. 'Think I'm just emotional right now. Been getting that way lately, when I'm hungover.'

'Uh-huh,' said Frey, not really listening.

'Maybe I should lay off the swabbing alcohol and go back to grog.'

'Maybe.'

They found the elevator soon after. It was little more than a small box with a folding gate, set inside a caged passage that rose up into the darkness. It was waiting at ground level, so Frey pulled it open and ushered everyone in. He could hear running footsteps approaching. The noise and the darkness made it hard to tell where they were coming from. The Samarlan hesitated, obviously considering the prospect of being crammed in there with so many people. This time it was Trinica who shoved him inside.

Frey pulled the gate closed and Roke hit the button. The elevator clanked and squealed and began to rise, just as a group of refinery workers ran into view. They were slow to react – it took them a few moments to spot Roke among the passengers – but when they did, they were furious. One of them pounded the button that called the elevator, but to no avail. Finally some of them started shooting, but by that time the elevator had moved high up into the darkness, and their shots only ricocheted off the protective cage.

The refinery fell away beneath them. As they rose over the machines, Frey could see more fires starting at the far end. Vats glowed with heat; troughs of molten rock were overflowing; steam engines were pumping at a distressing rate. One massive piston arm came loose and went spinning across the room to crash into a set of pipes on the other side. As predicted, the refinery was ripping itself apart.

I hope you know what you're doing, Samandra, he thought.

Then the refinery disappeared beneath them, and they were travelling through a short passage of concrete, with grey daylight at the top. A doorway to the roof. The elevator had almost made it when they shuddered to a halt.

'I reckon they found your master override switch, then,' Malvery said. 'Never doubt the Century Knights, that's what I say.' He eyed the gap between the top of the elevator and the bottom of the doorway, which was barely large enough for a man of Malvery's bulk to squeeze through. 'We cut it a little fine, though.'

There were gates across the doorway, which Frey pulled aside. Malvery gave him a boost and he crawled out on to the flat roof. Black chimneys rose all around him. Cold air chilled his cheeks, nose and forehead. He heard engines, and looked up to see the *Ketty Jay* approaching through the snowy sky.

'Right on time, Cap'n,' Jez said in his ear. 'Not like you to be so punctual.'

'I'm full of surprises these days,' Frey said, giving her a wave.

They were safe up here. The Century Knights would have their hands full defending the staff of Gradmuth Operations from their irate employees. And better still, he had Roke, a man who claimed to know where Grist was. In fact, when you thought about it, he'd done pretty bloody well. Trinica had better be impressed with *that*.

Frey walked to the edge of the roof as the others climbed out of the elevator and the *Ketty Jay* eased in to land between the chimneys. There was gunfire from below. Workers and mercs battling in the courtyard, taking cover behind anything they could find. From up here, the conflict seemed a lot less urgent than it had when he was down among it. Let them fight it out; it wasn't his affair. He had more important things to deal with.

He heard a commotion behind him and turned around to see that the Samarlan had started up on Silo again. Damn it, this was getting out of hand. He strode over there. Silo was walking away, his head down and his fists clenched, but the Samarlan was following him, yelling at him in his own strange language.

'What happened now?' Frey asked Trinica as he came closer.

'The Samarlan's annoyed because Silo got out of the elevator before he did,' said Trinica. 'It's not done, apparently.' Trinica looked up at him. 'Darian, I don't know how much more your man's going to take of this. That Samarlan seems to still think he's a—'

She never finished, because at that moment the Samarlan, angered that Silo was ignoring him, slapped him round the back of the head. Frey groaned and put his hand over his face.

'That's done it,' he said.

Silo rounded on the Samarlan, stared at him a moment, then smashed the butt of his shotgun into his mouth. The Samarlan staggered back, clutching his bleeding face, his eyes wide. He was making incoherent gasping noises, as if he couldn't catch his breath. Silo descended on him, his expression furious. He grabbed the Samarlan by his shoulders and began dragging him towards the edge of the roof.

'Stop him!' Roke cried in alarm. 'Unharmed! That was the deal!'

Malvery looked to Frey expectantly, waiting for the signal to intervene. But Frey had had enough of asking Silo to take the Samarlan's abuse, just so he could get some information. He'd been putting Harvin Grist before the needs of his crew for too long now.

'Sorry, Roke,' he said. 'Your mate's got it coming.'

'Bloody right,' muttered Malvery, with an approving nod.

The Samarlan didn't even resist as Silo pulled him along. No doubt he was still too shocked at being struck. He probably never even entertained the thought that Silo would throw him off the roof, until he was airborne.

They listened to his shrill scream all the way down. It was cut short with a faint thump. Silo walked back towards Frey, and stood before him.

'Feel better?' Frey inquired.

'Sorry I did that, Cap'n,' he said, but his head was held high and he looked prouder than Frey had ever seen him.

'No, it's me who should be sorry,' said Frey. 'You're a free man on my crew. You shouldn't have had to suffer that.'

He held out his hand. Silo took it and shook.

Roke was gaping in disbelief. 'You killed . . . you just . . . !' He took a step back from Silo, as if from a madman. 'The deal's off! You hear?'

He got another step before he heard the click of a pistol hammer being cocked, and felt the muzzle of a gun in the back of his head. Trinica was on the other end of it.

'You gave it a good try,' said Trinica to Frey. 'But that's enough of being nice. Let's do this quick and easy.' And she shot Roke in the back of the knee.

Roke dropped to the ground, trying to scream but unable to make a noise. Blood steamed on the snow-covered roof. Trinica walked round to stand over him. Frey and the others had instinctively stepped back. Suddenly, all his romantic thoughts of his old sweetheart had disappeared. This was the Trinica who'd robbed and killed and plundered her way across Vardia. Even without her make-up and attire, he could see it in her manner. Utterly cold. Utterly ruthless. No one was getting in her way.

'Now,' she said to Roke. 'Grist. Where?'

Roke just gasped at her. She shot him in the hand, pulverising it into a bloody mash of tendon and shattered bone. He found his voice then.

'He's in Sakkan! Two hundred kloms north-west of Marduk! Warehouse complex on the east edge of the city! That's where we always hid out. He moves his drugs through it. Heavily guarded! He's got his own hangar there and everything! Big enough for the *Storm Dog!*'

Trinica shrugged at Frey. 'That's where he is,' she said, and she shifted her aim to Roke's forehead.

'Trinica!' said Frey sharply. She looked over at him. He shook his head slowly.

'Whyever not?' she asked. 'This way he can't talk to anyone else.'

The stark logic in her voice chilled him more than the freezing air. Over the past month he'd almost begun to believe this side of her had faded away, and a new tenderness had replaced her steely brutality. The fact that he'd been mistaken came as unpleasant shock.

'Don't be like this, Trinica,' he said.

'But this is how I am, Darian,' she replied.

Roke whimpered and blubbered on the ground, his eyes fixed on the barrel of the pistol pointed at his head. Trinica's gaze was locked with Frey's.

Frey had seen enough murders in his time. He'd just watched his engineer throw a man off the roof. But that was done in anger, was heavily provoked and, to Frey's mind, well deserved. Roke might be a scumbag, maybe even a traitor, but he'd given them the information they wanted. To shoot him now was just too cold-blooded.

Or maybe it was just that it was Trinica holding the gun. Maybe, if she pulled that trigger, he'd lose her for ever.

Please don't be like this.

Frey's heart thumped in his chest. Snow drifted through the space between them. Seconds crawled past.

'Very well,' she said at last. 'As you wish.' Then she lowered her gun and walked off towards the *Ketty Jay* without another word. Frey let out the breath he'd been holding.

'I need a doctor!' Roke cried suddenly. He was cradling his destroyed hand, face slack with shock. 'Someone get me a doctor!'

Frey turned to Malvery.

'Don't look at *me*,' Malvery said. 'I've barely got enough supplies to look after you lot. I ain't wasting any on him.'

'Sorry,' said Frey to Roke. 'Looks like you're on your own.'

'Maybe you can ask one of the factory workers for help,' Malvery added maliciously.

Roke was still howling when they left him, and he kept howling until the sound of the *Ketty Jay*'s engines drowned him out.

Thirty-One

A Place For Partings – A Gift –
The Grog Hatch – The Paths Our Hearts Take Us

The *Delirium Trigger* hung at anchor over the docks, between the frozen land and the ice-blue sky. She floated silently on aerium ballast, linked to the ground by thick chains. Fresh welding scars and burn marks marred her skin, tokens of her battle with the *Storm Dog*. The patch-up job hadn't been pretty, but that was the price of speed.

Frey and Trinica stood by a wooden railing on a hillside path that overlooked the Yort settlement of Iktak. Here the path bulged outward, perhaps intended as a rest point, a place for carts to pass, or even a convenient spot to take in the view. Frey couldn't imagine it was the latter. There was little to view in Iktak, just a depressing, industrial knot of pipes and factories and grimy snow that never quite thawed. That, and the bleak tundra beyond, an empty expanse broken by streaks of shrubbery in toxic colours.

Frey had stood in this exact spot when he'd said his goodbyes to Crake, a month ago. Back then the *Delirium Trigger* had been going in for repairs. Now, it seemed they were all but completed.

A place for partings, then, he thought. For there was another one coming, and he'd feel this one even more keenly than the last.

After they left Endurance, a hasty conference in the cockpit had determined their next move. Fly to Iktak, collect the *Delirium Trigger*, and then move on Grist's hideout in full force. Trinica was confident that her craft would be ready. She knew the workshop and said it was the best in the North. She'd offered them enough to make sure her craft was repaired within a month. It appeared her trust hadn't been misplaced.

'It'll take a day, at least,' she said. 'Maybe two. Break in the new crewmen. Trial flight. Fire the guns. All of that.' She pulled her fur-and-hide coat closer around her shoulders. 'I won't take them into battle untested. Not against Grist.'

'Fair enough. He hasn't made a move this past month. Whatever he's waiting for, what's another day or two? Better to be ready, right?'

'Indeed.'

'I've a trip of my own planned, anyway.'

'Oh yes?'

'I had a talk with my crew.'

She turned towards him slightly. Black birds flapped through the air overhead, croaking. 'About what?'

'About everything. Grist, you. About why I was dragging them all over everywhere.'

'You told them about us?'

'Not everything. Enough.'

'How did they take it?'

'Well, after they'd picked themselves off the floor, I think they were glad to know. It explains a lot for them, I suppose.'

Trinica laid a gloved hand on his arm and gave him a wan smile. Frey felt his throat tighten suddenly and his eyes began to prickle. The moment of affection, this lightest of contacts, had caught him by surprise. He looked away and stared intently into the middle distance, forcing back the threat of tears.

Blood and dust, Frey! Hold it together! You're supposed to be a man!

'They wanted to try and get Crake back,' he said. 'I said yes. Least I could do. Jez thinks she might be able to talk to him. She knows what's eating him up.'

'What about Pinn?'

'Pinn's gone,' said Frey, a touch of regret creeping into his voice. He couldn't help feeling that it was mostly his fault they'd lost their best pilot. 'If he ever told anyone where he came from, they don't remember. Don't have the first clue where to look for him. If he wants to come back, he'll have to find us. But somehow I doubt the lad's got the brains for it.'

'Will you replace him, then?'

'I don't know,' he said. 'I suppose I'll have to, eventually. Won't be the same, though.' He scratched the back of his neck. 'You know, there's a little part of me that's gonna miss that fat, stupid moron.'

He studied the *Delirium Trigger*. A shuttlecraft was departing from the Iktak docks and heading up towards it. Perhaps it was carrying engineers, still applying finishing touches to the delicate mechanisms inside. Maybe, once all the major work was done, they'd moved it out of the hangar to make space for another craft.

Thinking about things like that stopped him thinking about other things.

'It's a good idea,' said Trinica. 'About Crake.' She sounded weary and unenthusiastic, but then she always did when she was depressed.

Frey rolled his shoulders. 'We could do with getting Bess back if we need to do any fighting on the ground. Nobody can kick your head off like Bess can.'

'Come on. It's not about Bess. You miss Crake, too. Admit it.'

Frey poked at the frozen ground with the toe of his boot. 'Yeah,' he said. 'A lot more than Pinn, anyway.' He looked over at her. 'You won't go after Grist while I'm gone?'

'I'll wait for you, Darian,' she said. But, tired as she seemed, she didn't say it with much conviction. Frey wanted more assurance than that.

'Trinica,' he said. He made her face him. He wanted her to know it was serious. 'I can trust you, can't I? Because if you turned on me again . . .' He trailed off, not knowing how to end it.

'You can trust me,' she said, more firmly this time.

Frey was satisfied with that. They stood together in silence for a time, watching the activity in the docks below. Aircraft taking off, engineers tinkering with engines, foremen directing the moving of heavy equipment.

'All this will be different, you know,' she said at length.

He knew what she meant. She meant the feeling between them. She meant herself. After this, she'd return to the *Ketty Jay*. She'd don her black outfit and chop at the hair that had grown during their time together. She'd put on her white make-up and her garish lipstick and those contact lenses that made her eyes monstrous. She'd become the pirate queen once more.

'It doesn't have to happen that way,' he said awkwardly.

'Yes it does. I can't be here with you and there with them. There's no weakness allowed in that world.'

He turned to her, swept his hand down to indicate her, head to foot. 'This . . .' He fought for the words. 'This isn't weakness. When you put on all that shit and turn into the queen bitch of the skies, *that's* weakness.'

She nodded faintly. 'Perhaps you're right,' she said. 'But I live in a world where men judge me by my appearance. If I came to them as I am now, they'd see a woman. Trinica Dracken – *Captain* Trinica Dracken – needs to be more than that.'

Frey felt a surge of frustration. Why did she need to be so obtuse? How could she agree with him and still refuse to see what he wanted from her?

This past month, he'd hardly given a thought to that hollow sense of worthlessness that had settled on him. In fact, it had stopped bothering him completely. Perhaps it was because, in trying to catch Grist and prevent a disaster, he'd been doing something vaguely noble and selfless for a change. Or perhaps it was because he'd been doing it with Trinica at his side.

But now change was coming, and he was afraid. He'd got used to having her around. He didn't want that to end.

Suddenly, he wanted to do something to stop her. It couldn't finish this way, with a weak and bitter goodbye. Once she was gone, once she was back with her crew, then all this would fade from her mind. He didn't want her to forget him. That would be the worst thing imaginable. Even if she came to hate him, he couldn't bear to be forgotten.

He slipped off his gloves, and pulled off the silver ring around his little finger. Then he held it out to her in his palm.

'Oh, Darian, please,' she said. 'Your ring? Isn't my word good enough for you? You want to keep track of me too?'

It wasn't quite the response he was expecting. 'I just . . .' he said, but as usual the words crowded up in his mouth and nothing much came out. 'I want you to have it.'

She looked at him oddly. 'Why?'

'Next time you're thinking of robbing me blind, I want you to look at this and remember . . . how good we were together.'

It had started out as a half-hearted attempt at levity, but that only made the finale more pathetic. Frey could feel himself turning red. Damn it, why were unfelt emotions so easy to express, when the real ones tied his tongue?

She didn't laugh. Her face was solemn, and she had a fragile look about her. 'Alright,' she said quietly. She slipped off her glove and held out her left hand.

He took it carefully. Handling her as if she was porcelain. Her skin was cold and dry. 'Maybe I can find you again, after all this is done,' he said.

'That might not be a good idea,' she replied.

'Never stopped me before,' he replied. Bravado made him feel a little less nervous.

He slipped the ring on to her little finger. Her fingers were smaller than his, and it didn't fit.

'It's kind of big, Darian,' she observed gently.

He tried the next finger, and it slid on perfectly and stayed there.

Her gaze flickered upward, met his, and held it a long time.

There was nothing in his head. A wilderness of thought, blasted white by the moment. There was only her, the planes and curves of her face, the intelligence behind those eyes. As long as those eyes stayed on him, everything would remain as it was, beautiful as frost. Her hand still lay in his, but now it was warm: thawed by his touch, perhaps.

All he wanted was that she'd never stop looking at him.

But then she drew back, and her gaze fell. She took her hand away from his, and put it back inside its glove. 'I must go,' she said. 'Goodbye, Captain Frey. I'll see you on your return.'

She walked away from him, back towards the *Ketty Jay*, not meeting his eye. He looked out over the docks and listened to her boots crunch on the snow until he could hear them no more.

He walked around for slow hours before he went back to the *Ketty Jay*. He wanted to give her time: time to change herself, time to leave. It was only after they were airborne and on their way back to Tarlock Cove that he realised the hollow ache, which had been absent all month, had returned.

Pinn woke with an explosive snort to find that everything was sideways.

It took him several seconds to locate himself and work out which way up the world was meant to be. The smell of tobacco smoke, grog and sweat hung in the air. A badly tuned piano plinked and clunked in the background. He heard laughter, snarls and curses.

He was lying face-down on the bar, one chubby jowl spread out under him like a cushion. His chin was wet with drool and spilled beer.

His head felt heavier than usual as he lifted it. It lolled this way and that, too weighty for his neck to support. He got it under control with some effort and blinked the crust out of his eyes.

'You look a little the worse for wear, sir,' beamed the bartender, 'if you don't mind me saying.'

Pinn did mind, but he didn't have the energy to do anything about it. He decided he needed a drink instead. He had a vague memory of putting some coins on the bar in front of him, ready to buy his next drinks. His last two coins in the world. He'd been staring at them glumly at some point before he passed out. Now they were gone. He couldn't even remember what he'd spent them on.

'Stand me a round, friend?' he mumbled, more in hope than expectation.

The bartender, a tall mustachioed man with an annoyingly lively character, just grinned ever wider. 'No need, no need! Hold still just a minute.' He leaned over the bar and peeled the missing coins off Pinn's face. 'There you go. That should cover it! A rum and a beer, was it?'

'Right,' said Pinn. The bartender busied himself with the drinks.

Pinn wiped his chops with his sleeve and gazed blearily into the mirror behind the bar. Something resembling a bewildered mole stared back. The little thatch of hair atop his head had been crushed into an unflattering slope. He licked his palm and tried to do something about it. When he couldn't work up enough saliva, he dipped his hand in a nearby beer spill and used that.

The bartender put the drinks down in front of him. 'Forgive the observation, sir, but you've got about you the air of a man who doesn't quite know where he is. Am I right?'

Pinn looked around the bar again. 'Yeah. Where am I?'

'The Grog Hatch, sir. Finest tavern in town.'

Pinn thought for a moment. 'And what town is that, then?'

The bartender was impressed. 'You *are* a free spirit, sir. Well then, I have the pleasure of informing you that you find yourself in the fine port of Kingspire. Home of the best spitted divehawk in Vardia. I urge you to try it, if you haven't already. Might I ask what brings you to this place?'

The bartender's conversation was making Pinn's head hurt. 'I was going somewhere . . .' he mumbled. 'My sweetheart's getting married.'

'Oh, how terrible! And you, sir, are racing to prevent it?'

'I was,' he said. 'Dunno how I ended up here.'

'Perhaps you were inclined to a have a drink to steel your nerve?' suggested the bartender, who'd begun cleaning glasses.

'Yeah.'

'And after several drinks . . . Why, a man alone in a place like this, he has needs, doesn't he? Needs a woman can't understand. Perhaps you took a fancy to one of the local doxies?'

'More than one,' Pinn grunted. He swigged his rum to clear the taste of previous rums out of his mouth.

'You must possess a surfeit of manly desire, sir.'

Pinn wasn't sure what that meant, but he liked the sound of it so he agreed. 'Damn right.'

'Perhaps you gambled a little, too?'

'Got to do a bit of gambling after you've done a whore,' said Pinn. 'That's the time to hit the tables. A man thinks best when his pods are empty. '

'And, if I may venture to extrapolate from your recent attempt to solicit refreshments, perhaps you've been here several days, spent all the money you have and now find yourself stranded, without a shillie to your name, and many kloms still to go to your sweetheart?'

'That's it,' said Pinn. 'Exactly.'

The bartender sighed dramatically. 'You have my sympathy, sir. Fortune is cruel to romantics.'

Pinn raised his mug of rum to that. This bartender was one wordy son of a bitch, but he was wise. He understood. You couldn't blame a man for cutting loose once in a while.

It had been a hard month, after all. Worrying about Lisinda, trying to work out what he should do. Suffering that bitch Dracken for the Cap'n's sake. Even after she peeled off the ghoul mask and it turned out she was hot underneath, he still hated her. Not enough that he'd have said no, but you didn't have to like a woman to sleep with them. It was simply a matter of letting the pressure off. A man had to let the pressure off every so often. Otherwise, he was apt to do all kinds of stupid things. That was just nature.

So the first thing Pinn did when he got out on his own was to let the pressure off. There was nobody giving him orders, nobody to stop him, nobody to make him drink coffee and sober up. It took him two days to spend all the money he had in the world.

It was only now, in the cold light of impending poverty, that he remembered why he'd stopped at Kingspire in the first place. In his haste to reach Lisinda he'd been pushing the afterburners hard, and they'd eaten up all his fuel. He was running on fumes when he touched down in Kingspire and, unless some kind of miracle had occurred in the meantime, that was still the case.

The bartender was right. It was like the world was conspiring against him. Trying to thwart his attempts to reach his sweetheart. If there really was an Allsoul, it certainly seemed to have a grudge against Pinn.

Miserably, he assembled a roll-up. He considered offering one to the bartender – it would be good to befriend him, since Pinn would be tapping him up for drinks later – but his tobacco was low and he wanted it for himself. He was just licking the paper when someone eased on to the bar stool next to him, arriving in a wave of strong perfume.

'Got one of those for me, stranger?' she asked.

She was plump, heavily rouged, and showing a terrifying amount of cleavage. Red hair spilled in curls over a mole-pocked expanse of white flesh. One of her front teeth slightly overlapped the other. She was at least twenty years older than him, but she dressed like a woman half her age.

He handed over his roll-up, as if in a daze, and lit it for her with a match. She took a drag and smiled at him. It might have been the booze, but Pinn thought she was the most beautiful creature he'd ever seen.

'Strange and mysterious, the paths our hearts take us,' said the bartender sagely. But nobody was listening to him, so he drifted off to the other side of the bar, where there was another drunken soul in need of a sympathetic ear.

Thirty-Two

Plome's Confession –
Conversations In The Sanctum – An Ending, Of Sorts

Summer had got hold of Tarlock Cove, and Jez was glad to feel the sun on her face. After all that time in the arctic north it was a pleasure to be reminded that not every day was a hostile one. She took winding lanes up the mountainside, past streets turned sluggish in the heat. The distant sound of crashing waves drifted up to her as the sea patiently battered at the coast far below.

The address that Crake had left with the Cap'n turned out to be a tall, narrow house tucked away down a well-kept cobbled alley. She approached the door and composed herself. Now that she was here, she felt nervous. She'd not seen Crake since that day on the *All Our Yesterdays* when her Mane side had taken over. By the time she was out of the infirmary, he was long gone. She had no idea what to expect from him.

Would he welcome her, or be angry? Would he resent her for coming, and scorn her attempts to talk him back to the *Ketty Jay*? Would he despise her for being part Mane? Or would he offer to help her, as she hoped? That was, after all, her reason for coming.

Yes, she wanted him back on the crew, for everyone's sake. Yes, she was concerned about his well-being and worried that he might be in some kind of trouble. But first and foremost, she needed him for his expertise. Because she had a daemon inside her, and who but a daemonist could drive it out?

If anyone could help her deal with what she was, it was him. But she'd never told him about her condition. He'd hinted in the past that he knew, or at least suspected, what lay behind her unique abilities. Yet she still hadn't spoken out. And then, on the very day it became obvious to all and she could hide it no longer, Crake decided to leave.

Just when she needed him most. Just when she could finally admit to him that she was part Mane.

Was it just bad timing? Or did he leave because of me? Does he fear me? Or does he fear what I might ask him?

No way to know. She should have talked to him a long time ago. Should have asked him to take care of the daemon that plagued her. But instead she'd suffered, because she didn't dare admit her secret.

In that, at least, they understood one another.

She rapped on the door and waited. After a few moments she heard footsteps, and the door was opened by a harassed-looking middle-aged man, stout and balding. This, she assumed, was Plome, the owner of the house.

'Yes?' he inquired, looking her over critically. It occurred to her that she should have worn something more impressive than her grey overalls, but she'd never been much interested in clothes or jewellery.

'I'm looking for Crake,' she said. 'Is he here?'

'And who might you be?' he asked suspiciously, studying her over his pince-nez.

'I'm Jez. I'm the navvie on the—'

But Plome's face had already lit up. 'Oh, thanks be! Come in, come in!' He hurried her inside and shut the door.

'He spoke about you,' Plome explained, as Jez found herself propelled down the hallway. 'Said you were the only one who knew about what happened to him. I'm so glad you're here. So very, very glad.' He stopped and seized her by the shoulders. 'You have to take him away!'

'Err . . .' said Jez, who was still catching up. 'That was the idea, actually.'

'Good! Good!' Plome cried. 'I thought it would be wonderful having him here, you know. Such an eminent daemonist to learn from. Oh!' He clamped his hand over his mouth, aware that he'd let something slip. 'You mustn't tell anyone!' he urged.

'Tell anyone what?'

'That I'm a daemonist. Just an amateur, you understand, but then, aren't we all? No professionals in our business!' He laughed nervously, produced a handkerchief and mopped his glistening pate. 'I'm in politics, you know. Running for the House of Chancellors. If anyone knew, it'd be the death of me.'

Jez held up her hands. 'Mr Plome. Calm down. I'm not going to tell anyone anything. Now what's happened to Crake?'

Plome was describing frantic little circles around the hallway, wringing his handkerchief. 'He's become a liability, that's what! Oh, don't think badly of me. I've been a good friend to him. I lent him money. I helped him in everything. He bought rare books, sought out other daemonists, gathered all the research he could. But he always needed more. And one time he emerged from the sanctum, ranting about daemonism, while there were guests in the house! Came damnably close to blowing my cover and sending me to the gallows!' He threw his hands up in the air. 'I've become a recluse! Trapped in my own home, guarding him! I spend every day dreadfully afraid that the madman in my basement will break out and the world will know I've been dabbling with daemons. It's a short trip from there to the noose, believe me, young lady! And I'm supposed to be in the middle of a campaign to become a Chancellor of the Duchy! My rival makes ground every day I'm not out there! The Tarlocks are breathing down my neck, wondering what I'm up to! It's a disaster!'

He was panting by the time he finished. Jez decided she'd heard enough. 'Show me where he is.'

Plome led her around the side of the staircase at the end of the hall. There a cupboard door lay hidden and out of sight. He began fumbling in his pocket for something.

'Through here?' Jez asked, and pulled the door open.

'Wait! Don't open that yet!' Plome said.

Jez felt a strange tingle through her body. Her senses tipped, threatening to send her into a trance. Then everything righted itself, and she was looking at a set of steps, leading down, just beyond the door.

'He's down there?' she asked.

Plome, who was holding a tuning fork in his hand for some reason, gaped at her. 'But . . . the glamour . . . You can see the stairs?'

Jez looked at him oddly. 'Of course I can. Can't you?'

Plome looked bewildered. 'Oh, my. It's time I thralled a new daemon to that doorway. This one's lost its fizz. You shouldn't have seen anything but an old cupboard.'

Jez was eager to see Crake. She headed down. There were deep scratches on the walls of the stairway, which looked relatively fresh.

'Don't tread on the third step from the bottom!' Plome called after her. Jez stepped over it obediently. She could feel the faint thrum of energy from the wood. Another daemon, she guessed. She wondered if it was any more effective than the last.

The sanctum was a mess. Electric lights buzzed behind their shades, but half the bulbs had died and not been replaced. Chemical apparatus lay half-disassembled. Muddled equations were scrawled on blackboards, overlapping one another. There was a huge brass vat against one wall with a window in the side. It was full of a murky yellow liquid and attached to various machines. A large, riveted metal device like a bathysphere stood in the centre of the room. Books lay face-down and open where they'd been thrown.

Crake was sitting at a desk, his back to her. He was scribbling in a notebook, with occasional pauses to consult an enormous hidebound tome. His blond beard and hair had grown out; he looked shaggy and untidy. Bess sat near the desk, dormant. She was wired up to a complex tangle of equipment.

Jez suddenly understood the scratches on the narrow stairway. They must have had quite a time getting her down here.

'Crake,' she said.

He jumped at the sound of her voice, and his pen nib snapped. He stared at the notebook for a moment, then swept it off the desk.

'I can't make it work, Jez,' he said. He got to his feet and began pacing back and forth, his hand on his forehead. Red-rimmed eyes searched the middle distance restlessly. 'I can't make it work.'

'You can't make *what* work?'

'This!' he snapped, gesturing towards Bess. 'It's impossible!'

Jez was shocked by the state of him. He was like a madman, full of frantic energy, waving his arms around, bubbling on the edge of mania. He stank of sweat.

'What were you trying to do?'

'I was trying to get her back! There were rumours, you see. Always rumours among daemonists. They said there was a way to bring someone back from the dead. If you just collected the right raw materials, you could put them in a tank, you could infuse it with the essence, the . . . the . . . *frequency* of your loved ones, that you'd recorded when they were alive. And the body would *grow* itself!

Bones would form and muscles knit and there they'd be, floating in the tank, the way they always were!'

As he spoke, his face was full of mad hope, like a crazed prophet; but then his expression twisted and turned to rage.

'Lies! All lies! There are no records! I've searched everywhere, I've asked everybody, and no one's ever done any such thing! I don't even know where to start, do you understand? It's so far beyond me I can't even *begin*!'

Jez was appalled. *That* had been his plan? She'd suspected that he'd left the crew to deal with the question of Bess, but this sounded like a far-fetched method of doing so, even to her. She began to worry that he'd taken leave of his reason altogether.

'You were trying to bring her back from the dead?'

'The dead!' he cried, pointing at her. 'That was my next thought! After all, *you* walk around without a pulse. Why not my Bess? But what was I to do? Her body's gone, Jez! Dust and worms! Am I supposed to murder someone *else* to provide her with a form? No, I couldn't. So I tried to find corpses, but when I saw them, I . . . I couldn't . . . I . . .'

'Wait, you did *what*?'

'Don't you dare judge me!' he shouted. 'Don't you dare! I'd do anything to get her back. But not that way. Not some stitched-up post-autopsy puppet of cold meat. I'd be exchanging one abomination for another. That wouldn't be my Bess. So I looked for another method, but there *isn't* one!' He raked his hand through his hair anxiously. 'And after that . . . after that I wondered if I could make her smarter, you know, something closer to what she once was. Spit and blood, at least that'd be *something*. But I don't have the slightest notion how to do it! I don't even know what I did when I put her *in* there!' He was pacing back and forth now, making wild gestures, so agitated that he could barely contain himself. 'And then I thought . . . I thought, what if I *did* rescue her from wherever she went? What if I *did* restore her, and my beautiful little niece woke up and looked at herself, and held up those metal hands in front of her, and realised what she was? Can you imagine such a horror? Trapped inside an unfeeling metal shell for ever, her only companion the man who put her there? It's . . . it's positively macabre! It's that kind of meddling that led to all of this in the first place!'

He stopped, stared at her, and suddenly the angry expression on his face wavered, his lip trembled and tears shimmered in his eyes. 'I can't bring her back,' he said.

'No,' said Jez. 'You can't.'

She pitied him. Blinded by guilt, desperate to atone for the crimes of his past, he'd wanted to achieve the impossible. But Bess's body was gone. He might have salvaged a part of her, but he'd never get back the girl he'd known and loved. Her skin, her hair, her smile – they'd rotted away in the grave. All he could do was move her essence from the vessel she occupied to another one. And that wasn't any kind of solution.

But he had to try. He had to prove to himself that it couldn't be done, that there was no way to save Bess. He needed to fail before he could be made to see.

'It's not as simple as life and death, Crake,' she said. 'You should know that. I'm technically dead. My heart doesn't beat. But I *am* Jezibeth Kyte. I'm as much Jezibeth Kyte now as I was the day the Manes caught me.' She looked at Bess: an empty shell, her essence departed to wherever it went when Crake sent her to sleep. 'All that you knew of your niece, all the things that made you love her . . . they're gone. Gone for good. And what lives in that suit is not that girl.'

Tears had started to fall. Crake was beginning to sob. He wiped his nose. 'Why are you telling me this, Jez?'

'Because you can't change things, Crake. What you need to realise is that your niece died that night. That golem is just a memory of her. But it's not your niece. Your niece is dead.'

Crake shook his head.

'Say it, Crake!' she urged him. 'It's been killing you every day, and it won't stop killing you until you accept it.'

'She's there!' he insisted, thrusting a finger at the armoured suit. 'I put her in there! It's up to me to get her out!'

'You can't!' said Jez, grabbing him by the shoulders. 'That over there, that's something else. And it loves you and it needs you to take care of it, but it's *not your niece.*'

Crake pushed her away with a moan of anguish. He spun around and lashed a mass of chemical apparatus off a nearby table, then snatched up the book he'd been copying from and hurled it at Jez. She stepped aside with ease.

'What do *you* know? What do *you* know about it?' he shouted at her. Spittle flecked his beard, and his bloodshot eyes bulged.

'I know the difference between being alive and being dead,' she said calmly. 'Better than anyone, I reckon.'

Crake rampaged around the sanctum, knocking over anything he could see. When he'd smashed or thrown anything he could lay his hands on, he wheeled drunkenly against the wall and leaned there, sweating and red and spent.

'Say it, Crake,' she said relentlessly. 'You can't save her. You don't have the power. She's dead. Say it.'

'Alright!' he said. 'She's dead! I killed her and she's dead and gone! Happy now?'

His words rang into the silence, and then his face crumpled and he began to cry. He hugged himself and slid down the wall until he was sitting on the floor. 'She's dead,' he said again.

'You have to accept that,' Jez said. 'Accept it. Make it a part of you. Move on.'

'Easy for you to say,' he muttered. He clambered unsteadily to his feet, his face hard with disgust. 'I know why you're here. I know what all this is about. You've a daemon inside you, and you want it out.'

'Well, yes, I—'

'Well, nothing! You think I haven't considered that? All this time when I suspected you were a Mane? I was your friend, Jez. You think I hadn't wondered if I could fix you?'

Jez had a sinking feeling in her guts. 'Can you?' she asked.

'No!' he crowed. 'No! No one can! Because you died, Jez! Because your heart doesn't beat! I could drive that daemon out of you, but it's the only thing that's stopping you being *actually* dead. Without that daemon, you're just a corpse. Accept *that*! Make *that* a part of you!'

Jez was shocked by the viciousness in his voice, the hate on his face, the glee with which he crushed her hopes. Tears prickled at her eyes. She struggled to maintain her composure. She'd hurt him, and he wanted to hurt her back. She understood that. It didn't make it hurt any less.

No wonder he left as soon as it was clear that she was a Mane. Maybe that was the spur he needed. He didn't want her to ask him. He didn't want to tell her that there was no help for her. That she was condemned to slowly turn into something else.

She fought to come up with some kind of argument, some way to persuade him that he was wrong. But his reasoning was infallible. In fact, had Jez not been so desperate to rid herself of the invader in her body, she might have seen it herself. Even someone who knew nothing about daemonism could have worked it out. But just like Crake, she'd believed what she wanted to believe, what was necessary to keep going. And just like him, she'd been doomed to failure from the start. Some things couldn't be changed, no matter how hard you wished.

But now that she came to it, she found there was none of the disappointment or sorrow or misery she'd expected. Instead she felt a bleak, sad sort of resignation. The peace of a prisoner as they walked to the gallows, knowing that all possibility of reprieve or escape was gone. Maybe she'd always known, deep down, that there was no going back.

'Alright,' she heard herself say. 'I believe you.'

'Good,' he said.

She walked around the room. 'There's no chance.'

'None.'

'The way I am is the way I am.'

'Exactly.'

She shook herself, brushed a strand of hair back from her face, and nodded. 'Then that's how it is,' she said quietly.

Crake gazed mournfully at the empty shell of the golem. 'That's how it is,' he agreed.

She raised her head. 'We'd like you to come back, Crake.'

The daemonist surveyed the room, strewn with the wreckage of his studies. 'Yes,' he said. 'I'm finished here.'

They held a small gathering on a hillside on the way back to Iktak. There was nothing to bury, so they simply raised a marker: a slab of metal that they'd scored with one of Silo's screwdrivers.

> *Bessandra Crake*
> *Beloved niece of Grayther Crake*
> *DY138/32–147/32*

The whole crew attended, except Pinn, who was no longer with them. Crake was glad of that. He'd only have asked moronic questions. The others understood well enough, though. They didn't know the dead girl, nor why Crake was honouring her now when she'd died two years ago. But they came anyway and kept silent. Because he asked them to. Because he wanted them there, and they were his friends.

And though they couldn't have failed to notice the similarity between the name on the grave and Crake's golem, he knew they'd never guess the truth. It was too terrible, too impossible. Easier to assume he'd named the golem in her memory.

On reflection, Crake decided they were right.

Bess herself – the *golem* Bess – stood off to one side, her ball clutched in her massive hands, shifting restlessly. She'd picked up on the mood and made sad cooing noises, but he wasn't sure whether she really fathomed what was happening here. If his niece truly was inside that armoured skin, he'd surely have seen more of a reaction. She was witnessing her own funeral, after all. But the way she behaved was no more than might be expected of a faithful dog.

The wind was warm, rippling the grass, and sunlight broke through the clouds to slide over the hills in great patches. Harkins had his cap scrunched in his hands. Malvery's head was bowed. Jez had tears in her eyes. Frey and Silo stood solemn and grim. Even the *Ketty Jay*, visible nearby, was a witness to this.

She's dead, he told himself. It still didn't feel true. But, on some level, something had changed. He'd begun to feel that, if he repeated it enough, he'd believe it. That was something, at least. That was hope.

No words were spoken. They simply stood and stared at the grave-marker. Silently sharing the emptiness of death.

After a time, Crake stooped and laid a small toy at the foot of the marker. A doll that he'd bought in Tarlock Cove. Bess had always been enchanted by the toys he bought for her. He used to pretend he made them himself, in his secret basement. It explained what he was doing in the wine cellar of her father's house, night after night. It had been her desire to see his mythical toy workshop that led her to sneak into his sanctum, on the night that was to end her life.

He heard the rustle and clank of leather and metal, and felt Bess arrive next to him. She looked down at the grave-marker, tiny glimmers of light glittering behind her faceplate. Then she bent down, and put her ball next to the doll.

Crake choked back a sudden sob. He rubbed his eyes with his

fingertips and smiled at her, as best he could. He put his hand on the cold armour plate of her shoulder and patted it.

'Good girl, Bess,' he said.

Then he turned away from the grave, to face the sympathetic gazes of his friends. He pulled in a deep breath, raised his head, and nodded.

'I'm ready,' he said. 'Let's go get Grist.'

Thirty-Three

Many Angles – 'She Doesn't Really Do Subtle' –
A Confrontation

Sakkan was a city of geometries, all slopes and angles. Situated deep in the frozen Duchy of Marduk, it didn't hide underground like many northern settlements, nor did it shelter in the lee of a mountain. Instead, it stood stern and resilient as the rock of the plateau it was built on. A summer dawn was breaking, hazy cloud choking a sky that was dull and bleached of colour. There was no wind, and no snow. The cold hung in the still air and seeped like liquid into the bones.

A tractor rumbled and sputtered through the quiet streets, surrounded by a wary escort of fifteen men and two women. It towed a trailer behind it, carrying a large, lumpy shape, concealed under a tarpaulin. The men and women moved quickly, with hurried steps, their eyes darting this way and that, hands never far from their guns.

Time was of the essence here. Word of the arrival of the *Delirium Trigger* and the *Ketty Jay* would soon spread. The element of surprise would be lost. That wouldn't do. They needed to hit their target hard and fast.

Frey glanced around the faces of his crew. Harkins had remained behind but Jez, Malvery, Silo and Crake were with him. They were focused and determined. There was a new confidence about them since Crake had returned and Jez had been accepted back into the fold. Malvery had even muttered about searching for Pinn once they were done with Grist.

Things were different between them now. The sense that their world was unravelling had faded, and that gladdened Frey immensely. The end was in sight. Maybe they *would* track down that porky idiot Pinn once they'd mopped up here.

He was cold, and rather scared, and it was far too early in the morning to get killed. But for all that, he felt a fierce kind of love for his crew right then. There was nothing quite like the camaraderie of men and women who faced danger together. It was a bond stronger than friendship. Going into battle with another person at your side was a level of trust altogether unknown in the world of the aristocrat or the peasant.

Besides, he really liked it when they kicked arse.

Marduk's second city was built almost entirely from the grey-black stone of the region. It clung to the hilly back of the plateau, rising in grim tiers above them, walled sections linked by sloping roads and winding switchback stairs. Stout towers stood defiantly against the threat of winter gales. The streets were austere but not bare. Monuments and statues of dukes and explorers looked down on neat squares and wide boulevards. Banks and powerful trading houses competed for the most impressive premises. Sakkan was a dark and hard place, but it hadn't forgotten how to be grand.

The tractor's engine sounded eerily loud in the quiet of the dawn. The man driving it was Balomon Crund, Trinica's bosun. He was a squat, ugly man with dirty, matted hair and a burn scar on his neck. Not too easy on the eye, but Trinica thought highly of him. He'd been her most loyal supporter in the mutiny that deposed the *Delirium Trigger*'s previous captain.

Frey could see why she trusted him. Though he was a taciturn sort, the signs were clear to a man of Frey's experience. Crund adored her. He'd seen it on the faces of several of her men: a certain sort of veneration, somewhere between affection, respect and awe. She'd made herself untouchable, put herself on a pedestal, and made them love and fear her. She couldn't rule by raw strength, so she'd fashioned them a cruel goddess, and let them come to her altar.

But the woman they knew wasn't the one Frey knew. That one had disappeared, it seemed, just as he feared she would.

The sight of Trinica in her make-up and black attire was jarring after a month of seeing her without it. But worse was the change in her behaviour. She was distant now, closed off from him. Her black eyes were empty and showed nothing. He told himself she had to be that way in front of her men, but he wasn't sure that was the whole truth. Perhaps she wore her personalities like a coat, to take off and put on as necessary. Perhaps the feelings he'd thought were growing between them had been the same: another woman's feelings, not those of a pirate queen.

He caught himself. Damn, what was happening to him? Since when had he spent this much time fretting about a woman? *Don't be such a sap!* he told himself.

The streets began to thin out as they came to the eastern edge of the city. Trinica's men led the way. She'd sent scouts ahead while Frey was off picking up Crake, and their reports had been encouraging. They'd found the warehouses Roke had spoken of, and apparently they'd seen Grist as well, and spotted the *Storm Dog* in its hangar.

The news made Frey restless with excitement. He'd wanted to fly in there and blast the place to pieces. Trinica had persuaded him otherwise. The Coalition Navy might not take kindly to an aerial assault on one of their major cities, she pointed out. Better to make it a ground assault. Take them by surprise. Catch Grist before he could even get his craft into the sky.

There were five in the assault team from the *Ketty Jay*, the rest from the *Delirium Trigger*. Harkins had been left with the aircraft, and instructed to stay in contact via the earcuffs. Frey would need the pilot's eyes in case things went airborne. The *Delirium Trigger* stood ready to take off at a moment's notice, at a signal from a flare gun Trinica carried. Just in case the *Storm Dog* got out of its hangar. Grist wasn't going to slip away again.

They passed early risers and late revellers, drifting through the streets. Many had heard of Trinica Dracken, and recognised her. They kept their distance, sensing trouble.

There'll be trouble for someone, alright, Frey thought.

The further from the landing pad they went, the more the city flattened and spread out. Eventually, they reached an industrial district of factories and warehouses. The roads became narrow, bleak and dirty. Walls crumbled, cracked by frost. The air smelled of chemicals, and the buildings were sooty with residue.

Crund brought the tractor to a halt just before the crest of a rise. Beyond, the road dipped down towards a group of blank brick warehouses huddled round a large aircraft hangar. The warehouses were surrounded by a formidable metal fence, ten feet high and tipped with spikes. A pair of guard towers stood overlooking the compound.

Frey got a better view with his spyglass. They were Yorts, their beards and hair knotted and braided, faces tattooed and pierced in several uncomfortable-looking places. They were carrying heavy repeater rifles, and appeared generally unfriendly.

He scanned the compound while the others pulled the tarpaulin off the trailer and checked their weapons. There were fifteen guards that he could see. One guard each.

Not good enough. Fair fights were for suckers. It was time to employ their secret weapon.

He walked around the side of the trailer, where Bess now lay uncovered. 'Wake her up, Crake,' he said.

Crake put a brass whistle to his lips and blew it. No sound was made, but Bess stirred and sat up. Trinica's men stepped back uneasily. Some of them remembered the golem from her rampage through the *Delirium Trigger* when she was berthed in Rabban during the Retribution Falls affair.

'Come on, Bess,' said Crake. The golem clambered down and the trailer groaned in relief. Trinica's men set about detaching it from the tractor they'd hired from the landing pad.

'Are your people ready?' Frey asked Trinica.

Trinica gazed at him in that cool, half-amused way she had. 'They'll do their part.'

The group split into two. Five of Trinica's men were staying behind with the tractor. The rest were coming with Frey and his crew, Trinica and her bosun included. Frey didn't feel good about Trinica fighting alongside him – he'd have preferred her safe and out of the way – but she wouldn't be dissuaded and he knew better than to try. She was hungry to get her own back on Grist. She wanted to be there in person when the big man went down.

'Get moving as soon as you hear the first gunshots,' he told the men who were staying behind. They acted as if they hadn't heard. They didn't take orders from anyone but their mistress.

Frey's group headed off the road and through back ways towards the compound. It was too early for many people to be around in this part of the city, so Bess could travel unconcealed. Walking through the heart of Sakkan in the company of an eight-foot golem would have brought the Militia down on them in minutes, but out here in the industrial district there was no one to see her.

One of Trinica's scouts led them, taking them down the hill by routes that kept them out of view of the compound. Soon enough they found themselves in the mouth of an alleyway between two grim storage facilities, looking out across a road at the fence that encircled their target. A warehouse lay just beyond it, blocking most of the compound from view. A guard tower overlooked both fence and compound, but the guards within weren't paying a great deal of attention to their job, being more interested in playing a game that involved punching each other in the arm and laughing a lot. Yort humour, Frey supposed.

Trinica nodded towards the fence. 'Tell your golem to be subtle, hmm? Get us in quietly.'

He cocked his pistol. 'She doesn't really do subtle.'

He motioned to Crake, who said a few words to Bess. Bess strode out across the road, took hold of the bars of the fence, and with one huge pull she ripped them out. Metal screeched and twisted and snapped as she tugged at the bars, dragging a great section of the fence with her. By the time she'd torn a hole big enough for them to get through, she'd also destroyed the fence for ten metres to either side.

'So I see,' Trinica commented dryly.

The racket had attracted the attention of the Yorts in the guard tower, who were yelling and pointing at her. One of them began taking shots with his rifle. The bullets just bounced off Bess's armoured hump. Other guards on the ground were running over to investigate the source of the disturbance, rounding the edge of the warehouse. They skidded to a halt when they saw her, swore in Yortish, and then scrambled towards what cover they could find.

'Aren't we going to help her?' Crake urged, fidgeting anxiously. They were still crowded in the alleyway, unnoticed in the commotion.

'Not with those guards still up above us,' said Frey.

'*Bess!*' Crake called. '*The tower!*'

Bess had stamped her way into the compound and was looking this way and that for enemies. The guards had opened up on her in earnest, and the irritating sting of bullets on her metal skin was making her angry. At the sound of Crake's voice she swung towards the tower and charged it with a bellow.

The tower was a metal scaffold, little more than a frame that supported the platform. It was sturdy enough under normal circum-stances, but it hadn't been designed to stand up to an enraged golem. Bess crashed into the base of the scaffold, smashing away one of the four legs and badly damaging another. The Yorts at the top yelled and flailed as the tower tipped slowly sideways. It toppled into the side of the warehouse, collapsing in a heap of mangled metal.

'*Now* can we help her?' said Crake.

Frey whistled through his fingers. 'Let's go!' he cried, and they broke cover and ran across the road, past the wrecked fence and into the compound.

The Yorts were slow to see them coming. They were too concerned with Bess, who was chasing around trying to catch them. It gave Frey a chance to find cover behind the wreckage of the guard tower. From there he could see around the side of the warehouse, giving him a good view of the compound. Ahead of him was a gravelled expanse with the fence and the front gate to his left. The second guard tower was on the far side, some distance away. The hangar was out of sight, around the other side of the warehouse.

'Fire!' Trinica called, and the air was filled with the sharp bark of gunshots. A withering volley of bullets cut down the Yorts as they fled Bess's wrath.

Their initial assault took out most of the first group of guards, but more were appearing from inside the buildings. Bullets began flying their way. Frey kept his head down. The crushed and twisted frame of the guard tower was hardly an impenetrable barrier.

'They're coming round the back of us!' said Jez. She heard them before anyone saw them, and that probably saved a few lives. They had precious seconds to line up and aim before a half-dozen Yorts rounded the other side of the warehouse, behind their position in the cover of the guard tower. They were cut down in a blaze of shotgun fire.

'Where are your people, Trinica?' Frey cried in annoyance. No sooner had he said it than there was a loud crash and a squeal of metal. He peeped through the wreckage of the guard tower and saw the front gate hanging by a hinge, with the tractor tangled up in it. Trinica's men had sent it plunging full tilt down the hill and were now swarming in behind it, shooting at the disoriented guards, who suddenly faced an attack on three fronts. Bess, meanwhile, was having great fun shaking the remaining guard tower and watching the guards fall out.

Malvery loosed off a couple of shotgun blasts and then ducked back into cover as a few more bullets came their way. 'We ought to get inside, Cap'n. Bit likely to get shot out here.' One of Trinica's men wheeled backwards and slumped to the ground, a red hole in his cheek. Malvery pointed at him meaningfully.

'Head for the hangar!' Trinica said. 'We can't let Grist get away.'

Frey nodded. 'Alright. Stay close to the warehouse. Go!'

They broke cover and ran low across the open ground, hurrying past the corpses of fallen Yorts. There were few guards left out here now; most had retreated to more defensible positions, terrified of the roaring golem in their midst. Bess was chasing two of the slower guards across the gravel. She caught one by his trailing leg, picked him up as if he was weightless, and used him to swat the other one into the fence.

'Bess! Come on!' Crake called. She looked up at the sound of his voice and lumbered over, still carrying the corpse of her latest victim, dangling by one shattered leg from her massive fist.

Crake eyed the body and turned faintly green. 'I don't think you need that any more,' he said. Bess obediently pitched the dead man into the distance.

They followed the warehouse wall to the corner. From there, they could see the back end of the hangar where the *Storm Dog* was hidden. An entrance led to a loading bay inside.

'Through there!' said Trinica. Frey scanned the ground before them, saw no guards, and went for it. He was halfway there when a pair of Yorts came running into sight. Silo and Malvery had spotted them, and they were gunned down before they could get a shot off. Frey pressed himself up against the side of the loading bay entrance and peered inside.

Trinica's scouts had been on the money. The hangar was cluttered with piles of supplies and criss-crossed with gantries. In their midst, looming over everything, was the colossal prow of the *Storm Dog*. Frey felt an angry sense of triumph at the sight.

Gotcha, you thieving, psychotic son of a bitch.

The hangar appeared to be empty, but Frey didn't like the look of the loading bay. Before them was a clear space where the tractors entered the building to pick up and deposit cargo. Stacks of crates were piled up on three sides. Perfect territory for an ambush. He hesitated at the door.

'What are you doing? Get inside!' Trinica cried, as she slammed up against the wall next to him. Bullets pocked the brickwork nearby: another group of guards, heading their way from the far side of the compound.

'I don't trust it!' he said. 'It's too easy! Grist's smarter than this!'

'Don't be stupid, Darian! How could there be an ambush waiting for us? He doesn't know we're coming!'

She was right. It was a surprise attack. Grist wouldn't have had time to organise an ambush. Frey was giving him too much credit. They were outside, exposed, and more guards were coming. There was no more time to deliberate.

'Move it!' he shouted, waving them through. Bess went first, closely followed by the rest of the crew. He ran after them. Trinica and her men loosed off a few potshots at their attackers and followed.

Jez was only a few metres in when she skidded to a stop. The look in her eyes as she turned back told him all he needed to know. She'd detected something with her heightened Mane senses that Frey had missed. 'Cap'n!' she cried. 'Go back! It's a—'

The loading bay door slammed down, shutting them in. Two dozen men sprang up from behind the crates, weapons levelled. The invaders' assault came to a stumbling halt.

'—trap,' Jez finished, belatedly.

There was the sound of weapons being primed behind them. Frey's heart sank and kept on sinking. He squeezed his eyes closed.

'Yes,' said Trinica. 'I'm afraid it is.'

Frey felt like he was tipping into a yawning void. Her voice seemed to come from far away. It didn't belong to the woman he'd known. It was a creature incalculably more terrible, the dark goddess that the men of the *Delirium Trigger* worshipped.

No. No, no, no. Not her. Not again!

Frey was no stranger to betrayal, whether suffering it or committing it himself. But this time, this single moment of utter, damnable *loss* . . . this one beat them all.

'Put down your weapons,' he heard himself say. His voice was flat. 'Crake, take care of Bess.'

He surveyed the faces of the men behind the crates. The men of the *Storm Dog*. He recognised the bald head and bulbous eyes of Grist's bosun, Crattle. He heard the clatter of weapons being thrown down, and threw down his own. Crake was muttering soothing words to the golem, who was making threatening movements towards the men.

He looked over his shoulder. Trinica was there, her pistol trained on his back. He might have been looking at a statue, for all the emotion she showed.

None of it had been real. None. All this time he'd been fooling himself. He should have listened to sense. He should have learned his lesson on Kurg, when she stole the sphere and dismissed him with barely a word. She was a fake, a ghost, a wreck. The ruined husk of the woman he'd almost married. Just because she knew how to act the way she once had, it didn't mean the emotions were real.

But he'd fallen for it. He'd neglected his crew, he'd ignored their protests, and he'd let her into their lives. All because he thought there was something there still worth fighting for. Some remnant of the past that he could kindle into life. A relic of the time before he'd run out on her, when things seemed honest and straightforward. When he'd loved with abandon, unafraid.

His eyes fell to the ring on her finger. Then he turned back towards the men training guns on them. He'd gone beyond fury or grief, into a numb kind of calm.

'I suggest you let my daemonist deactivate his golem,' he said, loudly. 'Otherwise she's liable to tear someone's head off.'

Crattle waved his gun at them. Crake held up one hand. 'Nobody shoot me, okay?' He slowly reached into his pocket, pulled out his whistle, put it to his lips and blew. Once again there was no sound, but Bess drooped and stopped moving, the life gone from her.

Trinica and her men walked around in front of them, and she took the whistle from Crake's mouth. 'Search them,' she ordered her men. 'The daemonist especially. He may have various devices about his person.'

She reached up and took the silver cuff from Frey's ear. Their eyes met, but she looked through him as if he was a stranger. 'Watch out for his cutlass,' she told her men. 'Keep it away from him. It's dangerous.' Then she moved to Jez and took her earcuff, too.

'The compass,' she said, holding out her hand. Jez gave her a glare of pure hatred and pulled the compass from her pocket. Trinica consulted it, checking that it did indeed point towards the ring on her finger, then tossed it to her bosun.

'Keep hold of that,' she instructed him, and he slipped it into the pocket of his coat.

'Found these,' said another of her men, holding up Crake's pocket watch and his skeleton key that could unlock any door. Trinica held out her hand and took them, too, putting them away with the earcuffs and the whistle.

Then they stepped back to make way for the man who'd come out from behind the crates and was walking towards them, a cigar clamped between his grinning yellow teeth. Frey stared levelly at him. Harvin Grist, of course. The bastard might have outsmarted them again, but Frey wasn't about to show an ounce of humility, or bitterness, or sadness at the way this had all turned out. He wouldn't give them that satisfaction.

'Captain Frey,' he beamed, then launched into an explosive coughing fit that left him red-faced and wheezing, somewhat undermining his moment of glory.

'Captain Grist,' said Frey. 'You know, I have a doctor here if you want him to take a look at that cough.'

'I'll happily pull your lungs out your arse for you,' Malvery added. 'Cure your cough in a jiffy.'

Grist recovered and slapped Malvery on the arm. 'Aye, I don't think that'll be necessary, but thanks anyway.' He straightened and took another drag on his cigar. 'Now where were we?'

'You were warming up for a good, hearty gloat,' Frey replied. 'But under the circumstances, y'know, just skip it and shoot us, eh?'

'Oh, there might not be any need for that,' said Grist. 'I could've had Trinica blow you out of the sky if I wanted you dead.'

'Yes,' said Frey, turning a slow gaze on her. 'I'm sure she'd have been delighted to do that.'

'Don't be a child, Darian,' she said. 'It's business. Grist made me an offer. I accepted.'

'Heard from Osric Smult that you two were lookin' for me,' Grist said, through a cloud of smoke. 'Couldn't find Captain Dracken, but I found the *Delirium Trigger* in Iktak. I reckoned she'd come back sooner or later, so I left a man there to make her a proposition when she returned.'

'What happened to revenge, Trinica?' said Frey coldly. 'What about *thousands will die*?'

Trinica tilted her head. 'I didn't feel quite so vengeful after I heard his offer,' she said. 'Everyone has a price. He exceeded mine.' When Frey kept on looking at her, she waved him away. 'Don't act hurt, Darian. You'd have done the same. You know as well as I do that your intentions weren't half as noble as you pretended. As soon as you got your hands on that sphere, you were going to sell it to the highest bidder. Your *thousands will die* wouldn't be quite so important, weighed against a fortune.'

He laughed bitterly. Laughed because she was so, so wrong. All this time, she'd never even believed him. She thought he was chasing the sphere for his own profit. But for once, on this matter, he knew his own mind absolutely. No amount of money was that important. That was a line he wouldn't cross. Whatever she thought, he had enough honour for that.

Besides, he could have had ridiculous wealth twice over, first with her and then with Amalicia. The easy path. But both times he'd turned it down. Whatever the hole in his life was, filling it with money wasn't enough.

'I don't know how many times I've got to tell you, Trinica,' he said. 'You don't know me half as well as you think. You might have a price. I don't.'

At that, he saw the first flicker of uncertainty on her face. The smallest fracture in her surety.

Good, he thought bitterly. *I hope it hurts, damn you. I hope you take it to your grave, and I hope you end up there real soon. I trusted you. But I reckon you don't know what trust is any more.*

Grist pointed to Jez. 'Take her,' he told his men. 'The Captain too. Everyone else, lock 'em up down below.'

Jez and Frey were pulled out of the group. 'Hey! She's just a navvie! What do you want with her?' he demanded.

The end of Grist's cigar glowed. 'She's the reason you're here, Captain Frey. See, I need a Mane. And it just so happens you've got one on your crew. Now ain't that a twist?'

Thirty-Four

A Genuine Piece Of History – All Is Revealed –
Crake And The Pocket Watch – Feline Suspicions – Jez Has To Choose

Jez stared at Frey's back as they were marched into the depths of the hangar at gunpoint. Grist and Crattle accompanied them, along with several of the *Storm Dog*'s crew. Trinica came, too. Perhaps she wanted to enjoy the fruits of her treachery.

The Cap'n walked with slumped shoulders, crushed by Trinica's betrayal. He tried to conceal his pain, but it showed anyway. He'd put every ounce of his faith in that woman, and she'd let him down. Even before the Cap'n had confessed to them that he had a history with Trinica, she'd seen the connection between them. She'd sensed the depth of feeling he carried.

And Trinica? What did *she* feel? Nothing at all, it seemed. Nothing at all.

Damn it, Cap'n. You're a good man, but you make the worst choices.

It occurred to her that she should be worrying about herself, rather than the Cap'n. It was her that Grist was interested in, not Frey. Because she was a Mane. She wasn't sure why that was important to their enemy, and she wasn't keen on finding out.

But she'd never known the Cap'n so *defeated*. It hurt her to see him diminished that way.

They were led away from the *Storm Dog*, down several sets of steps, along blank stone corridors lit by electric lights. Frey didn't speak, and neither did anyone else. Presently, they entered a small, chilly cellar, with walls that didn't match the modern construction of the rest of the hangar. It was as if they'd travelled a century back in time. There were two huge oak doors in the cellar floor, with heavy iron pull-rings and a complicated sequence of symbols carved into their surface.

Jez had been conscious of a growing unease as she drew closer to the cellar, but she hadn't known the source until she saw it. It was coming from those doors. The symbols were a daemonist's work, and though they had no force now, the memory of their power made Jez's skin prickle.

There was a sense of barely suppressed energy in the air. Something lurked behind those doors. She dreaded it, and didn't want to go further.

She must have slowed unconsciously, because one of the crewmen jabbed her in the back with the muzzle of his pistol. Ahead of them, two men were pulling the doors open. Beyond were worn stone steps. Crattle pulled a breaker on the wall. A row of lights, strung together with cables, began to glow in the stairway and the room just visible at the bottom.

'Ladies,' said Grist, bowing to Trinica and Jez. 'Cap'n,' he added, nodding at Frey. 'You're about to see a genuine piece of history.'

Grist led the way down. Jez followed with the rest of them. It sounded as if there was a crowd at the bottom of the stairs, a howling, shrieking horde whose cries bypassed the ears and went directly into the mind. They were getting louder with every step. She looked around at the others, distressed, but nobody else seemed to hear it. Was there agony in those voices? Terror? Or a fierce exultation? Every fibre in her body thrummed with the noise. A cacophony of ghosts, screeching out of the past.

What happened here?

The chamber at the bottom was another cellar, larger than the first. It was damp, freezing and gloomy. The edges of the bricks had been nibbled away by time. Mould grew in black patches. Electric lights had been placed on the floor, against the walls, but they did little more than push back the shadows.

This place was a sanctum.

Evidence of daemonism was everywhere. The centre of the room was dominated by a huge cage, a dodecahedron of rusted bars that stood on an octagonal pedestal. Symbols, similar to those on the doors, had been carved into the pedestal. Metal rods stood at the points of the octagon, one of them bent at an angle. Cables led from the cage to antique machines, as big as cabinets. Sections of panelling had come away from the machines to reveal broken cogs, springs, tiny gears and switches. There were lecterns with rotted books lying open on them. Seats were placed in rows, some tipped over and missing legs. There was a table, a chest, and a shattered chalkboard smudged with the suggestion of words and symbols.

The damage hadn't all been caused by the hand of time. The chalkboard had been broken by force. So had several chairs, and the panelling on one of the machines. There had been conflict here.

It was a reconstruction, Jez realised. Grist had found this place in disarray, and put everything back as best he could. She knew now what he'd brought them to see. The cries surrounded her, battering at her mind. The wails of the daemonists and the savage triumph of the daemons.

'This was where it started,' she said.

Grist put a fresh cigar in his mouth. The flare of the match lit up his face, turning it craggy and sinister. He puffed, drew in the smoke, and blew it out, surveying the room as if it were some grand vista.

'Right you are, ma'am. This is where they came, that day, to perform their secret ritual. Didn't know what they were messin' with, I reckon. Full of 'emselves. Explorers of the unknown. I ain't sure what they thought they were lookin' for—'

'But what they got were the Manes,' said Frey.

Grist regarded him from beneath his bushy eyebrows. 'Well. Seems my little surprise ain't so much of a surprise after all.'

'We dropped in on Professor Kraylock at Bestwark,' said Frey. His tone was dead, void of emotion. 'He filled us in on what your father was up to. He sent you his research, didn't he? Before he was killed.'

Grist took out his cigar and waggled the nub in Frey's direction. 'You're a smart one, Cap'n,' he said, impressed.

Frey looked at Trinica. 'Not that smart.'

Grist stuck the cigar back into place between his teeth. 'Women,' he commiserated. 'Can't live with 'em, can't feed 'em into a meat grinder and feast on their remains.'

Trinica showed no reaction, just gazed at him with eyes black as a shark's. Grist grinned and turned back to Frey. 'Ah, she ain't got anything to say. She's been well paid.'

Jez was finding it hard to follow the conversation. Just being here was like standing in the torrent of a river, trying not to be swept away. The memory of the Manes was everywhere here. She felt herself sliding into a trance, and fought it.

'You found this place through your father's notes?' Trinica asked.

Her head was tipped back and she was studying the ceiling, most of which was lost to darkness.

'Aye,' said Grist. 'Used to be there was a manse here. Belonged to a businessman, name o' Slinth. He was a big name in daemonist circles, back in the old days. This was his sanctum. Used to be some way outside o' town, but Sakkan's grown since then, turned into a city. They knocked the old place down, built a cannin' factory over it. Never knew the cellar was here. My Dad figured it out, though. I bought up the factory, so I could get to what was underneath.'

'Well,' said Frey, looking around at the dank room. 'It was certainly worth it.'

Grist didn't rise to the sarcasm. 'Thought there'd be answers here, but there ain't answers. The books were past savin'. Couldn't read what was on the chalkboards. This place is just a museum.' He coughed his hacking cough. 'Still, I put the land to good use. The warehouses, the hangar. You come in at night when no one's around to spot you. No records, no docking fees. Nice little place to hole up. And I can move my product through here without anyone takin' an interest.'

'Your father's reseach,' said Trinica. 'You still have it?'

'Safe in my cabin, don't you worry.'

'You're aware of the repercussions if it was made public? If it could be proved that the Awakeners have been using the daemonic techniques pioneered here?'

'Aye, I've got a notion. Would that offend you, Cap'n Dracken? You've a soft spot for the Awakeners?'

'I don't have a soft spot for anyone,' Dracken replied. 'I wondered if you were intending to take revenge on them. Your father was most likely murdered by an Imperator. I assume you knew that?'

'I figured as much,' said Grist. 'The thought had crossed my mind, I'll admit. But I've more urgent business to deal with first.' He broke out into a tremendous coughing fit that left him wheezing and watery-eyed. His crewmen shifted uneasily, glancing at one another.

'You alright?' asked Frey. 'Wouldn't want you to keel over and die. Much.'

Grist wiped spittle from his beard and went over to the small chest that was sitting on a nearby table. He opened it up. 'I'm touched by your concern, Cap'n, but I ain't keeling over anytime soon.' He took out the metal sphere that Frey had first seen on the Mane dreadnought. 'Not now I got this.'

Jez's attention fixed on the sphere. Smooth black metal with silver lines curving all over its surface. There was no symmetry to it – at least, no symmetry that a human would recognise – but as Jez stared at it, the pattern seemed to almost make sense, straining on the edge of recognition. There was a chanting in her head, louder even than the voices of the ghosts here. A wordless summons, from far away. Far to the north, behind the Wrack. The Manes. Wanting her.

'What is it?' she heard herself say. 'What have we been chasing all this time?'

'This?' he held it up. 'It's an alarm.'

Frey blinked. 'A what?'

'An alarm.'

'Not a doomsday device, then?'

Grist peered at it. 'Not really.'

'Oh.'

'It's a distress beacon,' Grist said. 'All dreadnoughts carry them. You remember I told you about that Navy report, when they found a downed dreadnought? I neglected to mention a couple o' things. Like how there were still Manes alive on it, and the Navy fought 'em back. And how one of 'em locked itself behind one of those daemonically guarded doors that your man Crake had so much fun gettin' through. And how, right after, a half-dozen dreadnoughts appeared. *Appeared*, Frey. A hole got punched in the sky, and they came sailin' through.' He puffed on his cigar. 'That takes power of a kind you and I can't imagine. Dad reckoned that whatever provided it, it was behind that door. And he was right.'

'What about the dreadnought we found?' asked Frey. 'Why didn't they use the sphere?'

'Maybe they didn't want to go back,' said Jez. 'They'd rejected the Manes. It killed them in the end.'

She shivered with the memory of the terrible, endless loneliness. *But that's how we all live, every day. Sealed up in our own little worlds. We only know of each other what we choose to show.*

Frey frowned. 'Listen, Grist. I had a chat with an Awakener, back on the *All Our Yesterdays*. He told me that thousands of people would die if that fell into the wrong hands. Now you're telling me it's just an alarm?'

'Oh, right,' said Grist. 'See, he was probably thinkin' of what'll happen when the alarm goes off. What'll happen to all the people in this city when them Manes turn up, after I activate this thing.' He turned and stared at Jez, his face hardening. 'Or rather, when *you* do.'

Crake sat with his back against the wall of the store room, and whistled a tune to himself.

'Dunno how you can be so damn calm, while we're cooped up in this place and the Cap'n and Jez are in who knows what kind of trouble,' said Malvery, who was pacing the floor. He walked up to the metal door that sealed them in, and hammered on it with his fist. 'Hey! We're freezing in here! Give us some rum, for pity's sake!' When he got no response, he pulled his coat tighter around him and continued to stomp up and down. Silo, sitting in the corner, watched him blandly.

'May I have your pocket watch, Malvery?' he asked. 'Trinica's men took mine. Presumably they thought it was possessed.'

Malvery took out his watch and tossed it over. Crake pressed the catch and the case sprang open.

'You late for something?' Malvery asked irritably.

'Oh, no,' said Crake. 'Right on time.'

He smiled wryly. It seemed like a long time since he'd smiled. As if a tombstone had been laying on his chest, heavy and cold, which was now gradually lifting away.

The grief he felt at the death of his niece was both old and new. He'd always known in his heart that he could never get her back, but he could never make himself believe it. Not until he'd tried. Now that he had, now that he'd seen the sheer impossibility of it, the weight of the task he'd placed upon himself was lessening day by day. It had taken Jez's harsh words to make him face up to himself.

It was strange. Bess, his niece, was dead. It was his responsibility, his hand that had wielded the blade. He would never shed the guilt of that. And yet he felt better now than he had for two years. He'd finally accepted what he'd done, instead of trying to change it.

It hurt. Of course, it hurt, like a bright blade in his guts. But it was a clean hurt. The pain of healing. Not the slow, grim death that he'd been trying to blot out with alcohol. For the first time since his niece had died, he saw light. Sharp and hard, but light. And he wouldn't look away, no matter how it brought the tears to his eyes.

Malvery was suspicious of Crake's smile. He narrowed his eyes. 'You've got something up your sleeve, haven't you?' He hunkered down next to Crake and poked him in the ribs with a meaty finger. 'What you up to, eh?' he asked.

'You remember the first time Dracken captured us?' he said. 'Just outside Retribution Falls?'

'Ain't likely to forget it. We all nearly got hanged on account of her.'

'We put down in the Blackendraft,' said Crake. 'An endless, trackless waste of ash, far as the eye could see. I put Bess to sleep so she wouldn't attack anyone and get us all killed. Trinica left her there when we flew off.'

'Right,' said Malvery. 'You were all in a gloom, thought you'd never see her again. But Jez found her. S'pose because of those Mane abilities she's got.' He paused. 'Never thought of that till now.'

'Yes. But if we hadn't got out of being hanged, or if Jez hadn't found Bess, then she'd have stayed asleep for ever. Like a metal statue in the middle of the wastes.'

'Where you heading with this, Crake?'

'Back in Marlen's Hook, you asked me if I'd done anything useful lately. Any new daemonic artefacts, any new techniques, that sort of thing.'

Malvery waved it off, embarrassed. 'Aw, mate. I was just giving you a kick in the arse, you know. Trying to get you to lay off the booze before you ended up like me.'

'I know,' said Crake. 'And I want to thank you for that. You and Jez, you both helped me a lot.'

Malvery shrugged. 'That's what friends do, right? They give it to you straight. Speaking of which, get back on the subject.'

'Look, the point was, what you said got me thinking. About that time with Bess. How it could happen again, and I might not be so lucky next time. If I put her to sleep, and I lost that damn whistle . . . then what? I might never be able to wake her up.'

'S'pose not. So what?'

'So, I taught her a few more whistles. A few more frequencies, you see. You can't hear them, and it takes a daemonist to make them work, but to Bess they're loud and clear. They make her do different things, rather than just put her to sleep indefinitely.'

'Like what?'

He looked at Malvery's pocket watch again. 'Like putting her to sleep for . . . oh, about half an hour.'

Malvery grinned. Crake grinned with him. Malvery took back his pocket watch and snapped the case shut.

'It's bloody good to have you back, mate,' said the doctor.

In the distance, the gunshots and screams began.

Something was amiss on the *Ketty Jay*.

Slag opened his eyes slowly and licked his chops. The fur around his face still carried the taste of rat blood. But it wasn't rats that had brought him out of his doze.

He got up and loped through the ventilation ducts, towards the cargo hold. Slag was the master of these hidden byways. It was his mission in life to keep them clear of invaders. The world outside was full of those curious beings that occasionally – unwisely – tried to touch him or pick him up. But they were too big to get into the vents. Here, it was Slag versus the rats. And while there had been some epic struggles in his time, fought against large and vicious opponents, Slag had always dominated. He'd never come across an enemy he couldn't beat. He didn't know the meaning of defeat.

He slipped out of the duct into the cargo hold. Cold air was blowing in from the outside, stirring his whiskers and chilling his nose. The cargo ramp was open. Sounds came to him from beyond: people shouting to one another, the clank of machinery, the roar of thrusters as an aircraft accelerated overhead. The sharp tang of aerium gas, vented from a freighter that was touching down. The busy industry of landing pads was terrifying in contrast to the safety of his enclosed world. It was an assault on the senses that confused and intimidated him.

The cargo ramp being open was not unusual. Slag padded out into the centre of the room and sniffed.

That was it. That was what had woken him.

The cowardly one had dared to come aboard.

He made a sinister crooning noise from low in his throat. The thought of that pathetic specimen on his territory made him angry. He listened, and heard scurrying footsteps in the corridor overhead, the main passageway that ran down the spine of the aircraft.

This wasn't the first time, either. He knew his prey had sneaked aboard several times recently. Sometimes Slag detected him and chased him away. Other times, he'd been busy in the depths of the aircraft, and all that was left when he emerged was the sour smell of fear and sweat.

Slag's instinct was to chase him off again. But he was an old cat, a veteran of many secret wars, and he'd learned a thing or two. He knew how the rats would keep coming back, no matter how many times he killed them. There were always more. Unless he hunted them down to their lair. Kill them there, kill the mothers, and the rats didn't come back.

He could chase off the intruder, but the intruder would return. It was time to take an altogether more crafty approach. He'd take the fight to his enemy.

Slag padded down the cargo ramp. He could see the enemy's lair, a few dozen yards away. The place where he slept and hid. The cowardly one was smugly content there, behind the transparent shell that sheltered him. Secure in the knowledge that Slag wouldn't cross the gap between the aircraft.

The sight of the Firecrow infuriated him. The shell was open, too. It was a taunt beyond endurance. His enemy thought Slag was too weak to come and get him. He thought that Slag was too afraid to brave the sky.

But Slag refused to be afraid of anything.

He went down to the end of the ramp. Beyond it, dozens of people worked around a huge metal craft. Tractors chugged past, hauling jangling trailers of metal pipes. The air stank of petrol. There were so many threats out there. Too many to keep track of.

Above him, beyond the jutting stern of the *Ketty Jay*, there was no ceiling. Only a rucked blanket of feathery whiteness, impossibly high. The sheer *size* of the outside crushed him. He crouched down unconsciously, flattening his ears, making himself small. Was the cowardly one *really* worth this? Wouldn't it be enough to simply chase him away again?

No. This had gone on too long. And Slag didn't know how to lose.

He put one paw out on to the cold surface of the landing pad, then looked around quickly, in case any of the roaring machines had noticed his transgression. He put his other paw down next to it.

Nothing happened. He glanced up at the sky. The hazy white blanket seemed to be staying up there.

He fixed his gaze on the enemy's lair. The open cockpit. The ladder rungs, built into the flank of the craft, that would take him there.

He moved his back legs forward, until all four paws were on the tarmac. His tail still lay flat on the lip of the cargo ramp. His last connection with the *Ketty Jay*.

The big people were occupied. The machines paid him no attention.

He steeled himself. Then he scampered forward.

For the first time in his long and violent life, Slag departed the *Ketty Jay*.

'Let me get this straight,' said Frey. 'You just said that activating that sphere would bring a horde of Manes down on us. So . . . er . . . exactly why would you want to do that? If you want to commit suicide, there's a gun in your hand. Do us all a favour.'

'Suicide?' Grist burst out laughing and ended with a wheeze. 'Oh, no, Cap'n. I ain't committing suicide. Just the opposite, actually.' He sucked on his cigar and let it seep out through his lips. 'See, I'm dying anyway. You may have noticed this delicate little cough of mine? Well, I got the Black Lung. The rot's eatin' me up from the inside. Docs said it were only a matter of time, and there weren't much o' that.' He held up his cigar and contemplated the glowing tip. 'Like I said, tobacco's a harsh mistress.' He stuck it back in his mouth and showed yellow teeth. 'But I don't wanna die, Cap'n Frey. I'm havin' too much fun livin'. And as far as I know, there's only one way to live for ever.'

Jez felt a jolt of horror as it clicked into place. 'You want to become a Mane,' she said.

Grist gave her a slow look. '*Now* you get it.'

'You,' said Frey, 'are bloody well cracked in the head.'

'Think so?' Grist walked slowly around the daemonist's cage at the centre of the sanctum. 'Live for ever, maraudin' the skies?' he cried, his growling voice echoing into the darkness. 'Part of the greatest crew in existence? Possessin' who knows what supernatural abilities?' He pulled on his cigar and blew out a plume of dirty smoke. 'Damn, I'll have my own craft in no time, mark my words. Man of my experience.' He nodded to himself. 'I can think of worse ways to spend eternity.'

Frey appeared to consider that. 'Nope,' he concluded at length. 'Still cracked.'

Grist gave him a look. 'Some things are worth riskin' *everythin'* for.'

'Why do it this way?' Jez asked. 'Why do you need the sphere?' She felt panic clawing at her. She saw what was coming.

'You know how hard it is to find a Mane when you want one?' Grist said. 'They come without warning, and they're gone in a flash. No pattern, no rhyme or reason. Here's a man desperate to meet 'em and, even with my dad's notes, I couldn't get close. So I'll bring *them* to *me*.'

'But why Sakkan? We could do this out in the snows. There's no need to unleash the Manes on all these people!'

'It's a gift,' said Grist. 'Best to announce myself with a bang, I reckon. "Here I am," I'll say. "And here's a thousand new recruits, an' all". I'll come to 'em as a hero.' He grinned. 'They won't be *dyin'*, you know. Those who don't resist, they'll be turned. And you of all people should know that ain't so bad.'

Jez looked around at Grist's crewmates, hoping that some of them would react to this insanity. What she saw was not doubt but excitement. These few were Grist's inner circle. Perhaps they, too, dreamed of immortality. At any rate, Grist had persuaded them to his way of thinking. There would be no help there.

'And what about you?' she said to Trinica. 'Presumably *you* don't care if a whole city is taken by the Manes.'

'You presume correctly,' said Trinica.

'You think he's going to just let you go after explaining all this to you?' she demanded, pointing at Grist. 'He'll betray you, just like he did everyone else.'

'Actually, ma'am, the only reason I'm explaining it at all is for Cap'n Dracken's benefit,' said Grist. 'Someone needs to know what happened here. Someone who can tell the tale of Cap'n Harvin Grist.'

He smiled nastily. 'Otherwise, how will they know me when I come back for 'em?'

Jez stared. He wasn't just after immortality in the literal sense. He wanted to be a legend. The smuggler who destroyed a city. Who'd joined with the Manes. And who one day might return at the head of a fleet of dreadnoughts. A man to strike fear into the hearts of everyone. They'd use his name to scare children. *Be good, or Cap'n Grist will come for you.*

'I'm a Mane,' she said. There was desperation in her voice. 'You don't need to do this. I can turn you!'

'Can you?' said Grist, sceptically. 'A half-Mane like you? I don't reckon so. I know what you are, Miss Kyte. You ain't the first. I had my suspicions back on the dreadnought, and I knew for sure on the Flashpan, after we'd dealt with the *All Our Yesterdays*. Should've taken you then, saved us all a lot of trouble. But I got you now.'

'Let me try!' she begged.

'You ain't capable of giving the Invitation,' he said. 'You ain't even accepted it yourself.'

'The Invitation?' said Frey. 'Is that what you call it?'

'Ain't what *I* call it. That's what it's called. But I got another use for a half-Mane.' He tossed the sphere to Jez. She caught it automatically. 'Make it work.'

Jez gazed at the sphere clutched in her hands. Just holding it made her nerves crackle. She'd known this moment would come, ever since Grist had confessed his desire to summon the Manes. No wonder nothing had happened during the month when they were searching for him. They'd been expecting news of some catastrophe all that time, and questioning why Grist, who finally had his prize, wasn't using it. Here was the answer. He didn't know how.

But nor did Jez.

'I can't,' she said.

Grist motioned to two of his crewmen. They seized Frey and pulled him over to a nearby table. One of them pressed a pistol to his head; the other was carrying a machete, and forced his hand down on to the wooden surface. Frey struggled and swore, but they were too strong for him. Trinica folded her arms and watched, not a flicker of distress on her face.

'Try,' said Grist. 'I done everything I could, but there ain't no notes on this thing in my father's research. And what I come to conclude is, it takes a Mane to activate it. You're only half o' what I need, but you'll do, I reckon.' His eyes were dark chips of stone beneath his heavy brows. 'So now I'm gonna give you one minute, then I'm gonna chop off your Cap'n's hand. Then I'll do the other one. Then I'll start on his feet. When I run out of limbs, I'm really gonna start hurtin' him. So I suggest you put your mind to the task, ma'am.'

Jez barely heard him. The crackling in her nerves had got stronger and stronger. The power in the sphere was reaching out to her, flowing into her, overwhelming her. She could feel the onset of a trance, the flip into the surreal other world of the Manes. She fought against it.

I can't be responsible for this.

Thousands of lives. All that death would be on her head. Because she was a Mane. Because of the daemon that dwelt inside her.

I can't.

The Manes would come, and they'd give the Invitation to anyone they could, and they'd kill everyone else.

But there was Frey, still struggling, even with a gun to his head. Frey, her captain, the man who'd given her a home on the *Ketty Jay* when she'd despaired of ever finding one again.

'Thirty seconds,' said Crattle, who was consulting a pocket watch. Trinica looked on, unmoved by Frey's plight.

It wasn't a matter of making it work. It was a matter of *preventing* it from working. The sphere *wanted* to be used. Its power leaped eagerly to her, threatening to tip her, to bring on the trance that she knew would be the final step in activating it. Once she let her daemon have its head, it would call its brethren. The eager voices from the Wrack howled encouragement, battering at her resistance.

All those people on one side of the equation. Frey on the other.

'Twenty seconds.'

How could she watch his hand chopped off, then another, then a foot? If she held out now, could she really hold out till the end? What if she crumbled halfway through? That would be worse than death to Frey, to leave him without hands, and she'd still have lost.

It came down to a choice. Between the man she knew, and the thousands she didn't.

'Ten.'

All those people. Because I'm a Mane. I should have died back there in the snows that day.

But she hadn't. And that was part of her now. For better or worse.

'Five.'

She gave up her resistance. The sphere took her like a flood. The trance was almost instantaneous. Between blinks, the world turned to a hyper-real twilight. Her senses became superhumanly clear. She could hear guns firing in the hangar, a sound that had been muffled by the rock until now. Something was up. Bess was awake. She could hear her footsteps.

'Four.'

But whatever help might come, it would come too late to stop Frey being maimed. And she wouldn't allow that.

'Three.'

The silver lines on the sphere glowed with a spectral light, beaming out from within. Crattle stopped counting. He stared, entranced.

Then there was a terrible shriek, a hurricane of sound that tore through the room and blasted her senses white.

And with that, it began.

Thirty-Five

No Ordinary Storm –
Bedlam In The Sanctum – Frey's Authority

Harkins clutched the shotgun tight as he came down the stairs into the cargo hold of the *Ketty Jay*. He was trembling with fear and an awful, nauseous excitement. Every shadow could be the one hiding his enemy. Part of him dreaded the sight of that damned despicable cat. Another part, that voice which sometimes got defiant when there was nobody around to challenge it, was hoping Slag would show his face after all. A squeeze of the trigger, a bloody puff of fur, and all his troubles would be over.

Oh, who was he kidding? The noise alone would probably scare him witless. He'd deliberated for a long time between pistol and shotgun, on that basis. In the end, he'd picked the one that most suited his shooting style. He always closed his eyes and cringed away whenever he fired at someone, so accuracy was impossible. The shotgun was louder, but the scatter effect made it a bit more likely that he'd actually hit something.

He swallowed and made himself go down the stairs. Crates and boxes and vents: all possible ambush points. He wished he hadn't come aboard at all. But he had to get a gun. That was the thing. He had to get a gun, to save Jez.

He'd sat with his heart in his mouth, listening via Crake's daemonic earcuff to the gunfight at Grist's warehouse. He thrilled every time she spoke. She was so strong, so capable. He imagined himself battling alongside her, grim-faced, felling guards with a keen aim. And after they'd won, she'd be kind to him. She'd offer soothing words and encouragement, the way she sometimes did.

But then he'd heard the hangar doors slamming. Jez's voice. 'It's a trap!' And he knew they were betrayed.

After that, there was little more than a garble. The earcuffs had been taken off them, it seemed. The signal, weak at this distance, became weaker still. Sounds were muffled. It was hard to tell what was going on. Once in a while, he heard voices he knew. The Captain's, for one. And Jez. Sweet Jez.

She was still alive. She was in trouble. And he was the only one who could help her.

The past month had been hard on him. He'd spent the majority of it in the Firecrow's cockpit. It would have been easier if they hadn't been hopping around towns in the arctic, but the Firecrow had no heating when the engines weren't running, so he spent his nights cocooned in blankets, shivering. Harkins wasn't a reader – in fact, he didn't do much of anything except fly – so a large proportion of his time had been spent staring into space and thinking of nothing. The need to relieve himself drove him out now and then. He'd head into whatever town was nearby and use what facilities he could find. His contact with the crew was minimal. The only person he saw with any regularity was Jez, who brought him his meals.

He'd looked forward to those visits with a mixture of anticipation and dread. He loved to see her. She'd usually inquire how he was doing, even though she was often distracted. He'd babble something, and his tongue would run away with him, and eventually he'd stumble to a stop. It was embarrassing that she should see him that way. She knew why he was hiding. He was afraid of the cat. He thought that maybe she seemed a little less kind to him nowadays, and wondered if it was something to do with that. Had he failed her? Or did she have other things on her mind? After all, it must be a burden being a Mane.

Pinn had told him the news, gleefully, during one of the rare moments when he wasn't depressed about his own sorry love life. 'Your girlfriend's a Mane!' he crowed. 'She's the walking dead! How'd that be, eh? Humping a dead one!' He leered horribly and made a pumping motion with his hips. 'I always pegged you as a necromofelliac.'

Harkins had never heard of one of those before, but it didn't sound like something he wanted to be. Still, he wasn't particularly concerned by the news. Alive or dead or some combination of the two, she was the same old Jez to him. What did concern him was how the rest of the crew began to talk about her after it became known that she was a Mane. They were mistrustful and uncertain. She didn't deserve that.

He tried to keep her spirits up when she came to visit him, but he always got tongue-tied. Did she think he was like the others, muttering behind her back? He hoped not, but it was hard to tell. Damn, why couldn't he just make his mouth say what his heart felt? Why was he born with a knot between his brain and his voicebox?

Well, actions spoke louder than words anyway. And he needed to be brave. That fat fool Pinn had deserted them good and proper, so there was no one left but him. He needed to be strong for Jez. Somehow, he was going to save her.

He wondered how he'd possibly find the courage to single-handedly defeat Grist's gang of smugglers, if he couldn't deal with one elderly cat.

He hurried down the stairs, across the cargo hold and down the ramp. The Cap'n would have chewed him out for leaving it open, but he needed his escape route clear. He'd left the hood of his cockpit up as well, just to be extra sure. If he spotted Slag, it would only take him seconds to reach the safety of the Firecrow.

He scampered off the *Ketty Jay* and came to a halt with a sigh of relief. The cat wouldn't follow him out here. Stupid animal. He closed up the ramp and locked it by punching in a code on the exterior control panel, located on one of the *Ketty Jay*'s rear landing struts.

That was when he saw what was happening to the sky.

The morning had been chilly and grey when he entered the *Ketty Jay* in search of the weapons locker. A shapeless haze of cloud had hung overhead, and the sun had been low on the horizon, shining with a sharp, glittering light.

But things were different now. The sky had curdled and darkened. The wispy, inoffensive sheet of cloud had turned thick and black. Pulses of light flickered in its depths. A strong, icy wind had struck up, blowing the ear flaps of Harkins' cap against his cheeks. Despite the gathering storm, the sun was still visible in the east, between the cloud and the horizon: a shining pupil in a slitted eye. It cast a spectral light over the bleak vista.

Harkins didn't like this. Not at all. There was an eerie, oppressive quality to the atmosphere. He had keen senses when it came to detecting threats. He'd had a lot of practice at being scared, and he was good at it.

This was no ordinary storm.

The clouds were moving, but it wasn't the wind that was pushing them. They were swirling, slowly at first but getting faster, as if stirred by a spoon. Gathering, becoming dense, drawing inward towards a single spot. At that point, the pulses of light had reached a frenzy. The cloud roiled and turned. Silent lightning threw out giant sparks.

Harkins became aware that he was making a low, distressed moan. His feet were rooted to the tarmac. The crewmen of nearby craft had stopped their work and were looking up. Tractors sputtered to a halt as their drivers tipped back their caps and squinted skyward.

This was bad. Somehow, he knew this was very, very bad.

The pulses of light at the point where the clouds were gathering became faster and more frequent. They accelerated to a flickering strobe, and finally to a dazzling burst of whiteness that bleached the city below. The observers shielded their eyes and turned away.

The cloud had collapsed in on itself, and was being sucked away like water down a drain. It was as if the very sky was being consumed, eaten up by the hungry maelstrom.

And out of this sky, through the tunnel of the great, swirling vortex, came the dreadnoughts.

Frey blinked. For a few seconds, all he could see was white. Then darkness began to soak into the picture, giving form to the shapes around him. Fuzzy shapes and blurred colours made themselves known.

Uh? he thought, which was pretty much the best description he could come up with for his mental state at the time.

His body was pins and needles all over, numb and painfully a-tingle at the same time. His tongue lolled in his mouth, barely under his control. There was a loud whistle in his ears.

Gradually he came back to the world, as his overloaded senses restored themselves.

He was in the ancient sanctum somewhere beneath Grist's compound. People were picking themselves up off the ground. Grist was nearby, shaking his head, dazed. Trinica was getting to her feet, leaning heavily on a table in case her legs betrayed her. Jez lay on her side, eyes open, staring into space. The metal sphere was no longer in her hands.

Then he heard something. A rapid thump, growing louder. Like someone running. Someone very heavy.

He looked up.

Bess.

The sanctum doors were set horizontally in the roof of the sanctum. The golem plunged through them like a cannonball, crashing on to the stairs with a roar. Her tiny eyes glimmered behind her face-grille, bright in the gloom.

Bess was in a rare fury this morning.

Panic seized the room. Grist's men scrambled to their feet, flailing and disoriented, desperate to escape the terror that had descended on them. But there was no way out except past Bess.

She thundered down the steps and backhanded the nearest man into the wall with enough force to shatter the brickwork. Her charge brought two more men within her reach, who were too slow to get out of the way. She snatched them up by their necks and smashed their heads together, splattering herself in blood, bone and brain matter. Frey winced. That had to hurt.

Grist and his men had found their guns by now, and were rushing for whatever cover they could find, aiming futile shots at the enraged golem in their midst. Crake, Silo and Malvery came scrambling through the ruined doors and opened up with their own weapons, picking their targets. One of Grist's men caught a bullet and went down, clutching the back of his leg. He fell into Bess's path, and she stamped him flat.

Frey didn't know how his crew had got out or how they'd got their guns back, but he was damned pleased to see them. He turned his attention to Jez, who was still immobile, eyes unfocused. He went to check her breathing, then realised there was no point. He poked her in the nose instead. She blinked. A sign of sort-of-life. Good enough for the moment.

The sphere. Where was the sphere?

He cast about for it. There! It had rolled free of Jez's hands and was lying near the base of the pedestal, beneath the daemon cage.

Grist had seen it too. Their eyes locked across the distance between them. Then both ran for it at the same moment.

Frey raced through the corridor of gunfire. Bullets scored the air around him. Bess was a bellowing mountain in the gloom, flinging furniture this way and that. But all his focus was on that sphere. He wasn't even sure what he'd do with it, now that it had been activated. But he knew he didn't want Grist to have it.

Both captains lunged together, and both laid hands on the sphere. They fell into a scrabbling tangle, each fighting to pull the prize from the other's grip. Grist's grimacing face was close to Frey's: hot, smoky breath, the smell of sweat and dirt. His eyes were dark with madness, that terrible rage that Frey had seen before. Frey fought hard, but Grist was a bull, who outweighed him by some considerable fraction. The contest was brief. Grist yanked the sphere from his fingers, and as Frey clutched for it, he drove a clublike fist into Frey's belly.

Frey stumbled away, hunched over and winded. Grist broke off in the other direction, but his momentum carried him into Trinica, who was retreating towards the back of the sanctum, seeking cover. Grist bowled her over and they went down in a mess of limbs, fighting one another for purchase. Grist came up first, dragging Trinica with him, but he didn't let her go. Instead he wrapped one thick arm round her throat – the one carrying the sphere – and with the other he drew his pistol and shoved it into her ribs. He backed away towards cover, with Trinica as his shield.

Grist's men had been decimated by the surprise attack. The last of them were being slaughtered by Bess or picked off by gunfire. The golem had just seized one of Grist's crew, and was raising him triumphantly over her head with both hands, ready to fling him to his death. Only Grist's bosun, Crattle, was still in the fight, hiding behind a bullet-riddled lectern, and the remainder of his life could be counted in seconds.

Frey saw, with a sudden flood of horror, what would happen next. He fought to drag in a breath.

In moments, it would be over. Grist was dead meat. He didn't have a chance. They'd turn their weapons on him, and gun him down, and that would be that.

But to get to Grist, they had to go through Trinica.

He found air at last. Sucked it in and yelled.

'STOP!'

His voice rang out with a volume and authority he hadn't realised he possessed. Friend and enemy alike froze, fingers on triggers.

Silence fell, broken only by the crescendo wail of Grist's crewman as he flew across the room to crunch against the far wall.

Bess made a bubbling noise in her chest that somehow managed to convey an apology.

All eyes went to Frey. Grist stood where he was, his gun in Trinica's ribs. Crattle stayed in hiding, hardly daring to believe his reprieve. The crewmen of the *Ketty Jay* waited expectantly.

He knew he should let his men loose. He had the power. Kill them all, Trinica too. Be done with all the bitterness and betrayal. It would be so damned good to see her die right now.

But he couldn't. Even with all the anger and hate inside him. This woman was a millstone around his neck, and yet he couldn't bring himself to get rid of her. She was his penance and his punishment. Of all the women he'd wronged, she was the only one that counted. She'd carried his child, and killed it too. Like a vengeful ghost, she followed him out of the past, taking on whichever shape best enabled her to hurt him. He'd never be free.

He wanted her gone. He so desperately wanted her out of his life. But she'd never leave him alone until she was dead, and he couldn't handle that eventuality. Her absence from the world would rob him of something vital, something he needed in order to keep on going. Without it, all that was left was that hollow feeling, the dreadful, indefinable *lack* that had inspired this whole sorry escapade in the first place.

A grin spread across Grist's face. The advantage was lost. Grist had figured him out. 'Thought so,' he said. He looked at Frey, down at Trinica, and then back to Frey again. 'Ain't that nice?'

Trinica watched him, her face blank. Was she afraid? Was she silently pleading with him to save her? No. Perhaps she simply didn't care if she lived or died. But how could he tell, in the end? How could he trust any emotion from her ever again?

He waved at his men. 'Let 'em go,' he said.

Malvery had his shotgun aimed squarely at Trinica and Grist. His eyes flicked from the gunsight to Frey.

'You what?' he asked, his voice flat with disbelief.

'You heard me.'

'You can't let them walk away,' said Crake. 'Not with that sphere. We'll need it if there's any hope of undoing what's been done.'

'Nobody's undoin' a bloody thing,' said Grist. 'We're walkin' out of here, sphere an' all, or your Cap'n's little missy gets a bullet.'

'Cap'n,' said Malvery, his voice tight with suppressed anger. 'She's a lying, backstabbing bitch and she ain't worth it.'

'I know, Doc,' said Frey. 'No one knows it better than me. But if any one of you pulls his trigger, it's the last thing you'll do as a crewman on the *Ketty Jay*.'

It wasn't often he had to threaten his crew nowadays. But they needed to know that he meant it. This wasn't a moment for dissent.

Malvery glared at him hard, and for a moment Frey thought he might actually do it: just blow them both away, Trinica and Grist alike, and take the consequences after. But then he spat on the ground, swore the foulest oath in his armoury, and stepped aside. Bess and the others followed his lead, clearing the way for Grist, Crattle and Trinica to get to the stairs.

'Get out of my damn sight,' Frey told Grist and his prisoner alike.

They left without another word. Grist circled close to the sanctum wall, keeping Trinica between himself and the guns trained on him. Crattle stayed close, looking grey, shaken by his close shave. Trinica didn't take her eyes from Frey's the whole time. He didn't flinch from her gaze. Damn her. Let her know that he was unbowed, even after this. It was through his mercy that she lived. She'd better know that.

Then they were gone, up the stairs and away. Weapons were lowered. Malvery kicked a chair to pieces in frustration. Frey closed his eyes and took a breath. Trinica was gone. He felt lighter already.

Crake went to Jez, who was stirring again. She seemed to have been hit harder than the rest of them by the effect of the sphere. Even now, she was dazed and distant. Frey joined them and hunkered down alongside.

'You alright, Jez?'

'I'm okay, Cap'n, I'm . . .' she trailed off, then looked around in alarm. 'They're here,' she said. 'The Manes. They're here.'

'Then we shouldn't be,' said Frey. He got to his feet. After all that had passed between him and Trinica, it felt good to deal with something he could understand. A crew. Orders. Action. 'I've had just about enough of this whole bloody mess. Grist, Trinica, the sphere . . . damn 'em all to a cold grave. What's done is done. We tried to stop it and failed. The people of this city can take care of themselves. We're not paid to be anyone's guardians.' He surveyed his crew. 'Back to the *Ketty Jay*. We're gone.'

'First sensible thing I've heard out of your mouth for a month,' Malvery grumbled.

Crake drew Frey's cutlass from his belt and tossed it to him. 'Here you go, Captain. We stopped off in the hangar to pick up our things after Bess broke us out.'

Frey caught it. His face was reflected in the blade. Grim and stony. *That* was the Frey he wanted to be now. Frey the Heartless. Frey the Invincible. Frey the Untouchable.

That's right, he thought. *Captain Frey. You've got your craft and you've got your crew. Anyone else can go hang.*

He thrust his cutlass into his belt and stalked out of the sanctum.

Thirty-Six

Harkins Takes To The Air –
The Streets Are Overrun – A Fortuitous Encounter

H arkins had spent a lot of his life being afraid. He knew fear in its many forms, from the blind panic of a gunfight to the poisonous, chilly unease that he felt whenever he tried to have a conversation with anyone. But this was a different order entirely. This was a crushing, brutal, animal terror that bypassed the conscious mind altogether and sent wild sparks down every nerve. He couldn't move and yet he was desperate to flee. He wanted to crumple into a ball but he couldn't take his eyes off what was happening.

The Manes were coming.

The landing pad was mayhem. Men ran back and forth, yelling oaths, howling at one another to get into their craft, get airborne, get out of here. Tractors were abandoned with cargo still in the trailer. Pilots threw themselves into cockpits and took off without a care for nearby aircraft. Fighters flew overhead, dangerously low. The space above the pad was full of lumbering hulls and speeding wings. A crash was only a matter of time.

Beyond, and all around, the dreadnoughts were descending on Sakkan. They sank out of the maelstrom, through the eerie half-light. Black, ragged iron monsters, a dozen or more. The damned ghosts of a frigate fleet, come from the land of the dead. As they neared the ground, ropes snaked from their decks. The Manes swarmed down them, scampering head-first, hand over hand. They wore human shape, but they were far from human. They dropped to the ground like spiders and were lost from sight.

Jez is one of them? *I don't believe it! I won't believe it!*

The thought of Jez brought his mind out of a tailspin, enough to pull a coherent thought together. He should run. He should get in the Firecrow and flee while he still had the chance.

But what about Jez? What about his plan to rescue her? What about being brave?

Taking on Grist's gang single-handed would have been easy compared to this. The Manes were dropping all over the city, infesting the streets that lay between him and her. Trying to reach her would be suicide. And then he'd *still* have to take on Grist's gang singlehanded.

It was too much for his fragile courage. An impossible task. He felt his resolve failing under the weight of the Manes' presence. But even though he couldn't bring himself to go to her rescue, he wouldn't run out on her either. He couldn't do that. He was a coward and he knew it, but there were limits. If he left now, he wouldn't be able to return. The shame would be too much, even for a man who lived his life ashamed.

What could he do, then? What could he do?

Then, as he looked frantically this way and that, he caught sight of something. Aircraft in the distance, heading *towards* Sakkan instead of away. They came from the east, beneath the black clouds, silhouetted by a low, glowering sun. Frigates, by the size. Maybe ten of them, flying in formation, approaching at top speed. There was only one organisation he knew of that could summon ten frigates and have them fly with that kind of discipline.

The Navy! The Navy is here!

His heart lifted a little. A ray of hope. How had they got here so fast? Well, he wasn't in any mind to complain. The Navy was here. There would be a battle over Sakkan, as well as in the streets.

The realisation spurred him, and he found the strength to move. On the ground, he was worse than useless: a pathetic shell of a man. But in the sky, ah, *there* he wasn't so meek. Up there, his enemy respected him. And if they didn't, they soon learned to.

He needed the safety of the cockpit. He could seal himself inside. Within the protective canopy of windglass, he was the master of his own small world. There, he had a chance. If he had to stay, if there was to be a fight, then he'd take it to the air.

A siren had begun to sound in the distance, a low, sinister yowl that floated over the rooftops. It was joined by another, from the far side of the city. He ran for the Firecrow, and was halfway up the ladder to the cockpit when there was a shriek of metal from behind and above him. A wave of heat and pressure shoved him in the back. He looked over his shoulder to see two fighter craft spinning towards the ground, trailing flame. A cacophony of screams rose from the far side of the pad. The crashed fighters hit the ground, ploughing through men and aircraft alike, sending up blooming fountains of fire in their wake.

Harkins scrambled into the cockpit, pulled the canopy shut, and activated the aerium engines. He was usually obsessive about pre-flight checks, but not this time. He was desperate to be off the ground, to get up into the freedom above. He flicked the thrusters to ready and grabbed the flight stick.

A moment. Something was amiss. For an instant, he thought he caught a whiff of a familiar scent. The foul musk of that damned cat, that it sprayed all over the *Ketty Jay* to mark its territory.

Then he looked down into his lap, and realised that his crotch was sodden in a great dark patch.

Ah, he thought. *That must be it.* He'd been too scared to notice.

The Firecrow sat up on its wheel struts and rose from the ground. Harkins scanned the busy sky above him. A space in the frantic traffic. He lit the thrusters and flew.

'Cap'n! To your left!'

Frey turned just in time to see one of them come lunging out of an alley, right by his shoulder. A flash impression of yellow eyes, a gaping mouth full of rotten teeth, an animal snarl. Terror paralysed him, but not his blade, which moved of its own accord. The cutlass slashed out in a horizontal arc and halved the creature's head. Frey stepped aside instinctively as the Mane's ragged, sinewy body staggered past him. It fell to its knees and tipped to the floor, gore spilling from its skull cavity.

They'd stumbled into a nightmare. The eerie light of the low sun combined with the black ceiling of cloud made everything seem fractured and strange. The dreadnoughts slid overhead, like the shadowed hulls of ships passing above the graves of drowned men. The grim, cold streets of Sakkan were littered with bodies and echoed with distant cries. And here were the Manes. The ghouls of the sky, terror out of legend, sprung suddenly to awful life.

The shout that saved him had been Malvery's. Frey spotted him nearby. The doc was in trouble himself. He and Silo were backing down the street together, shotguns firing. Three Manes were approaching. They ran and leaped in jerky zigzags that made them tricky to hit. Malvery winged one, sending it twisting to the ground. The shock of the bullet would have taken a human out of action, but the Mane sprang back to its feet and came on again.

'Bess!' he yelled. He needed to give orders, take control. He pointed at the enemy. 'Deal with 'em!' Then he aimed with the pistol in his right hand.

Three Manes. One was slow, one was damned fast, and the other one shifted restlessly from place to place like a jumpy kinetoscope he'd seen once in a travelling show. One moment it was there, the next a half-metre to the left, then back again in the blink of an eye. He'd seen Jez flicker the same way, back on the *All Our Yesterdays*.

He sighted on the slower one: a bulky, muscular monster, skin stretched like parchment over taut muscle, wearing little more than tatters and rags in the arctic chill. His own hands were freezing and numb, but he still squeezed off a shot. Non-lethal wounds didn't seem to slow them, and he knew from experience with Jez that they didn't need a heart. *Aim for the head, then.*

He did, and he missed.

Bess pounded up the street to cover their retreat. She tackled the Manes fearlessly. The Manes faltered. Presumably, they were accustomed to their enemies being afraid of them; but Bess was afraid of nothing. Frey took another shot at the bulky one, who was too occupied with Bess to evade. The shot wasn't good – his fingers slipped a little as he fired – but he got lucky. There was a small puff of red mist from the Mane's head, and its legs crumpled beneath it.

The two remaining Manes swarmed over Bess. They battered and scratched at her uselessly. She flailed about like a bear who'd disturbed a wasp's nest. The others aimed, but none fired. They couldn't shoot without hitting the golem.

'Fall back!' he yelled at the others. 'Bess can handle them! They can't hurt her!'

They obeyed gladly. Nobody wanted to get into a stand-up fight with the Manes. They just wanted to get back to the *Ketty Jay* alive. Malvery, Crake and Silo backed off while Frey and Jez covered them.

He cast a quick glance at Jez, who was standing next to him, sighting along a rifle. She'd shaken off the daze that had taken her after she'd activated the sphere, and now she was hard-faced and sharp.

'You okay?' he muttered to her.

'You mean, am I okay with shooting at my own kind?'

'Right.'

One of the Manes, a female with long, tangled hair, jumped off Bess's back, giving up on her. It came running up the street towards them. Jez narrowed her eye and squeezed the trigger. The Mane flickered, shifting left and right so rapidly that seemed it was in three places at once. Jez hit it anyway, dead in the forehead. It spun off its feet and crashed to the cobbles.

'I've picked my side,' she said.

The final Mane was quick, but it couldn't dodge Bess's grasping hands forever. She snagged its ankle, pulled it writhing into the air, then grabbed its head in one metal hand and pulled it off, dragging a length of bloody spine with it.

They headed off in the direction of the landing pad. The sloping, angled streets of Sakkan were in chaos. People ran with no destination in mind. The unnatural fear brought on by the dreadnoughts had turned them into panicking sheep, fleeing the wolves among them. A man bolted screaming across their path, closely pursued by a Mane, which ignored them totally as it chased its prey into a side alley.

They didn't intervene. There was nothing they could do. They had enough on their hands.

I tried to stop this! Frey thought angrily. *I tried my best! But now it's every man for himself.*

The Manes were up above them, springing from roof to roof. Strange, feral howls drifted over the city, punctuated by gunfire and the shrieks of the unfortunate citizens. Frey's crew were spotted from time to time, but the Manes sought easier prey than an armed gang. They hunted the vulnerable, those who were alone and unarmed. That was how they worked, according to the stories. They took the ones they could, and killed the ones they couldn't. The few who got away lived to spread the stories.

Frey's mouth was dry. Were it not for Bess, they'd have been dead by now. The Manes were coming from all directions, and they weren't like ordinary opponents. They had no weapons but they attacked without fear, running on to their enemies' guns. They were relentless, confident in their speed, able to absorb most wounds with impunity. But Bess was an obstacle they couldn't handle. They hadn't found a way to hurt her yet.

Frey and his crew retraced the route they'd taken to Grist's warehouse, following the major roads. It was uncomfortably open and exposed, but he couldn't risk getting lost. Besides, he suspected that the narrow alleys and side streets were where the Manes liked to catch their prey. At least out here he could see them coming.

Trinica.

He tried to cast her out of his mind, but couldn't. His last sight of her was burned on his memory. That face, those eyes; in the end, she'd given him nothing. No gratitude, no condemnation, no love or hate. A blank. And yet still he felt as if she was disappointed in him. Like he'd committed a betrayal.

I saved her bloody life! he told himself. And yet by doing so, he'd thrown her to the sharks.

She'd done worse to him, it was true. But no matter how strong the argument, he couldn't convince himself. No matter which way he turned it, he didn't seem to win. Even after everything she'd done to him, he felt like he'd abandoned her. And it gnawed at him as they fled.

His thoughts were interrupted by a commotion behind him. They stopped and turned, guns ready. Several dozen people came fleeing out of a cross-street and raced towards them. They sprinted past, eyes wide, flailing and stumbling as they went. The sight of Bess didn't cow them in the slightest: they were already maddened with terror. One woman ran straight into the golem and knocked herself cold. Frey could do nothing but brace himself against the stampede and fend off those who looked like they were about to bowl him over.

In moments, the crazed crowd had passed. The crew looked at one another, rather amazed that nobody had been trampled.

'Well,' said Malvery. 'They were in a hurry for something.'

'What worries me,' Crake said, 'is what they were hurrying *away* from.'

Frey felt his stomach sink. As the screams of the crowd faded, he could hear howls and shrieks, swelling, multiplying, rolling towards them like a tidal wave.

'*Run!*' he cried, and they turned tail and followed the departing crowd just as a horde of Manes exploded from the cross-street and came tearing hungrily towards them.

Frey's boots pounded the cobblestones, as fast as he could manage, driven by the fear of what was behind him. The noise of the horde was terrible: their wild baying seemed to be meant for him alone. He was amazed to see Malvery accelerating away ahead of them, arms pumping; the overweight, alcoholic doctor had found a surprising well of vigour all of a sudden.

Panic crept in at the edges of his thoughts. They'd never outrun their pursuit. The Manes were faster, and they wouldn't tire. They'd be caught, and then there would be the teeth and filthy claws and – worse, perhaps – the Invitation.

I don't want to be like them! I'm too damned handsome to be a ghoul!

He'd sell himself dearly, if it came to that. He wouldn't let them take him alive.

The street dipped ahead of them, heading into a sunken square surrounded by towering rows of merchant's offices and banks. Gunfire and the dull thump of an autocannon sounded from within the square. Frey's heart lifted. A squadron of Ducal Militia? Whatever it was, it was hope. At least the militia were liable to be on their side. And they had a big gun.

He poured on the speed and burst into the square just behind Malvery. Scattered Mane corpses lay about, a few citizens among them. The crowd that had passed Frey earlier were scattering in different directions, dividing between the square's various exits. Striding through their midst were five figures Frey recognised.

Samandra Bree, Colden Grudge, Eldrew Grissom, Mordric Jask. And at their head, the bulky, grizzled figure of Kedmund Drave, the Archduke's most feared troubleshooter.

He'd hoped for a squadron of militia. He got five Century Knights. Given the choice, he'd have taken this option any day.

He staggered to a halt in front of Samandra. She tipped her tricorn hat back with the barrel of a shotgun and gave him a dazzling smile.

'How's this, then? You again?'

'Yeah,' he panted. 'It's me.' He stuck a thumb over his shoulder. 'And I brought some friends.'

Samandra looked past him at the squealing horde of Manes piling down the street towards the square. 'So you did.'

Thirty-Seven

The Battle Over Sakkan – Harkins Is Put Upon –
Emanda – Many Manes – 'Choppin' Time!'

The Navy frigates ploughed on towards the city, shedding fighter craft like glittering shards. Windblades streaked away ahead of the flotilla, joining up in formation as they raced to engage the enemy. The dreadnoughts were still out of range of the frigates' artillery, but that would change in a matter of minutes. The battle was about to begin.

Harkins kept to the edges of the battle zone, palms clammy and mouth dry. The Manes ignored him, as they ignored all the aircraft that were fleeing Sakkan. But Harkins wasn't fleeing. He was waiting for the Windblades to arrive. If he couldn't defend Jez on the ground, he could at least defend her in the air.

The dreadnoughts had risen away from the city streets and were readying themselves to meet the attack. They kept no formation that Harkins could recognise, but there was still an unmistakable co-ordination in their movements. They shifted and circled in perfect sync. It was a fluid defensive strategy that kept them moving, kept them separated, and made them difficult targets.

Harkins listened to the Firecrow's engines. He concentrated on the feel of the flight stick in his hand, the reassuring certainty of the instruments on his dash, the press of the seat against his back. It helped steel his nerve. He needed to slow his heartbeat, to fight the tightness in his chest and the sickness in his stomach. To overcome the terror of the battle to come.

Even the smell of the cockpit made him feel safe, the stink of his own sweat and the urine soaked into his trousers. Except that, every now and then, he still caught the scent of cat musk.

No. Just his imagination. He was all alone. Even the voices of his crew had gone silent. He'd heard gunshots and muffled voices, and a scuffle, and something bellowing that was probably Bess. After that, he didn't recognise any of the speakers, except one that he thought might have been that stinking bastard Grist. But wherever the ear-cuffs were now, they weren't with Jez. He could only hope that she hadn't been hurt.

Get out of here, said the panicked, fluttering voice of cowardice. *She's gone. Probably dead. More dead than usual, I mean. There's no sense joining her. Just take off.*

But that would be the final admission that he was worthless. The humiliations he'd suffered at the paws of the *Ketty Jay*'s cat had whittled his pride to a shred, but it was the last shred he had, and he didn't want to let go of it. So he gritted his teeth, wiped his nose on his sleeve, and tried to think brave thoughts.

You can't hurt them anyway, the voice persisted. *What are you going to do? Your little machine guns against armoured frigates? You won't even scratch them.*

That was true. But Harkins wasn't planning on attacking the dreadnoughts directly. He'd heard stories about the Manes. The dreadnoughts had more than cannons to defend themselves.

As the Windblades approached, the dreadnoughts released their Blackhawks.

They slid from recesses in the flanks of their mothercraft and swooped out into the sky in a dark flock. It chilled Harkins to see them, and he had to withstand another assault on his resolve. They were so damned *unnatural.* Their wings swept far forward, curving to either side of the cockpit. The front end of the cockpits were round windows, through which their hideous pilots could be seen. Their very shape defied the laws of aerodynamics. Aerium engines had long since removed the need for wing lift in aircraft, but it should have been impossible to bank and turn at speed with their wings slanted so far forward, like the tines of a meat-fork. There was no tail assembly or rudder, only a blunt back end housing a thruster. How did they *steer?*

But however they did it, they did it well. Unlike the dreadnoughts, the Blackhawks flew in threes or sixes, in formations so tight they seemed suicidal. Yet they yawed and dived all together, like birds or bats, as if all the pilots were of exactly the same mind. Their co-ordination was literally inhuman.

You really want to fight these?

He really didn't. But he was going to anyway.

The Windblades' assault had been carefully timed so that they'd reach the enemy just after the frigates came into range. The effect was shattering. The sky over the city detonated in a terrifying thunder of smoke and flame. Great chains of explosions ripped among the dreadnoughts, sending the Blackhawks wheeling away. For a few brief moments, the enemy were in disarray, their formations buckled by the force of the fusillade. The Windblades lanced through the artillery haze and opened up with their machine guns.

The first assault was devastating. The sleek Windblades cut into their enemy, guns spitting, ripping through exposed flanks and keels. The Blackhawks tried to evade, but the ferocity of the attack over-whelmed them. Some went plunging earthward, trailing smoke. Others were torn into dirty balls of fire, their wings spinning away through the sky.

But the Windblades' dominance was short-lived. The Blackhawks snapped back into formation with unbelievable speed. Shattered groups of fighters merged into units, locking in as if drawn together by magnets. The Manes were on the counter-attack faster than anyone could have predicted. The Windblades found themselves surrounded and under fire in moments.

A second wave of artillery came in, this time aimed at the dread-noughts. The powerful guns of the dreadnoughts bellowed in reply. At this range the shots were speculative, but still deadly if they hit home.

Harkins shuddered and shook in his cockpit. He was flying high and to starboard of the main body of Mane craft. Below, beyond his port wing, he could see down on to the deck of one of the dread-noughts. It swarmed with nightmarish figures, leering and strange. Some wore rags, others wore motley, still others strode among them in outlandish armour. He saw one that was a giant, at least eight feet tall, arms bulging with veined muscles and a neck thick as an ox's. They manned deck guns, ran back and forth with ammunition, or took potshots with rifles as the Windblades flew by. A filthy horde, yowling and shrieking, terrifying in aspect.

His hands gripped the flight stick hard. Blackhawks and

dreadnoughts alike had ignored him so far. It wasn't too late to back out. How could a man face up to such daemonic savagery?

Leave. Just go.

No.

She's dead. It's not worth it. Live to fight another day.

But what if she wasn't? He couldn't bear the disappointment in her eyes if she knew he'd left her.

They'll kill you!

He gritted his teeth and let out a high wail that was his best approximation of a battle cry. Then, before he could think any better of it, he thrust the stick forward and plunged into the fray.

The sound of the Firecrow's engines rose to a scream as he dived. Below him were three Blackhawks, flying across his path, apparently oblivious to him. He didn't much fancy taking on three, so he looked about for a single Blackhawk, one that was damaged or detached from the flock. There were none to be seen. It was three, or nothing.

Three it was. He wouldn't let himself back out now. He'd do it for Jez.

He took aim, accounting for speed and distance with an expert eye. He sucked in a deep breath, let it out, and squeezed the trigger.

The brash clatter of his machine guns made him jump. They seemed exceptionally loud. By firing them he'd broken his silence, and invited the attention of the enemy.

But the Blackhawks paid the price for ignoring him. His first salvo caught the formation squarely from above, ripping through the body of one of the craft and tearing the cockpit and pilot to pieces. The other two reacted before he could bring his guns to bear on them. They spiralled away crazily, spinning and turning, drawing G-forces that would have made a human pilot pass out.

Harkins pulled out of his dive and raced away, hoping their evasive tactics would make them lose sight of him. Now that the surprise attack was over, he feared retribution.

But his tactic was useless. The Blackhawks air-braked and came climbing towards him, hard and steep. A third one appeared from nowhere, slipping into formation to replace the one he'd destroyed. Suddenly Harkins found himself pursued by a trio of aircraft, a three-clawed pincer reaching up towards him.

'Oh, this isn't bloody fair at all!' he squealed, as the air around him filled with tracer fire. He threw his craft left and right: diving, rolling, spiralling. Yellow incendiary bullets blazed past his wings. The Blackhawks shot past him. They braked, split apart, and in seconds they were back in formation again, right on his tail.

Harkins craned around in his seat, trying to catch sight of them. He jinked left and then dived, evading them by instinct alone. A salvo of bullets shredded the air where he'd been a moment before.

He tore down towards the heart of the conflict, risking the artillery barrage. Anything to get them off his back. Between evasions, he contorted himself in his cockpit, attempting to locate them. But the bastards were nailed to his blind spot and wouldn't be thrown off.

His heart was thumping and his face was glistening with sweat. This was exactly what he'd feared would happen. The Blackhawks were out of his league. Messing with them was an invitation to get killed.

Oh blimey, damn and shit, what've I just got myself into?

Explosions all around him. Pummelling blasts of sound and flame and fury. He shrieked against the din. The Firecrow was thrown this way and that. He plunged past the flank of a dreadnought and caught a flash impression of the decks, seething with Manes like maggots on a carcass.

Then the explosions faded, and he still wasn't dead. He slammed into a sequence of manoeuvres that pushed him to the limits of his endurance. Turns so steep that his vision sparkled and his head went light. Crushing dives that send the blood pulsing hard in his sinuses and forehead and threatened a red-out.

He pulled up, head pounding. *That's the best I've got*, he thought. *There's nothing more.*

Machine guns opened up on his tail. Bullets chipped his starboard wing. He spun away with a curse, craned over his shoulder, and caught a glimpse of them. Right there, as if they'd never been away. They'd matched him move for move, implacable, just waiting for him to stop for an instant so they could shoot at him again.

They weren't going to let up on him. He could dodge about as much as he liked. They'd be waiting when he got tired. Harkins felt the sick panic that came with the certainty that he was going to die.

You should've run when you had the chance.

'Shit!' he screamed, pounding the dash with his fist. 'Shit! Shit! Shit!'

Machine guns sounded in a rattle. Harkins closed his eyes.

Sorry, Jez.

An explosion from behind him. His eyes flew open, and he twisted around in his seat.

Behind him one of the Blackhawks was spinning towards the city below, minus a wing. The other two moved to dodge the barrage of bullets slicing up at them from below, but they were too late. The bullets smashed into the flank of the second Blackhawk and sent it spiralling sideways. It crashed into its companion, who was still in close formation. The two of them tangled in a squealing collision and exploded.

'Waaa-hooo!' cried a familiar voice in Harkins' ear.

'Pinn?' he said in disbelief.

The Skylance came spinning through the cloud of smoke left by the destroyed Blackhawks.

'The one and only!' Pinn said. 'Here to save your sorry arse again!'

Pinn cackled. Damn, it was good to be alive! And there was nothing that made him feel quite so alive as murdering some dumb bastard who couldn't fly their aircraft as well as he could.

He glanced at the ferrotype hanging from his dash. A new face was in the frame where Lisinda's had once been. A face infinitely more beautiful to Pinn's eyes. Those red curls. That expanse of white bosom. The adorable way her front teeth overlapped.

Emanda.

He'd already forgotten what his previous sweetheart looked like. She'd faded from his memory without a picture to remind him. Well, who cared anyway? Let her be with her new man. She'd regret it one day, when Pinn was a hero and word of his exploits spread far and wide. She'd weep into her pillow when she saw the ferrotypes of him in the broadsheets, with Emanda on his arm. Someone better, prettier, more witty and charming than her. Someone more perfect in every way.

The face in the frame brought the memories flooding back. Wonderful days in Kingspire, a heady haze of booze, cards and bedplay. He'd borrowed some of her money and turned it into ten times the amount. Just having Emanda by his side put him on a winning streak. And she never left his side, except when she was on top of him, or under him, or in any other position they could think of. Damn, that woman had an appetite! And Pinn liked a woman with appetite.

How had he ever thought he wanted to be with Lisinda? She was a small-town girl with a small-town way of thinking. He'd dreamed of returning as a hero, but could he ever have settled into the dull, homely life she promised? No! What a lucky escape he'd had! The kind of life that Emanda offered, *that* was a life fit for a hero. *That* was the kind of woman he needed. A woman who could match him drink for drink, and who'd lead him to bed afterward.

After a few days of blissful, overwhelming happiness, the fateful moment came. They'd been lying together in bed, drunk, and she'd thought he was asleep. She'd leaned over and slurred quietly in his ear.

'You know, Artis Pinn, I think I'm falling in love with you.'

That was when he knew she was the one. The only one he'd ever love. His heart thrilled at the realisation. He pretended to be asleep until he heard her begin to snore. Then he slipped out of bed, picked up a pen, and scribbled a note.

He couldn't remember the exact words he'd used. He was barely sober enough to hold the pen. But he knew his lover would understand, the way she understood everything about him. He had to go, the note said, but he promised he'd be back. When he was rich. When he was a hero. When he was worthy to be with a woman like her.

And with that, he slipped away. He fuelled up his Skylance with the money he'd made, and asked about till he found the town of Endurance. He got there just in time to see a flotilla of Navy frigates departing at speed. Going by past experience, he reckoned it'd be more than likely that the Cap'n was tangled up in this somehow, so he tagged along. When he got close enough to Sakkan, he began to pick up Harkins' fearful blubbering through his earcuff. After that, it was just a matter of tracking him down.

He'd arrived just in the nick of time, it seemed. The way heroes were supposed to.

'You ready to get back in there, you shuddery old dog?' he asked Harkins.

'I suppose, I . . . Wait a . . . No. Yes. Ready.'

'Alright. Follow me down.'

'Pinn?'

'What?'

There was a pause. 'It's . . . that is . . . I'm . . . er . . .' He stopped and collected himself. 'It's good to see you,' he said at last.

Pinn felt a smile spread across his face. 'Good to see you too,' he said, and was surprised to find that he meant it. Then he shoved his flight stick forward and dived towards the enemy, whooping all the way.

Time to make himself a hero. Emanda deserved nothing less.

The Manes came in a flood. The Century Knights were waiting for them.

They stood in a line, guns raised, in front of the massive stone fountain that formed the centrepiece of the sunken square. They'd had only seconds to organise themselves, but they did so quickly and smoothly at an order from Kedmund Drave. They were a well-oiled unit, disciplined and deadly. The Archduke's elite: the best of the best.

Frey and his crew stood with them.

When they first met the Knights in the square, Frey had half a mind to keep on running and let the Knights deal with the Manes at their back. At least they might slow the pursuit a bit before they were overwhelmed. But he'd made a snap decision, and, absurdly, decided to stay. He'd begun to feel a faint cameraderie with Bree and Grudge, enough that he'd feel like a rat for bailing out on them. Their paths had crossed several times over the last year and a half, and they'd saved his life in the past.

Maybe it was because he needed to do something honourable, because Trinica had treated him so dishonourably. Maybe it was just the pull of childhood fantasy. Every boy – and many girls – grew up wanting to be a Century Knight. Fighting alongside them came a close second.

Or maybe – and more likely – it was just because Samandra Bree was damned cute and he didn't like the idea of letting her get her face eaten by a Mane.

The horde hadn't expected resistance, perhaps. Certainly not on the scale they faced now. They came through the narrow bottleneck where the cobbled street entered the high-walled square. Over a dozen guns opened up on them, and they were mown down like wheat.

Frey and his men aimed and fired into the thrashing mass of Manes, hoping to hit whatever they could. The Knights, in contrast, were astonishingly accurate. Whenever Samandra Bree fired one of her twin shotguns, or Mordric Jask his large-calibre pistols, it was a headshot. Colden Grudge's autocannon was less precise, but he made up for it with his sheer destructive power. Each bolt tore through several Manes, smashing through limbs and ribs and skulls. They howled as they were shredded into bloody meat.

But the withering hail of bullets couldn't hold them back for long. One by one the defenders stopped to reload. For the Knights, it was a well-drilled manoeuvre accomplished with impressive speed. For Frey's crew, it was more a matter of fumbling the bullets into their chambers and trying not to drop any.

The Manes took advantage of the lull. They were relentless, leaping over their fallen, scrambling and slipping through the tumble of shattered bodies. The defenders couldn't catch them all, and the Manes began to break through the bottleneck and spread into the square.

'Bess!' said Frey. 'Get in there!'

Bess didn't need a second invitation. She thundered forward through the hail of bullets and crashed into the Mane horde. With her arms outstretched, she took up half of the width of the bottleneck. She scooped up the Manes and forced them back with sheer, unstoppable strength. The Manes scratched and bit at her, but it was like attacking a cliff face. With Bess narrowing the gap, the flow of Manes into the square was choked off.

Grissom and Jask turned their attention to those Manes that had made it through. They picked off their targets before they got within five metres of the line. The ghouls twisted and rolled to the ground, bearing holes in their foreheads.

Frey took a moment to reload, glancing around at his crew through the acrid haze of gunsmoke. Malvery and Silo were grim-faced. Crake was scared out of his wits. But it was Jez that concerned him. Did she regard the Manes with hatred, or did it pain her to kill them? Did she feel each death, or was she glad of the slaughter? He couldn't say, but he worried for her state of mind.

It was only moments before the flood began to overwhelm Bess. Even though her body blocked them, they clambered over her, or ducked beneath her huge arms. The area around the golem was piled with Mane casualties, but they showed no signs of abandoning their assault. If anything, the deaths of their fellows had increased their frenzy.

The dam burst a second time, and this time the weight of numbers was too great to withstand. The Manes poured into the square. The defender's gunfire became unfocused as their targets spread out, and more of them broke through as a result. The balance had tipped. They couldn't be held back.

'Stay together!' Drave shouted, more for the benefit of Frey's crew than the Knights.

The Knights chose their targets with icy precision and took them down. The air was a terrific percussion of rifles, shotguns and pistols, underpinned by the steady report of Grudge's autocannon and the artillery detonations from overhead. There was no use taking cover, since the Manes weren't firing back. This was a game of nerve. Crake had lost his: he was trembling visibly as he fired. Malvery was getting panicky, blasting every which way. But Frey and the others drew strength from the men and women at their side. They aimed and fired steadily, and though the breaking wave of Manes came closer and closer, they were made to pay dearly for every metre they gained.

But nothing could stop them.

Frey's pistol fired empty. No time to reload. He shoved it in his belt and drew his cutlass. He knew now they'd be overrun. The battle would go to close quarters.

Bring it on, then!

He was awash with adrenaline. His teeth were bared in a snarl. All the anger and disappointment and hate that had been inspired by Trinica's betrayal sharpened in that moment to a fine point. It didn't matter whether he lived or died. It just mattered that somebody paid.

Some of the others drew weapons, ready for hand-to-hand fighting. Kedmund Drave pulled out a huge two-handed sword. Others stuck to their shotguns or rifles. They'd use boots and gun butts to fend off the enemy long enough to get a point-blank shot in. To his right,

Eldrew Grissom threw open his greatcoat, revealing an array of knives like the inside of a butcher's cupboard. He selected two gleaming cleavers.

'Choppin' time!' he yelled, with a crazed glint in his eye, and he went to work.

The Manes attacked all at once, jagged nails reaching out, mad faces behind them. Frey stepped to the fore, led by his cutlass. There was little he could do but surrender to its will. He could almost hear the singing of the daemon within as it took control, slashing in broad arcs, dismembering this and severing that. For his part, he simply concentrated on not getting hurt.

But for all the efforts of Frey and his crew, it was the Knights who held the Manes back. They moved like quicksilver, slipping fluidly between positions, always where they were needed. Whenever two Manes tried to take on Frey at the same time, there would be a Knight at his side to assist him, or one of his enemies would go down with a bullet in the brain. Even Drave and Grudge, who were more cumbersome in their heavy armour, seemed untouchable. They didn't have the speed of their companions, but they anticipated every strike and moved to counter it before it came. The Manes couldn't match them.

For a time, Frey lost himself. All thought disappeared in a bloody chaos of limbs and blades and teeth. His hands were spattered red. His breath rasped loud in his ears, heart pumping hard. His jaw clenched as he swung again and again, chopping away the grasping hands of the enemy. Fingernails raked his cheek. He found the owner, just as its head exploded, blown apart by somebody's shotgun.

When would it stop? When would they give up?

Behind him, he heard a cry. Crake. He risked a glance, and saw that one of the Manes had broken through. An awful, red-eyed, ragged thing. It had seized Crake's gun arm and was biting into the meat of his hand. Frey's blade came down on its neck. Crake staggered backwards, the thing's head still clamped tight to his flesh.

Then suddenly Bess was back among them, drawn by her master's voice. She'd abandoned her post and was ploughing into the Manes from the rear, scooping them up and flinging them in all directions. The Manes faltered, looking over their shoulders. The Knights had no such hesitation, and took the advantage. They shot and cut at the creatures, driving them back, gaining a little space and a few precious seconds to regroup.

A piercing shriek sounded over the square, stilling them all. Even the Knights froze at the sound. Even Bess. They sensed something. A signal, perhaps. Frey wiped blood from his face and searched for the source.

There it was. A Mane, eight feet tall, the same height as Bess. This one was clad in belts and bands of black leather armour, criss-crossing its thin yellow body. Buckles and straps hung from every part of it. Even its face was half-hidden by overlapping straps. What little could be seen of it was glowering, hollow-eyed and fearful. It carried two long, thick chains, far heavier than a man could lift. They hung from bracelets on its wrists, and as Frey saw it, it swung one and lashed it through the air like a whip, and screeched a second time.

A leader, a general. Come to rally them, to lead the final charge.

But no. The Manes were stepping back now, retreating. Bess turned quizzically towards Crake, looking for direction. He was grey with pain, but he managed to hold out his good hand. *Stop. Don't do anything.*

The Knights had the same idea. They stood ready, but nobody fired a shot. The Manes backed away, turned and ran out of the square the way they came. The general waited until they'd all passed and then stalked after them, without even a backward glance at the Knights, or the dozens of fallen Manes that littered the flagstones of the square.

Frey sagged, and let out a trembling breath. They'd given up. Just like that. The cost of the fight was too high for them. He exchanged a glance of happy disbelief with Malvery. The doctor swung his shotgun up on his shoulder and whistled.

'S'pose we showed *them*, eh, Cap'n?' he said.

'I s'pose we did,' he said. 'Go see to Crake, will you?'

'Right-o,' said Malvery. He went over to Crake, who'd flopped to the ground, holding the bloody head of the Mane in one hand. Its teeth were still buried in the other. Yellow eyes glared at him malevolently over his knuckles.

'Ooo. Nasty,' said Malvery, as he squatted down.

Crake wasn't in the mood for small talk. 'Get this damned horror off me,' he said.

Malvery pulled out a length of bandage and some disinfectant salve from his inner pocket. 'This ought to hold you till we get back to the *Ketty Jay*.' He felt around the Mane's head with an expression of disgust until he got his fingers between its teeth. 'Now,' he said, 'this might hurt a shitload.'

Crake's yell of pain echoed off the walls of the austere banks and imposing merchant houses that overlooked the square. Samandra Bree, who was standing with Frey, winced in sympathy.

'Poor feller,' she said.

'He'll be okay. It's only his gun hand. He's a bloody disaster with a pistol.'

Crake noticed them looking at him and waved weakly to her. She waved back. 'Glad you're back, Grayther Crake,' she called.

'Me too,' he said, though without much conviction.

'I notice you're missing one, though,' she said to Frey. 'Where's the blonde?'

Frey felt his mood curdle. 'She's gone,' he said.

'Oh,' said Samandra. 'My sympathies.'

'Yeah.' Frey checked his crew were alright, scanned the square, then looked into the sky, where the Navy and the dreadnoughts were battling. A Windblade went shrieking overhead in a death-plunge and crashed a dozen streets away. Screams and howls drifted over the city. Havoc was all around them, but this square was theirs. They were safe here for the moment. The Manes wouldn't come back.

'How'd you find us?' he asked, while he waited for Malvery to patch up Crake.

'Roke. We found him on the roof of the refinery. Good of you to leave him alive, by the way.'

'Hey, I'm a decent sort. We only needed a head start.'

'Well, you got it. When we caught up with him we weren't in the mood to be patient any more.' She winked. 'And there weren't no one around to see.'

'So you left word for the Navy and headed here.'

'They turned up right after you left. Drave with 'em. We went ahead with Drave, and they came fast as they could after. Not fast enough, I guess.'

The other Knights were reloading, idling in defensive positions in case anyone else should try to surprise them. Kedmund Drave, perhaps hearing his name, came over and joined them. He was the leader of this little group, a man with brutal features and silver hair cropped tight to a scarred scalp. He wore a suit of dull crimson armour, moulded to the contours of his body, and a black cloak. He regarded Frey with an expression that suggested he hadn't forgotten that time when Frey had emptied a shotgun into his chest at point-blank range.

'Where's Grist?' Drave demanded. 'I assume he's responsible for all this?' He waved up at the clouded wound in the sky.

Frey pointed back in the direction they'd come, where the black rectangle of the *Storm Dog* was lifting up above the city.

'There,' he said. 'And he's got the sphere.' *And Trinica.*

'Let me guess,' Drave said. 'You went ahead and tried to get it back yourself, instead of letting the Knights do it. Things went horribly wrong. Am I close?'

'No, you're pretty much dead on,' said Frey.

'You're turning out to be a wretched pain in my arse, Captain. I should arrest you all now and save you doing anything else stupid.'

'I think you've got bigger fish to fry right now, don't you? Protecting the citizens of Sakkan from a rabid mob of arctic ghouls, and all that?'

Drave gave him an iron stare. Frey stared back.

'Lucky for you that we do,' he said at length.

'I'll take what luck I can get these days,' Frey said, turning away. 'Malvery, are you done? We're out of here!'

Crake was on his feet now, his hand wrapped tight in bandages. He came over sheepishly and gave Samandra a little bow.

'Enchanted to see you again,' he said. 'I can only hope for better circumstances next time.'

She gave him a smile and touched the peak of her tricorn hat. 'Lookin' forward to it, Grayther Crake.'

'Alright, alright, you two can snuggle up later,' said Frey impatiently. He gave the Knights a quick salute. 'Good luck, you lot.'

'Same,' said Grissom. 'Get going.'

'Back to the *Ketty Jay*!' Frey called, and they headed out of the square, with Crake looking over his shoulder every now and then until Samandra Bree was out of sight.

Thirty-Eight

Frey Plots A Course –
Bait And Ambush – The Stowaway

Frey ran into the cockpit of the *Ketty Jay* with Jez hot on his heels. Behind him, boots clattered in the passageway as the crew went to their stations. Silo was heading for the engine room. Malvery clambered noisily up the ladder to the autocannon cupola.

Crake drifted in as Frey and Jez raced through the pre-flights. He was holding his bandaged hand, looking forlorn and slightly useless. Malvery's patch-up job was sloppy, but proper medical attention would have to wait till later.

'Did you shut the cargo ramp behind you?' Frey asked. 'Don't want any Manes getting in.' He glanced at Jez, then added wryly, 'One's more than enough.'

Jez gave him a quick, humourless smile of acknowledgement. Frey wished he'd kept his mouth shut. Whatever she felt about shooting down all those Manes, it wasn't a matter to be taken lightly. She was cool, efficient, grim. That was how she coped, he reckoned. Burying herself in her task. She'd think about it all later.

Was that how people were supposed to deal with things, he wondered? Shutting them out, closing down? It had been Frey's method of choice up till now, but damned if it had done him a scrap of good.

'Jez. Come up here. See if you can spot Harkins.'

Harkins and the Firecrow had disappeared from the landing pad. With the earcuffs gone, he couldn't talk to them. They'd have to rely on the old-fashioned methods they used before Crake came aboard.

Jez left her station and joined him, peering out through the windglass at the jumble of fighters and frigates in the sky above. Tracer fire tracked across the black ceiling of cloud. Above it all, the great churning hole in the sky, flashing with its own private lightning.

He hit the aerium engines, flooded the tanks, and the *Ketty Jay* began to lift.

'You know, that vortex is going to stay open until the sphere is deactivated or destroyed,' said Crake. 'They're going to keep coming.'

Frey didn't need telling. He was well aware that some of this was his fault. He'd helped Grist get his hands on that thing.

But he'd done his best to stop it, too. It wasn't as if he'd intended this. Those lives weren't on his shoulders. It wasn't his responsibility to save them. He was going to fly away and leave them to their fate. There was no sense in sharing it. Maybe his conscience wouldn't be exactly clean, but he could live with a certain level of grubbiness.

He spun the *Ketty Jay* slowly as she rose, giving Jez a panorama of the battle overhead.

'I see them!' she cried.

'Them?'

'Pinn's with him!'

Crake groaned. 'Really?'

Pinn! Pinn was back! And that meant they were all here, the whole crew, for the the first time in what seemed for ever. Six men, one woman (kind of), a golem and a cat. With Pinn's return, the balance was restored. The crew that had been forged in the firefights and fiascos of Retribution Falls were together again. And suddenly it felt like anything was possible.

The corner of Frey's mouth curled up. 'Pinn,' he said. 'Well, well, well.'

Jez clutched his shoulder and pointed. 'Cap'n! There!'

Her tone told him that she'd spotted something other than the pilots. He followed the line of her finger, but saw only dreadnoughts, one sliding behind another. An explosion rattled the cockpit, too distant to harm them. He looked again.

'The *Storm Dog*,' she said.

He could see it now. A small black bar, angled steeply upwards, sliding like a slow blade through the chaos. It was ignored by Navy and Mane craft alike.

They're not trying to escape. Where are they heading?

He traced their path to its end. His face went slack.

'You must be joking,' he murmured.

They were heading for the vortex. And Trinica was on board.

Suddenly Frey couldn't breathe. It was as if an iron band was tightening around his chest.

On some level, he'd always believed that Trinica would be alright, that Grist would release her once her purpose was served. Once he'd got away there was no point in killing her. Trinica was a survivor. She'd survive. If he hadn't thought that, he couldn't have left her in Grist's hands.

But now he was seized with an awful certainty. Grist would have kept her as a hostage until he was well away from Frey. That meant she was on board the *Storm Dog*. Grist was taking her with him, to the place where the Manes came from. Trinica and the sphere. And they wouldn't be coming back.

She wouldn't be coming back.

Ever.

Again.

He lit the thrusters and hauled on the flight stick. The *Ketty Jay* lurched forward, her prow tilting up towards the blackened, eerie sky.

'Get on the electroheliograph to Harkins and Pinn,' he ordered. 'Get their attention. Tell them to keep the Blackhawks off us.'

Jez caught the urgency in his voice. She darted back to her station and began tapping at the switch, flashing coded messages from the lamp on the *Ketty Jay*'s back.

'Malvery!' he yelled. 'Shoot anything that comes near us!'

'Navy too?'

'No, not the bloody Navy!'

'Right-o. Should be more specific, then, shouldn't you?'

Frey drowned him out by opening the throttle to maximum. The *Ketty Jay* blasted away from Sakkan, up into the dark morning. As they rose, Frey saw the devastation that had been visited on the city below. Sakkan was pitted and scarred with the impact of fallen craft. Crashed frigates had ploughed furrows through entire districts, leaving fire and rubble in their wake. A pall of oily smoke was spreading into the air.

Ahead of them was a deadly muddle of swooping fighters. Frigates and dreadnoughts exchanged artillery, battered heavyweights duking it out. Frey flew fast and straight, right through the middle, climbing steeply.

'Err . . . Cap'n?' Malvery called from the cupola. 'Can't help noticing that we're heading towards the terrifying vortex.'

Frey didn't reply. He kept going, face hard and jaw set.

'We're going after the sphere?' asked Crake, who was hanging on to the doorway. Frey thought he detected a certain pride in the daemonist's voice. The possibility of a noble act appealed to him.

'We're not going after the sphere,' he said. The citizens of Sakkan could fend for themselves. He had other priorities.

'We'd better not be going after that pestilent white-skinned cow you're sweet on,' Malvery warned.

Crake stared at Frey in wonderment. 'You are, aren't you? Even after everything she's done to you. You're going to try and save her.'

There was a strangled cry from the cupola. Jez joined Crake in staring at her captain. He glanced at her. There was something like admiration in her eyes.

'Some things are worth risking everything for, eh, Cap'n?'

He faced forward and hunched down in his seat. 'Damn right.'

Harkins whimpered as the air was shredded by tracer bullets, lethal fireflies darting past his cockpit. He threw his craft into a roll, and came out of it in a hard dive. His face and scalp reddened as the blood was forced to his head.

Three Blackhawks on his tail. Again.

'Pinn? Pinn? What's . . . how . . . Where are you?' he demanded.

'Five more seconds,' came the reply in his ear.

'I don't *have* five more—' he began, but then he saw Pinn come in from his starboard side, machine guns flashing. The Blackhawks were caught in a shattering rain of lead. One swerved to evade, hit its neighbour, and all three went down in a raging ball of flame and metal.

'Yeah, you do,' said Pinn.

Harkins slumped back in his seat and wiped sweat from his forehead with his sleeve. He wasn't sure he liked this bait-and-ambush game they were playing, but he had to admit it was effective. The Blackhawk pilots flew well, but they were unpractised in a real battle. Tight formation was all well and good for aerobatic displays, but if one member of the squad was hit in just the right way, even the inhumanly synchronised Manes couldn't avoid a mid-air collision. A fact that Pinn was exploiting.

The Navy were finding their opponents harder to handle. The Windblades hadn't got the trick of dealing with the Blackhawks yet, and they were being whittled down. The dreadnoughts and frigates were engaged in cumbersome manoeuvres, each trying to find an advantage. But the Navy had only a limited amount of craft, while more and more dreadnoughts were appearing through that frightening gateway in the sky.

To make things worse, the Navy were handicapped by the need to protect their citizens. They were doing their best to draw the dreadnoughts away from the city because they didn't want any more aircraft crashing down on Sakkan. But the dreadnoughts were staying put. Perhaps they realised their advantage; perhaps they wouldn't abandon their crews, running riot in the streets below.

The Navy aimed to disable rather than destroy. The Manes had no such compunctions. The massive aircraft exchanged barrage after barrage, but the Manes had the best of it.

We're not going to win this one.

Harkins passed a Navy frigate that was listing to one side, dipping slowly and unstoppably towards the streets below. It seethed smoke from a huge tear in its hull. Harkins didn't want to think about what would happen when it reached the ground. He was too busy thinking about himself. Trying to stay alive.

How many more lucky escapes would he get before his number was up? How much longer could he keep doing this? Combat flying was a young man's game. He didn't have the constitution for it any more. The physical and mental stresses were too much. He was getting seriously worried that he'd suffer a heart attack at some point, if he wasn't blown out of the sky first.

And yet, what else was there for him? Flying was the only thing he could do, and the only activity he really loved. Take that away, and there wasn't much left.

No, he was trapped in the cockpit till the end. That was plain.

Just let me live through this.

'Hey!' It was Pinn. 'Down there! To your starboard.'

He looked, and his eye was drawn by a sharp, rapid flash. An electroheliograph. It took him a moment to recognise the blocky, ugly shape of the *Ketty Jay*. And there was only one person aboard who could operate an electroheliograph that fast.

Jez!

His heart filled and swelled in his chest. A brown-toothed grin split his lips. Jez! Alive and well! He was overcome with joy, and for a few seconds he could do nothing but beam like an idiot.

'They're signalling,' said Pinn. 'I think it's . . . er . . .'

Harkins remembered himself. Quick, quick. What was she saying? It was a code, designed to speedily transmit a message without the need to spell it out. *Defend us.*

'Yes, ma'am!' he said happily.

'What?' Swept up in the heat of the moment, he'd forgotten Pinn could hear him.

'Nothing. They need us to, er, keep the Blackhawks off them, I suppose.'

'Where are they heading? They're flying *into* the battle.'

'Let's just do what they say!' Harkins snapped, surprising himself.

Pinn sounded equally surprised. 'Alright, alright. Let's get down there.'

Harkins tipped the Firecrow into a dive, keeping a wary eye out for Blackhawks. It *did* seem that the *Ketty Jay* was aiming itself into the heart of the conflict, but he had to assume the Cap'n had his reasons.

His train of thought was interrupted by an artillery shell, which exploded uncomfortably close to him and made him yelp. Concussion shoved at the Firecrow and jolted him in his seat, hard enough to make his cap fall off. The engines groaned as they cut through the disturbed air, then settled back to their usual pitch.

Harkins wasn't a vain man, but he didn't much care for showing off his balding pate, and he felt naked without his cap. He groped around for it in the cockpit, keeping his eye on the skies. When he couldn't find it at his feet, he reached under the seat.

His hand closed on something. Something warm. Something that was all tangled fur and stringy muscle.

'Oh, no,' he said quietly.

With a yowl like the shrieks of the damned, Slag exploded out of hiding and sank his claws into Harkins' calf. Harkins wailed operatically, kicking his leg this way and that in an attempt to dislodge his attacker. But the cat was hanging on as if his life depended on it.

Harkins' flailing hand brushed against his cap, which had fallen down the side of his seat. He scooped it up and and began to beat at the cat with it, maddened by agony.

'Harkins!' Pinn said. 'You getting laid in there? What in rot's name is going on?'

The drone of his engines ascended as the steepness of his dive increased. He wasn't even holding the flight stick any more. He was faintly aware that his aircraft was out of control, but the danger of that seemed dim in the face of the more immediate peril.

Slag released him at last, surrendering to the flurry of blows. He bolted into the footwell, where he ran around between the foot-pedal controls, screeching and hissing. Harkins tried to pull his legs up, but he was strapped in to his seat and he couldn't get far enough out of the way. His leg seared with pain and his trousers were wet with blood.

Pinn was shouting in his ear, but he wasn't listening. His entire attention was focused on the cat.

Slag shot out of the footwell, under his seat and behind him. Harkins fought to turn around, desperate to keep his attacker in view. Having that monster in front of him was bad enough; having him out of sight was worse. But his straps foiled him. He thrashed against them, fumbling for the release, but his hands were clumsy. G-forces were pressing him against his seat. His head was thumping as it filled with blood.

'Pull up! Harkins! You're diving too steep! Pull up!'

The city spun and veered beneath him. Terrifyingly solid, filling his view. The engines had reached an alarming pitch.

Instinct took over. The Firecrow was tumbling. He grabbed at the stick and fought against the roll. He needed to stabilise before he could level off. Otherwise, he wouldn't know which way was up.

There was the sound of fabric ripping. Claws on the back of his seat, ascending fast. Then the hot, stinking weight of Slag landed on his shoulders. The claws sank in, bringing exquisite and unbearable torture. Harkins abandoned the flight stick, beating at himself, consumed by panic.

'*Harkins!*'

He couldn't hear. The cat was howling. He twisted and contorted himself, trying to get the evil creature off him. The claws detached from his shoulder, scrabbled at his back, slashed his scalp. He couldn't get a hold of his attacker. Caught between two dangers, he lunged for the flight stick instead, which was jolting about of its own accord. His fingers grasped at it and slid away. His hands went back to Slag, who was launching a fresh attack on the nape of his neck, caterwauling at the top of his lungs. The hard, cold streets of Sakkan rushed up towards him.

You're going to die!

Then something clicked in among the panic and confusion. The cat's howling. Harkins had never known that sound to come from Slag before, but he knew an old friend when he heard it. That was the sound of fear.

Slag was scared. Out of his mind. He hadn't been hiding under the seat waiting to pounce. He'd been *cowering*, terrified of the sky and the noise of the plane and everything around him.

And with that knowledge came fury. He wouldn't go out like this! Not after everything he'd lived through. Dogfights, crashes, dozens of near misses. The whole point of being a coward was *not* to get killed. But Slag didn't seem to get that. He was just a dumb animal, too scared to know what was good for him.

More scared than Harkins, in fact.

Harkins reached over his head, and found a confident grip on the scruff of Slag's neck. He hauled the cat off him, ignoring the blaze of pain as the claws came free. He dangled the struggling animal in front of his face.

'Bad kitty!' he screamed, and punched the cat as hard as he could in the face. Then he slung his limp and cross-eyed adversary over his shoulder, into the back of the cockpit, and grabbed hold of the flight stick.

The Firecrow was speeding towards the ground, buffeted by the winds, corkscrewing crazily. He gritted his teeth and attempted to counter the roll. His head felt like it was going to burst. The cat was forgotten. There was only him and the Firecrow.

But there was no contest of wills here. Here, even if nowhere else, Harkins was the master.

The craft responded. The spin slowed and stopped. Harkins found the horizon above him. Now he was stable. He stamped on the air brakes and wrenched back on the stick.

'Harkins! Pull up, you stupid bugger! You're going down!' Pinn yelled in his ear.

'*I know!*' Harkins yelled back. '*Don't you think I know?*'

The Firecrow began pulling up. He was still braking hard, but not hard enough. He thumped the valve to flood the tanks with aerium, lightening the craft so the brakes would work better. He was close enough to see the people running in the streets below, and the Manes chasing after them.

'Come on! *Come on!*' he yelled at his craft. The nose was coming up level . . . slowly . . . slowly . . . too slowly . . .

'*Come on!*'

The Firecrow screamed down the length of one of Sakkan's main streets, its underbelly scraping the ground with the slightest of touches, sending a fountain of sparks out behind it. Then it was up, up, up, soaring over the rooftops and back into the blessed sky.

Harkins closed his eyes and breathed out.

'Harkins?' It was Pinn. 'You okay?'

'I'm okay,' he said quietly. His mind had gone blank, so he said the only thing he could think of. 'I just punched out the cat.'

There was a long pause from the other pilot. 'You did *what*?'

Thirty-Nine

'This Might Very Possibly Be A Stupid Idea' – No Turning Back –
The Biggest Chicken Of Them All – A Private Message

The *Ketty Jay* rocked and trembled, pushed by the concussive forces of the artillery exploding all around them. Frey's shoulders were hunched, as if by making himself smaller he could somehow shrink the *Ketty Jay* and present a harder target. His gaze was fixed on the stormy vortex ahead of them, a vast, flashing swirl of heaving cloud. Shells flitted across his path to smash into the flanks of Navy frigates that loomed on his port side. Windblades darted past them, with squads of Blackhawks in pursuit.

Frey powered through the crossfire, and hoped.

Crake's eyes were wide as he stared at the flickering, churning maw in the sky, waiting to swallow them up, as it had swallowed the *Storm Dog*.

'Captain,' he said. 'This might very possibly be a stupid idea.'

'Very possibly,' Frey agreed. But his determination was unshakable. He hadn't felt this certain about anything for a long time.

Grist might have been the wrong side of sane, but he wasn't suicidal. On the contrary, he was desperate to live. Frey had to believe that the other captain knew what he was doing when he plunged into that vortex. And where the *Storm Dog* went, the *Ketty Jay* could follow.

Probably.

Pinn was on his wing, nipping and harrying the Blackhawks, drawing them away as best he could. Malvery was firing at any that came near, without much success. He never had been a brilliant shot with the autocannon. Harkins was nowhere to be seen. They'd lost sight of him a few minutes ago, when he suddenly dived away from them.

The *Ketty Jay*'s thrusters were labouring. There was a distressing knocking noise coming from deep in her guts. The freezing temperatures she'd endured of late had done nothing to improve the precarious state of her prothane engine. It was a testament to Silo's skill that it was still operating at all.

He pushed them hard anyway, climbing out of the plane of conflict where the dreadnoughts and frigates were slugging it out. Gradually the explosions fell behind them and the sky became less crowded. He focused only on his goal, ignoring the dangers all around him as if he could bring them through unharmed by sheer force of will.

Come on, girl, he told his beloved aircraft. *You can make it. I know you can.*

'Cap'n!' called Malvery. 'Stray Blackhawk! Coming in on our tail!'

'Where's Pinn?'

'He's run off the others! I reckon—' The rest of his reply was drowned out by the autocannon. Then: 'I got him, Cap'n! I—'

He was interrupted by a huge explosion, terrifyingly close. The *Ketty Jay*'s stern end was shoved hard. Multiple impacts peppered the craft, ringing through the hull. Frey reached for the controls to correct, but the *Ketty Jay* was still on course. Instead, he turned in his seat and yelled up to the cupola.

'Doc? Doc, you okay?' He looked at Crake, who was hanging on to the doorway. 'Crake, see if he's okay.'

Crake leaned out into the passageway and looked up the ladder that led to the gunnery cupola. 'Malvery?'

'I'm alright,' he said. 'Bit deaf. The awkward bugger blew up a few metres off our tail.'

Frey didn't have time for relief. Jez grabbed his shoulder and pointed. 'Cap'n!'

The vortex had grown huge now, as they sped up and out of the conflict. Emerging through the cloud, right in their path, was the scarred bow of a dreadnought. It dwarfed them, like a cargo ship bearing down on a rowboat.

Frey pulled the flight stick to the left. Nothing happened. He tried again, then moved to the right, then shoved it desperately in every direction. Still nothing happened.

He couldn't steer.

His pupils dilated to tiny points as he stared at the enormous aircraft bearing down on them.

'Uh-oh.'

★

Harkins spared a moment to check that his unconscious stowaway was in no danger of waking up, then headed back towards the *Ketty Jay* as fast as he could.

'Pinn! Where are you?'

'What happened to—'

'Never mind what happened to me. Where's – um – where's the *Ketty Jay*?'

'Heading for that great big bloody rip in the sky. Don't ask me why. I'm going back to 'em now.'

'*Back?*' Harkins was appalled. He'd left them?

'I had to draw off a few Blackhawks . . . er . . . wait a minute.'

The tone of Pinn's voice alarmed him. 'What do you mean, wait a minute?' He flashed at full throttle through the battlefield, ascending hard. 'What's wrong?'

'The Cap'n's playing chicken with a dreadnought.'

'He's *whaaaaat?*' Harkins screamed. He came out of the main body of the battle, up into clearer sky, and spotted them immediately. The *Ketty Jay* was heading right into the centre of the vortex. A dreadnought, many times their size, was lumbering out of it. And neither looked at all like getting out of the way.

Jez!

He angled the Firecrow towards them and put on all the speed he had.

'Shrapnel in the tail assembly!' Malvery called from the cupola. 'I can see it! It looks like it's coming loose! Waggle the flaps more!'

'I'm waggling as hard as I bloody can!' said Frey, waggling.

'Dump out the aerium tanks,' Jez advised. 'We'll sink underneath her.'

'We dump those tanks, we'll go off course.'

'Isn't that the idea?'

'We go off course, we'll miss the vortex. We miss the vortex, we might not be able to get back to it. There's no telling when or if we'll have steering again.'

'You want to chase the *Storm Dog* with *no steering*?' Crake cried in disbelief.

'We are going into that vortex!' said Frey.

'There's half a million tons of metal in the way!' Jez shouted.

'They'll move,' he insisted.

'No, they won't!'

Frey's hand hovered above the valve that would execute an emergency purge of the aerium tanks. The *Ketty Jay* would dip out of the dreadnought's path, but he'd never get her bow up again if he did. Not with that shrapnel in the tail assembly.

Hitting that valve meant giving up on Trinica for ever. Not hitting it meant that he and his crew would end up splattered across the keel of that dreadnought.

He took his hand away.

'They'll move,' he said.

'They won't move!' Harkins shouted at his captain, as if Frey could hear him. He didn't know what the Cap'n was thinking, but he was furious at him for gambling with Jez's life like that. Either the dreadnought hadn't noticed them, or whoever commanded it had decided to run them down rather than waste ammunition. The *Ketty Jay* would crumple like tinfoil against that armoured keel.

Why doesn't the Cap'n just pull out of the way?

Maybe they were in trouble. Maybe they *couldn't* move aside. In that case, a collision was inevitable. In that case . . .

He raced towards them at full throttle. He wasn't sure what he could do about the situation when he got there, but a fierce determination blazed in him nonetheless. He was heady from defeating Slag, and he felt invincible. Somehow, he'd save them. He'd save *her*.

Pinn was further away, approaching from another angle, yelling pointlessly at the Captain. He was as alarmed as Harkins, and just as powerless to intervene.

Then an idea slipped into Harkins' head. Powerless? Him? Not any more. After all, he'd just punched out a cat. Taking on a dreadnought seemed like the next logical step.

There was no time to think about it, anyway. No time to listen to the voice in his head that screamed, *'What are you doing?!!?'* He felt a hard calm overtake him. The kind of calm he'd once possessed in battle, before all those crashes and lost comrades broke his nerve. A colder, more dispassionate part of himself seized control, quelling the panic that beat at his mind. His brow creased into a stern frown, and for the first time in years, he felt like someone to be reckoned with.

He slowed as he matched the *Ketty Jay*'s course, flying in a few dozen metres above them. Ahead was the dark metal landscape of the dreadnought. The *Ketty Jay* was heading dead into its keel, but Harkins was approaching above the level of the deck.

He could see the Manes emerging from hatches in the deck, swarming out like cockroaches. No wonder there had been nobody firing the guns. Presumably it was too dangerous to be up on deck when they passed through that swirling vortex. Too dangerous for Blackhawks as well, he guessed. That was why they were smuggled through in the bellies of their mothercraft.

Far back on the deck stood a command tower, a black pile of spikes and rivets with armoured slits for windows. If there was a captain, he'd be there, along with the pilot. So that was where Harkins was heading.

He cut the thrusters further, coming in slow to give his enemy a chance to react. Then he flew over the *Ketty Jay*, leapfrogging her in the air, and headed straight for the command tower.

'You want to play chicken?' he muttered. 'Well, I'm the biggest chicken of them all!'

He didn't fire his machine guns as he came. He refused to. He'd leave them in no doubt of his intentions. He'd let them know he wasn't going to pull away.

He'd let them know he was going to ram the command tower, and if their captain valued his inhuman life, he'd move aside.

The Manes were scrambling to the deck guns, but they wouldn't get there in time. The dreadnought cruised towards him, framed by the flashing churn of the vortex. Harkins squared his shoulders and flew straight.

His heart slammed against his ribs, his muscles rigid as he held the Firecrow steady. The dreadnought was huge now, growing faster and faster. The Firecrow juddered and rocked around him. The thrusters roared in his ears.

I'm not moving. He projected his thoughts at his opponent. *Are you?*

'Harkins, what the shit do you think you're doing?' Pinn asked. 'They're Manes! This is *not* the time to grow a backbone!'

Pinn. He was the worst of those who laughed at him. Well, one way or another, no one would be laughing after this.

He was coming up on the deck of the dreadnought. Close enough to see the faces of the scurrying figures there. They howled and pointed. Perhaps they sensed his intention, but they couldn't stop him.

Closer. His hand began to shake on the stick. Doubts ate away at his resolve. What would it feel like to die? What would come after?

Closer. He was passing over the bow of the dreadnought. Suddenly all the bravado he'd gained from beating up a cat deserted him. The cowardly voice in his head rose to a shriek. His arms trembled with the effort of resisting the urge to pull away.

Don't do it!

Don't do what? Don't carry on, or don't crack and flee?

The deck streaked past beneath him. The tower rose ahead. He was still aiming right for the bridge. The wind shook and battered the Firecrow, as if the whole craft might come apart.

He gritted his teeth to clamp down on the blubbering wail rising up from his chest. The black metal slab of the command tower thundered towards him, the promise of fiery oblivion with it.

Just this once, he thought. *Just this once. Be a man.*

Then there was a deafening blast of escaping gas, and the command tower tilted as the frigate vented its aerium tanks on the starboard side. The dreadnought listed hard and dipped. Manes went scrabbling and sliding across the deck towards the gunwales. Harkins rolled to his own starboard as the bigger craft bowed aside, and the Firecrow raced past the command tower, wings vertical, with half a metre to spare.

Harkins blinked in shock. The dreadnought was diminishing behind him, the vortex gaping ahead. He unclipped his straps and twisted to look over his shoulder.

The dreadnought was venting on its port side to level itself up, but the added weight was making it sink fast. As it moved out of the way, he saw the *Ketty Jay*, flying over the top of the dipping craft, trailing in his wake.

'Wa-hooo! You crazy bastard!' Pinn was ecstatic. 'That was the bravest damn thing I ever saw!'

A tentative smile spread across his face. That *had* been brave, hadn't it? And even better, he was still alive to enjoy it.

He turned away from the vortex, back toward the *Ketty Jay*. The electroheliograph on her back was flashing rapidly. *Break off. Don't follow. Meet at Iktak.*

Harkins understood. The fighter craft would likely be destroyed in the unknown stresses of the vortex. Maybe the *Ketty Jay* would, too. But there was nothing he could do to prevent that now. His part in this, and Pinn's, was over.

But he'd done himself proud. At least he could say that. He'd done himself proud.

He gave the *Ketty Jay* a tilt of his wings as he approached, acknowledging the message. Then, just before they passed each other, another message flickered from the electroheliograph.

It took him a moment to decipher it, by which time he was already heading away from the battle, with Pinn following after. It was a private communication, from Jez to him.

Nice work, hero.

Harkins was so happy he thought he might die.

Forty

The Vortex – Jez Reads The Wind –
Among The Dead

The *Ketty Jay* groaned and screeched as she was flung this way and that. Rivets popped and gauges cracked. Thrusters squealed as they chewed up the roiling air.

Slowly but surely, she was coming apart.

Crake hung on to the cockpit doorway for dear life. Frey fought the controls as if he'd forgotten they didn't work. Jez clutched at her maps and instruments, which were sliding all over the desk of the navigator's station.

The cockpit was dark, lit only by occasional blasts of brightness from outside. Grey cloud flurried past the windglass, whipping and switching in the hurricane. They were in the heart of the vortex. Jez didn't think they'd come out of it in one piece.

They'd all been shocked by Harkins' display of bravery, how he'd faced down the dreadnought. Nobody had thought him capable of that, least of all the Cap'n, who'd been singing his praises until the winds took hold and he had bigger things to deal with. Now, he was probably wishing Harkins hadn't been quite so courageous. Following the *Storm Dog* into the maelstrom seemed like less and less of a good idea with every passing minute.

Jez felt like she was emerging from a daze. Activating the Mane sphere had been like a hammer blow to her mind. The energy released, the sheer *force* it took to tear open a rift to another place, was colossal. All those in the ancient sanctum had been stunned by the detonation, but Jez had caught it worse than the others. The sphere sent out a cry for help, loud enough to resonate across the planet, to jar the senses of Manes everywhere. Unbraced and unpractised at dealing with her new, inhuman awareness, she'd been overwhelmed.

Since then she'd been operating on automatic. Her faculties were all in place, but her Mane senses were deadened. Down in the streets of Sakkan she'd killed Manes without compunction, and felt nothing for the loss. She knew the Cap'n worried for her, but he needn't have. There was no kind of tribal kinship there. She was part Mane, but she didn't owe them loyalty. They'd press-ganged her. She hadn't chosen to be one of them.

Now her Mane senses were recovering, and a new awareness was seeping in. Ahead, she sensed something: a vast, ominous presence, growing stronger as they ploughed clumsily through the clouds. The Manes. They were going to where the Manes came from, and their nearness threatened her. She felt herself slipping into a trance.

No. Not now. You could lose yourself for good, here.

But despite her best efforts, it was happening. She fought to resist, but it was all she could do to stop herself going under entirely.

She could sense the aircraft around her, like a living thing. She felt the shift and grind of its mechanisms, the stresses on its tortured joints. She could smell the fear coming off Crake, and plot the swirl of the clouds that whipped at the windglass. The darkness didn't affect her. She saw everything with uncanny definition.

Hold it back, she told herself. The temptation to let herself go, to allow herself to be subsumed in the daemon that shared her body, was terrible. Here, so close to the Manes, its pull was fierce.

But she wouldn't let it win. Her crew needed her now. They needed Jez the navigator, cool and collected. Not a wild Mane in their cockpit.

The craft surged to port, hit an air pocket and plunged. Frey hollered with amazed joy.

'What are *you* so happy about?' asked Crake, who was looking green.

Frey ignored him. 'Doc!' he yelled through the doorway. 'Can you see that shrapnel? Is it still stuck in our tail?'

'Can't see it,' came the reply. 'Then again, I can't see bugger all else, either!'

Frey swooped the *Ketty Jay* to starboard. She bucked against the wind shear. Metal howled and something burst deep in her guts.

'Wind must have blown it clear! I can steer again!' Frey said.

'Well, can you *stop* steering?' Crake replied. 'We were doing better before!'

Jez surged to her feet. 'Cap'n,' she said. 'Let me fly her.'

Frey was shocked by the request. He'd always guarded his place in the pilot seat jealously, and only ever let her fly when he wasn't there to do it. She didn't know the *Ketty Jay*'s quirks like he did.

'We're breaking up, Cap'n,' she said urgently. 'But I can ride the winds. I'll get us through.'

He gave her a long stare.

'Let her try!' Crake urged him.

'Alright,' he said. He slipped out of the seat, his expression faintly resentful. Jez took his place, grabbed the stick, and closed her eyes.

There was an invisible swell coming up from beneath. She angled the wings and let them be carried on it. It should have been a battering ram against their hull. Instead they were lifted, firmly but steadily, like a swimmer on a wave.

'I can get us through,' she said again, and now she knew that she could.

The winds in the vortex were a labyrinth, a three-dimensional maze of turbulence. Jez saw it in her mind's eye, all the impossible complexities laid out before her. She tracked changes in the currents as they began to happen, knots and valleys in the wind. By the time they reached her, she'd corrected their course to take advantage. She flew as birds flew, at home with the mysteries of the sky.

As she went, she sank further and further into the trance. Her entire concentration was focused on her task, and there was little left to resist the pull of the daemon inside her.

There were voices on the wind. Some called out, some screamed in pain, others murmured as they went about their industry. Drowning them all out was the alarm, the cry of the sphere, pulsing at her mind. It drew her with a primal urgency, like the wail of a newborn draws its mother. Its distress was her distress. Her brethren needed aid. She wanted to help.

The dreadnoughts were beginning to evacuate the Manes from Sakkan. She knew that, without knowing how. They covered for one another, beating back the beleaguered Navy, and let down their ropes for their crew to climb, bringing the newly Invited with them. The sphere was no longer in Sakkan, so they were gathering their people and preparing to give chase.

Even with her best efforts, the *Ketty Jay*'s passage through the clouds was violent. She couldn't react fast enough to account for every variation in the vortex. The craft shivered and whined as she was pummelled from all sides.

But gradually, the chaos eased, and the jolts came less often. Finally they reached still air, a featureless blank of grey cloud. Jez sat back in her seat, her expression vacant.

'You did it,' said Crake, after he'd swallowed a few times to get some moisture back into his throat.

'Nice work, Jez,' said Frey. 'Bloody nice work.' He got out of the navigator's seat and slapped the bulkhead. 'She's a tough old boot, the *Ketty Jay*!'

'Cap'n,' said Jez, her eyes distant. 'Cloud's thinning out.'

A light was growing ahead of them, and the temperature had dropped noticeably. Frey and Crake pulled their coats closer around them and crowded up behind Jez. Their breath steamed the air, despite the *Ketty Jay*'s internal heating system.

The picture faded in gradually, until at last the land opened up before their eyes.

'Oh, my,' whispered Crake.

The haze in the air had diminished but not disappeared, giving the panorama a bleary, dreamlike quality. The sun shone, weak and distant, forcing the barest illumination through the shroud. Beneath them, a dim white world was laid out, an ocean of ice and snow as far as they could see. Cliffs surged abruptly into the sky at steep angles, as if they'd exploded up violently from beneath. Some lay splintered against one another, smashed by epic, millennia-long conflicts. The plains were rippled with sastrugi, great breaking waves, flash-frozen. Distant mountains loomed high and bleak. At their feet was a wide, low shadow, all curves and angles, glowing a faint shade of green.

'By damn,' said Crake. 'Is that what I think it is?'

'Yes,' said Jez. 'It's a city.'

Even Jez couldn't believe what she was seeing. A city of Manes, here in the arctic. To the others, it was barely visible, but Jez's vision was far superior to theirs. The city was all circles and arcs, built from black granite without much thought for human ideas of symmetry.

The majority of the buildings were low and round, stacked in uneven layers, half-circles and crescents and S-shaped curves. Among them stood sharp towers of shiny, glassy black, slender stalagmites that thinned unevenly towards their pinnacles.

The stacks and towers were linked by a complicated sequence of curving, covered boulevards that fractured and split in all directions. The buildings were like points on a diagram, the boulevards a web of connections between them. A seething green light soaked upward from the ground around the city, but Jez couldn't see what was making it. It was too far, even for her.

'Where are we?' asked Frey.

'We're at the North Pole,' said Jez. 'On the far side of the Wrack.'

Crake licked his lips nervously. 'Cap'n . . . what we're seeing here . . . no one's ever been here.'

'No one's ever been here and *come back alive*,' Frey corrected. 'I'll bet the second part's the trickier of the two.' He scanned the sky and pointed. 'There they are.'

The *Storm Dog* was a few dozen kloms distant, hanging in the air, her thrusters dark. A dreadnought lay alongside, firmly attached to Grist's frigate by a half-dozen magnetic grapples. There was no sign of life or movement on either craft.

'They've been boarded,' said Jez.

'Get us over there, fast,' Frey told her. 'Crake, with me. Let's get tooled up.'

Crake held up his bandaged hand. 'I might sit this one out, Cap'n. I can't fire a gun. I'd be dead weight out there.'

'We can't bring Bess,' Jez added. 'That kind of craft, she'd barely get through the corridors.'

Frey cursed under his breath. 'Alright, Crake. You and Bess make sure the *Ketty Jay* is still here when we get back. Come get a weapon for Jez while she's landing us.' Then he left, calling for Silo and Malvery.

Crake lingered a moment, until Frey was out of earshot. 'You think he's crazy?' he asked Jez. 'Dragging us through all of this for Trinica?'

Jez just stared ahead. 'I wish I felt half as much for somebody as he does for her,' she replied.

Crake nodded in understanding. 'You should be careful what you wish for,' he said, and with that he was gone.

She brought the *Ketty Jay* in over the *Storm Dog*'s deck. The blare of the sphere prevented her from sensing any Manes on either craft, and she didn't know how to tune it out. But whether they were unobserved or simply ignored, their approach drew no reaction.

'Cap'n!' she shouted back into the aircraft. 'You got clamps on this thing?'

'Rack on your right! Second switch!'

She flicked it and lowered the *Ketty Jay* carefully, venting aerium as she went. When she was close enough to the *Storm Dog*'s deck, the newly magnetised landing skids sucked the aircraft down with a hefty thump.

Crake returned to the cockpit as she was getting out of her seat. He threw her a rifle. 'Cap'n says get down to the hold, double quick.'

She began to hurry past him, but he stopped her with a hand on her arm.

'Good luck out there,' he said earnestly.

She snorted. 'We're due some, I reckon.'

Frey led the way down the cargo ramp, wrapped tight in a greatcoat, breath steaming the air. Malvery, Jez and Silo followed in his wake, pointing their weapons in all directions, searching for enemies. They were met with a profound quiet.

The deck of the *Storm Dog* was empty. The deck of the dreadnought, looming on the starboard side, was similarly deserted. The blurred sun shone hopelessly through the mist. A lonely wind stirred the air.

It was freezing. Their exposed hands were already turning to icy claws, and their cheeks and foreheads burned. They waited for an ambush. None came.

'Well, I like this,' said Malvery. 'Easiest suicide mission I ever did. Can we get inside before my bollocks turn to snowballs?'

Silo pointed towards a doorway on the deck. It was hanging open, and the top of an iron ladder was visible beyond.

They clambered down the ladder, which had become cold enough to rip at the skin of their hands, and came out into the narrow passageways below. Jez had been right: Bess would never have fit down here. This was no luxury craft like the *All Our Yesterdays*. The interior was cramped and functional. It was just about possible to walk two abreast, shoulder to shoulder, but that was all.

Tarnished metal surrounded them, lit by electric lights powered by the frigate's internal generator. It smelt of oil and sweat, and a dry, musky scent that Frey recognised from the crashed dreadnought on Kurg. The scent of the Manes.

One of the lights further down the corridor was cracked and flickering. Lying beneath it was a man whose jaw had been torn away from his face. Frey eyed the corpse uneasily.

'Where are we heading, Cap'n?' Malvery asked.

'Captain's cabin?' Frey suggested. 'Most likely place to find Grist.' *And Trinica.*

'Right-o,' said Malvery. He looked up and down the corridor. 'Where's that, then?'

'They usually put it towards the stern on this type of craft,' said Jez. She took the lead, and Frey followed with a fresh speed in his step. The sight of the dead man had sparked a new fear in him. Would he find Trinica like that? Her face ruined, eyes glazed in death? The woman he'd almost married, shredded like a carcass in a slaughter-house, reduced to meat and sinew?

He didn't dare think about it. She was somewhere on this aircraft. He'd find her. That was all.

They hurried through the corridors, passing more corpses on the way. Most of them were Grist's crew in various states of dismemberment, but the occasional Mane was tangled up among them. The stink of blood made Frey's gorge rise. Malvery, who'd seen more innards than the rest of them put together, was unmoved.

'Why do I get the impression something's gone horribly wrong with Grist's plan?' he said. 'They don't seem too interested in taking new recruits, do they?'

'Pick it up, Doc!' Frey snapped. 'Let's get what we came for and go.' He was afraid they were already too late. They could hear dull explosions and gunfire on the lower decks, echoing up through the ventilation system. The howls of the Manes drifted faintly through the passageways as they ran.

Jez's prediction was spot on, and she led them right to Grist's cabin. But when they got there, the door was open and it was clear that it was empty. Frey burst into the room nevertheless, and began turning it over, throwing open cabinets and rummaging along shelves. He was searching for a sign of her, some assurance that she was still alive. He needed to know that he wasn't risking his own life and the lives of his crew for nothing.

'They've been driven down below,' said Jez. Her eyes were out of focus and she seemed to be having trouble concentrating.

'*Where?*' he demanded. 'This aircraft is bloody gigantic! We'll be slaughtered if we go running about down there.'

'That's as good an argument as I've ever heard to bail out while we can,' Malvery said.

Frey stopped his search for a moment and fixed the doctor with a hard glare. 'We're not going anywhere without her.'

'Worth a try,' said Malvery, and delivered a sulky kick to a severed hand that was lying nearby.

Frey needed to keep moving, keep thinking, make a plan. He was full of restless energy that demanded an outlet, but he couldn't just rush off headlong into a horde of Manes. Something was nagging at him. Being here, in Grist's cabin, had reminded him of something. It slid around frustratingly in his mind until he pinned it down.

'*Your father's research. You still have it?*' Trinica's question to Grist, while they were down in the sanctum.

'*Safe in my cabin, don't you worry.*'

Frey's eyes fell on a large chest in the corner of the cabin. One of the few places he hadn't already searched. He pulled it out, and found that it was shut tight. He shot off the lock. Malvery jumped at the sound.

'You trying to give me a heart attack?'

'Think!' Frey said, addressing Jez. 'You know this type of craft. Where's the most defensible place? If you were Harvin Grist, where would you go?'

He tried to think of the answer himself as he opened the chest. Looking for Maurin Grist's research was a tactic to keep him occupied, to prevent him from doing anything stupid. His thoughts were on Trinica, and how to save her.

Inside the chest were piles of documents and accounts, bound up in folders. On top of them lay a large manila folio of papers. He picked it up and ruffled though the papers within. It took only a few glances to establish the subject matter. He rolled them up absently and stuffed them in the inner pocket of his greatcoat.

'Come on, Jez!' he said, because he couldn't find an answer himself.

'Engine room,' said Silo.

Jez's face lit up. 'He's right. On a frigate like this, it must have walls a foot thick.'

Frey snapped his fingers at the Murthian. 'Engine room. Then that's where we're going.'

Forty-One

The Engine Room –
Intruders – Time Runs Out

M alvery and Silo backed up the passageway, laying down gunfire as they went. A half-dozen Manes swarmed towards them, sinewy limbs stretching out, jaws gaping. But lever-action shotguns were devastating in a confined space.

Blood sprayed the dirty walls. The men kept firing until nothing moved.

'Not that way, I reckon,' said Malvery. He took off his glasses and wiped them with his thumb. Silo was calmly reloading.

Frey gazed at the sickening clutter of bodies through the haze of gunsmoke. 'We'll never get down to the lower decks like this.' He ran his hand through his hair and swore. Every moment might be Trinica's last, but he couldn't get to her. The deeper into the *Storm Dog* they went, the more Manes they came across.

He could hear them howling down below. The sound was terrifying. Even if they could fight their way in, he doubted they had enough ammo to deal with those kind of numbers.

'What are they doing down there?' he muttered to himself.

Jez responded as if the question was directed at her. 'Can't tell,' she said, her voice faint and dreamy. 'The sphere . . . it's too loud. They want the sphere, that's all. They're not interested in us.'

He exchanged a glance with Malvery. They were losing her. The longer she stayed here, the more her mind drifted out of focus. Soon, she'd be no use to them at all. They had to get her away. But he wasn't leaving without Trinica.

What if Jez turned Mane, right here? Could he bring himself to shoot her, if she became one of them?

He didn't like that idea. He hurried to change his train of thought. 'The engine room on a craft like this, it'll be huge, right?' he said.

415

'Should think so,' said Malvery.

'There's got to be a back way in, then.'

Silo's eyes widened suddenly. 'You're right, Cap'n.'

'I am?' he asked, surprised.

'Most every engine room got an escape hatch, 'n case fire cut you off from the door. All kinds o' things go wrong in an engine room. You don't wanna be stuck in there when they do.'

'The *Ketty Jay* doesn't have one,' said Frey.

'Ain't the first safety regulation you broke,' Silo pointed out.

'S'pose not,' said Frey. 'Let's get looking for it, then. Jez!'

She blinked out of a daze.

'Escape hatch!' he barked at her.

'We're on the deck above the engine room,' she said. She thought for a moment. 'Could be anywhere around here. In the floor.'

'Split up, get looking!' said Frey.

'Split up?' said Malvery, pointing at the pile of dead Manes cluttering the corridor. 'Bad idea, Cap'n.'

'Just find it!' said Frey.

They hurried up the passageway, scanning the floor, investigating likely alcoves and side corridors. The gunfire from the lower decks had ceased, but since Jez had said that the sphere was still broadcasting, he had to assume the Manes hadn't got hold of it yet. That meant Grist was still down there. Trinica too.

His thoughts were interrupted by a screech and a flurry of limbs, as a Mane launched itself out of an open doorway just ahead of him. It crashed into Malvery, hard enough to knock the bulky doctor off his feet, and sank its teeth into his shoulder. Malvery rolled around bellowing as Silo and Frey tried to grab hold of the ragged ghoul. The very touch of it was appalling: taut muscles sliding under clammy skin. They pulled it away far enough for Malvery to get his boot into its throat. He slammed it against the wall, put his shotgun to its temple, and fired. Frey shuddered as he was pelted with brain flecks.

'Bastard!' snarled Malvery, as he dusted himself down and got to his feet. His face had turned red with anger. He pulled back his coat to examine his shoulder, which was dark with blood.

Frey spat in case any bits of Mane skull had got in his mouth. 'You alright, Doc?'

'Got a good chunk of me,' he grumbled. 'Coat got the worst of it.' He rolled his shoulder and sucked in his breath through his teeth with a hiss. 'I'll live.'

They found what they were looking for a few minutes later, tucked away in a short, dead-end corridor. It was a pressure hatch, set into the floor, with a turn-wheel in the centre. Frey spun it and pulled it open. A ladder led down.

'Whaddya know?' said Malvery, amazed. 'It's actually here.'

'Reckon the Manes don't have escape hatches like this,' Frey said. 'Didn't occur to them to look.'

'Guess they skimped on the safety regs, too,' Malvery said.

The ladder led down on to one of the gantries that surrounded the monstrous engine assembly. It was the size of a small building, a mass of oily pistons, gears and magnets, nestling inside a web of walkways. Inside that structure, prothane was processed ready to feed to the thrusters, and aerium was pulverised into gas. It was dormant now, but it still radiated heat from recent use. The room was sweltering. Metal parts ticked and grumbled as they cooled. Shadows lurked in the folds of the room, hiding under pipes and in corners.

Frey heard voices from somewhere within the room. The echoes mangled the words, turning them ghostly and strange, but he caught the tone. Angry and fearful. Desperate men arguing.

And then, calm and measured, a woman's voice.

Trinica!

A surge of excitement ran through him. It *had* to be her! It wasn't too late, then! He could rescue her, bring her out the way they came in, and get back to the *Ketty Jay*. The Manes wouldn't stop them. They didn't care as long as they got the sphere. All he had to do was deal with Grist.

But as well as the voices, he could hear the Manes. They were howling outside, pounding and scratching at the door. The echoes made it seem as if they were everywhere, trying to claw through the very walls.

The sound chilled him. The Manes would find a way inside some-how. He was dreadfully sure of that.

Silo closed the hatch behind them. Frey searched ahead for Grist and Trinica. The walkways were made of grilles and bars; it was possible to see through the gaps underfoot, to the levels below. But he could find no sign of them, and he decided they must be the other side of the engine assembly.

He turned to his crew and put his finger to his lips. Jez didn't react. She had her head cocked, listening to the wails of the Manes outside. Silo had to shake her by the shoulder to make her focus.

'Concentrate!' Frey hissed.

She nodded, but she was already slipping away again.

He led them down a set of steps to a lower level and began to circle round the greasy bulk of the engine, alert for danger. It stank of aerium and prothane, strong enough to make his head feel light. The door of the engine room came into view below, visible through the intervening mesh of walkways. It was stout metal and shut tight. Frey felt slightly reassured. Not even Bess would get through that in a hurry.

Then he saw movement. At first he thought it was a trick of his vision, a product of the fumes in the air. When he narrowed his eyes and peered closer, it became more pronounced. No mistake, then. It took him a moment to work out what he was seeing, and a while longer to believe it.

An arm was slowly coming through the door. Reaching out of the solid metal, as if its owner was no more substantial than smoke. As Frey watched in horror, a shoulder followed, and a head. It was a Mane, this one ethereal and elegant, a slender figure with a deathly pallor, wearing tattered robes. Its face was that of a handsome young man, with thin lips and high cheekbones. But its eyes were pale and blank like a cave-fish.

They can *walk through walls!* he thought, remembering his conversation with Professor Kraylock at the university. *Some of them, anyway. The rumours were true.*

It came on, inch by inch, as if moving through treacle. All that metal did nothing more than delay it. It would come through, this ghostly figure, and open the door from the inside. Then its fellows would flood in, and that would be the end.

Time was running out.

Frey approached the corner of the engine assembly. The voices of Grist and his men became suddenly loud. Frey realised they were nearer than he thought, and stopped.

'We hold 'em here!' Grist's gravelly voice.

'Cap'n, this has all gone to shit!' That was Crattle, his bosun. 'They ain't interested in makin' us immortal like them. They're killin' *everyone.*'

'What you say?' said a third voice. 'You *wanted* 'em to turn us? What kind of crazy scheme you dragged me into, you piece of—'

A gunshot made Frey jump. There was a slithering noise, and a body hit the floor.

'Any more dogs wanna bark?' Grist asked. 'No? Then firm your damn jaws. They'll be comin' in eventually. We'll meet 'em here.'

Frey looked back at his crew. Malvery and Silo were pressed up close to him, primed, waiting for the word to go. But Grist and his men were dug in, no doubt facing the engine room door. By the sounds of it, they were too busy arguing to notice the Mane stealthily slipping inside, but even so, Frey didn't like the idea of a frontal assault on their fortified position.

He raised his hand and made a twirling motion with his upraised finger. Malvery made the same motion, frowned and shrugged. Sign language for: *what's that supposed to mean?*

'Go around,' Frey mouthed to them, indicating with his hand. Not for the first time, he wished he commanded a highly trained bunch of soldiers instead of a ragtag mob of rejects in varying stages of alcoholism.

Malvery understood the second time. They sneaked back the way they came, skirting the engine assembly on its other side. Frey wanted to get behind Grist, to catch him by surprise.

As they passed the entrance, he glanced down from the walkway. The Mane was three-quarters into the room, pulling its trailing leg through the door. He marvelled that Grist's men hadn't seen it yet. He guessed they must be settling in to their positions, loading their guns, doing anything but looking where they should be.

The Manes were coming, and soon. Their shrieks sounded ever more eager, reaching a new pitch of frenzy. He had to force himself not to run.

Hold your nerve. Blunder in and you'll get everyone killed.

He needn't have worried. At that moment, Grist and his men spotted the phantom slipping through the door, and the racket of gunfire drowned out all other sounds. Frey threw caution to the wind and ran, hurrying along the walkways, until finally he saw them.

They'd taken position at one corner of the engine assembly, on the floor of the chamber. They'd piled up a barricade of parts and equipment between the protruding iron pipes, and were hiding there, facing away from Frey. There was Grist, a hulking, hateful figure in a grubby greatcoat, wreathed in smoke as ever. The sphere was wrapped up in a coat at his feet. He had a pistol in one hand and a cutlass in the other, ready for hand-to-hand combat if things should come to that. Next to him was his scrawny, gaunt bosun, bald skull shining with sweat.

With them was Trinica. Black-clad, white-haired, crouching at the barricade with the rest of them, a pistol in her hand. Trinica. Alive and kicking.

His reaction was not what he'd expected. Bitterness tinged his relief. He suddenly remembered the burn of her betrayal. It angered him to find her like this: not as a prisoner, but ready to fight on Grist's side. Of course, even enemies became allies when necessary, and she was probably only being practical. But it upset his vision of the grateful maiden, waiting to be saved, and that spoiled things.

All he'd wanted to do, ever since he saw the *Storm Dog* disappear into the vortex, was to rescue Trinica. But now he knew that wasn't quite right. He wanted to rescue the *idea* of her. To salvage the possibility of love as he'd once known it. But the reality was considerably more complex and messy.

How was it that life never worked out the way it did in his head?

Well, anyway, they were here now, and he was bloody well going to rescue her. If only so he could hold it over her later.

There were six of them in all, including Trinica. Along with Grist and Crattle were two sturdy-looking thugs and a scared engineer. Another man lay face-down, shot through the chest. All of them, except Trinica and the corpse, were occupied with shooting at the Mane, to no effect. Trinica, sensibly, was saving her ammo.

Keeping well to their rear, Frey took the opportunity to descend from the walkway to ground level. Shooting down on them from an elevated position seemed like a good idea at first, but the walkways provided little protection from return fire, and Frey didn't much fancy catching a bullet between the legs.

He reached ground level a dozen metres behind Grist's position. Silo followed him down, and Malvery was just stepping off when

Crattle yelled, 'The Manes are coming in! Get ready!' Then, warned by some intuition, the bosun looked over his shoulder, and saw Frey and his men.

They needed no other signal. Frey, Malvery and Silo opened fire.

Their first shots, instinctively, were all aimed at Crattle, who'd raised his pistol towards them. He jerked and twisted, bloody spray punching from his back, and went sprawling to the floor. The rest of Grist's crew had a few seconds to react. It wasn't enough. Silo and Malvery chambered new rounds, picked their targets, and blew them away. The last of Grist's men, the engineer, managed to get off one wild shot before he, too, was killed.

While his companions took care of the others, Frey aimed at Grist. But a dozen metres wasn't an easy distance for Frey, and Grist was quick for a big man. Frey took three shots, but somehow Grist slipped between them, and Frey hit nothing.

Trinica hadn't been as fast to appraise the situation as Grist had. She wasted an instant on shock, surprised by the sight of Frey. Then Grist came lunging towards her. Too late, she raised her pistol to shoot him. He cannoned into her, knocking her weapon aside. They rolled together along the ground, and he ended up with one huge arm around her throat, gun pressed to her head. He slid backwards until he came up against the barricade, and lay there, with her lying across him as a shield.

Grist grinned. Stalemate. Again.

Not this time.

Frey raised his pistol and aimed it at Grist's head, where it protruded from behind Trinica's. She was struggling in the captain's grip, but she didn't have his strength.

At that moment, there was a triumphant howl, multiplying rapidly in volume. The door was opening. The Manes were getting in.

'We gotta go, Cap'n,' Malvery said.

I might hit her, he thought, sighting down the barrel of his pistol. His hand began to tremble. *I might kill her.*

'We gotta go!' Malvery yelled at him, as the shrieks of the Manes got louder still.

Take the shot, he urged himself.

Her eyes met his. Maybe it was wild fancy, but he thought he spotted a flicker there. A crack in the façade. Fear. There had been a time when she'd genuinely not cared if she lived or died. But something had changed now. She wanted to live. He saw it in her.

Don't leave me. Don't let me die.

Malvery and Silo were backing away now, towards the steps. The cries of the Manes had reached a deafening pitch. He heard the slap of their feet as they raced into the room. At any moment they'd come flooding round the corner of the engine assembly to consume him.

Take the shot or run! he told himself. But he couldn't do either. He couldn't tear his gaze from hers. There was a longing there, he was sure of it. Regret.

I wish this were different, she said to him.

The Manes came into sight, a filthy tide of tooth and nail, and he knew it didn't matter whether he took the shot or not.

Then something moved. Dropped like a cat from an upper gantry, to land right in the path of the Manes. A jumpsuited figure with a dark brown ponytail. She threw back her head and howled. The horde, as one, came to a stop before her.

Jez.

Jez, and yet not Jez.

Forty-Two

The Invitation – A Mouthpiece –
The Last Stand

S ister.
   Comrade.
   Beloved.

The hurricane of joy that met her almost swept her away. A thousand voices, risen in greeting. At last their discordant song made sense. They were no longer terrifying, but wonderful. They were welcoming her. Welcoming her as one of them.

She'd fought the daemon inside her every inch of the way, in those long years since the day of her death. Frightened of the temptation it presented. Terrified of being subsumed. Desperate to keep hold of herself.

But when she saw the Manes break into the engine room of the *Storm Dog*, when she saw her crew – her *friends* – standing in the path of that savage fury, she abandoned her resistance at last. This time, it was no hostile invading force that took her against her will. This was a surrender.

Strength surged into her body. Confusion was replaced with clarity of thought. She sprang from the walkway where she'd lingered unnoticed, in a daze, while her friends shot down Grist's men. And the Manes halted before her.

But these Manes were not the horrors she knew. She saw past skin and muscle and bone, to the cascade of harmonics within, a music that could be seen and sensed in all its marvellous subtlety. Each Mane was a symphony to themselves, yet each had movements and passages in common. The daemon that possessed each of them was one entity split among many bodies. That was the uniting force. Otherwise, they were as different as earth and sky. The Manes were human, only more so. So much more, that they'd passed beyond the understanding of the beings they once were.

She was still herself. They welcomed her, they wanted her, but it was Jez that bathed in their love. The same Jez it had always been. It was a delight she could never have imagined.

What had she ever been afraid of?

She wanted to speak, but speech was impossibly clumsy. There was no need, anyway. Her thoughts were transparent to them. Yet still she tried, forming words with her mind, because she knew no other way.

Not these, she thought. *You must not harm them.*

And the Manes knew what she knew. They shared her memories of Frey, of her crew, her time aboard the *Ketty Jay*. They sensed her gratitude at being given a home when no one else would give her one. They learned how the crew had accepted her, even in the face of their own ignorance and fear of the Manes. They saw the beautiful simplicity of their friendships.

She knew, then, that they wouldn't be harmed. Not by any hand here.

And yet, for all this astonishing *completeness* that she felt, there was greater yet to come. She'd connected with them on the most rudimentary level. The intoxicating sense of kinship and understanding was only a fraction of what she might feel, if she took the Invitation wholeheartedly.

The daemon inside her had accepted her surrender, but only temporarily. It didn't want her unwilling. The Invitation was just that: an invitation. It could be refused. It was just that very few ever did, with this heaven of belonging within their grasp. Who, when offered this, would choose the lonely isolation of humanity?

Jez was only partway there. To be a Mane in its fullest sense meant accepting the Invitation. And she knew that there was no returning from that.

They spoke to her without words.

Will you join us?

Frey's gun was still levelled at Grist's head. Grist's gun was pressed against Trinica's, at a considerably closer range. Jez was on the far side of the barricade, crouched like a cat. The unearthly howl she'd made was dying away in her throat. The Manes stood at bay before her.

Nobody dared make a move.

What in the name of buggery is going on?

Then Jez straightened and turned. Frey saw the awful change that had been wrought in her, just like on the *All Our Yesterdays*. Her face was not physically different, but something else lived behind it now. Something feral and mad, something *other*. It was in her posture and her expression, and above all in her eyes. She jarred against his senses, and terrified him.

Then she spoke. Her voice was straining, gasping, horrible, as if she was unfamiliar with the workings of her own throat. A flock of whispers that coalesced into sound.

~ *This one speaks for the Manes* ~

'Jez?' said Malvery. 'That you?'

~ *This one is she. She is our mouthpiece. We have lost your way of speech. You are mute to us, as we are to you* ~

Frey felt his skin crawl. He summoned up a little defiance for form's sake. 'What have you done to her?'

~ *Nothing she has not chosen. Be calm, Captain Frey. You and your crew will not be harmed. This one places great value on you* ~

'Her, too,' Frey said immediately, pointing at Trinica. 'She's done you no wrong.'

Jez didn't reply to that. Instead, she said, ~ *Captain Grist. Let the woman go. Bring us the sphere* ~

'No funny business, Frey,' Grist warned.

Frey put up his weapon. Grist let go of Trinica, and she scrambled out of his grip and backed away from the Manes towards Frey. Frey moved closer, carefully, as if fearing a sudden move would lead her to be snatched from him again. Relief crashed in as his hand closed around her wrist and he pulled her towards him. He felt a fierce desire to take her in his arms and hold her, but something in her manner prevented it. She was no longer the kind to be held and comforted.

Grist had picked up his cutlass from where it had fallen during the struggle with Trinica, and shoved it in his belt. Now he retrieved the sphere from where it lay, bundled up in a coat. He stepped past the barricade and walked towards Jez, still clutching his pistol in his right hand. 'You know why I came here, don't you?' he said.

~ Yes ~

'Give me the Invitation.'

~ We know what you want ~ She took the sphere from Grist and stared at it, brow furrowed in concentration.

Frey felt the air go slack. It was as if some tight wire, that had been tugging at the edge of his mind, had quietly snapped. The sensation was noticeable only by its absence. He hadn't realised he was detecting the sphere, even in the faintest way, until it stopped broadcasting. Now, finally, it was silent.

'I brought you a thousand new recruits,' said Grist, eyeing Jez warily. 'My offerin' to you. All I want's to be one of you. To live always. It's all I want.'

Jez's gaze went from the sphere in her hands to Grist. *~ We came to find the sphere. We came believing that our long-lost brethren were in peril. But there were no Manes there ~*

'I had to find you,' Grist said. A note of uncertainty had crept into his voice. 'It was the only way.'

~ Hundreds of our kind and yours have died today, Captain Grist. All so you could come here before us ~

'I did what had to be done,' he growled. Even in the face of a crowd of Manes, he prickled at having his decisions questioned. He addressed the horde defiantly. 'Don't pretend you're strangers to killin', yourselves!'

~ We kill to survive. What your kind call kidnapping, we call recruitment. We must grow in number, and we have no other way of reproduction. But the sight of us inspires terror in your kind. They are apt to resist. We are forced to defend ourselves ~

'Aye,' said Grist. 'But it all adds up to a whole heap o' bodies, whichever way you cut it.' He swept the Manes with a hard stare. He wasn't a bit afraid of them. 'Now, I've proved myself, ain't I? I want the Invitation.'

~ No ~

Grist's face darkened. 'No?'

~ We are not monsters. We do not want you ~

Grist drew a cigar from his pocket, put it in his mouth, and lit it with a match. A dangerous calm had settled on him. 'Am I to understand,' he said, puffing, 'that after two years of searchin', after turnin' over every rock and stone in Vardia, after I lost my whole damn *crew* and chased you to the North bloody Pole . . . That ain't *enough?*'

~ *It will never be enough. We do not give the Invitation to everyone. Some are unsuitable* ~

'Unsuitable, you say? You realise, o' course, that by refusin' me, you're condemnin' me to death from the Black Lung?'

~ *You should not concern yourself. Your death will come considerably sooner than that. You are far too dangerous to be allowed to live* ~

Grist surveyed the ranks of ghouls before him. 'I reckon you're right, at that.' Then he turned around and looked over his shoulder. His eyes met Frey's across the barricade between them. Frey could see the suppressed anger there, his fury at being thwarted at the last. He'd come all this way, and lost.

Grist gave him a grudging salute. Frey returned it just as grudgingly. Both of them knew that he'd reached his end, but Frey couldn't help respecting him for the way he faced it.

'Well,' he said, 'death, then.' He spun around, switching his pistol to his off-hand and drawing his cutlass. 'Which o' you bastards wants it first?'

With a roar, he ran at the Manes, firing his pistol as he came. They fell on him in a howling frenzy as he plunged into them, cutting and slashing this way and that, shooting point-blank at his opponents until his bullets ran out. With long nails and crooked teeth they tore at his skin and raked at his face, but he shook them off time and again, bellowing his defiance. He hacked off limbs and heads to his left and right, a gory and fearsome figure amid the thrashing mass. All control had left him now: he was berserk with rage, more animal than man, a force of nature. As feral as the Manes that surrounded him. At last they pulled him under, overwhelming him by weight of numbers, but a moment later he struggled to his feet again, throwing them back with irresistible strength. They flung themselves at him, biting and scratching, rending strips of flesh from his arms and shoulders, but he battered them away.

'*Come on!*' Grist howled. '*You ain't even tryin'!*'

Frey stared, appalled by his courage. Grist was surrounded by pieces of dead Manes, a butcher in a slaughterhouse, bleeding from dozens of wounds. He was visibly weakening, but he still kept his feet. No matter how they fought, they couldn't bring him down.

In the end, it was his own blood that did it. He slipped on the slick floor, and disappeared beneath the tide. This time, he didn't come up again.

They savaged him as he struggled on the floor. They plucked out his eyes and tore out his tongue. They ripped his belly open and pulled his innards from them in great loops. They gnawed his hands while he still thrashed, peeled muscle from bone, *shredded* him.

Frey had never heard screaming like it.

Then, at last, it was over. As much as Frey had hated Grist, he was glad when they were done, and silence returned. As if at a signal, the Manes began to retreat, melting away into the depths of the craft. What was left of Harvin Grist was scarcely recognisable as human, a bag of red and broken bones connected by strips of sinew.

Malvery cleared his throat. 'In my professional opinion,' he said, 'that feller is dead.'

Jez, who'd stood apart from the fighting, walked up to Frey. ~ *The sphere is deactivated. The vortex is closing. You must move with haste* ~

'What about Jez? You ain't keeping her!' Malvery said.

~ *We do not hold her captive. She has chosen her path* ~

'Oh, aye? And what path is that?'

~ *She was given the Invitation. She refused* ~

'I didn't know you could *refuse*,' Frey said. 'Of course she refused, then! Why wouldn't she?'

~ *Few do. You cannot understand the choice she has made* ~

Frey wasn't going to argue about it. But the creature before him was still not Jez, his navigator. 'Then what is she, if she's not one of you?'

~ *A half-Mane* ~

'Wasn't she one already?'

~ *It is different now. She has accepted her Mane side, as we have accepted her humanity. She no longer resists us. In time, she will learn to control those aspects of us that she bears, or find others to teach her* ~

'There are others?'

~ *Some are agents of our cause in the world beyond the Wrack. Others tread their own way. One day our kind and yours will meet, in war or peace. On that day, there may be need of those who can bridge the gap between us* ~

Frey was too tired and numb to take it all in. It was all too much for

428

him right now. He just wanted to go. He wanted to take his crew and Trinica and leave as fast as he bloody well could.

~ *She chose you over us, Captain. That is a rare honour indeed* ~

Then a shadow passed from her, some dark alter ego departing, and she sagged and staggered. When she raised her head, the feral look was gone from her. The shift in her aspect was subtle but unmistakable. She was back. She pushed some loose hair away from her forehead and gave them a wan smile.

Malvery thundered over to her and swept her up in a bear hug, planting a huge kiss on her cheek. Silo came next, and laid his hand on her shoulder. Their eyes met, and a certain understanding passed between them, something that Frey had no knowledge of. But whatever it was, the half-Mane navigator and the silent Murthian shared something in that moment. Unless Frey was mistaken, Silo was proud of her.

Frey joined them, and hugged her too. She was the smallest on his crew, but sometimes she was tougher than all of them. To have her back, to be *chosen* by her, filled him with a nameless gladness. She was precious, like all of his crew, and it was only then that he truly realised what a loss it would have been if she'd left them.

Jez laughed as she pushed him away. 'Give a girl some space, you bunch of lunks!' she said. 'We don't have time for all this. That big hole in the sky isn't going to be there too much longer, and I for one am not staying. So anyone who doesn't want to spend the rest of their lives stuck at the North Pole . . . *run for it!*'

By the time they came up on the deck, the dreadnought was detaching itself and pulling away from the *Storm Dog*. Other dreadnoughts were in the sky, droning out of the grey mist, shadows that took on shape and detail as they approached. Returning combatants from Sakkan, some smoking from wounds in their hulls.

Frey and the others sprinted back to the *Ketty Jay*. The crew fanned out to their posts, fired by their captain's urgency. Frey put Jez in the pilot's seat.

'Get us out of here!'

Jez didn't need any further invitation. She released the magnetic clamps and had the *Ketty Jay* airborne in moments. It was only when she lit the thrusters that Frey realised something was badly wrong.

'Silo!' he called. He pushed past Trinica and Crake, who were just arriving in the cockpit, and headed down the corridor towards the engine room. He stuck his head through the open door. 'What's that noise?'

'Engines are iced, Cap'n,' came the reply. The *Ketty Jay*'s engine room was like a miniature version of the *Storm Dog*'s. Silo, as usual, was invisible, lost somewhere in the walkways. 'She can't take these temperatures. There's cracks in the tanks.'

'Hold her together! Just till we get out!'

Silo didn't bother to reply to that. Frey returned to the cockpit, listening anxiously to the clattering noise coming from the thrusters. Trinica and Crake hovered about. They could do nothing to help.

'She sounds bad, Cap'n,' said Jez, whose mental clarity had apparently returned. She seemed no worse for her experience. In fact, she seemed considerably better.

'Don't push the thrusters if you can help it,' he told her.

'I'll do what I can.'

The *Ketty Jay* moved away from the *Storm Dog*, leaving her hanging in the sky, empty and abandoned. In another time and another place, Frey would have cheerfully stolen her. But all he wanted now was to get to safety in one piece.

The bleak world of ice and the strange city in the distance were lost to sight, as Jez turned the craft away and took them into the deeper mist. They slipped past the dreadnoughts that were gliding in the other direction. Later, maybe, he'd think about the things he'd seen here, and marvel at the day's events. For now, he was too preoccupied.

Trinica was watching him. Her mind was a mystery, as it ever was. He'd known better than to expect gratitude, but it still rankled that he'd had no word of thanks from her. No words at all, in fact. He'd risked his life and the lives of his crew to come here and get her. They might yet all die on her account. Wasn't that worth a little praise?

Instead, she studied him as if he was some new and mildly fascinating thing she'd never noticed before. Her attention made him slightly uncomfortable.

You stabbed me in the back and I saved your life in return. I'm better than you. Live with that.

He was conscious of an awkward pressure against his ribs. Irritably, he opened his coat and pulled the rolled-up sheaf of papers from his inside pocket. Since Crake was nearby, he held them out to him.

'What's this?' Crake asked.

'Grist's father's research. Apparently it's compelling evidence that the Awakeners have been using daemonism to create Imperators.'

'They've *what?*' Crake exclaimed. He snatched them from his grasp. 'Give me that!'

'Yeah, didn't I mention it? When you were away we went to Bestwark University, and we met—'

'No, you bloody well did *not* mention it!' Crake began leafing through the papers excitedly, their predicament suddenly forgotten.

'To tell you the truth, I sort of forgot about it till I was in Grist's cabin. Didn't seem all that important.'

Crake stared at him, aghast. 'Do you know what this *means?*' he asked, brandishing the folio.

'Reckon so. If it got into the Archduke's hands, it could help bring down the Awakeners, or something,' he said offhandedly. He didn't much care whether the Awakeners were around or not, but Crake certainly did.

'Spit and blood! This is incredible!'

'Yeah, well, enjoy it,' said Frey, listening to the labouring thrusters. 'It won't be so incredible if the prothane engine doesn't hold out.'

The mist closed in around them, and the wind began to pick up fast. The *Ketty Jay* started to shake and rattle. Jez stared out into the gloom. What she was seeing, Frey couldn't tell. The route back was invisible to him, but she seemed to know exactly where she was heading. She twitched the flight stick, banked and dived. Frey steadied himself against the navigator's desk. It was going to be rough.

The wind buffeted them as they flew further in, and Jez was forced to manoeuvre more and more. There was a screeching noise coming from the port thruster. Frey bit his lip and hoped. If the thrusters failed now, they'd be tossed about in the tempest until they came apart.

If only he'd had the time and money to get the parts Silo had been asking for. If only he didn't live this hand-to-mouth, breadline existence. If they died today, it would be his mediocrity that was to blame.

You can do it, girl, he thought, addressing his aircraft. *Hang on.*

The *Ketty Jay* bucked and surged as she fought through the storm.

Lightning flickered in the clouds. Frey felt useless. He wanted to be doing something, but there was nothing he could do. Having given up his seat as pilot, he was just a passenger. He watched Jez, or gazed out at the mist, or listened to the disturbing sounds coming from the engine. Mostly, he willed the aircraft to stay together, and tried to keep his balance as they were jostled around. There were safer places to be while the *Ketty Jay* was fighting through such savage turbulence, but no one would leave the cockpit.

Time ticked by. Moment after agonising moment. Frey lost track of it altogether.

'Not far now,' Jez said.

Frey exchanged a cautiously optimistic look with Crake. Crake, who was clutching the papers tight in one hand and steadying himself with his other, gave him a brave smile. Maybe they'd make it after all.

Then the thrusters coughed and hacked and, with a final bang, the engine blew out.

No.

Frey felt himself go cold. The world seemed deadened, the silence profound. The injustice was like a blade under the breastbone. To have got so close. So close, and to fall at the final hurdle.

No.

Outside was the endless, empty grey. They drifted, somewhere in the vague, strange space between the Wrack and Sakkan.

No.

Then the wind hit them, and this time there was no way to ride it. The *Ketty Jay* was flung hard, throwing Frey off his feet. He crashed into Trinica and they went down together, sliding along the floor to fetch up against a bank of instruments. Crake was thrown against the navigator's station. He cracked his head on the side of the desk and fell senseless to the floor, papers scattering all around him.

Jez stabbed at the ignition frantically. The thrusters didn't respond. Frey tried to get to his feet, but the *Ketty Jay* plunged, and he was lifted from the floor and slammed down hard. Jez wrestled with the controls, but her efforts were futile.

Everything was futile.

They were shaken like a rag in a dog's mouth. Without thrust, they had no control. Everything not fixed down went flying about the cockpit. There was the squeal of tearing metal from the corridor. The jolts came fast and from all directions, making it impossible to find their feet. Something snapped and crashed down in the cargo hold. The windglass cracked.

The craft was breaking up. And there was nothing any of them could do about it.

Frey crawled across the floor towards Trinica. One of her black contact lenses had fallen out in the chaos, revealing the green eye he knew. That eye was the one he focused on. The eye of the woman he'd loved. There was the woman he'd risked it all to save. And she was scared; he could see it. Frightened of the end. She didn't want it to be over.

He reached out a hand to her. She snatched it and clutched it hard. Her hand in his. He could think of worse ways to die.

At least he'd tried, he thought. It was reckless, headstrong and stupid, but it was real and it was worth it. With a little more luck, he'd have made a story that every freebooter, raconteur and drunk would have told for a decade. The man who went into the Wrack, rescued the dread pirate Dracken, and came back to tell the tale. They'd all know the name of the *Ketty Jay* then. If he never did anything else, at least he'd have done that, and made a tale worth telling of his life.

He just needed a little more luck. But everyone's luck ran out sometime.

'Cap'n!' Jez cried. 'Cap'n, look!'

The tone of her voice drove him to his feet. He pulled Trinica up with him, and they staggered a few steps to clutch the back of Jez's seat.

Bleary lights in the mist. *Electric* lights, and a huge shadow behind them. Another dreadnought? No, dreadnoughts flew without lights. Then what?

'It's the *Delirium Trigger*!' said Jez, an amazed smile breaking out over her face. 'It's the bloody *Delirium Trigger*!'

And it was. Vast, ugly, brutal, looming from the cloud. The wind couldn't threaten a frigate of her size. Thick snakes uncoiled from her shadowy decks and slammed into the hull of the *Ketty Jay*. Magnetic grapples, clamping on. The lines went taut, and the *Ketty Jay* began to move through the storm, hauled inexorably forward by the *Delirium Trigger*'s massive engines. They were pulled towards the mouth of the vortex, and the safety of the world they knew.

Frey couldn't believe it. It didn't seem possible. Jez was cheering in her seat, but he just stared, gaping, unable to credit their reprieve.

'How did they find us?' he asked. 'In all this mist, how did they find us?'

Trinica held up her left hand before him. On her finger was the silver ring he'd given her. The ring that was linked to a compass, which Trinica had given to her bosun when she took it from Jez, back in Grist's hangar.

He looked from the hand to her. She smiled at him. A genuine, beautiful smile, that filled him with such happiness it made tears prickle at his eyes.

Forty-Three

Spit And Polish –
Malvery's Joke – Farewell

The Yort engineer led the way up the *Ketty Jay*'s cargo ramp. Frey and his crew followed him in, looking around curiously, as if they'd never seen their own aircraft before. A blast of icy air and a flurry of snow chased past them. Beyond, in the grey glare from outside, there were tractors and hangars, and Yorts walking back and forth. They were in dock at Iktak, where the *Delirium Trigger* had recently been repaired, and the *Ketty Jay* more recently still.

'We had to put in a whole new engine assembly,' the engineer was saying. 'Fixed up your thrusters, too, but the guts of 'em were good, so we kept most of it. Blackmore P-12s.' He grinned. 'They don't make 'em like that any more.'

The engineer was a short man, but stout, making up in width what he lost in height. A well-attended gut hung over his belt, but his shoulders and arms looked stuffed with cannonballs. Orange hair fell down his back in braided ropes, and his jawline was outlined with studs of metal.

'We did over your control system and some of the internals. She ought to fly better now, at any rate. Don't know how you kept her together all this time. Your Murthian's a bloody genius.' He thumbed at Silo.

Frey was finding it hard to keep up with his accent. All Yorts spoke Vardic, but it was so heavily inflected that you had to pay strict attention to get any meaning out of it. He suspected they did it on purpose, thorny buggers that they were.

'Sounds like you did a thorough job,' he said uneasily. He was worried that the *Ketty Jay* wouldn't be the same old girl he knew. After fifteen years of flying her, he'd learned to compensate for all her little tics and problems. They were part of her character. He felt bad about losing them.

The engineer didn't notice. 'Lot of environmental damage on the hull, so we gave her a patch and weld, scrubbed her out. Basically did her over, top to bottom. She'll be better now than when you bought her.'

That's what I'm afraid of, Frey thought. Then he told himself to stop being a grouch. He'd just had his aircraft given an all-over service by one of the best workshops in the North, and it hadn't cost him a shillie. That put a smile on his face.

'I can't wait to fly her,' he said. 'She looks great.'

She *did* look great. She'd been polished up so she looked factory-new. And Frey had never seen the cargo hold so tidy. His crew looked amazed. Like him, they'd never realised there was so much space in here.

'Anything you couldn't fix?' Frey asked, half-hopefully.

The engineer pointed to an air duct, where Slag was hiding, watching them malevolently. 'Your cat's disposition,' the engineer replied. 'Damned thing kept attacking us whenever we went near the vents.'

'The cat?' Harkins scoffed loudly. He made a lunging movement towards the vent. Slag took fright and disappeared in a scrabble of claws. Harkins crossed his arms and looked smug. 'Who's scared of a cat? You *are* about twenty times his size, after all.'

Everyone turned to look at him. The engineer gave him a flat glare.

'Er . . .' said Harkins.

'Don't mind him,' Frey told the engineer. 'He laughs in the face of danger.' He slung his arm around Harkins' shoulders. Harkins tensed up, as if expecting to be hit. 'May I introduce my outflyer, "Fearless" Harkins. You know, one time, he played chicken with a dreadnought and won!'

'Him?' the engineer asked.

'Hey, *I* could have done that, if I'd got there in time!' Pinn protested. 'I'd have won, too!'

'I'll leave you all to have a look around, eh?' the engineer said, somehow making it a threat directed at Harkins. Then he stomped off. Frey took his arm away and Harkins relaxed visibly.

'"Fearless" Harkins, eh?' he said, glancing sidelong at Jez.

'Don't let it go to your head,' Pinn grumbled.

The crew scattered throughout the craft, keen to see what had been done. Only Malvery stayed behind with Frey.

'I bet they even cleaned the infirmary,' Frey said.

Malvery snorted. 'About time someone did.'

'How's the shoulder?'

'Fine. Crake's hand's healing up okay, too. It won't lose any mobility.'

'He seems better these days,' said Frey. 'Happier. So does Jez.'

'We all do, Cap'n. Been through the wars, come out alive. This is the second time we pulled off something we really shouldn't have got away with. The lads are getting confident, I reckon.'

Frey and the doctor considered the empty hold. The subdued clamour of the docks filled up the silence.

'Thought I was losing you lot for a while there,' Frey said eventually.

'Who, us? Nah.' Malvery said. 'Where would we go?'

'Off to find new sweethearts, like Pinn?'

Malvery roared with laughter. 'Chance would be a fine thing.' Then his laughter tailed off and he harumphed uneasily.

'What is it?' Frey asked, sensing something wrong.

'Actually, Cap'n,' he said. 'About that. I've got a confession to make. You know that letter from Lisinda that Pinn got?'

Frey groaned. 'Oh, Doc. You didn't.'

'Well, you know. I thought he was full of it, always talking about that bloody girl of his. Thought I'd call his bluff. To tell you the truth, I posted it a couple of months ago, when I was leathered. Forgot all about it till it turned up in Marlen's Hook.'

Frey pinched the bridge of his nose in exasperation.

'Well, I never thought he'd actually *go*, did I?' Malvery protested. 'I'm fond of the lad, myself.'

Frey took a deep breath before replying. He thought about all the trouble he'd have faced if Pinn hadn't come back, and he'd been forced to find a new pilot. He wondered if their fight over Sakkan might have turned out differently. Harkins might have been shot down by the Blackhawks. They might never have made it through at all.

But they *had* come through. They were all safe and well. Given that, it was hard to be angry at Malvery, even if he thought he probably should. The doctor was too much of an affable sort. Besides, no harm was intended, and Pinn seemed more spry than ever since his return.

'I think, on balance, you did him a favour,' he said. 'But keep it to yourself, eh? And *don't do it again.*'

'Aye, Cap'n.' Malvery said with a grin. 'I'll be good.'

Frey sighed. His aircraft might have been fixed up like new, but his crew were just as they'd always been. Argumentative, dysfunctional and ill-disciplined. Yet for all that, he was glad of them. Individually, they were hopeless. But somehow, when they were all together, they became something greater than the sum of their parts.

He couldn't believe there had been a time when he'd almost let them slip away from him. What had he been thinking? It was a dirty world out there, and these were the only true friends he had. You didn't throw that away. Not for money, fame or anything else.

He heard quiet footsteps on the cargo ramp. Malvery turned. 'You've got a visitor,' he said.

It was her. Trinica. Without her make-up, without her contact lenses. Not the pirate queen, but the woman beneath. She'd come as herself. Just the sight of her warmed him.

'Morning, ma'am,' said Malvery, as she joined them.

'Good morning, Doctor.'

Malvery looked at Frey, then back at Trinica. 'Think I'll make myself scarce. See what they've done to the infirmary.' He slapped Frey's shoulder and strolled off, whistling.

Frey barely noticed. All his attention was on her. Her hair was still uneven and ragged, but she'd made the best of it for his sake. She was wearing a hide coat and furs against the Yortland cold. There was nothing of glamour about her, but still she mesmerised him.

Her eyes searched his with that strange curiosity he'd noticed in her gaze ever since he'd rescued her from the *Storm Dog*. As if she'd never seen him before. As if he was some fascinating artefact that she was trying to puzzle out.

Then she looked away, and began to examine her surroundings. 'I came to see if everything was to your liking.'

'Haven't taken her up yet,' he said. 'But they told me they did a complete overhaul. Reckon she'll fly like a dream now.'

'You're disappointed,' she said, with a tiny smile. 'You'll miss her quirks.'

'Yeah, a little.'

'You always did like to do things the difficult way.'

'Can't argue with that,' he said. 'Thanks for fixing her up. Really. I bet they did a fine job.'

'It was the least I could do,' she said. The space between their sentences felt heavy with unspoken words. Then, as if it had just occurred to her, 'I have some things I should return to you.'

She produced a handful of small objects from her coat. Crake's paraphernalia, that she'd taken from him in Grist's hangar. The earcuffs, the skeleton key, the brass whistle, the compass and pocket watch. When she'd given them to Frey, she began to take the silver ring off her finger.

'Not that,' said Frey, holding up his hand. 'That's yours.'

She hesitated. 'And the compass?'

'That's mine.'

She smiled reluctantly. 'Very well, Darian,' she said. 'As you wish.' And she slipped the ring back into place.

'So where now for you?' he asked, before he could begin to feel mawkish.

'I believe I might pay a visit to Osric Smult, a certain whisper-monger of my acquaintance. He and I have unfinished business. And you?'

'Bestwark University. We'll go see Professor Kraylock. Reckon he'll know what to do with Maurin Grist's research.'

'It'll be a powerful blow to the Awakeners. Have you thought what will happen if they discover you were behind it? Are you certain you want to stir up the big fish?'

'Crake would never forgive me if I didn't,' he said. 'Besides, I got kind of sick of all this small-time grubbing about I've been doing. You have to take a risk now and then, right? That's the point. If you don't take a risk, you'll never do anything worth half a shit.'

In fact, the idea of stirring up the big fish had begun to hold a certain appeal for him. He was a man who'd always tried to avoid the notice of everyone stronger than he was. He'd always preferred to deal with bottom-feeders, the dregs of the world, people who he reckoned he could safely outwit. He'd considered it a sensible

strategy, since it had kept him alive thus far. But just staying alive wasn't enough any more. It wasn't sufficient to drift through a middling existence, making little impact on anyone, to slip quietly into an obscure death with only the fond memories of a few friends to mark him.

He wanted to be someone. He wanted to make a difference. It was a feeling he hadn't had since he was a boy.

He'd been haunted by a sense of worthlessness for some time now, but no longer. He'd done something extraordinary, and all of Vardia would know it. This time wasn't like the last, at Retribution Falls, when his involvement was secret and he'd been only interested in saving his own hide. This time he'd done something no one had ever done before, and what was more, he'd done it for someone else's sake.

What will I leave behind? he thought to himself. *A damn good story. A tale they'll tell over and over. And that's enough.*

She seemed to catch his thought. 'You know, they're all talking about you in the taverns. What you did.' She raised an eyebrow. 'They drew their own conclusions as to your motives. I suppose it appeals to the doomed romantics.'

'I thought you wouldn't want it getting out. Can't be good for your reputation.'

'Men will talk,' she said. 'I can't stop that. My crew have rather revised their opinion of you, it seems.'

'And what about you?'

She didn't answer that, but her gaze flickered awkwardly away from him. Frey cursed himself. He'd meant it to sound light, but the conversation had taken a sudden turn into territory that neither was comfortable with.

'Darian,' she said softly. 'I'm not what you imagine me to be.'

'I know,' he said. 'And you've done your damnedest to prove it.'

'What you feel . . . It's meant for somebody who died a long time ago.'

'She didn't die. She changed, that's all.'

'Yes. She changed. Into something you don't want.'

'Don't tell me what I want. I *know* what I want.'

She looked up at him, and a wry expression creased the corners of her eyes. 'That's not like you at all, Darian.'

What he wanted was to gather her in his arms. It was a physical

need. The barrier between them was almost unendurable. But he felt that to do so would be to shatter something that had been built between them, some delicate and fragile understanding. He knew what she'd been through in those years they'd been apart. The touch of a man, any man, would most likely not be welcome. And he had no right to her, anyway, after what he'd done. As hard as it was to stop himself, it would be worse if she rejected him, or coldly suffered his embrace.

So he didn't reach out to her, as much as he was desperate to. He resisted, for her.

'You came after me,' she said quietly. 'Even after all my cruelties. You didn't let me go.'

Frey didn't know what to say to that.

'You won't stop trying, will you? No matter what I do.'

'No.'

Slowly, tentatively, she raised her hand, brushed her fingertips down his chest. She stared at the buttons of his coat, as if contemplating them fiercely. Then she slipped closer, and pressed her body against him. Her arms slipped around his waist, and her head leaned against his shoulder. She breathed in the smell of his coat and sighed.

'Don't,' she said.

It was as if it had only been minutes since he'd last held her, instead of a decade and more. The feel of her was familiar and new all at once. She fitted into him perfectly. For a few precious moments, everything was tranquil, and a wonderful peace spread through him. Then, as if afraid to let it last, she stepped away from him. She gave him one last look, and there was something of sadness in her gaze, but something of happiness too. Then she left him.

He stood in the empty cargo hold, staring after her. Back she went, back to the *Delirium Trigger*, back to being the pirate queen whose body she inhabited. He knew he should have felt bereft, but he didn't. Instead, a broad smile broke out on his face.

There was hope. After all this time, there was hope. The thought of it lit him up on the inside.

His friends were alive and well and together again. His craft had been made over, better than new. The drunks were singing his praises

in every tavern from here to the Samarlan border. And maybe, just maybe, Trinica didn't want to kill him any more.

'Frey, my boy,' he said to himself. 'Things are looking up.'